DEMONIC POSSESSION

Magda turned from the heavy door, her cold gray eyes almost phosphorescent in the blue light. "This had better be good, Sherone."

Sherone started to tell her about Heather and the tarot cards, but Magda stopped her. "We've been over this before. It's nothing. A Sensitive duplicates a set of cards spelling out the name of a demon with which she's had previous contact. This is to be expected."

"But Magda," Sherone insisted nervously, "she called him up again, without trying. Right in my own bedroom!"

"Impossible," Magda replied firmly. "She can*not* channel Azgaroth at will. He must be summoned deliberately."

"Magda, he was *there*. Like he's following her, or maybe waiting for her—"

Magda smiled a hard smile. "Why would a powerful demon like Azgaroth be so interested in an ordinary teenage girl?"

"Perhaps," said a voice from the darkness, "we can find out...."

THE ULTIMATE IN SPINE-TINGLING TERROR FROM ZEBRA BOOKS!

TOY CEMETERY (2228, $3.95)
by William W. Johnstone
A young man is the inheritor of a magnificent doll collection. But an ancient, unspeakable evil lurks behind the vacant eyes and painted-on smiles of his deadly toys!

SMOKE (2255, $3.95)
by Ruby Jean Jensen
Seven-year-old Ellen was sure it was Aladdin's lamp that she had found at the local garage sale. And no power on earth would be able to stop the hideous terror unleashed when she rubbed the magic lamp to make the genie appear!

NIGHT WHISPER (2901, $4.50)
by Patricia Wallace
Twenty-six years have passed since Paige Brown lost her parents in the bizarre Tranquility Murders. Now Paige has returned to her home town to discover that the bloody nightmare is far from over . . . it has only just begun!

SLEEP TIGHT (2121, $3.95)
by Matthew J. Costello
A rash of mysterious disappearances terrorized the citizens of Harley, New York. But the worst was yet to come. For the Tall Man had entered young Noah's dreams — to steal the little boy's soul and feed on his innocence!

Available wherever paperbacks are sold, or order direct from the Publisher. Send cover price plus 50¢ per copy for mailing and handling to Zebra Books, Dept. 3371, 475 Park Avenue South, New York, N.Y. 10016. Residents of New York, New Jersey and Pennsylvania must include sales tax. DO NOT SEND CASH.

BLOOD SABBATH

LEIGH CLARK

**ZEBRA BOOKS
KENSINGTON PUBLISHING CORP.**

To Carla White

ZEBRA BOOKS

are published by

Kensington Publishing Corp.
475 Park Avenue South
New York, NY 10016

Copyright © 1991 by Leigh Clark

All rights reserved. No part of this book may be reproduced in any form or by any means without the prior written consent of the Publisher, excepting brief quotes used in reviews.

First printing: April, 1991

Printed in the United States of America

PROLOGUE:

the invocation

"Children of the Wicca! Arise!"

The strident female voice shocked sixteen-year-old Heather Roberts out of her distracted reverie. She got to her feet along with the twelve other members of Magda Prokash's coven. They formed a circle inside the larger circle outlined in coarse rock salt around a black altar with four black candles.

Crystal wind chimes revolved slowly overhead, reflecting broken light from flickering candle flames. A gust of dry, smoggy Southern California air blew in from the hot San Fernando Valley night outside, fluttering lace curtains, sending the wind chimes into a mad terpsichorean whirl.

Heather sneaked a furtive glance at her watch. It was almost midnight. *I'll be in deep shit when I get back*, she thought, *no matter what I tell Mom.*

Heather and her mother, Karin Roberts, did not see eye to eye on everything—like Sherone Livingston, for example, Heather's best friend, the blond girl standing next to her in the circle. Karin suspected Sherone of being a little too wild for her own good and of keeping even wilder company. Outwardly Sherone seemed normal to the point of imitation, with her dyed blond shoulder-length hair and every-day-at-the-beach tan. Sometimes she wore odd necklaces with strange stones and jewel-studded belts with short decorative swords, *athamés*, stuck through them. But Sherone got better-than-average grades and seemed to lead an ordinary teenage social life.

If Karin Roberts had even remotely suspected that Sherone Livingston was a member of a Wicca, or witches' coven, and that she had talked Heather into coming with her this Tuesday night to Magda Prokash's to participate in ceremonial magic, Karin would have taken immediate preemptive action and grounded Heather for life.

Sherone nudged her friend. "Go with the flow, okay?" She nodded at the black altar. "Don't fight it."

I'm fighting boredom, Heather thought, but asked, "Sherone, will anything ever, you know, happen?"

Sherone's brown eyes narrowed. "Just wait."

I've been waiting! Heather thought, more than a little impatient now with her best friend. It was Sherone who had convinced her this whole thing would be fun, like a Halloween party, with witches, magic, secret spells. But it had to be on a school night, Tuesday night. *This Tuesday night,* Sherone had insisted, *when the moon is full!* And it had to be at Magda Prokash's. *Magda's a wise and powerful witch,* Sherone had whispered, *really deep into the elements.*

That was why Heather now stood inside a salt-outlined circle with twelve other people she didn't even know, except for Sherone, in the front room of a tacky Valley tract house, worlds away from the large, expensive home she shared with her mother in fashionable Encino. She was there to see a magic show.

And check out the guys. *Really sensitive guys,* Sherone had promised, *not like the one-night hitmen at school.* There were a few guys at Magda's that night. The interesting ones seemed to be deep into meditation, breathing evenly, going with the flow. A skinny guy with straight dark hair and a sharp nose leaned forward, eyes closed, meditating. A curly-headed blond lifeguard-type looked up and grinned at Heather. She looked away, thinking, *Another macho superjerk, just like Kurt.* Kurt Pritchard was her official boyfriend, but they had been having problems lately.

"Children of the Wicca! *Attention!*"

Magda Prokash stood in the center of the circle before the black altar and its small bronze statue of a nude woman with a cat-demon's face and a horned crown in the shape of a crescent moon. The statue was disturbing, but it had nothing on Magda Prokash. She stood there: short, stocky, gray hair cut tight around her broad head, round face almost featureless except for the cold, hard gray eyes. She wore a brown monk's robe with a deep cowl and heavy rope sash. In her right hand she held a gnarled wooden staff.

"Attention!" Magda Prokash rapped on the hardwood floor with her staff. "The hour of invocation has come."

A buzz of excitement swept the circle. Sherone punched Heather's arm. "*Now* see what happens!"

"And with the hour also comes the fear." Magda Prokash's voice dropped low. "For make no mistake, Children of the Wicca, what we attempt tonight is precarious. No idle love spell. No simple charm for health and long life." Her cold gray eyes transfixed the circle. "Tonight . . . we raise the demon."

A chill seemed to settle over the room, despite the hot night outside. Heather ran a hand through her long red hair. *This is such bullshit*, she thought. She knew it was just a game of make-believe, like a Saturday-night horror movie.

Even so, she felt the chill.

"Join hands," Magda commanded, "and close the ring of dark eternity."

The coven obeyed.

Magda pointed with her staff to a man-size triangle outlined in rock salt on the hardwood floor, its base angles almost touching the edge of the circle. The triangle was covered with a layer of charcoal briquets spread over tinfoil.

"Behold the sacred triangle, sign of three. A trap to catch a demon from the darkness beyond this world."

Heather, staring at it, felt her stomach tighten.

Magda Prokash nodded. "Set it afire."

A small, dark-skinned girl with eyes like midnight picked up a can of charcoal lighter. Heather turned to Sherone to make a wisecrack about barbecued demons. What she saw in Sherone's eyes stopped her. The dark-skinned girl squirted lighter fluid generously over the charcoal briquets. Then she struck a wooden match. The hiss of sulphur seemed unnaturally loud. She threw the match into the triangle. It tumbled end-over-end, a fiery miniature torch. The triangle burst into flame. Shadows appeared on the far wall. Heather squinted at the burning brightness.

Magda Prokash raised her arms, the wooden staff clutched tightly in her right hand, and intoned solemnly, "By the Ancient Gods who came before us . . ."

The flames leaped up.

"By the Dark Ones who ruled at the beginning . . ."

A hissing rose from the flames, clear and penetrating, like the drone of some monstrous insect.

"By Astarte, crescent-horned Queen of Night . . .

"By Dagon, god of Dark Waters . . ."

This is such bullshit, Heather repeated to herself, sweat breaking out across her upper lip. *This is such—*

"By Baal, drinker of blood . . .

"By the Nine Circles and the Nine Stairs . . .

"By the Seven Stars and the Seven Moons . . ."

Magda Prokash threw her arms wide. The wooden staff seemed alive, a serpent about to strike.

The hissing stopped abruptly.

"Speak, Demon!" Magda thrust her staff forward. "Speak! I command you!" She gasped for breath. *"Reveal to us your evil name!"*

At first, nothing.

Only the crackling of flames inside the triangle.

Then the hissing began anew, growing gradually louder. And louder. Heather plugged her ears.

"Sherone." She turned to her, frightened. "That sound . . ."

Sherone frowned at her. "What sound?"

The hissing stopped again, sputtering into silence.

Heather took her hands from her ears.

Magda Prokash was staring thoughtfully at her, gray eyes hooded. She turned to the dark-skinned girl. "Wants to play games with us, does he? Aracely, bring the tarot deck. We'll have to do a ten-card divination just to learn his pesky name."

Aracely glanced at the burning triangle. "Something powerful's caught in there, Magda."

"Bring the cards."

Heather whispered to Sherone, "What's a ten-card divination?"

"You'll see."

Aracely returned with a tarot deck. Magda Prokash drew from it, placing the cards faceup in a crosslike pattern on the hardwood floor. The other coven members crowded forward, craning their necks to get a better view as the cards were laid down, one after the other.

Hanged Man.

Six of Cups.

Six of Swords.

Seven of Pentacles.

Knight of Pentacles.

Tower.

Death.

A shocked murmur swept the circle. Heather glanced at Sherone. But Sherone was staring intently at the last tarot card. The Card of Death. A pale rider on a pale horse: a skeleton in a suit of armor astride a white horse, visor raised to reveal a grinning death's-head beneath the helmet.

"My God, Magda." Aracely shuddered. "The Death Card!"

"That's only seven," Magda Prokash said. "We need three more."

"NO!"

Heads swiveled toward the speaker. It was the skinny boy with the sharp nose and straight dark hair, his lean face tight with tension.

"You know what the Death Card means, Magda." He nodded at the burning triangle. "We've got something in there we can't control. *Close the ceremony!*"

Magda Prokash looked at him critically. "You came here, Brian, of your own free—"

"The Death Card means *stop*. It means *black magic*."

Angry murmurs rose from the circle.

Magda Prokash smiled. "Black magic. White magic. It all depends . . . Some would say that calling forth a demon is *always* black magic—regardless of why you're calling him, or what you plan to make him do."

"It's not fair, Magda!" Brian brushed lank hair back from his face. "No one controls a really powerful demon. *No one*. And we've got new people here . . ." His eyes met Heather's briefly, then glanced away, back to Magda Prokash's cold gray eyes.

"The initiates will be safe," she said. "All will be safe. So long as we stand together inside—"

"JUST SHUT DOWN THE GODDAMNED CEREMONY, OKAY?"

"Brian . . ." She paused. "Are you afraid?"

He glanced at Heather, then looked down. "No," he muttered. "I think this is a real chickenshit thing to do, Magda—pulling a Death Card, then going on ahead with it anyway—but I'm not afraid."

10

She smiled. "Then why all the fuss?"

She turned and drew another card from the tarot deck. Five of Swords.

She stopped.

"Two more," Aracely whispered.

Magda shook her head. "No. We have our name. Look." She knelt, arranging the cards on the floor before her. "Hanged Man. *A*. Six of Cups. *Z*. Six of Swords. *G*. Seven of Pentacles. *A*, again. Knight of Pentacles. *R*. Tower. *O*. We skip the Death Card, the one that bothers Brian so." She looked up in his direction. "And finally, Five of Swords. *TH*. Put them all together and we have a name. A-Z-G-A-R-O-T-H. Azgaroth." She turned the name over in her mouth, savoring its strangeness, its guttural harshness. "Azgaroth . . ."

The hissing sound started again, more fierce this time. Heather plugged her ears again, but it did no good. The sound continued, increasing in volume *inside her head*.

"Azgaroth . . ." Sweat glistened on Magda Prokash's broad upper lip. "*Azgaroth!*"

The hissing grew louder, sharper inside Heather's skull.

She unplugged her ears and turned to Sherone. "Tell her to *stop!* That boy's *right!*"

"That boy," Sherone tossed her head in disgust, "is such a total jerk."

Heather winced at the terrible hissing. "Sherone, he's *right!*"

"Look, Magda knows what she's doing, okay? *She learned its name!*" Sherone's brown eyes burned with excitement. "Once you know their name, you can make them—"

"AZGAROTH!"

Magda Prokash stood erect in the center of the salt circle, gray eyes clouded, breasts rising and falling heavily as she struggled for breath.

"REVEAL YOURSELF TO US!"

The hissing skipped abruptly to an ear-splitting *scrreeeeeeeeeeee*... Heather jumped back from the painful sound. Her right foot scraped over rock salt.

A hand gripped her shoulder. "Stay *inside* the circle!" Sherone spoke through clenched teeth. "No matter what happens, *don't step outside!*"

Heather nodded. But she was not listening. Her frightened blue eyes flashed across the dimly lit room. Revolving wind chimes. Burning triangle. Bronze statue of the nude cat goddess. Tarot cards in order on the floor, spelling out the demon's name. Awestruck faces of coven members. Magda Prokash's head thrown back in ecstasy as she called upon the demon.

Heather's heart beat wildly inside her chest. The squealing sound filled her head, digging into her brain. A hotter, stronger gust of wind burst into the room from the darkness outside. Wind chimes whirled. Candle flames flickered. Magda Prokash lifted the wooden staff above her head. Sparks flew from the burning triangle.

I've got to get out of here! Heather thought, panicked. *I've got to get—*

The candle flames flickered once again, then went out.

The fire inside the triangle seemed to grow dark. Its light dimmed, but still continued to burn with an eerie, opaque glow.

Heather bolted.

She stumbled out of the circle, scattering coarse rock salt crystals across the hardwood floor.

"HEATHER!" Sherone screamed, grabbing for her.

The squealing sound stopped. The room fell silent.

Except for a slow, steady pounding, deep and loud, like the amplified beating of a gigantic human heart.

Heather stopped, gasping for breath.

She saw the blackness then. *Felt it.* Across her flesh, inside her body, within the dimly lit darkness of the room. A blackness so horribly unclean, so palpably evil, that Heather shrank from it, her heart filled with terror.

She tried to turn back toward the safety of the circle,

away from the blackness.

Away from its evil.

She opened her mouth to scream. No sound came out. She could hear the skinny guy, Brian—miles distant he seemed now, separated from her by a vast body of dark water—calling to Magda, begging her to do something. *Jesus, help me!* Heather screamed silently inside her head. *Somebody please! Help me! Mother!*

The blackness wrapped itself around her, slowly, loathsomely.

The wind began to howl outside like a maddened beast.

Flames leaped higher within the burning triangle.

Then there was nothing but blackness.

PART 1
EARTH

chapter 1

the forgotten gods

Milton Bromley frowned over his black-framed glasses at the eight-inch-tall statuette on the polished mahogany tabletop. "I'm not saying it's not interesting." He pursed his lips. "But is it . . . right?"

The bronze figurine depicted the bare-torsoed body of a man with the head of a jackal.

Karin Roberts tried to smile. "Mr. Bromley, I don't think I have to defend a superb Egyptian Middle Kingdom bronze. Its authenticity has been documented by the catalogue for the 1965 British Museum Exhibition. As for its artistic integrity—"

"Mrs. Roberts." Milton Bromley held up a pudgy, well-manicured hand. "Please. No one here questions your decision to include this particular piece in our upcoming exhibition. Agreed, gentlemen?" Bromley nodded formally to the other board members seated around the long mahogany conference table. When he turned back to Karin Roberts, his pursed lips had become a cupid smile. "We *all* trust your integrity, my dear."

Karin turned on her best good-little-girl smile, thinking, *You pompous asshole.* She had worked with Milton Bromley for more than eight years now, and it would be four years this October since her divorce from David had been finalized. But she would always be "Mrs. Roberts" or "my dear" to Milton Bromley, chairman of the board of the Barringer Foundation and director of the Barringer Museum. It did not matter that she had taken her B.A. with honors at Berkeley, same with the Ph.D. at Harvard, or that she had more practical experience with exhibitions than the chairman and his fellow board members put together. Nor did it matter that she had just as much right to the title "Doctor" as Dr. David Roberts, distinguished heart surgeon and ex-husband. None of it mattered. She was "Mrs. Roberts"—except when Bromley disagreed with her. Then she became "my dear."

Probably the same thing he calls his wife when they argue at home, Karin thought. That was the problem with rich and powerful men. They never had to raise their voices in an argument, because they already owned whatever they were arguing about. Karin took a deep breath and brushed back a lock of her dark brown hair. *Lighten up*, she told herself, cranking up the good-little-girl smile a few extra watts. *Nobody likes a bitch, even if she's right.* A cigarette would have helped just then. But there was absolutely no smoking at board meetings. Milton Bromley, a reformed three-pack-a-day man, was strict about enforcing this rule.

Bromley had taken off his black-framed glasses and was now tapping them reflectively against the palm of one hand. "It's not that we don't think your little dog-headed man is a kind of art . . ."

"Jackal-headed," Karin corrected him. "He's Anubis, jackal-headed god of the underworld in Egyptian mythology."

Bromley smiled pleasantly. "Forgive me, my dear. *Jackal*-headed. In any event, none of us dislikes your little jackal. For my part, I'm rather amused by him. But we are wondering . . ." Bromley wrinkled his forehead, making his bald head look like an onion under pressure. "We wonder if an entire exhibition of such things—

some of them far more unpleasant than our little jackal-headed friend . . ."

"Like the rat god from India?" Karin asked. "Or the spider god from Sri Lanka?"

"Precisely." A faint grimace ruffled Bromley's composure. "We fear that a whole show of that type might possibly upset some of our, ah, regular and generous patrons."

Scare away your angels, you mean, Karin thought. In the backstage world of art museums, "angels" are the wealthy patrons whose donations make possible major acquisitions and expensive exhibitions like the one Karin was preparing, *The Forgotten Gods: Religious Images in Ancient and Primitive Art.*

"Mr. Bromley." Karin turned from him to the other board members, struggling to keep her smile in the process. "This is a major exhibition. We'll be displaying priceless items on loan from great museums and private collections around the world. We've all been working on this for months." Karin lost the struggle and her smile collapsed into a look of hurt bewilderment. "Now you're telling me you want to back out because you think it's going to frighten away paying customers." Anger flared briefly in Karin's dark blue eyes. "When did we stop being a major Los Angeles art museum and turn into . . . a theme park?"

Several board members cleared their throats.

"My dear," Bromley began.

Robinson Parker leaned forward. "We all think you're doing a great job, Karin. We know this show's going to boost our reputation here at the Barringer. And we'll have you and your fine staff to thank for it. But . . ."

Robinson Parker, gray-haired and deeply tanned, was a senior partner with a major Los Angeles law firm. Like most good corporate attorneys, he chose his words carefully, preferring awkward silences to awkward statements.

Karin finished the sentence for him. "But you want it

to be a big commercial success. A box-office smash."

Milton Bromley nodded. "Precisely."

Karin turned to him. "Maybe we could mix in a few Impressionist favorites. Renoir women and children. Ladies with pink parasols. Boating on the Seine. Or even better, how about a Disney retrospective? Six Decades of Animated Magic?"

Bromley regarded her with an unfriendly stare.

Robinson Parker, ever the diplomat at board meetings, interceded once again. "I think what Milt's getting at here—and we all agree with him—is that this exhibition, even though it's first-rate, is maybe just a little *too* austere. It's a great teaching show. The local universities will love it. And don't get us wrong, Karin, we want shows like this. But . . ."

Parker hesitated again. "Some of those gods and goddesses are pretty creepy. Human sacrifices, things like that. We know the Barringer's a great cultural institution and we accept our responsibilities along that line. But, like it or not, we're also in show business. Most people go to an art museum to have a good time." Parker cleared his throat. "We don't want to scare all those folks away, you know."

Karin nodded, eyes respectfully lowered. "I understand, Rob. But I hope all of you understand," she looked up, "that I'm not trying to turn the Barringer into a research museum. I *want* people to come and see this show. I want them to enjoy it. I think they will." She turned back to Bromley. "But if some of them are shocked or offended, that's part of the risk of art." Karin leaned forward, her blue eyes bright with conviction. "Great art expresses the whole range of human emotion. It's not just pretty pictures."

Bromley smiled pleasantly. "You may be quite right, my dear. None of us are qualified to debate the point with you. But some of us, along with our more generous patrons, are old-fashioned enough to think that art should elevate the human spirit, not cast it down into the gutter."

Karin started to object, but Bromley added, "There is also the matter of, ah, religious sensibilities. All these pagan gods and goddesses—indulging in licentious sexual behavior, eating babies. Some of our devout and generous patrons may take this the wrong way."

Karin thought, *Always looking out for your angels, aren't you?* But she said, "Mr. Bromley, this show's historical in its approach. We're not trying to convert anyone."

Bromley nodded patiently. "Of course not, my dear. *You* know that. *We* know it. But will our devout and generous patrons see things the same way? And what about our, ah, less cultivated museum-goers? The occult bookshop crowd? Might they not also misunderstand, in a somewhat different way? Those frightful statues of Baal, Dagon, the pagan gods of darkness . . ."

Karin sighed. "Mr. Bromley, nobody takes that sort of stuff seriously."

"You'd be surprised, my dear, by what people believe."

Karin sighed again. "Okay. I concede. I'm supposed to be head curator. But you gentlemen control the pursestrings. I'll cancel the show."

A frown line creased Bromley's smooth brow. "You'll do nothing of the sort. As Rob Parker has already pointed out, we are firmly committed to your little experiment. What we want from you at this point is not cancellation, but rather, ah, modification."

Karin's eyes narrowed. "What kind of modification?"

"That's your department, my dear. But if you're soliciting suggestions, perhaps you could include some representative art works from the sacred Judeo-Christian tradition. Sort of a comparative religious approach."

Karin smiled. "Equal time for the other side?"

Bromley nodded. "Something like that. As I recall, Madonna and Child paintings are always popular, especially nowadays—babies being all the rage, even with

21

women old enough to know better."

Karin nodded, defeated. "Okay."

Robinson Parker cleared his throat. "I think Milt's given us some good ideas of what changes we all want to see in the show. Since we'll have two more meetings before it opens, I'd like to table this discussion for right now and give Karin time to work on the changes. We can get into details at another meeting."

The other board members agreed. After discussion of some minor details, the meeting was adjourned.

Outside the boardroom, Robinson Parker caught up with Karin on the way back to her office. "Congratulations on keeping your cool. I think Milt was trying to get under your skin."

Karin smiled. "He succeeded."

"Well, you didn't show it. That's the main thing. He can be a real son of a gun when it comes to the PR angle of a show. Maybe that's why he's the most successful fundraiser the Barringer's ever had."

"Thanks for coming to my rescue in there, Rob. But don't expect me to agree with your defense of Mr. Milton Bromley. He may be good at hustling bucks, but he doesn't know how to run a museum."

Parker gave her a critical glance. "Hustling bucks is just as important as setting up a show. An art museum's still a business, Karin, only it's a lot less profitable than a gas station and it costs a hell of a lot more to run. That's why we need the angels. And the Milt Bromleys to take care of them. But you know all this."

Karin knew. Underneath the excitement of the shows and the acquisitions, it was just money. It was always money. David had married her for her money, to get through medical school. When he got established and started making his own, he left her. And it wasn't even her money. It all belonged to her mother, Maureen O'Connor Magnusson, who had inherited it from her father, Cornelius Joseph O'Connor, a red-faced, irascible Irishman who had turned a small beer distributorship into a major liquor industry. Sometimes Karin wished that Grandpa O'Connor had lost his money so she would have been forced to earn the important things instead of buying them. But then her flinty honesty stepped in. *Without Mom's money and connections*, she told herself, *you never would've landed this job, even with all your fancy-ass degrees.* She owed it to Maureen Magnusson and Maureen's friends—the handsome and debonair Robinson Parker, the fat and powerful Milton Bromley. Just thinking about it gave Karin the beginnings of a world-class headache.

"Well," Parker briskly changed the subject, "give my regards to your mother and father. We missed them at the Music Center last Wednesday." He hesitated. "And by the way, Brett sends his regards to you. He told me he never knew how hard museum curators worked until he started going with you."

At the mention of Brett Courtney, Karin stiffened.

Parker cleared his throat. "I know your mother thinks highly of Brett. So do I. He's one of the fastest-rising young partners in our firm. He's got a great future. I'm happy for both of you."

Karin looked sharply at Robinson Parker. "You make it sound like we're engaged to be married. We're not. We've been out together a few times. I'm not even sure we're dating seriously."

"I think Brett thinks you are."

"Maybe he does."

Parker smiled. "Keep up the good work on the show, Karin. It's going to be great. We're all pulling for you. Even Milt."

Inside her own office, the first thing Karin did was light up a cigarette. Then she took off the jacket to her blue silk suit. Karin had the soft, milk-white skin of her mother and her daughter, Heather. But the voluptuous female figures on both the O'Connor and the Magnusson sides of the family had passed right over her to land on Heather with a double vengeance. While her daughter was a red-haired Irish-Scandinavian goddess with *Penthouse* proportions, Karin was tall, nearly five feet eight inches, and slim. Her perfect oval face was framed by wavy dark brown, almost black, shoulder-length hair.

Her secretary looked up from the word-processor. Barbara Kappelman was a short, intense woman with a sharp nose and lively dark eyes. "I'll tell you my bad news first; then you can tell me yours, okay?"

Karin nodded, drawing a cup from the Mr. Coffee machine. "Sounds like a deal."

"First," Barbara counted off on her fingers, "Keith Michaels called from New York. They've got the Sumerian fertility god statue all crated and ready to drop in the mail. But it seems Keith baby can't get it insured. So, no insuree, no mailee."

"Shit." Karin dumped non-dairy creamer into her coffee. "Can't he ever do anything right?"

"Apparently not without step-by-step instructions. Second, Nigel Harris called from London. Looks like the boys in Leningrad are playing coy again and they will not, repeat *not*, let us borrow the gold Scythian animal god from the Hermitage after all, *glasnost* or no *glasnost*."

"God*damn* it!" Karin slammed down her coffee cup. "That deal was okayed months ago! It should *be* here by now!"

"Actually," Barbara cocked an eyebrow, "don't let on I told you, but the thing's with Nigel. Seems our Soviet friends mailed the statue to London for transfer to New York, then got cold feet. Nigel wants you to call him on the p.d.q. so you two can reach out and double-team the Hermitage with a long-distance conference call."

"Jesus, Barb." Karin slumped down into her desk chair. "What next?"

"Brett called."

Karin groaned. "That's news?"

"Hey, girl, have a heart. This boy's on fire. Even asked *me* if you'd go to dinner with him. I told him I don't handle your personal calendar, but I'd be glad to chow down with him anytime. But he's only got eyes for you, baby. So *puh-leeze* call this poor man back."

Barbara counted off her fourth finger. "Heather called. She knows she's grounded because of last night—"

Karin's head snapped up. "Damn right she's grounded! Coming home at two in the morning after spending all night doing God knows what with Sherone Living—"

"Now, now, let's not jump to conclusions. By the way, which one is Sherone? The tough little blonde with those leather skirts slit all the way up the hip?"

"The same. What did Heather want?"

"Permission to go over to Sherone's after school—" Barbara held up a hand to silence Karin. "Just for a little while. She'll be home by dinner, she says."

"Any more surprises, Barb?"

"I've saved the best for last. Your momma done call you, girl."

"Oh Jesus."

"She said," Barbara imitated Maureen Magnusson's imperious tone of voice, "'You tell that daughter of mine not to get so busy she forgets to call back her only mother who needs to talk to her.' This has been a recording. Now," Barbara leaned forward, "she didn't say why she was calling, but here's what I think. I think poor desperate Brett called her up and asked her to run interference for him." Barbara sat back triumphantly. "So, tell me, how did it go with you and Bear Bromley?"

"Knock, knock." Sandy Weatherford stuck her blond head into Karin's office. "We want to hear this too, okay?"

"Yes indeedy." Dodge Andrews followed Sandy in, a cigarette held delicately in his left hand. "Sandy and I must hear *every* word that adorable little bald man said to you. I swear, he has got *such* hot pants for you, Karin! Any day now he'll start coming on to you in the breakroom, positively *begging* you to help him commit an unnatural act."

Sandy raised her eyebrows. "Is Bromley into that?"

Dodge gave an exaggerated shrug. "I'm sure *I* wouldn't know, personally. But I should think *any* kind of act with Teddy Bear Bromley would be highly unnatural."

Dodge Andrews was a short, fastidious young man with a neatly trimmed beard and a recently completed apprenticeship at the Metropolitan. Despite his frivolous style, he had a jeweler's eye for details of color, shape and texture. Sandy Weatherford was a pleasantly dumpy blonde from an old and rich New England family. She reminded Karin of her dull cousin Marte Magnusson, the one who wanted to marry an auto mechanic so she'd always have someone to keep her car running. But Sandy's plain face concealed a razor-sharp brain with a photographic memory. She could digest whole catalogues and retrieve a single date or reference almost instantaneously.

Karin told them what had happened at the board meeting.

Sandy shook her head. "Bromley . . . Where does he think we can round up enough Madonnas at the last minute? Make a midnight raid on the National Gallery?"

Dodge threw back his head and laughed. "Wait! I've *got* it! We can borrow the Small World puppets from Disneyland! I can see it now . . . The Forgotten Gods! All Singing! All Dancing!"

Sandy's round face turned serious. "If you want us to help you with this, Karin . . ."

Karin shook her head. "Thanks, Sandy. I need you and Dodge to keep working on the show. I'll take care of Mr. Bromley's modifications."

Dodge gave a sigh of mock irritation. "All right, Karin. *We* can take a hint. Sandy and I will now traipse out quietly, leaving you to bear your heavy cross all alone. But if you need any help sticking pins in your Bromley doll, just give a whistle."

After they were gone, Karin asked Barbara, "Why can't Heather be more like Sandy?"

Barbara got up to check and make sure Sandy and Dodge were really gone before she came back and said, "Because Heather's a knockout, that's why. Beautiful girls have a harder time of it. So many choices. Us uglies have our goals laid out early in life. It's called the law of diminishing opportunities."

Karin smiled. "If that's her biggest problem, I guess I don't have much to worry about, do I?"

"You got that right."

"But it's still hard raising a teenager, Barb."

"Always is. All you can do is listen, try to understand, but don't take too much shit."

Karin nodded. "I guess so. But I worry about Heather. I get this feeling when I look at her sometimes that she's really going to put me to the test before we're through. It scares me a little."

"It should." Barbara folded her arms across her desk. "I hope you won't take this the wrong way, Karin, but I doubt if you've ever been really tested before in your whole life."

Karin looked hurt. "I was divorced, Barb."

"So was I, honey. It don't count."

Karin thought, *You mean it doesn't count because I have money*. She lifted her chin. "Money doesn't buy happiness, Barb."

"No," Barbara agreed. "It buys the next best thing."

"Which is?"

"Freedom from unhappiness."

Karin smiled in spite of herself.

Barbara frowned. "Hey, kiddo. You want to return any of those calls this year?"

Karin lifted the receiver and started to dial, thinking, *Just you wait and see how I pass the Big Test, Barbara Jean Kappelman*.

But then she thought of Heather again, and for some reason she felt uneasy.

Very uneasy.

chapter 2

fast lane

Sherone waited outside English for Heather.
Heather seemed to be dragging as she walked out of the classroom into the noise and confusion of B Hall. There were dark shadows beneath her blue eyes. Her shoulders slumped. In her baggy black trousers, cinched at the ankles, and her green utility vest over a white T-shirt, she looked like a dispirited prisoner of war.

Sherone sighed. "God, that was *so* boring. I hope you took notes." She frowned at Heather. "You okay?"

Heather nodded, not looking okay. "Sure."

Sherone studied her carefully. "Still bummed out about . . . last night?"

They stopped at Heather's locker. She started working the combination lock. Bobby Keefer, a short kid with hair waxed straight up from his head, squeezed the back of Heather's neck as he passed.

"Hey, beautiful!" Bobby turned around and walked backward, arms thrown wide. "Give me a higher love!"

"Get screwed, bozo," Sherone called after him.

"Baby, baby. I'm *workin'* on it, okay?"

Sherone turned back to Heather. "Still pissed? Want to talk about it?"

Heather slammed the locker shut. "I am *not* pissed. And I do *not* want to talk about it. Okay?"

Sherone nodded. "Sure."

They walked out of Module B into the painfully bright Southern California sunshine of the Quad, Heather still dragging, Sherone keeping a respectful silence. The low stone benches around the Quad were filled with students talking, eating junk food, listening to Walkman headphones or just taking it easy. Severy Academy was a coeducational private secondary school with light college prep and heavy tuition. It sprawled over several grassy acres in the Pacific Palisades east of Malibu. The parking lot was crowded with Japanese compacts owned by the faculty and German and Italian sports cars driven by the student body. Most of the students were dressed in Rodeo Drive trendy, some of the more avant-garde in Melrose Avenue outrageous. Hairstyles were cut according to fashion. Everyone looked tan, fit and rich.

Sherone said hello to friends as they passed. Heather kept looking straight ahead, feet dragging. A tall blond boy left a group of his friends to come over and walk with the two girls. He had a good build and hair stiff with styling mousse.

"Hi, Kurt." Sherone smiled, tossing her head.

Kurt Pritchard said hello, but he was looking at Heather. His teeth gleamed white against his smooth tan skin. "I called you last night but you were out."

Heather said, "Really?"

"Yeah, really. Your mom said you went out with Sherone. So where were you?"

Heather rolled her eyes. "God, he talked to my *mother*."

Sherone moved in closer, bumping her hip into Kurt's. "He talked to your mother and he actually *listened* to what she said."

Kurt persisted, "So where'd you guys go?"

"We went to *The Rocky Horror Picture Show* at the Chinese," Heather said. "We saw it three times in a row."

"Bullshit. Where were you?"

"We worked out all night at Sports Connection," Sherone said, "with this whole roomful of hunks. It was, like, a totally rad experience, you know?"

Kurt stared at her. "I'll bet you had a great time, Sherone." He turned back to Heather. "So what did you do while everyone else was busy with Sherone?"

Sherone sneered. "Thanks, Kurtis darling!"

Heather shook her head, face tense at the thought of what really had happened last night. "Kurt, don't be such a jerk, okay?"

"I call you up and you're not there. So I wonder where you are. That's bein' a jerk?"

Heather said, "Leave me alone, Kurt."

"Leave you alone? Fuck." Kurt turned and stared at the blue Pacific lying hazy in the distance. "I *ought* to leave you alone."

"Leave me alone just for right now, okay?"

He turned on her. "What's the matter, Heather? Somethin' better come along?"

Sherone put a hand on Kurt's shoulder. "Look, give her a break, would you? She had a really bad night last night. She is, like, totally stressed out, okay?"

Kurt did not like or trust Sherone Livingston. He wished Heather would find another friend, someone like Paige Benson, his best friend Troy's girl. Paige was cute, nice and rich. Sherone was cute. And bitchy and poor. That canceled out the cute part, especially her being poor. Sherone wasn't POOR poor. Her dad made a living as a freelance photographer. But she was the nearest thing Severy Academy had to a scholarship student. Some people liked Sherone because she was always out there on the edge, farther out than anyone else dared to go. But the trouble was, Sherone liked going over the edge, and taking people with her. She also had a mouth on her and liked to push other people around. As Kurt had learned from his father, a successful mini-series producer, nobody has the right to push other people around unless he's got an exclusive option, in writing.

Kurt turned from Sherone to Heather. "Okay. I'll back off. I'll leave you alone for a while, all right?"

Heather smiled. "Thanks, Kurt. You're sweet."

"Yeah." He looked down at his high-top Reeboks, then back up again. "Want to go out this Saturday?"

That was one of the last things Heather wanted to do, but she was grateful to Kurt for giving her some space and she said, "Sure."

He put an arm around her. "Pick you up at seven?"

She nodded, looking down. "Okay."

Kurt walked back to his group of friends.

Sherone called, "Bye-bye, Kurtis!" thinking, *You fucking son of a bitch . . .*

Heather walked on without her. Sherone hurried to catch up. Heather was dragging forward, shoulders slumped.

"You don't have to take that," Sherone said, falling into step beside her. "If you don't like him, it's okay to say no."

"He was trying to be nice."

"So what? Just a few seconds before he was acting like a real asshole. So he acts nice for maybe, like, a minute, and you roll over and give him whatever he wants."

"Sherone." Heather shot her a warning glance. "Back off, okay? You and Kurt and everybody. Just *back off.*"

Sherone put a hand on her shoulder. "You need to talk about it, okay?"

"I told you, I'm *not* talking about it!"

"You need to." Sherone nodded at the parking lot. "Let's go out to my car."

"Sherone, I don't want a cigarette."

"So don't smoke one. But we need somewhere to talk. Someplace private." Sherone started to pull Heather toward the parking lot. "And *I* want a cigarette."

Out in Sherone's cherry-red Volkswagen beetle, she lit up a cigarette. Heather coughed. Sherone rolled down the driver's window a crack. Heather stared out the windshield at the parking lot. Bright sunlight streamed in through the glass. Students and teachers crossed back and forth on their way to and from cars. The cigarette smoke irritated Heather's nose. She sneezed.

She had tried to start smoking. Twice. Each time she coughed more than she smoked. Sherone told her she just had to get used to it; then it would be fantastic. But Heather wasn't so sure. Lately she had begun to notice that most of life's fantastic experiences were turning out to be real downers when they actually happened. Alcohol. Cigarettes. Witchcraft.

Even sex.

Of course, sex had not quite happened for Heather yet. Not officially. When Sherone wanted to give her a bad time, she would call her "Southern California's only certified sixteen-year-old virgin." In truth, she had gone pretty far with Kurt. But if the real thing turned out like cigarettes, or witchcraft, she wouldn't be missing much.

The thought of witchcraft brought a sudden image of Magda Prokash's cold gray eyes. Heather shuddered.

Sherone asked, "Why won't you talk about it?"

"Because I don't want to."

"You're thinking about it. I can tell."

Heather clamped her mouth shut.

Sherone approached the subject carefully. "You think something . . . happened?"

Heather looked up at her. "Sherone, I heard those *sounds*. Hissing. Squealing. And then, when I ran out of the circle . . ." Tears started to form in Heather's blue eyes. "Sherone, I could *feel* the darkness! *I felt it all over my body!*"

Heather started to cry.

"Lighten up, okay?" Sherone put a hand on Heather's cheek. "Just lighten up a little."

Sherone saw again Magda Prokash's hard gray eyes. *She must not remember*. Magda had spoken slowly, deliberately. *What she remembers must be denied. What she remembers did not happen.*

Sherone felt a hot steel wire coiling itself up inside her stomach.

She cleared her throat with difficulty. "Heather, whatever you think happened . . . It was only like a bad dream, okay?"

Heather shook her head, sniffling. "It was no dream!"

"Heather, you passed out. That's all. You were out for just a little while. Only a few minutes. We were getting ready to call, like, the paramedics. Then you got up and everything was cool." Sherone drew a deep breath. "You were scared. But you were okay. Okay?"

Heather turned away from Sherone. "The darkness," she whispered, "was everywhere."

Sherone felt a sudden chill invade her heart as she remembered the darkness and what had been within it, and what had happened then. The sunlight streaming in through the car's windshield was hot. But Sherone was shivering.

She swallowed hard, tensing her muscles to stop the shivering. "Heather, you've got to believe me. *Nothing happened*. Trust me. Okay?"

Heather wiped at her eyes. "Nothing, huh?"

Sherone nodded, still shivering. "Zilch."

Heather looked at her searchingly. "You wouldn't bullshit me, would you?"

"Hey, am I your friend or what?"

Heather smiled and put her arms around Sherone, hugging her close. "You're my best friend. My *only* friend." Tears sparkled in her blue eyes.

Sherone patted her on the shoulder. "You're still a little wired. It was your first time."

Heather pulled back. "And my last."

Sherone protested, "Alls you have to do is get—"

"—used to it and it'll be fantastic," Heather finished for her. "Thanks, Sherone. But once is enough."

"You'll change your mind."

"Yeah? Watch me."

Sherone stubbed out her cigarette, then closed the

ashtray. "Want to come by my place after school? I still got that old Madonna video."

"Sure." Heather smiled, then stopped. "I forgot! I'm grounded."

"Come on. Nobody gets grounded anymore."

"I am. No shit."

"For how long?"

Heather shrugged. "Until my mom gets over being pissed about last night."

"It'll only be, like, for an hour or two. You'll be home by dinner."

"Sherone, I'm *grounded*."

"Ask her if you can stop by for just an hour."

"I don't have to ask. She'll say no."

"So ask anyway. Moms are like everyone else. They talk big. But it doesn't mean much."

Heather shook her head. "You don't know my mom. When she says no, she means *no*."

Sherone nodded in apparent agreement, thinking that Karin Roberts, with her stubborn integrity, could be a real pain in the butt sometimes.

chapter 3

the Golden Road

Late afternoon sunlight fell on the green trees and spacious lawns of the Nelson G. Barringer Museum. It was a hot, dry September. Smog lay thick and brown on the horizon. But the landscape of the Barringer seemed unnaturally lush and green with the foliage of an endless springtime. The tree leaves and grass blades shimmered with moisture droplets, though no rain had fallen on Los Angeles for more than five months.

Karin came down the wide marble steps of the front entrance. Engraved on the lintel above the heavy front doors in pseudo-Roman capitals was the inscription:

BEAVTY IS TRVTH, TRVTH BEAVTY
THAT IS ALL YE KNOW ON EARTH
AND ALL YE NEED TO KNOW

Karin smiled skeptically. She had no problem with Keats's famous aphorism. But she wondered what possible significance it could have for Milton Bromley and the other board members.

She got into her car, a white Jaguar XJ6. Karin would have preferred something cheaper, more practical. She once considered buying a van or jeep to haul frames around in on weekdays and drive to the mountains on weekends. *Probably why I got the Suzuki Samurai for Heather*, she thought, buckling up her seat belt and shoulder harness. The Jaguar was a gift from Karin's mother, Maureen Magnusson, who knew that a museum curator should not be seen on the street in anything less. *Why can't mothers just buy the cars they want for themselves,* Karin wondered, *instead of forcing them on their daughters?*

Karin tuned her FM to a drive-time traffic report and headed out of the museum parking lot toward the nearest freeway on-ramp. The Barringer was located on an expensive piece of land in the foothills of the San Gabriels. Its fancy address and distance from downtown Los Angeles gave it a rather exclusive reputation—something Milton Bromley worked hard to play down. *Bromley'd be happier,* Karin thought, *if we put the show on at Dodger Stadium.*

Traffic slowed to a crawl on the freeway. Karin put a Mozart cassette in the tape deck, lit a cigarette, then leaned back against the headrest, ignoring as much as possible the crush of metal and fumes around her. Her home in Encino was not far from the Barringer as miles go. It might have been possible to drive it in thirty minutes with open freeways. Under normal rush-hour conditions it could take an hour or more.

Afternoon sunlight filtered down through murky haze, turning buildings and hillsides into ghostly apparitions. Sunlight glared into the eyes of westbound commuters. Karin pulled down her visor. It did no good. Sometimes she wondered why she put up with it all, day after day: the drive to work and back, the endless hassles with Bromley and the board members. She had enough money, in a trust fund administered by her mother, to live comfortably for the rest of her life without working. But working, she knew, was her only reason for living.

Work's all I've got now, she thought. There was

Heather, of course. But teenage girls live their own lives in their own special worlds, no mothers admitted. She couldn't make Heather the center of her life, not unless she wanted to spend the rest of it worrying about someone who was never there. It was her work, despite the headaches and the Bromleys, that kept her on track. *Without it,* she thought, *I probably wouldn't get out of bed until Heather came home and turned on her videos.*

It was not a good situation, living for her work. Karin knew that. She had seen the television specials on workaholics and the messes they made of their lives. *You cannot, honey girl,* her mother Maureen Magnusson had insisted, *you simply cannot continue living alone like this with nothing to occupy yourself except that damn musty museum.*

Karin agreed. But what were the options? Volunteer work? Health clubs? Marriage to someone like Brett Courtney?

She grimaced at the thought. Then she felt embarrassed, and guilty. It wasn't that there was anything wrong with Brett. In fact, he was perfect, a state-of-the-art modern man—rich, handsome, sensitive—in the words of Annie Newmar, Karin's younger sister, "such a really super guy." But Karin knew that if she had to make a choice, she would rather go crazy alone at the Barringer than try to live with someone like Brett Courney. *I've been to that movie,* she told herself, *and I left before it was over.*

Most of Encino is flat, but part of it rises up into the hills that form the north side of the Santa Monica mountains. Karin lived in the hills, 117 Camino de Oro, the Road of Gold. Once, years ago, when she and David were younger and still in love and they first came out to look at the place with the real estate agent, Karin had found it a wonderfully romantic name. The Golden Road that leads to home. Now, from the other side of those years, it sounded tacky and ironic, like "Funland" as the name for a rundown, unfun amusement park. A friend who once complimented her on the address was surprised to hear Karin refer to it as the Road of Fool's Gold.

As Karin pressed the remote control to the garage door, she noticed that Heather's dark blue Suzuki Samurai was not parked in the driveway. She frowned and turned off the Jaguar's engine. She felt her anger rising, but told herself, *She's just doing this to test me—she'll be home soon.* The garage was attached, but Karin liked to walk out across the driveway unless it was after dark. She ducked underneath the automatically closing garage door, wondering where Heather had really gone with Sherone that afternoon.

As she headed for the front door, Hyung-Joon Kim came hurrying across the lawn toward her, a clump of withered blossoms in his right hand. Hyung-Joon Kim was the elderly Korean gardener who had worked for Karin as long as she had owned the house.

"Good afanoon, Meesa Robbers." He bowed formally.

Karin smiled. "Hi, Hyung-Joon."

"Meesa Robbers . . ." Hyung-Joon Kim held out his handful of withered rose blossoms. "Rose busha all wanna die."

Shit, Karin thought, looking at the dead flowers. She had spent time and money putting in her rose garden. It was one of the few things about the house she still liked.

"What's wrong with them?" she asked. "Disease?"

Hyung-Joon shook his head firmly. "No disease."

"What is it then? Too much sun? It's been so damn dry. Maybe they haven't been getting enough water."

Hyung-Joon Kim looked offended. "Rosa busha *aways* getta righta amounta *eva*thing. Sun. Wata. *Eva*thing. Theesa flower," he raised the limp blossoms, "they juss wanna die."

Karin frowned. "It must be the soil. We'll have someone come out and test it."

"No soil!" Hyung-Joon Kim was adamant. "Soil *good.* Wata good. *Eva*thing good. Flowers juss wanna die."

Karin felt her headache returning. "Okay, Hyung-

Joon. Thanks for telling me. I'll think of something."

Hyung-Joon Kim bowed to her, then walked away shaking his head and muttering to himself, "Juss wanna die."

Karin unlocked the front door and stepped inside. The central air conditioning felt crisp and cool, a welcome contrast to the hot, smoggy air outside. Karin moved through the entranceway into the large formal living room. The furniture was black leather against stark white walls and carpeting. David had loved the melodramatic effect. *Just like the Cabinet of Dr. Caligari!* Karin had grown used to it eventually—enough so that she had never got around to replacing it during the four years since David left.

For some reason, thinking about David and his furniture made her feel moody, depressed. She got out a Johnny Mathis compact disc and popped it into the sound system. The sugary strains of "Misty" filled the air. Karin mixed herself a gin and tonic at the black marble bar that separated the living room from the dining room.

Then she opened the sliding glass door and stepped out into the pool area. The house was built around the swimming pool, creating an atrium effect that gave each room a picture-window view of the pool. Johnny Mathis singing "Misty" followed her outside, piped over an outdoor speaker setup. Karin walked slowly down the length of the pool, looking at the still, blue reflection of the house in the water. Her high heels echoed off the pavement. She sipped at her drink.

She hardly ever swam in the pool anymore, but she liked looking at it like this at the end of the day. Some nights, when she really felt out of it, she would sit by the pool for hours, watching the water turn dark as the sun set, then continuing to watch as outdoor lights and lights from the house shimmered on its surface. Heather sometimes had pool parties for her friends. But most of the time it sat there undisturbed, maintained meticulously once a week by Esteban the pool man.

The telephone rang. Karin went back into the living room. There was an extension by the pool, but the answering machine was in the living room. Like most people, Karin used it as a screening device for calls she did not want to receive. Some clicks sounded, followed by Karin's voice on tape:

"Hi. You've reached (818) 986-4433. We're not in right now. But if you leave your name, number, the time you called and a brief message after the beep, we'll get back to you as soon as possible. Remember, wait for the beep. Thanks for calling. . . . BRREEEEEEP."

Karin sat down on a black leather sofa and took a sip of her gin and tonic.

More clicks. "K.M.? It's Annie. Hey, listen up, kid! You and Brett gonna go sailin' at the marina with me and Sam this weekend or *what?* I mean, we got to know before the weekend, right? And that's almost *here!* So *call* me, okay? Bye!"

Karin reached over and punched a button on the answering machine to see who had called while she was at work.

More clicks. "Karin Marie? This is your mother speaking. I suppose I don't have to tell you that. But sometimes I wonder. I really do. You never call me. You never answer my calls. And, of course, you *never* stop by to see me. I might as well be living in Cleveland. In fact, if I *were* in Cleveland, I suppose you might call me more often than you do now. Well, I guess I'd better get off before this damn machine of yours cuts me off. Please call me back, darling. Right now. Before you forget about it. I know you're busy. But that's no ex— BRREEEEEEP."

More clicks. "Hi. This is a personalized computer message from Valley Realty World, your one-stop center for home buying in the San Fernando Valley. Have you thought about taking advantage of the equity in your home by refinancing your first trust deed and getting cash back? With interest rates at an affordable—"

Karin shut off the machine and lay back against the

sofa cushions. She supposed she should call her mother and Annie. But not right now. Not after Bromley. Later, maybe.

The telephone rang. Karin's tape message echoed across the living room.

"—for the beep. Thanks for calling.... BRREE-EEEEP."

"Karin?" The voice hesitated, then started again. "Karin? This is Brett. Sorry you're not there. We just seem to keep on playing telephone tag. I left a message at your work. Guess you didn't get it. Anyway, I'd really like to talk to you—"

Karin sighed and picked up the receiver. "Brett?"

"—and if you can't get me there, *please*, leave a message on my home—"

"Brett! It's *Karin*."

"Karin? Hey, Karin! Is that you?"

"It's me."

"I can't believe it. Phone contact at last! You sound great. How've you been?"

"Okay," she lied.

"That's great. I tried to call you at work."

"I know. You said so on the tape."

He laughed. "Guess I did, didn't I? So, how's the new show? Still comin' right along?"

"Comin' right along."

"Keeps you pretty busy."

"Yeah, pretty busy." *Why*, Karin wondered, *does every conversation with him have to sound like it's happening inside an echo chamber?*

"They keep me pretty busy over here too," Brett said. "Lots of acquisitions and mergers. But you know what they say: all work and no play..."

"Right." Karin started rubbing the place where her head hurt. She knew what was coming next.

"Say, listen. It's been a while since I've seen you."

"It's been just about a week."

"A week's a long time."

41

Why do you keep stringing him along like this? she asked herself. *Just tell him you want to break it off, then go ahead and do it.* But it wasn't that simple. Karin couldn't cut someone off the way you turn off a television set. That was David's way. Telling her there was someone else, that slutty little big-boobed intern from Boston who talked through her nose. Dropping it on her casually one night like a nuclear bomb over what she had thought was a romantic dinner at Spago's. It was David's way. But it wasn't hers. Besides, Brett Courtney was a nice guy. Karin hated shutting down nice guys, even if they bored her.

"—to see you again. Maybe dinner. A show. Maybe just dinner. Whatever you feel like. How's tomorrow night sound?"

"What's tomorrow night?" Karin stalled. "Thursday?"

"Uh—" Brett checked something—a watch, a desk calendar. "Thursday. Right."

Tell him no, she told herself. *Tell him you've already made plans.* But the only plans she had were to work late on the show, going over the physical details one more time, checking out the displays, the lighting. It wasn't really necessary at this stage. Dodge and Sandy had that part under control. All she could hope to accomplish would be to get in their way and on their nerves. A good head curator knows when to leave competent assistants alone. And Karin was very good.

But the museum and the show were her life. Without them she had nothing to fill up her empty evenings.

"Well? How about it?" Brett's voice had the nervous uncertainty of someone who expects to be turned down.

Okay, she thought, *you win. For now.* But she did have important work planned for Friday morning. She had no intention of coming in hung over from a late night dinner with Brett Courtney. "What if we move it from, say, Thursday to Friday?"

"Friday's fine with me," Brett answered hopefully.

Karin resigned herself. "So where are we going?"

He almost sighed with relief. "There's this great new sushi bar in Little Tokyo. All the visiting Japanese businessmen go there, so you know it's got to be good."

Raw fish, Karin thought, and her stomach flipped. What she really felt like was ribs. But Brett worked hard to keep up with these trendy things. You couldn't ask a guy like that to take you out for ribs.

"Sounds good," she said.

"I'll stop by your place at 7:30, if that's okay."

"I didn't think lawyers called it quits till 8:00."

"I'll leave early."

"Still remember where I live?"

"117 Camino de Oro. Encino, California."

"Hey, Mr. Memory."

"That's all they teach you in law school."

"Brett . . ."

"Yes?" His voice had a hushed expectancy.

"You think they'll have anything besides sushi at this place?"

"You mean something like sukiyaki?"

"I mean anything except sushi."

"I think they have boiled eel."

Boiled eel, Karin thought. *Jesus*. "I guess I'll stick with those little cucumber rolls."

"*Kappa maki*." Brett knew the Japanese names for the sushi pieces. That was all part of it. "They have great *kappa maki*."

"Great." Karin tried to put a smile in her voice. "Well, talk to you later."

"Don't work too hard on your show."

"Don't get caught in an unfriendly merger."

They said goodbye and hung up. P.T. Barnum, the family cat, an overweight gray-and-white Persian, hopped up onto the sofa and nestled comfortably against Karin. She stroked its head absentmindedly and thought seriously of unplugging the phone before her mother or Annie called back.

She was still thinking about it when Gabriela Garcia walked into the living room, rubbing something off her hands with a cleaning rag. Gabriela was a stout middle-aged Mexican lady with a dusky complexion and large dark eyes. She supported a son and two daughters in a modest stucco bungalow in Montebello, and a mother and two aunts in Tijuana. She had worked as a housekeeper for Karin ever since Heather was born. During Karin's difficult graduate studies at Harvard, Gabriela had practically raised Heather by herself.

Karin smiled at her. "How's it goin', Gabriela?"

"Karin . . ." Gabriela pronounced it *Kahreen*, the way Karin's great-aunt Ilse Magnusson did. "You see this stuff?" Gabriela raised a hand smeared with something black and sticky like tar, but also fine and powdery like crumbled ash.

Karin got up from the sofa. "What is it?"

Gabriela shook her head in disgust. "I find this stuff all over the top of her dresser, on the carpet too. The mess, my God."

Karin grabbed at Gabriela's hand. "What's she doing in there? What *is* this?"

"You come with me. I show you." Gabriela cocked her head reproachfully. "Then maybe you tell me what the hell kind of thing go on around here, okay?"

chapter 4

card trick

Wes Livingston, Sherone's father, lived in a modest redwood ranch-style tucked away in one of the more obscure corners of Topanga Canyon. Topanga is right on the edge of the San Fernando Valley, not far from Santa Monica or Beverly Hills. But it makes you forget you're anywhere near a city. Deep arroyos. Steep, twisting roads. Manzanita. Boulders. Trees. Cacti. A wild, woodsy feel to the place. It reminds you that Los Angeles, second largest city in the nation, is only half-civilized, only partially reclaimed from the wilderness surrounding it.

Heather gunned her dark blue Suzuki Samurai up the winding ribbon of a road that led to the Livingston place. Sherone trailed after her in the cherry-red VW, the bug grinding its guts out in second to negotiate the almost vertical ascent. Heather pulled into the dirt-and-gravel driveway in a cloud of swirling dust. Her brakes rocked the little jeep. She turned off the engine. The cooling motor ticked and pinged. She got out and looked over the deep arroyo that dropped down from behind the house. A red-haired Irish setter, Sean O'Casey, ran out to greet her. Heather patted him on the head. Sherone's VW came sputtering up into the drive.

Heather turned to her. "You guys have a really super view from up here, you know?"

Sherone got out and walked over to where Heather was watching the play of late afternoon sunlight along the far canyon wall. "What good is it? My dad'll never sell. Alls you can do is take pictures. Or toss empty beer cans over the side."

Heather scoffed. "Your dad would *never* do that."

Sherone patted Sean O'Casey. "All the time."

"Bull-loney."

Wes Livingston was an active conservationist as well as a serious nature photographer. That was one of several reasons why he and Sherone's mother had eventually divorced. Serena James felt her own acting career would have gone somewhere with a husband who was a fashion photographer or a promotional stills man for a major studio, anything except what he was—a "bugs and birds boy," as Serena put it. Wes Livingston occasionally took glamor assignments to pay the mortgage and buy food. But his role model was Ansel Adams, not Richard Avedon. *Ansel Adams shot in black and white, for Christ's sake,* Serena would remind him, as if only real losers did that. Wes Livingston worked in black and white when his editors let him get away with it. Mostly he did color specials for travel magazines and calendars.

Serena had left him for a retired Italian producer with a neo-Pompeian villa in Beverly Hills. It was a relatively happy divorce. Wes and Serena were glad to be free of each other's value systems. When Sherone missed her mother, she drove down to Beverly Hills for a visit. She never stayed long.

Sherone peeled a yellow Post-it note off the front door. "Glenda's at the lab."

Glenda McGuiness had lived with Wes Livingston for almost three years now. She was an associate professor of zoology at UCLA.

"Where's your dad?" Heather asked as she followed Sherone and Sean O'Casey into the small living room with its cheap furniture and large blowups of nature studies.

"Bora Bora, I think," Sherone answered, rummaging through the refrigerator for snacks.

"Bora *Bora?*"

"Someplace like that. Some island where the women all run around bare-ass naked. The kind of scene my dad can really get into."

"Your dad's not like that."

Madonna begged her papa not to preach while Heather and Sherone sat on Sherone's quilt-covered bed listlessly watching the VCR. Sean O'Casey lay on the floor at their feet, panting happily with his tongue hanging out. The girls were drinking Diet Coke and eating chocolate Häagen-Dazs ice cream and Doritos. Heather poked moodily at her ice cream with a soggy Dorito. Sherone watched her.

"Still stressed out about it, aren't you?"

Heather frowned. "Drop it, would you?"

"I don't see—"

Heather turned fiercely on her. "You don't see because it didn't *happen* to you! *It happened to me.*"

Sherone shook her head. "Heather, nothing hap—"

"*Drop* it, Sherone."

Sherone persisted. "'It' happened. What's 'it'?"

"Drop it or I'm leaving, okay?"

"Like hell!" Sherone leaned forward suddenly, so close their noses almost touched. "You tell me what's wrong with you."

The video cassette came to an abrupt end. Madonna stopped singing. The television screen went blank. Sean O'Casey whimpered and licked his chops. Outside the nightbirds started calling in the twilight. Cars shifted gears in the distance to climb steep hills.

"What are you afraid of?" Sherone demanded.

Heather shrugged.

"You said you don't believe in witchcraft."

"I don't."

"Then how can you be afraid of something that isn't even real?"

"It doesn't have to be real to bring bad luck." Heather swallowed. "Bad luck just . . . happens."

"Like flunking English, huh?"

Heather looked up, blue eyes frightened. "I mean *bad* luck. Like dying. In a wreck. Or from cancer. My mom dying." Tears glistened in her eyes. "*Really* bad luck," she whispered.

Sherone regarded her solemnly. "You're not afraid of what happened last night at Magda's. You're afraid of the future."

Heather said nothing.

Sherone went over to her chest of drawers and pulled something out of the top drawer. When she came back and sat down on the bed again, Heather could see that it was a deck of tarot cards.

"There are ways," Sherone confidently shuffled the cards, "of finding out about the future."

"No thanks." Heather reached for her purse. "No more black magic for me."

Sherone put a restraining hand on her friend's arm. "This is *not* black magic."

Heather shook her arm free. "Forget it, Sherone."

"Heather . . . Tarot cards have been used for, like, thousands of years to tell the future. It's not magic. It's more like, you know, weather forecasting."

Heather rolled her eyes. "Give me a break."

"It's no more magical than palm reading. But it's a lot more accurate. Remember Madame Morvena?"

Madame Morvena was a palm reader at a psychic fair they had gone to last year. She had gotten almost everything wrong.

Heather sniffed. "Big deal. A fortune cookie's better than her. Besides, you can make those cards say whatever you want."

"That's not true!" Sherone persisted. "They have very definite meanings."

Heather countered, "Then you just draw the ones with the meanings you want."

"I don't draw them," Sherone said. "You do."

Heather's face grew serious. "If there's bad luck ahead, maybe I'm better off not knowing."

"There's no bad luck," Sherone said.

"How do you know?" Heather demanded.

Because Magda promised me you wouldn't be hurt, Sherone thought guiltily, her heart fluttering inside her chest. But she said, "I just . . . know." She held out the shuffled deck. "Cut it, then draw a card."

Heather reached for the remote control. "Let's watch the video again."

"Draw a card, Heather."

"You draw one."

"You want to *know* what the future holds? Or just be afraid of it?"

"I want to watch the video again."

"You're afraid, aren't you?"

"The hell if I am."

"Then draw a card."

Heather hesitated, then reached out and drew a card, and turned it over.

A young man dressed in medieval hose and doublet hung upside down by one foot from a tree in the shape of a cross, arms tied behind his back, a brilliant nimbus encircling his head.

The Hanged Man.

"Sick." Heather grimaced at the bizarre card face. "I'm going to be crucified upside down. Just like St. Peter." She remembered the ghastly fate of the apostle from her parochial school days.

"That's not what it means! The Hanged Man represents a giving of yourself to a new way of life. Opening yourself up to new ideas and new people."

"Why's he hanging like that? Anti-gravity boots?"

"Cute. It's like, you know, a reversal. A big change in the way you look at things, okay?"

Heather did not want to admit it, but some of this was starting to make a little sense. So far.

Sherone said, "Draw another card."

Heather drew one and turned it over.

Like something out of *Hansel and Gretel*, two children in medieval dress filled a row of large cups with flowers against the backdrop of an old-fashioned thatched-roof cottage.

The Six of Cups.

"This one," Sherone explained, "means you're looking back at your childhood, but now you know that's passed and you're ready for new things and new people."

It's starting to sound like a horoscope, Heather thought, and drew another card.

A medieval ferryman poled his boat across smooth water toward a distant shore, six swords standing straight up in the boat, blades downward, a female passenger and a small child sitting huddled on a plank in the middle of the boat, their backs to the viewer.

The Six of Swords.

Heather squinted at the card. "Looks like something out of a fairy tale."

"It means a journey by water," Sherone said.

"Thanks, Sherone. I can see the guy's paddling a boat. What does it *mean?*"

"It means you're going to be making some kind of big change or crossover soon."

Heather drew another card.

A young man in medieval tunic and hose leaned meditatively on his hoe in the middle of a large field, staring at a bush with seven pentacles, five-pointed stars inscribed within circles.

"This is a good one!" Sherone cried excitedly. "Seven of Pentacles. It means you're going to be real successful and make lots of money, or marry someone with lots of money."

"Like Kurt, huh? Thanks a lot. Really makes my day, knowing I've got that to look forward to."

"Hey, *you're* drawing the cards."

Heather sighed and drew another one.

A man in full medieval armor, visor raised, sat astride a black horse and looked out across a distant plain, holding in his right hand a circle inscribed with a five-pointed star.

The Knight of Pentacles.

"He's searching for something," Sherone explained.

"A Christmas tree to hang the ornament on."

Sherone ignored that. "So it means you're searching for something too. Something very important. But you're, like, real particular about your search, okay?"

That part pleased Heather, so she said nothing.

And drew another card.

A terrifying bolt of lightning flashed down from a dark sky, severing the crown of a mighty tower as flames burst from its windows and hapless inhabitants fell openmouthed and screaming into the abyss below.

"The Death Card!" Heather jumped to her feet. "The one that witch lady—"

Sherone pulled her back down onto the bed. "You airhead, it is not the Death Card. That one's got a skeleton, remember? This is the Tower."

"It's still bad luck." Heather was uneasy. "You can tell by looking at it."

"It's not always bad luck," Sherone explained calmly. "Sometimes it just means like, you know, a really big change in your life."

"Oh sure, right. Like getting hit by lightning and falling a thousand feet from some building."

"Heather, you are *so* literal—"

"That's because it's *my* card and *my* bad luck!"

"The Tower doesn't always mean bad luck," Sherone insisted. "It can mean a sudden change or something."

Heather looked at her reproachfully. "Anyone can tell that card means bad luck and you know it."

"It *can* mean that," Sherone admitted. "Like an accident or something. But not necessarily a fatal one."

51

"Oh great. Just the kind where you wind up crippled in a wheelchair for the rest of your life. Screw this shit." She picked up the remote control.

Sherone sighed. "Heather, you've got to be patient and look at all the cards. One card never tells the whole story."

Heather fiddled with the remote control.

"Just one more card," Sherone asked, "please?"

"No. This is getting boring."

"Are you feeling afraid again?"

Heather glared at her, and drew another card.

Beneath a storm-dark sky a powerful man stood gloating savagely over two men cowering hunch-shouldered and defeated before a seacoast, their two swords lying useless on the ground, two more swords resting on the victor's left shoulder, a fifth sword held downward in his right hand, blade planted firmly in the earth.

Sherone hesitated. "I'm sorry, Heather . . . This one's pretty bad."

Heather looked up. "What do you mean?"

"Five of Swords," Sherone explained slowly. "It's not a real powerful card or anything. But it's not good."

"What do you *mean*, Sherone?"

"It means someone may threaten you with physical violence . . . or even try to attack you."

"Oh *great!*" Heather tried to laugh, but fear caught at her throat. "That's just really great, Sherone! I'm worried about what might happen because of last night, so you tell me, relax, nothing's going to happen. Except maybe I'll just get raped or killed by some sleazebag. Thanks a *lot*, you asshole!"

"Don't call me an asshole!" Sherone snapped back, hurt. "*You* drew the stupid cards."

"Fuck your cards!" Heather grabbed the deck and threw it across the room, cards scattering like confetti.

"You jerkhead." Sherone got off the bed to pick up the scattered cards.

Heather clapped her hands at Sean O'Casey. "Come on, boy! Come here." The Irish setter got up and trotted over to her, tail wagging happily. "Let's go outside and fetch sticks or somethin'." They headed for the living room and the front door.

"You leave my dog alone," Sherone called from the floor.

"He's more fun than you are," Heather called back.

"Screw you!" Sherone shouted; then she added, "Don't throw any sticks over the edge. He's so dumb he'll try to go after them."

The front door slammed shut.

She can be such a shithead sometimes, Sherone thought, picking up the cards. But it wasn't all Heather's fault. She knew that. Why did she have to draw the Five of Swords? It was such a rotten card. There was no way you could make it sound good. Sherone wished she could do readings like Magda Prokash. Magda's always came out right, no matter what cards you drew.

Sherone got to her feet with the reassembled deck and went over to the bed to gather up the seven cards Heather had drawn.

Her heart seemed to stop.

She blinked her eyes, rubbed at them, looked again. There was no mistaking it.

Her heart started throbbing inside her chest. Her mouth went dry. She stared at the seven cards lying on the bed in the exact order Heather had drawn them. Hanged Man. Six of Cups. Six of Swords. Seven of Pentacles. Knight of Pentacles. Tower. Five of Swords.

The same seven cards Magda Prokash had drawn.

The seven cards that spelled the demon's name.

AZGAROTH.

Sherone turned and looked around the room. The angles seemed to warp suddenly. Lines no longer ran true. A floorboard creaked long and loud in the next room. She could hear Sean O'Casey barking excitedly outside and Heather calling to him. But they sounded far away, very far away, like voices from another world. An ugly smell, foul and evil, wafted up from out of nowhere. The black night outside pressed in upon the open windows of Sherone's bedroom, seeming almost to ooze through them like a malignant, living effluence.

"Shit," Sherone whispered as she stared at the cards again and the terror took hold of her. "Oh *shit*."

chapter 5

candlelighter

Heather drove home alone in the dark.
She had patched up the quarrel with Sherone and each girl had apologized for whatever hard words she might have said to the other. But Heather was still tense, her nerves like shorted wires. The images of the tarot cards kept coming back to her, slipping sideways into her mind, along with Sherone's ominous interpretation of the Five of Swords . . .

. . . may threaten you with physical violence . . .
. . . or even try to attack you . . .

Heather shuddered. God*damn* those fucking cards! *Bad luck,* she thought bitterly, *bad luck no matter how you read them.* She wished she could forget about them.

And whatever had been in the bedroom with her and Sherone.

Something had been there, something undeniably real and forceful, yet undefined, a Presence felt but unseen. It wasn't just her imagination or a bad case of nerves. You could feel it kicking off heat like an open oven door.

That was the real reason why Heather had left the bedroom so abruptly. She was angry with Sherone and her tarot cards, but she was terrified of the Presence.

Outside in the cool night air, throwing sticks for Sean O'Casey, watching the large dog run barking after them, Heather had started to feel a little better. But she was still aware of the Presence—whatever it was—staring out at her from Sherone's lighted bedroom window, a sentient watcher.

Silent. Unblinking. Unknown.

She parked her Suzuki Samurai in the driveway of 117 Camino de Oro. A few lights were still on. She turned her key quietly in the front-door lock, hoping her mom had left on the lights and gone to bed or out for the evening. The door opened soundlessly. A shadow leaped out at her. Heather gasped, shrinking back within the door frame. Then she saw it was P.T. Barnum, the fat gray-and-white Persian.

"Hey, P.T.," she whispered, bending down to stroke the cat as it brushed against her legs, purring loudly. "How ya' doin', baby?"

A larger shadow slipped out from behind the door.

Heather jumped, giving a small cry of alarm; then she got angry. "Mom!" she shouted, breathless. ". . . scare the shit out of me like that!"

Karin Roberts looked critically at her only child. "This is what you call getting home by dinner?"

Heather sighed, looking at her watch. "Mom, it's only a little after eight."

"Since when do we eat at eight?"

Heather stifled a Häagen-Dazs belch. "I'm not hungry."

"I'm not surprised. But you don't have to wait till you're starving. The idea is to come home when you promise."

Heather dropped her eyes. "Okay, I'm sorry."

"So what were you and Sherone doing all this time?"

Heather shrugged. "Telling my fortune with tarot cards."

Karin stared. "Heather, honestly, I thought you gave up on that nonsense when you were eleven."

"It was Sherone's idea."

Maybe Bromley's right, Karin thought. *Maybe more people believe in this than I think.* "Did Sherone make a believer out of you?"

Heather shook her head no, trying to clear it of the mocking Five of Swords. "No way. Forget that."

Karin sighed. "Anyway, if you decide you're hungry later, Gabriela made chicken enchiladas. You can heat some up in the microwave."

Chicken enchiladas were one of Heather's personal favorites. But she honestly didn't feel hungry and she told her mother so.

"Suit yourself." Karin's voice turned hard. "Now let's cut the bullshit. What have you been doing in your room?"

Heather looked startled. "Huh?"

"Don't 'huh?' me!" Karin was trying to be reasonable about this, but she felt her anger sweeping her forward like a powerful current. "I asked you a question. I want an answer. *What have you been doing in your room?*"

Heather frowned, truly confused now. "Nothing special. The usual. Sleeping. Getting dressed."

Karin shouted at her, "Don't get smartassy with me, Heather Michelle!"

"I'm *not!*" Heather shouted back, upset now because her mom was never like this. She didn't grind people. Her dad used to do that sometimes, but her mom, never. "What do you *think* I've been doing, anyway?"

"I don't know," Karin answered quietly. The hardness in her voice was replaced by a worried, almost frightened tone. "I don't know at all. But I think you better come here and explain it to me." She headed for the hallway to the bedrooms.

Heather followed, an unpleasant tightness in her stomach. *What's wrong with her tonight?* she wondered. *I didn't come home that late!*

Heather's room, like the four other bedrooms in the house, looked out over the swimming pool. Lights reflected off the still water. It was a typical girl's room—if the girl had some money. There was a color television with its own VCR. Posters of Madonna and Tom Cruise hung on the wall. An expensive exercycle gathered dust in one corner. A three-way full-length mirror stood near a double-size clothes closet. Additional clothes racks held the overflow. The room's carpeting was deep-pile light blue. The telephone had its own answering machine and computerized control board with speaker phone. The full bathroom had a jacuzzi in the oversize tub and a sunlamp in the ceiling. Stuffed animals crowded the king-size bed: giraffes, whales, tigers, a baby Godzilla. The Cabbage Patch doll that usually completed the stuffed zoo was missing.

Back when Cabbage Patch kids were the hottest act in town and people were actually fighting over the ugly things in department stores at Christmas, Heather had decided that she had to have one. She was almost too old for dolls, even then, but as she explained to her mother, this was more than just a doll. It even came with its own birth certificate. Karin had a bad time finding one. She finally had to buy from a black market operation in Beverly Hills that charged more than two hundred dollars per doll. It all seemed worth it at the time. Heather was delighted. She christened the doll Jenny Lee. It occupied a place of honor on her teakwood dresser, staring out at the world with blank eyes and a round, insipid face.

Tonight Jenny Lee was not in her accustomed spot.

In her place lay a small heap of charred, twisted fragments coated with fine ash. Someone had set the doll on fire.

Heather's mouth fell open. "Oh no," she breathed softly. "No!"

She reached out toward the scorched remains, then withdrew her hand suddenly, as if the ashes might still be hot.

"You could have burned down the dresser," Karin

said, her voice unsteady, "and the whole house along with it."

Heather turned to her. "I didn't *do* this!"

Karin looked at her and said nothing.

"You think I did?"

"There's no need to yell."

Heather's eyes started to water. "God! I cannot believe you! You think I did this . . ." She turned away.

Karin reached for her. "Honey . . ."

Heather whirled around, eyes red, tears dribbling down her cheeks. "Why would I set fire to Jenny Lee?"

"Heather . . ."

"I loved her!" Heather was shouting now. "I wouldn't try to *h-h-hurt*—" Her voice broke. The tears came again.

"Honey, I know you wouldn't do something like this on purpose," Karin said, still trying to sound reasonable, even though her own voice was near breaking. "But you must have lighted one of those candles Sherone gave you and then forgot—"

Heather looked up, blue eyes swimming with tears. "I didn't light any candles! And if I did, I would've blown it out before I left for school! What do you think I am? *Stupid?*" She choked on a sob. "You always thought I was stupid."

"Heather!"

"You don't really love me." Heather's eyes were still red and swollen, but there was a coldness to them now. "You're just looking for some reason to get rid of me. Like because I tried to set fire to your shitty house by burning up my own doll in my own room."

Karin's head snapped back as if stung. "This has gone just about far enough, young lady."

Karin had been furious when Gabriela showed her the melted wax and the charred remains of the doll. Growing up in Southern California, Karin learned early to fear fire as the most terrifying of natural disasters, far more devastating than earthquakes. Fire was like a real-life vampire, pretending to be dead while actually biding its time, waiting for just the right moment to come howling back to life, destroying everything it touched. When she saw the damage in Heather's room, Karin's first thought had not been for her daughter's safety. It had been: *Fire!*

Heather must have left a lighted candle burning, Karin reasoned. How else could it have happened? But there was no point pushing it any further, not right now. Heather was upset. Karin had expected her to confess and then apologize in that easy way teenagers have: *Sorry, Mom, I didn't mean to, okay?* But she had not expected this violent outburst, these real tears of fear and righteous indignation.

Heather, still swallowing sobs, picked through the blackened remains of Jenny Lee. She turned to her mother, red hair falling loose on her shoulders, pale cheeks ruddy from the tears. *Most girls look awful when they cry,* Karin thought to herself, *but Heather's gorgeous even when she's miserable.* Then she frowned and wondered why she should be thinking something like that.

Heather lifted a piece of fire-melted plastic. "You really think I did this, huh?"

"No," Karin said. "I don't. Okay?"

Heather kept picking through the ash pile.

"Don't get your hands all dirty with that. Gabriela can clean it up later. You better get to bed. You had a late night last night."

Heather said nothing.

Kids, Karin thought wearily. *It's like war.*

"I really don't think you did it, Heather. At first I did. But I was wrong. Okay?"

Heather nodded. "Okay."

"Get to bed, honey. You need some sleep. Don't forget about those enchiladas if you're still hungry." Karin closed the bedroom door behind her.

Outside in the dark hallway she wondered if Heather was just lying to cover her ass or if maybe she had done it and then blocked it out, suffered a temporary memory lapse. Perhaps Gabriela should arrange for an emergency appointment with Dr. Goldstein. Healthy sixteen-year-olds don't have memory lapses. Then the dreaded word slithered into her mind: drugs. *Christ!* Karin thought, her heart chilled by real horror, *what if she and Sherone were over there doing drugs?* Karin knew Heather was smart on that subject, and she trusted her, to a certain extent. But she did not trust Sherone Livingston. Maybe it would be a good idea, Karin decided, if Heather saw a little less of Sherone. Dr. Goldstein could check for drugs as part of a regular physical.

Inside her bedroom, Heather was crying over her burned doll with all the unrestrained passion of an eight-year-old. Tears rolled down her cheeks. She drew in great quivering gulps of air. In truth, she hadn't cared for the doll that much. Just last week she was thinking about retiring Jenny Lee to the back of the closet. But now that the doll had been so wantonly, maliciously destroyed—*trashed!*—it was as if a part of her childhood had been destroyed along with it, the part that loves dolls and balloons and birthday parties with cake and ice cream and hates to give them up and finally does so only under crushing peer pressure but deep down inside never really does. That part of Heather wept for the ruined Jenny Lee.

Another part of her cried for fear of what had happened at Magda Prokash's house last night and in Sherone's bedroom just this evening. But she would not admit that to herself, that she was weeping over a damaged toy because she was afraid, horribly, helplessly afraid.

When she finished crying, she felt better, as if the tension gripping her for the past day and night had somehow been released.

She went over to her bed and flopped down full-length on it. She stared at the ceiling with its authentic imitation 1920s-style wood-blade fan. She thought about the tarot cards and wondered, *Why did I let Sherone talk me into that shit anyway?* She remembered the slick, slightly greasy feel of the cards as she drew them. She shuddered at the memory.

... may threaten you with physical violence ...
... or even try to attack you ...

Stop it! she commanded herself. *Stop it right now!* She sat upright in the bed, heart thumping against her chest. She glanced at the dresser.

And tried to scream.

The dresser was running with blood.

It spilled out over the sides of the teakwood top, dripping down thick and ropy onto the pale blue deep-pile carpet. It welled up from the scorched limbs of Jenny Lee, the Cabbage Patch Kid. Only now those torn limbs seemed to be raw and bleeding inside, with little knobs of bright white bone protruding from the severed arms and legs.

Heather felt the half-digested ice cream and Doritos come rumbling up into her throat. She leaped out of bed and ran over to the window. She fumbled at the lock, raised the window and stood there gasping for breath, shoulders rising and falling. The night air was cool. The hot, dry Santa Ana winds of the previous night at Magda Prokash's seemed to have vanished like a bad dream.

I wish it had been a dream, Heather thought, taking in deep breaths of cool air. *I wish—*

She remembered the blood on the dresser.

It was not easy to force herself to turn and look at the dresser again. But Heather was no coward. *If you can't face it in your own room*, she told herself, *you'll never be able to face it anywhere.*

She turned.

The dresser was clean. There was no blood on the teakwood top. No blood ran down over the brass drawer handles and onto the pale blue carpet. Heather let out a slow, steady breath. Then she took the top sheet off her bed and draped it over the dresser. It looked grim and ghostly now, like a piece of stored furniture in a dark warehouse. Heather got into bed and pulled the heavy quilt up over her, tucking it in around her shoulders and chin. She was shivering. Just minutes ago she had been burning up and now she was freezing. She curled up beneath the quilt and lay on her side, staring out the window, locked again now, but letting in pale moonlight through clear, cold glass.

She did not look at the dresser, not even once. She knew there would be nothing to see even if she did look, nothing but a dresser covered by a sheet.

But she took no chances and did not look.

chapter 6

exhibition hall

The display lights came on. Admiring "Oohs!" and "Ahhs!" broke from the gathered museum staff. Dodge Andrews pushed a button. A row of red lights flashed on and off in synchronized alternation, producing the effect of flickering firelight across a four-foot-high statue of a grisly bull-headed demon, claws spread wide, huge mouth gaping like the entrance to some pagan hell.

The onlookers applauded.

It was a statue of Baal, the Canaanite fertility god, on special loan from the Louvre.

"Dodge," Karin beamed at him, "that looks great!"

Milton Bromley squinted at the statue through his black-framed glasses, red lights reflecting off his shiny bald head. "Mr. Andrews, I fear your talents are being wasted here at the Barringer. Hollywood calls."

"Actually," Dodge said, his face dead serious, "I wanted to have a tape track positively *filled* with wild orgiastic cries—you know, like that *divine* madness with Yul Brynner and Gina Lollobrigida in *Solomon and Sheba?* But Karin said no."

Karin had to bite her tongue to keep from laughing.

Bromley nodded approvingly at her, then said to

Dodge Andrews, "I have absolute confidence in Mrs. Roberts's judgment. That is why she is head curator while you, my boy, are on probationary assistant status." *And,* said the tone of Bromley's voice, *damn likely to stay that way if I have anything to say about it.*

"Over here, Mr. Bromley." Karin pulled him away before Dodge had a chance to respond. "Here's our contrasting piece to the Baal statue. A magnificent fifteenth-century German St. George and the Dragon, on loan from the Nelson Gallery in Kansas City."

Footsteps echoed off the cavernous walls and ceiling of the Barringer's main exhibition hall as Bromley and the museum staff moved over to admire the subtle carving and polished highlights of the lindenwood statue. An earnest St. George sat astride his charging steed and thrust a spear downward into a creature that looked more like a bloated snake than a dragon.

Bromley nodded his approval. "Charming, my dear. But don't we have enough, ah, monsters in this show already? I thought we were striving for *balance.*"

"St. George is a traditional Christian symbol of the triumph of good over evil," Karin explained, moving Bromley away from the lindenwood statue as she saw Dodge Andrews catching up with them. "We thought St. George would make a nice contrast with Baal. Defender of the Innocent versus Destroyer of the Innocent? You see?"

Bromley nodded. "Interesting."

"Now over here," Karin brought him to a halt in front of a Madonna and Child by a minor sixteenth-century Italian master, "we have the Virgin and the Christ Child, and on the other side—Dodge, hit those lights, would you?"

The museum personnel gasped. Some of them stepped back. A bank of strobe lights flashed across a seven-foot-high bronze statue of Kali the Terrible Mother, Great Destroyer and Preserver, the eight-armed Hindu goddess of life and death. The stuttering strobes created an eerie illusion of movement. The eight arms of the angry-faced goddess seemed to ripple like snakes.

Bromley frowned. "Ingenious. More of Mr. Andrews's handiwork, I presume?"

Karin smiled proudly. "Dodge is a genius at lighting."

"Perhaps," Bromley suggested, "we could trade him to Disneyland."

Dodge moved up behind Bromley. "I wanted to make the feet move too, but Karin said the budget wouldn't stretch that far."

Bromley turned a cold stare on him. "Who knows, Mr. Andrews? Perhaps you could make it swish while you're at it."

Dodge started to say something, but Karin spoke first. "Dodge, turn the strobes off, please."

Dodge hesitated, looked from Karin to Bromley, then back to Karin again. He went to shut off the lights. The strobes winked out. The overhead lights came back to full strength.

Karin looked at Milton Bromley. "I thought you wanted this show to be more accessible."

Bromley nodded. "Accessible, my dear. *Not* vulgar."

"Mr. Bromley." Karin took a step closer. "There is nothing vulgar about it. We're trying to shake out some of the stiffness, and so far I think we're doing great. Of course, if you don't agree—"

"My dear," Bromley interrupted her, "no one is disagreeing with you."

"You're just telling me what to do."

Bromley smiled patiently. "I'm *asking* you to find a way to reduce—or eliminate—these cheap carnival effects."

"And," Karin asked coolly, "if I don't?"

"Ah, but you will." Bromley flashed a no-back-talk smile. "Because I and the other board members want you to. And because you're a reasonable woman." He adjusted his suit-coat lapels with an arrogant flourish. "Don't worry about a thing. We have the utmost confidence in your reasonableness, my dear."

Karin looked down at the marble floor.

"I'll check in again tomorrow to see how things are coming along." Bromley walked away, his footsteps ringing off the marble walls like echoes from a tomb.

"You know, Karin," Dodge said quietly, "for one awful moment there I was afraid you were going to haul off and actually *hit* Teddy Bear Bromley."

"If he'd hung around any longer, I might have." A pained look crossed Karin's face. "Dodge, you're brilliant and we love you. But can't you learn to keep your mouth shut?"

Dodge let out an exaggerated what-could-I-do? sigh. "Karin, Karin. I was only *teasing* the big silly."

Karin looked at him sternly. "Dodge, Bromley does not tease. No way. Ever. Remember that, okay?"

"You are being just *too* severe, Karin. I am sure Teddy Bear Bromley has a warm, wonderful sense of humor if only you'd give him the chance to show it."

"I've worked with him for eight years, Dodge. He has less sense of humor than a motorcycle cop. So back off, okay? We don't want him shutting us down this close to the opening."

Barbara Kappelman stepped forward. "Karin, the gold Scythian animal god's finally made it from the Hermitage."

Relief showed on Karin's face. "Thank God! I was beginning to—"

"It's not here. It's in New York."

Karin stared, her mouth open.

"It may not get any farther west," Barbara explained. "Seems a Soviet cultural affairs attaché at the U.N., some guy named Ivanov, doesn't want to part with it unless he gets an official assurance that it won't be used for any anti-Soviet propaganda."

"Christ!" Karin exploded. "What the hell does he think we're going to do? Use it as a bargaining chip?"

"I think," Barbara said, "what he really wants is just

67

for someone to call him."

"Fine." Karin nodded wearily. "Got his number?"

"In on your desk. But before you call, would you please talk to your sister, who's holding on line two?"

"Annie's on hold? What's wrong?" Half-formed images of accidents, rapes, drug overdoses flashed through Karin's mind. "Is it about Heather?"

"I don't think it's serious, Karin. She just said she wanted to hold for you." Barbara smiled. "The only really serious call you got was from Brett. He wants to make sure you don't forget about your dinner date with him this Friday."

Karin smiled bleakly. "Yeah, right."

Inside her office, Karin lit a cigarette with one hand and punched the hold button with the other. "Hello, Annie?" No answer. Karin's fingers tightened on the receiver. "*Annie?*" Still no answer. "ANNIE!"

"Hey!" Annie Newmar cried. "Not so loud, K.M.! Had to put you on hold for a sec. How ya doin', kid?"

Anne Ingrid Newmar was a full nine years younger than her big sister Karin—"the child of my old age," as Maureen O'Connor Magnusson liked to call her, although in fact their mother had been only thirty-three, five years younger than Karin's present age, when Annie was born.

"Pretty busy here with the show," Karin said, "but otherwise I'm okay, I guess."

"Hey, kid, if you're busy, you're happy. You're one of those guys *born* to be busy. Know what I mean?"

"Sorry I didn't call you back," Karin began, "about going sailing with you and Sam this weekend—"

"Not to worry, kid. Deal's off."

"—but I've been so tied up with this damn show . . ." *And besides,* Karin thought, *my idea of Hell is a long Saturday afternoon stuck in a small boat with Brett Courtney and Laughing Sam Newmar.* "I tried to call you this—"

"Earth to K.M.!" Annie shouted, laughing. "Earth to K.M.! Hey, do you *ever* listen to what I say? The deal, mon, she is, like, off, *comprende?* Sam and I won't be sailing off into the sunset this Saturday. And neither will you."

"Why not?"

"Mom's having us all over for a barbecue."

"Ah shit." Karin sat down heavily in her desk chair. "*Shit!*" She pounded the desk with a clenched fist. The burning tip of her cigarette fell off onto the polished desktop. She quickly blew away the glowing ashes. "Thanks, Annie. I needed to hear that."

"Hey, don't blame me. It's Mom's idea."

"Tell her I'm sick," Karin said. "Tell her I'm confined to my bed, doctor's orders, for at least three weeks."

"Careful there," Annie warned. "If Mom thinks you really *are* sick she'll rush right over and take care of you."

"Jesus, you're right." Karin knew that nothing aroused the maternal instinct of Maureen Magnusson like the prospect of caring for, and bossing around, a sick child. "Shit! Why now? Why couldn't she have waited until *after* the show was open?"

"Come on, K.M.," Annie tried to encourage her. "Lighten up! Nobody likes going over there. But it won't take all day. Sam and I don't plan on showing up until about noon."

Annie Newmar was a perpetually cheerful young woman with light blond hair, blue eyes and a figure that, while not quite as voluptuous as her niece Heather's, was still a knockout by anyone's standards. She had the O'Connor milk-white skin, but she kept hers burnished to a golden honey-brown by spending a lot of time outside in the eternal Southern California sun. *The reason she's always so goddamn cheerful,* Karin thought, *is because she never does anything, and neither does Laughing Sam.* In fact, Annie did things. So did Laughing Sam. But they were the things most people do on Hawaiian vacations. Annie Newmar was content to live off her inherited income and share it with her husband. In its own way, it was a very happy marriage.

"I'll bet Brett's disappointed," Annie went on. "But what the hell, bring him along to the barbecue."

Karin winced at the thought. "Thanks, Annie. But no thanks."

There was a brief silence; then Annie said, "You don't like him all that much, do you?"

"Oh, he's okay," Karin said, guilt nudging her in the ribs.

"Sure he's okay. But do you like him?"

"He's a nice guy, all right?" Karin's voice was on edge. She didn't like being pressured about this by her baby sister. Nor did she like the way Annie, with her usual scatter-brained accuracy, had zeroed right in on the truth.

"I think he's a super guy," Annie said. "But what do you think?"

Karin let out an exaggerated sigh. "He's not exactly the man of my dreams, if that's what you're getting at."

"Hey, don't feel bad, K.M. Not everyone's lucky enough to have a fun guy like Sam."

Karin bristled. "I wouldn't take Sam Newmar if he came wrapped in gold leaf with twenty-four-carat diamonds shoved up his ass."

Annie laughed. "If he came like that, I'd trade him at the Swap Meet for somethin' really good! Hey, K.M.! *Lighten up!*" Annie turned, for her, more serious. "Look, all bullshit aside, it's cool if you're not crazy over Brett. It's not a law or anything that you have to like him."

"Thank you, Dr. Ruth."

"No charge to family members. But I'm not through prescribing yet. I think—" Annie turned from the receiver and yelled, "No, Adam, the cat does *not* want to go into the microwave. So just—that's right, just let him out. And leave him *alone,* okay?" Annie turned back to the receiver. "Anyways, I think what you need right now is a whole new perspective on everything. Brett, the show, the whole nine yards. No shit, K.M., this show has got you so wired, I can't believe it. You need to get back in touch with yourself. You need to tap into the Power Source."

Karin closed her eyes. "Annie, not now. Please."

"Power Source" was a God-word with Annie Newmar. She had a normal suburban interest in metaphysics and the occult. Normal, that is, for Southern California. She believed in astrology and channeling and reincarnation. She attended psychic fairs and visited numerologists, and knew that from time to time she had visions, usually in her dreams, of the Other World, a world just as real and substantial as this everyday take-it-for-granted one. But Annie carried the whole thing a bit further than her Hollywood Hills neighbors. She believed passionately in the "Power Source," or *psi* phenomena, all those inexplicable goings-on that fascinate parapsychologists, things like telekinesis and precognition and poltergeist hauntings. Annie was her usual cheerful self about it. But any time a glass broke or a door slammed shut by itself when her five-year-old son Adam was home with her, she would look at him curiously and wonder, *Could it be?* Adam, a normal kid, was not affected by any of this. But Annie believed.

"Honest, K.M. You ought to—"

"GODDAMN IT, NO!"

"Okay." Annie backed off, startled by her sister's unexpected fury. "Okay, Karin. Whatever you say's cool."

Karin sighed. "Sorry, Annie. I didn't mean to blow up at you. It's just— I've had it up to *here* lately with psychic bullshit. Heather came home late for dinner last night after a tarot card reading with a friend of hers and I think it bothered her a lot. Heather, not the friend. This morning at breakfast she asked me if you could really tell the future through cards—"

"Well," Annie said thoughtfully, "sometimes you can."

"Fine, Annie. I know you believe that. So do a lot of other people. I don't. And I don't want Heather getting caught up in that Never-Never-Land crap."

"You know what they say, K.M. Don't knock it till—"

"I've tried it. It's a crock of shit."

"When did you try it?" Annie asked innocently.

"All right," Karin admitted. "So I never tried it. You don't need to taste a rotten egg if you can smell it. I've read about this stuff. I've seen those phoney psychics exposed on television."

"There's lots of phonies out there," Annie agreed. "Just like in anything else. Didn't you tell me once that forgeries are a big problem at the museum? How to tell the real paintings from the fakes?"

Annie had her there. Karin said nothing.

"You're a pretty honest kid, K.M.," Annie continued in her bright, cheery voice. "If you had the chance to hear some super-famous scientists talk about the Power Source, I bet you'd give 'em a fair hearing, huh?"

Karin saw where this was leading. "Annie, I'm awfully busy right now."

"It just so happens that *two* world-class premier parapsychologists are speaking tonight—"

"Annie—"

"—and it also just so happens that I have *two* tickets which I'd hate to see go to waste—"

"—so you thought of me," Karin finished it for her. "Where's this revival show taking place, Annie?"

"It's not like that, Karin. Nobody's going to be bending spoons with their mind or anything. These two guys are *scientists*. They both have Ph.D.'s."

"That doesn't mean a damn thing," Karin said, remembering all the idiots she had met in graduate school with Ph.D.'s and beyond.

"They're going to be talking at Hoskins tonight at eight," Annie said.

Hoskins College was a small, private four-year college in Santa Monica with a reputation, gained in the quiescent '80s, for being radical.

"They were supposed to speak at UCLA, but the psych.

department strong-armed the administration and the deal fell through. Come on, K.M.! Give it a chance!"

"Annie..."

"I'd hate to think that my big sister with her own Ph.D. refuses to spend just one evening—"

"Okay, okay. Eight o'clock. Where do we meet?"

"At Michael's after you get off work," Annie offered. "I'll buy."

"Thanks, but I've got to stop by home and talk with my gardener about some problems we've been having. I think I'm losing all my roses, Annie."

"What a bummer, K.M." Annie knew how much Karin loved her rose garden. "Maybe it's the soil."

"It's *not* the soil. Where do we meet at Hoskins?"

"Wilton Auditorium. Easy to find. Right in the middle of campus. If you have any trouble, just ask a student. I'll be on the front steps with the tickets." Annie hesitated. "Does this mean you're really going?"

"Yeah," Karin said. "That's what it means." *How do you let yourself get talked into so many things you don't want to do? Weak will? Or practice?*

As Karin hung up the receiver, Barbara Kappelman said, "Don't break for the ladies' room just yet. You've got an urgent person-to-person call from New York holding on line three."

Karin groaned. "Couldn't you take a message, Barb?"

"He said he wanted to hold."

Probably the Soviet cultural attaché from the U.N., Karin thought grimly, *ready to start an international incident.*

She braced herself, then punched line three. "This is Karin Roberts."

chapter 7

connections

There was silence on the other end of the line.

At first Sherone thought she had been disconnected. She leaned forward, straining to hear, receiver pressed up against her ear, the other ear covered to block out the sounds of Severy Academy students whooping and yahooing in the background as they milled back and forth across the Quad at lunchtime.

"Hello?" Sherone said softly. "Magda?"

Someone from the passing crowd, a friend maybe, whacked Sherone on the shoulder as she stood in front of the bank of four pay phones near the south side of the Quad. She stumbled under the impact. Regaining her balance, she glared at the passersby, then turned her back on them, right hand covering her ear, left hand holding the receiver tight against her head.

"Magda?" *Maybe it's the wrong number,* she thought.

"My child." Magda Prokash did not say it with any warmth. "Why are you calling me here?"

"I'm sorry, I— Magda, it's *important!*"

"You know I don't like to be called here, Sherone. And yet, knowing that, you have called. Why?"

"Magda, if this wasn't important I wouldn't bother

you with it, honest." *Shit!* Sherone thought, *she's good and pissed now*. She could almost see Magda's cold gray eyes clouding over, the frown lines furrowing her forehead.

Magda Prokash seemed to hesitate. "If it's truly important, my child, all the more reason not to discuss it over an open line. All the more reason to come here."

"Here" was The Heart of Darkness, an occult shop on Van Nuys Boulevard in the San Fernando Valley. Sherone and the other coven members referred to it as The Heart.

"Magda," Sherone protested, "I'm at school!"

Magda ignored this. "I've told you many times, my child, we are in constant danger. There are people who would destroy us if they could. We must protect our—"

"MAGDA!"

The line went silent.

"Magda," Sherone continued, glancing nervously at passing students out of the corner of her eye, "last night I was doing this tarot reading for Heather, okay?"

"You called me here," she said, "to tell me this?"

"Magda, *please*. There's more. The first seven cards—" Sherone's voice dropped to a hushed whisper. "They were the same seven you drew that night. The seven cards that spell . . . his name." Sherone waited breathlessly.

Magda might have been responding to a polite inquiry about the weather. "The girl is a Sensitive. It is not uncommon for the aura of a Sensitive to affect persons and objects around her. Who drew the cards?"

Sherone hesitated. "She did."

"You see? Her aura determined the cards she drew. And her aura still retains a powerful impression of . . . Azgaroth."

Sherone shuddered at the name. Magda's voice seemed to change as she pronounced it, growing deeper, coarser.

Sherone said, "After Heather drew those cards, she threw down the rest of the deck and ran out of the room.

She was scared. Really scared. I was scared too." Sherone paused. "It was like he was *there* with us."

"Impossible. We control him, not the other way around. He is not free to come and go at will. If that were true..." Magda seemed to waver at the brink of uncertainty. "Then it could be dangerous. Very dangerous." She drew back from the brink. "But it is not true. You saw the departure of the demon with your own eyes. You felt the heat of the demon wind as it blew through the circle. You remember what happened."

She remembered all right. Christ, did she remember. Sweat broke out on Sherone's forehead as the memories rushed back. Screaming at Heather, calling her back inside the circle. Screaming at Magda, begging her to help, *please*. And Magda just standing there like some sort of graveyard statue, watching the spectacle unfold before her.

We cannot help her, Magda had intoned. *It is death to step outside the circle now.*

Sherone remembered the flames leaping up from the triangle, bursting like sparks from an explosion, one of the sparks getting into the eye of that blond surfer kid, Don whatever his name was, and him screaming, clawing at his eye. And Heather . . . standing there, taking off her clothes, slowly, solemnly, a blank-faced, unsmiling stripper. *Heather, wake up!* Sherone had screamed at her. *Put your clothes back on!* But Heather did not hear her, or did not respond. She finished taking off all her clothes. Then the lights came over her. They seemed to wrap around her, like waves or ribbons of light, lights ranging from dark purple to pale pink to bright burning red. The other coven members watched in awe and horror. *Oh God, don't let her die!* Sherone had prayed, tears spilling down her cheeks. *Please don't let her die!*

She did not die. She rose. The lights seemed to lift her up several feet off the ground. It was impossible, absolutely impossible. But Sherone *saw* it—or thought she did. Heather started turning slowly, like a three-dimensional object revolving in space. A wind hotter than the hottest, driest Santa Ana roared through the open window, scattering glowing charcoal briquets and crystal wind chimes, whipping at the clothes and hair of the coven members. People screamed and covered their eyes. Then the wind stopped.

Now, Magda announced, *it is safe to step outside.*

Sherone had rushed from the circle then, and over to where Heather lay limp and naked and motionless on the hardwood floor.

"Come over and see us," Magda said, snapping Sherone out of her unpleasant memories. "And bring her with you. The Sensitive. We can have her draw more cards. I can help you do a better job of reading them. Have a good day, my child. Blesséd be."

"Magda . . ."

"Yes?" Irritation edged the older woman's voice.

Sherone hesitated, then burst out with it. "She remembers. *She remembers some of what happened.*"

Sherone could feel the change. She could almost feel the receiver growing cold in her hand, ice-cold, pressed up there against her ear, as if someone had started to flash-freeze it.

Magda asked, "What does she remember?"

"Not much," Sherone admitted, her heart starting to flutter in her chest the way it did when she ran too fast on a hot day.

"Exactly what does she remember?"

"She knows something happened. She knows about the lights." *Except,* Sherone thought with a crazy backward logic, *she thinks the lights were blackness.* "She thinks . . . *he* appeared." Sherone swallowed, forced herself to whisper it. "Azgaroth."

The silence on the other end lasted so long Sherone thought once again that she had been disconnected.

When Magda spoke, her voice was heavy. "Deny the reality. She must not know." Magda's voice cut like a knife through the static on the line. *"She cannot know."*

"But, Magda—"

The line went dead. There were some clicks, then the buzzing of an empty line.

"Magda?" Sherone clicked the switch hook. *"Magda?"*

Sherone looked up from the pay phone. There were fewer students crossing the Quad now. Lunchtime was winding down. Familiar and unfamiliar faces filed past. One of them was Heather's.

"Heather!" Sherone slammed down the receiver and ran after her.

Heather glanced up at Sherone, then kept walking.

"Heather!" Sherone called. "Wait up, would you?"

Heather did not slow down.

Sherone caught up with her, breathing hard. "Look—"

Heather stopped and turned around so abruptly Sherone almost bumped into her. "Sherone," she said, her voice low but angry, "if you ever want to talk about, you know, interesting stuff again, hey, that's cool. But if all you want to do is keep on rappin' about tarot cards and witches' covens—"

"Heather!" Sherone glanced around apprehensively, mindful of Magda's warning. "Not so loud, okay?"

"—if that's your idea of a fun time, then you just go find somebody else to have fun with. I don't want to hear *any* more about that shit."

"Heather—"

"Not one fucking word!"

Before Sherone had time to answer, Heather turned abruptly on her heel and walked off.

Great, Sherone thought, *this is really great. Magda's on my ass and my best friend hates my guts.* She felt like sitting down right there on the sidewalk and crying. But she was already late for her next class, Political Theory, so she headed in that direction.

Heather kept on walking, her pace quickened by anger. *Damn her,* she thought, *and damn her fucking tarot cards!* But it was not only Sherone and her cards that had

Heather upset. She was thinking about the burned remains of her doll on the dresser, about being accused by her mother of setting fire to the doll, about the blood that came from the doll, running down the sides of the dresser, pooling on the thick bedroom carpet.

Did I really see it? she asked herself for what must have been the hundredth time. *Or did I just imagine it?*

"Heather! How's it goin'?"

Troy Taylor, Kurt's best friend, waved at her from across the Quad. Shorter than Kurt, with blond-streaked light brown hair and a wiry build, Troy wore the constant sneer of a guy who thinks he has it all covered.

Heather returned a polite wave.

"Guys goin' out tonight?" Troy called.

Heather shook her head and tried to smile. "Studying!"

"Yeah, right." Troy cranked up the sneer. "You and my dead uncle. Catch you later."

Heather was glad to see Troy turn back to his circle of male friends clumped around one of the stone drinking fountains in the Quad.

Her thoughts returned to the blood. It *couldn't* have been real. She knew that. When she got up this morning she forced herself to go over to the dresser and look down at the light blue carpet beneath it. There was no blood, dried or fresh. She ran a bare foot across the carpet. It did not have the slightly stiff feel of newly washed carpet. She touched the thin film of dust on top of the dresser. *If there was blood and it got wiped up,* she reasoned, *then the dust would've been wiped up too.*

But if it wasn't real, why did she see it last night?

"Heather," the voice said.

She looked up. Paula Kratzer was standing under a palm tree with a guy. Heather thought she knew him from somewhere, a class or something, but she couldn't place him. Paula had tightly curled brown hair, braces on her teeth and a nervous laugh. She always made the top three percent of her class and never dated. Heather talked with her sometimes. Today she didn't feel like talking with anybody. But Paula started it. You had to say something.

Heather smiled at her. "How's it goin', Paula?"

"Okay, I guess." Sunlight glinted off her braces. "I've got papers for Psychology, Political Theory and English. And I've got a lab test for Physiology. Otherwise, it's okay."

Paula was one of those people who actually told you how it was going when you asked. Heather turned from her, still smiling, and nodded at the guy, wondering where she had seen him before.

"The hardest thing about Physiology," Paula explained, an earnest frown on her face, "is that you have to dissect *rats*. The big, hairy, gross kind that crawl up out of sewers. Can you believe that?"

The guy smiled at Heather. But it was not one of those cocky male everything's-under-control-babe smiles.

"—*this* much formaldehyde." Paula indicated with her hand. "You know what I mean?"

Any casual observer could have seen that Heather and the guy were interested in each other. Paula finally picked up on it too.

"Oh, yeah." Paula laughed her nervous laugh. "Heather, this is Brian. Brian, Heather."

Heather and Brian exchanged hellos. Then Heather placed him. It was like being hit by lightning. The bright sunshine of the Quad seemed to dim suddenly and be replaced by the dark, candlelit interior of Magda Prokash's dreadful house. *It's him!* Heather thought, astonishment rushing through her as she remembered the dark-haired, sharp-nosed boy who had stood up to Magda and challenged her about the Death Card, the one who had tried to make her stop the ceremony.

Heather's eyes grew wide as she stared at Brian.

Paula stopped talking about Physiology. "Guess I better get goin'." The nervous laugh again. "So long, you guys." She hurried off toward Module C.

"You were there that night," Heather said to Brian.

"So were you." He hesitated, then asked, "Are you okay?"

"Sure." Heather lifted her chin. "Why shouldn't I be?"

"No reason." Brian looked uncomfortable, like someone who has said the wrong thing.

"Nothing happened." Heather's eyes narrowed. "Sherone told me that."

"Sure." Brian nodded in agreement. "Sherone's got that right. Well, gotta run. Class in D."

"Just a minute."

Brian paused.

Heather stood with her arms crossed, studying him. "Did something happen?"

Brian glanced at his watch. "I'm gonna be late."

Heather reached out and grabbed his shoulder. At her touch, Brian obediently turned around. His eyes were shiny. Heather took away her hand.

"You can leave it there if you want."

Heather shook her head. "Don't get any ideas. I'm going with Kurt Pritchard."

"I know."

"What *happened?*"

Brian looked at her, started to say something, then said, "Ask Sherone."

Heather moved in on him until they were standing eyeball-to-eyeball. "I already did. She either lies straight out or tries to shine me on, just like you are. I need to know what happened, Brian."

He glanced around the Quad. "This isn't exactly the best place in the whole world to talk about it."

"Where do you want to talk?" Heather asked, adding as an afterthought, "Remember, I'm going with someone."

Brian mulled it over. "How about the Cove?"

The Cove was not a cove at all but a stretch of rocky

beach down below Severy Academy. Crashing waves and limited access by roads guaranteed some privacy. It was a favorite place for afterschool rendezvous of all sorts.

Heather frowned. "Can't we use the library?"

"Not really."

"I hope Kurt doesn't find out."

"Maybe you better ask Sherone instead."

Heather's head snapped up. "What time? Today? Right after school?"

"Uh, sure," Brian said, taken aback. "Okay."

"See you then." Heather walked off toward Module B.

Brian McNulty stood there in the middle of the Quad, watching Heather walk away from him, wondering if maybe this was one of those dreams that seem so realistic, right down to the smallest detail, that you almost start to believe it's really happening—then the clock radio goes off.

In another part of the Quad, two girls stood and watched Brian McNulty watching Heather Roberts. One of them, Paige Benson, Troy Taylor's girl, ran a perfectly manicured nail along a delicate, carefully painted lower lip. The other girl, Belinda Leonard, Paige's best friend, crunched M & M's out of a crumpled bag.

Belinda pulled down her sunglasses and looked at Paige over the top of them. "Shouldn't Kurt maybe know about this?"

"No, not yet." Paige smiled a slow, patient smile. "Later."

chapter 8

dead things

Karin Roberts examined the tufts of grass in her right hand. Hyung-Joon Kim stood beside her, his Dodger Blue baseball cap cocked back on his bald head. The old Korean gardener looked at the grass tufts, then at Karin, his eyes large and owlish behind rimless glasses. The sun was setting, turning the smoggy sky a vivid orange-pink, bathing Karin's front lawn in harsh, surrealistic light.

"Grass die," Hyung-Joon Kim said finally.

Karin looked at the tufts and said nothing.

"First rosa busha die. Then grass." Hyung-Joon Kim pointed to the orange and lemon trees lining the driveway. There were more in back. "Next, tree die. Evathing die."

Karin said, "You must be doing something different."

"No do *ana*thing different!" Hyung-Joon Kim was indignant. "Do evathing same. Same wata. Same fertiliza. *Eva*thing same. Ona thing different, these plant, they juss wanna die."

Karin shook her head, feeling the tears gather. *Christ*, she thought, *why does everything have to go wrong this week?* "It's got to be the soil, Hyung-Joon. Something must have happened to it."

"No *soil!*" Hyung-Joon Kim's voice, though rising slightly, was still under perfect control. But he was almost beside himself with frustration, unable to make himself clearly understood in this strange, difficult language fate had forced on him so late in life, unable to make this kind but simple-minded woman see that it had nothing to do with the soil or the water or even with the plants themselves.

It had to do with the other things, the things his grandfather had told him about many years ago when he was an old man and Hyung-Joon Kim only a small boy living in the mountains north of Seoul. There were things in this world that had power over other living things. These powerful things were not necessarily good or bad, like gods or demons. But they had wills, likes and dislikes. Now one of these things had decided it did not like his employer's grass and rosebushes. And that was that. There was nothing to be done about it. But how could he make her understand this?

"Soil good," he tried. "Wata good. Fertiliza good. Grass and rosa busha, good too. But . . ." He gave up. There was no way to say this in English. "Evathing juss wanna die."

Karin threw down the grass tufts, wiping away a tear with her other hand. "Fine, Hyung-Joon. I understand. But I don't accept it, okay? I don't see why everything that's been growing nicely here for all these years just suddenly starts to die for no reason. There must be *something* you can do."

Hyung-Joon Kim shook his head. "Ona thing, dig up *eva*thing. Start ova. Or cova up evathing with that." He pointed at the concrete driveway.

"Great." Karin sighed. "Then I'll have the largest parking lot in the Encino Hills." A tear trickled down her cheek.

Hyung-Joon Kim looked down at the dying grass underfoot, withered and yellow. He was sorry for his employer's grief. It was sad when any living thing died.

But that was part of life. Things live, then die. Couldn't she understand something that simple?

Karin blew her nose. "You're a great gardener, Hyung-Joon. And I know you've really tried. But maybe I'll have to have a specialist come out and analyze the soil."

What good would that do? Hyung-Joon Kim wondered. The specialist would just give fancy names to everything, like his grandson Theodore Kim, who had completed a B.A. in physics at Berkeley last spring and now talked about light, ordinary light, as waves and particles. You could name the fact of the dying plants anything you wanted. But what could you *do* about it?

"Maybe there's some kind of stuff they can spray," Karin said hopefully, but not sounding very convinced. "Some super hormone or—"

Three sharp blasts from a customized auto horn cut her short. Karin and Hyung-Joon Kim both turned toward the sound. A white Rolls Royce Silver Shadow rolled up onto Karin's driveway. Maureen Magnusson was behind the wheel, her fiery red hair visible even through the tinted glass. Karin had once hinted to her mother that most people who own a Rolls Royce usually retain a chauffeur to drive it. Maureen Magnusson easily could have afforded a chauffeur. *But that's not the point, honey girl,* she explained to Karin one day. *Why should I buy the most expensive car in the whole world and then let some . . . immigrant have all the fun of driving it?* As in the other areas of her life, what Maureen Magnusson owned, she ran.

Karin waved, forcing herself to smile. "Hi, Mother!" She started for the Rolls, thinking, *Shit, what timing.*

Maureen thrust a leg out into the driveway, groping for the concrete with an expensive Gucci pump. "Karin Marie!" she called in a ringing voice. "Are you going to come over here and help your poor old gray-headed mother out of her car? Or are you just going to stand there and gape while she struggles?"

Maureen climbed gracefully out of the Silver Shadow

and stood up straight, smoothing the wrinkles from her clothes. She had on a white silk long-sleeve dress and white leather pumps. She carried a black handbag and wore a wide black leather belt with a gold buckle. One of several characteristics that she shared with her former son-in-law, David Roberts, was a taste for the dramatic juxtaposition of black and white. *That dress,* Karin thought, drawing nearer, *looks exactly like my living room.*

"You don't realize it at your tender age," Maureen said, patting her red hair back into place, "but we old ladies have trouble getting in and out of cars. And although you think of me as your dear mother who never ages, I've got news for you, Karin Marie. I am a full sixty-two years of age. And I look and feel every minute of it!"

In fact, Maureen looked good for her age. Tall, just under Karin's height at a sprightly five feet seven-and-a-half inches, she had a trim but voluptuous figure and a pale white complexion heavily rouged and flamboyantly set off by piercing green eyes and unruly waves of fire-red hair. At one time it had actually been that color, or close to it. In those days she had looked very much like that other Maureen, O'Hara, in *The Quiet Man* with John Wayne, a lovely girl, strong and willful, with an alternately sunny and sullen Irish disposition. Since her early forties Maureen Magnusson had been helping her hair along, as she put it, with a light red color rinse. *If God didn't want me to color my hair,* she told Karin, *He wouldn't have made rinses so easy to use.*

Maureen reached out and folded Karin into a warm embrace, kissing her noisily on the cheek. "My, but it's *good* to see you! Good to see you and hold you, just to make sure you're still here. If I had to depend on your phone calls, I would have reported you missing weeks ago."

Karin squirmed slightly in the embrace. "Mother, I've been busy."

"Busy, busy!" Maureen shook her flame-red hair with a theatrical flourish. "Karin Marie, we are *all* busy. *Life* is busy. Only the dead are not busy."

"I know that, Mother." She felt—she tried not to, but she felt it anyway—the blood rising to her cheeks, the anger swelling inside her like a dark summer storm. *What the hell does she know about being busy?* Karin thought furiously. *When has she ever done anything except butt into other people's lives?* Karin stifled her thoughts the instant she had them. *I love her*, she told herself firmly, *and she loves me too, she really does.* "I really have been busy at the museum," Karin said. "The new show and everything."

"'And everything.'" Maureen Magnusson fixed her daughter with sharp green eyes. "And just what does 'and everything' mean? Don't get sloppy with your speech habits, Karin Marie. Please! If you must get sloppy with anything, let it be that damn musty museum. But don't, honey girl, *don't* start speaking like one of those pathetic young people who can't utter two words together without inserting a 'you know' or a 'like' or an 'and everything.'"

Karin bristled. "I do not speak badly."

"No one suggested that you did, honey girl." Maureen patted her daughter's cheek, flashing a radiant smile. "All I want you to do, Karin Marie, is be *conscious* of your speech and speak well."

"I *do* speak well!"

She hasn't been here five goddamn minutes and I'm arguing with her! Karin realized with mixed fury and despair. She tried to bring her anger back under control.

"And where is that lovely red-headed granddaughter of mine?" Maureen scanned the driveway for Heather's Suzuki Samurai. "Out with some boy, I suppose." She shook her head, smiling with obvious pride. "You can't stop that, Karin Marie. The boys will take an interest in her. The *normal* ones, that is." Maureen sighed. "There seem to be more of the *other* ones every year."

"She's not on a date," Karin said. "Heather has a steady boyfriend, Kurt. But she doesn't really date all that much."

"Kurt Pritchard?" Maureen's interest rose. "That's Jack Pritchard's boy, isn't it? Jack has done *so* well for himself with those mini-series."

So well he hasn't had time to raise Kurt properly, Karin thought, but she would never say that to her mother, not unless she was looking for a long, high-decibel argument. Maureen Magnusson rated people according to money or fame, with money taking the lead. *You can become famous with enough money,* Maureen told her, *but fame doesn't always make you rich—like the father of Heather's little friend, Sherone what's-her-name, the famous photographer who never earns a dime.*

Karin had got into it with her on that one. She had her own reservations about Sherone, and she didn't know Wes Livingston very well, had met him only once in fact, that time he picked the girls up at the Madonna concert at the Universal Amphitheatre and drove Heather home. But he seemed like a nice man. And he was an artist who did work he loved and believed in. People like that rated very high on Karin's list, whether they ever earned a dime or not.

"I *do* hope Heather will be sensible about a fine young man like Kurt," Maureen went on. "It's so easy for lovely young girls to be romantic instead of sensible—"

The ready retorts threatened to burst from Karin's lips. Sensible? Since when had Maureen O'Connor Magnusson, most romantic and impulsive of women, ever learned anything about being sensible? And who said Kurt Pritchard was a fine young man? Had Maureen ever met him? Karin had, and she knew— *I am not going to let her get me into this,* she told herself, trying hard to remain calm. *I am not going to—*

"—marry someone they simply won't be happy with, no matter what they think. Or . . ." Maureen shot a green-eyed glance at her daughter. "Or marry someone who's perfect for them, then let him go because they aren't sensible enough to appreciate a good man once they've got him."

Karin pulled back, stung by the words. "If you're making a not-too-subtle reference to Dr. David Roberts—"

"Who else would I be talking about, Karin Marie?"

That did it. Every time she talked with her mother, Karin told herself that this time she wouldn't be drawn in, this time she wouldn't let the taunts get to her. But like all people, Karin had a Wall, a point beyond which you couldn't push her—without having the bricks come down on your head.

Karin controlled her voice with difficulty. "Mother, I'm not going to stand here and listen to you dissect my marriage—"

"Who's dissecting—" Maureen began, a sweet smile on her face.

"—praise David to my face—"

"Who's praise—"

"—and blame *me* for whatever went—"

"No one is blaming you for anything, Karin Marie!" Maureen Magnusson thundered, drowning out her daughter with sheer volume.

"The hell if you aren't!" Karin shouted back.

Hyung-Joon Kim, who had been quietly tending to one of the dying plants, looked up in astonishment as the women's voices rose. It was not good when women shouted at each other like men.

"Unless." Maureen's voice dropped suddenly to a soft, reasonable register. "Unless, of course, you're blaming yourself, honey girl."

Karin thought she might burst a blood vessel. "I am *not* blaming myself!"

"Honey girl," Maureen frowned sympathetically, "I know it's never easy to admit when you've made a mistake."

"Mistake?" Karin's mouth dropped. "The only mistake I made was to marry that selfish, money-grubbing egomaniac in the first place."

Maureen's sympathetic frown hardened into one of

judgment. "No marriage ever fails because just one partner is selfish, Karin Marie. Because just one refuses to understand or forgive."

"What was I supposed to forgive?" Karin's blood was up now. "His fucking around with every cute nurse who turned him on?"

Maureen Magnusson shuddered delicately. "Don't use vulgarities in front of your mother, Karin Marie."

"*He's* a vulgarity!"

Maureen ignored that. "Men," she began calmly, "are not perfect creatures, God knows. But it is a woman's duty, and a woman's privilege, to understand when a man's physical weaknesses—"

Karin had been through all this before and there was only so much she could take. "Mother, that's bullshit."

"Don't use that word in front—"

"You've never faced up to what really happened with David and me," Karin said, her voice rising. "You made up your own little fantasy about it. Because that's easier than admitting that your wonderful daughter married a no-good bastard and paid for his medical school and internship and residency and got his practice established and then one day he dropped her like a used towel for some slutty intern he was banging on the ER night shift."

A tear rolled down each of Maureen Magnusson's heavily rouged cheeks. Karin started crying too. God, how she hated that! She wasn't crying because of David or the memories of what he did. She was crying because whenever her mother started crying she did too, just like one of Pavlov's reflex-conditioned dogs. It made her feel six years old again and helpless.

"Karin Marie." Maureen shook her head sorrowfully. "Oh, honey girl! It's hard. I know how hard it is to love a man who hurts you."

Maureen did not speak from personal experience. Karin's father, Harald Magnusson, was one of the kindest of men. A quiet research scientist, he was completely devoted to his difficult, demanding wife.

"Mother." Karin wiped at her tears. "I *did* love him. But he didn't give a damn whether I loved him or not. Because he didn't love *me*."

"But honey girl." Maureen's voice quivered like an Irish tenor's. "If only you'd forgiven him, if only you'd forgiven him with all your heart, he would have stayed. I know my Davie would have stayed."

Karin's tears stopped like water from a turned-off tap. "Sure. If I'd gotten down on my knees and groveled, and let him keep spending my money and using your connections and ignoring his daughter and treating me like shit—sure, he might've stayed. Who wouldn't? Thanks a lot, Mom, but no thanks. He wanted to walk with Miss Tits and Ass. I let him walk."

Maureen sighed deeply. "Honey girl, it's not good for you to live alone like this."

"Mother, I'm thirty-eight years old. I can take care of myself. Besides, I'll have Heather for another two years, at least. She still hasn't decided where to go for college." *And she may not get in if her grades don't improve,* Karin thought, but she wouldn't say that out loud. As far as Maureen was concerned, Heather was a genius. If she had problems at school, it was because her teachers were fools. Karin knew better. Heather did not like school and did not work at it. Her grades showed it.

"My darling granddaughter's a joy to your life as she is to mine," Maureen agreed. "But Karin Marie, women *need* men. They really do, honey girl."

Karin regarded her mother critically. "You make it sound like drug addiction. If a man and woman share a loving relationship, that's one thing. But no woman should ever need a man so much she's willing to let one treat her like a doormat."

Maureen Magnusson's green eyes darkened. "Davie did not treat you like a doormat!"

"No, he treated me like his personal slave. Someone to arrange his social life for him. Someone to show up with at functions, the attractive dutiful doctor's wife.

Someone to raise his daughter for him and be on call as an easy lay whenever he had bad luck scoring on his own."

"My, my." Maureen smiled cynically. "Aren't we bitter today?"

"I'm not bitter. It's just the truth." *All right*, Karin admitted to herself, *so I am a little bitter. Who wouldn't be?* But it was still the truth.

"Well, you can say what you want about Davie Roberts," Maureen said, an affectionate light in her eye. "But he's a fine man, and the father of your darling daughter. And *I* think he deserves a second chance."

Karin laughed at that. "Look, Mother, if you think he's so great, why don't *you* ask him back? Invite him to stay with you and Dad in Beverly Hills. He'll probably take you up on it."

"If I thought it would help bring the two of you back together again," Maureen lifted her head proudly, "I'd do it right this minute, as God is my witness!"

She probably would, too, Karin thought. David Roberts was the one great exception to Maureen Magnusson's otherwise inflexible money-before-fame rule. David's Scots-Irish family did not have any money. And even now that he was established as a heart surgeon, his yearly income was less than a tenth of his former mother-in-law's. He had all the greed and other bad habits attributed to him by his ex-wife. But he also had a world of Celtic charm. Immensely likeable, he could win someone over on first acquaintance. And he was handsome, not in a too-pretty male-model way, but with the kind of sturdy masculine good looks that inspire trust as well as affection. David Roberts did not just impress people. He dazzled them. Maureen Magnusson was among the bedazzled.

She sighed. "But I don't think it would do much good, Karin Marie. I really don't. I think your mind's all made up about Davie. I don't think you're being the least bit fair. But then, I'm only your poor old gray-headed mother. What right do I have to tell you how to live your life?" *Every right in the world*, said Maureen's hard green eyes. *And if you had the sense God gave a field mouse, you'd pay attention to what I think.*

Hyung-Joon Kim came up to the two women, bowing politely, a withered rosebrush in his hands. "Meesa Robbers," he said gravely, "theesa rosa busha die. I toss him out."

Karin's heart ached at the sight of the desiccated plant. It was a Peace Rose, one of her favorites. "Can't we keep it for at least another day, Hyung-Joon? Maybe run it over to Beckmeir's for analysis?" Albert Beckmeir, PLANT DOCTOR®, was Karin's most trusted garden consultant.

Hyung-Joon Kim shook his head firmly. "No good, take docta. Plant dead. Betta throw way."

"Look here," Maureen interrupted, stepping between Karin and Hyung-Joon Kim. "I think you have things just a bit backwards here, mister."

Hyung-Joon Kim looked up at the tall red-headed woman glaring down at him. "Theesa plant—"

"You work for my daughter," Maureen said. "You don't tell her what to do. She tells *you*. And you damn well do it. If you want to keep your job."

Hyung-Joon Kim was now truly at a loss for words. He was also a little frightened, not for himself, but for his employer and the harmony of her house. This woman, the one with the burning red hair, was dangerous. She knew everything. She would listen to nothing. Her angry ignorance might threaten his employer's harmonious relationship with her surroundings. It was most unfortunate that this ignorant woman happened to be also the honored mother of his employer.

"Do I make myself clear?" Maureen demanded.

Hyung-Joon Kim bowed his head and said nothing.

"What's wrong? Can't you speak English?"

"Mother." Karin frowned. "Lay off Hyung-Joon. He's just doing his job. And he's probably right. It won't do any good to take the rosebush over to Beckmeir's."

Karin looked past her mother to the old Korean gardener. "Hyung-Joon, throw the rosebush away. And please throw away any others you think are dying."

Hyung-Joon Kim bowed and left.

Karin started for her front door, still not looking at her mother. "I've got to get going. I'm meeting Annie on the Hoskins campus tonight at eight. Some psychic-ESP lecture."

"How nice," Maureen said in one of her pleasant voices. "I hope you'll keep an eye on your younger sister in case she decides to abandon her husband and little Adam and run off to follow some guru."

"It's not that kind of lecture, Mother."

"And I also hope," Maureen went on, a sharp note entering her voice as Karin continued to walk away without looking back, "that you and my darling grandchild plan to show up at the little gathering your father and I will be hosting this Saturday."

Karin stopped and turned around. "Mother, I told you I'm awfully busy right now."

"So busy you can't take the time to come and spend a few hours with the only father and mother you have in the whole world, Karin Marie?"

How has Daddy put up with it all these years? Karin wondered. *How did I put up with it all the years I lived there?* Then she realized, *I'm still putting up with it.* "We'll be there, Mother," she said. "I don't know how long we can stay—"

"Karin Marie, you know me better than that!" She walked up to her daughter and embraced her in a sudden bear hug. "The length of the visit doesn't matter one bit. It's the fact that you *care* enough to come and see us."

After more hugs and kisses and goodbyes, Karin stood on the driveway waving to her mother as Maureen Magnusson backed the white Rolls Royce out onto Camino de Oro, stopping to honk at a gray Volvo that stood idling in the street blocking her way.

As Karin watched the white Rolls disappear at the end

of the block, she felt a sudden chill in the air, as if a cold air mass had come swooping down over the Santa Monica mountains without any warning. It wasn't really cold. The air was turning pleasantly cool. But there was a chill to it, a dark, menacing chill that seemed to settle around Karin and the house she lived in with her daughter and without a man, a house surrounded by dying plants that her faithful gardener tended to no avail.

A house under some kind of siege.

Bullshit, Karin thought brusquely, pushing it out of her mind. *My poor old gray-headed mother just got on my nerves, that's all*. Picking up the pruning shears from where Hyung-Joon Kim had left them lying on the lawn, Karin clipped off a few still unwithered blossoms from a drooping rosebush. Then, blossoms held carefully in one hand, she turned and headed for the front door.

But as she walked, she felt the chill again.

And shivered.

chapter 9

SECRETS

When Heather finally reached the Cove, after descending four long flights of weathered wooden stairs from a grassy clifftop to the rock-strewn beach below, she thought that Brian McNulty had stood her up.

Breakers crashed against the rocks out to sea. Gulls drifted overhead on extended wings. Slashes of bright pink, magenta and orange glowed against the far horizon.

She was alone on the beach.

The strong salt wind cut through her clothes, swirling her long red hair. English and Comparative Government texts rode heavy as iron weights in her designer backpack. She felt like a jerk, agreeing to meet here with Brian McNulty and then actually expecting him to show up. *He's probably laughing about the whole thing right now*, she thought, wondering if anyone had seen her talking with Brian and then told Kurt. Kurt had such a shitty temper. He could get pissed off over nothing. Not that she cared whether he did. It wasn't like she loved him or anything. But she didn't want to do something totally retarded, something that really was her fault, and then get caught at it. Especially when the only reason for meeting Brian was the hope that he might tell her what had happened that night. Tell her at least that *something* had happened, that it wasn't all in her head the way Sherone—

Something touched her arm.

Heather screamed and jumped back, almost tripping over a sand drift.

"Hey," Brian said, "take it easy, okay?"

He stood there with one hand reaching out for her, the other in his jeans pocket. The sea wind blew his straight dark hair back from his face, making it look sharper, more angular than ever. He had on one of those pastel pink *Miami Vice* shirts. *Probably thinks it makes him look like Don Johnson,* Heather thought, her nose wrinkling in disgust at Kurt's favorite macho star. Then she looked again and saw that Brian McNulty was nothing like Don Johnson or Kurt Pritchard.

"You better lighten up a little," he said to her. "You look like somebody just scared the shit out of you."

Somebody did! Heather thought, heart still pounding inside her chest, but she said, "I'm okay."

They started walking slowly down the beach.

Heather took a deep breath and brushed back some loose strands of red hair from her face. "You're late," she said to Brian.

"Sorry. Got sort of delayed. There's this real chilled-out short little dude, okay? Weasel grin on his face." Brian demonstrated. "Runs around with your boyfriend."

Heather said, "Troy Taylor."

"Yeah." Brian nodded. "Tells me to be real careful about who I see after school." Brian mocked the deep voice of schoolyard toughness. "Like he was *warnin'* me, you know?"

"Troy can be a real jerk."

"So why hang around with him and Kurt?"

Heather looked up sharply. "If this is what you came to talk about, forget it."

Brian held up a hand. "Just kidding, okay?" But the

serious-eyed redhead in front of him was not in a kidding mood, and Brian picked up on this. "I didn't come to talk about your friends. I want to talk about, you know . . ."

Heather hesitated. "I don't remember much about it. I remember how you stood up to that witch lady, though." She smiled, barely. "You were pretty cool about that."

Brian shrugged in the fading daylight. "It didn't do any good. She went ahead with it anyway." *Even after drawing the fucking Death Card,* he thought to himself.

"But the thing is," Heather insisted, "you stood up to her. You weren't afraid."

In fact, he had been scared shitless. Scared of Magda. Scared of the Death Card. Scared of the consequences of going on. He had every reason to be scared. The details of that night came back on instant replay, precise to the last image, like a videotape inside his head. He saw Heather rush outside the rock salt circle, panicked. He knew she'd be killed if she left the circle's protection. He started to follow her. Then he realized that if he stepped outside the circle he would die too. Magda just stood there, watching it all with hard gray eyes.

Brian shook his head to clear it of bad memories.

Heather was looking at him thoughtfully. "You've been to one of those before, haven't you?"

Brian shrugged. "Maybe."

"You believe in it?"

"Not entirely."

"What does that mean? Yes? No? Or sort of?"

"It means," Brian said, "that maybe some of it's true and maybe some of it's not." He looked out at the ocean, darker now, reaching up to meet the darkening sky. "There's lots of weird shit out there in the world. Not all of it makes sense."

Heather remembered the blood dripping from the dresser in her bedroom. "You got that right," she muttered, moving in closer to Brian, wishing all of a sudden that he would put an arm around her, just to keep her warm, then moving away again the instant she found herself wishing that.

"Who knows what's real and what's not?" Brian continued. "This guy I went to school with in Beverly Hills, he used to rap on about that all the time. Are we real? Is the world real? Is reality really real? I mean, hey, give me a break. If something's real, you'll know it."

"Is witchcraft real?" Heather asked.

"Maybe."

"If it's not," Heather paused, "why'd you go to Magda's that night?"

Brian debated silently whether or not to tell her. He kicked at a pile of wet sand.

"Well?" Heather demanded.

"I went," Brian said, "because . . . Because of what she was trying to do."

"Which was?"

He swallowed. "You know, summon a demon."

It all came back to Heather with jolting clarity: the terrible hissing from the flames, the squealing that dug into her brain like a knife, the darkness that fell on her when she broke from the circle. Her forehead felt damp, her mouth dry.

She looked up at him. "Brian." Her voice cracked. "What really happened? After I ran out of the circle?"

He said nothing, remembering. Watching Heather that night, his mouth open, waiting to see what would happen to her. Waiting, in terror, to see how she would die. But she did not die. She stripped. Heather started taking off her clothes, methodically, mechanically. She pulled the T-shirt up over her head, then unsnapped her bra. Brian remembered that part, how she looked without her clothes. He used to think real girls never looked like that, like Pets or Playmates of the Year. He thought all the really good stuff was just lighting or trick lenses or airbrushes. But there were no tricks that night, just Heather, up close, all real, soft white skin, full breasts with—

He glanced down to see if his erection was visible

through his jeans. It wasn't, really, not unless you knew it was there and were looking for it.

He looked up, blushing. Heather was staring at him with an intensity that unsettled him. She looked very serious, for a girl.

"Brian," she said, "what *happened?*"

"Uh," he cleared his throat, "Sherone tried to stop you. She yelled at you to come back."

"Thanks. I remember that. What *else* happened?"

"Uh . . ." He didn't want to tell her. He had planned to, at first, when she agreed to meet him here at the Cove. He thought she was a foxy babe and he wanted an excuse to talk to her. It had seemed like a good move, telling her about how she stripped in front of everyone, but telling it real chilled-out and totally in control, watching her close to see how she reacted. It didn't seem like such a good idea now. For one thing, he could see she was really stressed out over that night at Magda's. She didn't even remember what happened, like she had a memory loss or something.

For another thing, he liked her. He liked her a lot. *Which is pretty fucking ridiculous, man,* he told himself, *because you've only known her for, like, maybe fifteen minutes max.* It didn't matter. He liked her. And not just because she looked like that Pet of the Year whose name he could never remember, the one in the hot tub. He liked her the way you like a friend you've known for a long time, someone you care about.

"*Brian* . . ." She was getting impatient.

"There were these lights," he said.

"Lights?" She frowned at him, not following. "You mean the black candles?"

"No. I mean lights like . . . *waves* of light. Streaks of different colors. Zippin' around all over the place like special effects in a movie."

Heather raised a skeptical eyebrow. "Who made the lights? Magda? Or someone she hired?"

An uncertain look entered Brian McNulty's brown

eyes. "I don't know. I just know they were there."

Heather frowned, trying to remember. "It got dark. *Real* dark. Like the darkness was trying to wrap itself around me, trying to get *inside* me." She shuddered at the memory, closing her eyes. Then she opened them and stared at Brian. "I don't remember any lights."

Brian nodded. "They were there. Different strips of light. Wrapping you up like some magic trick."

"I remember the darkness moving over me," Heather said slowly, her unfocused eyes staring out to sea. "It seemed to *cling* to me, like I was naked and there was only darkness next to my skin, pressing against me, all over my body."

"Right," Brian agreed. "Only it was lights, not darkness."

Heather's eyes snapped back into focus. "I said it *felt* like I was naked." She stopped walking. "I had my clothes on."

Brian nodded in agreement. "For sure."

Heather's blue eyes narrowed. "I *kept* them on, didn't I?"

He said nothing.

She stared at him for what must have been two full minutes. Then she uttered an embarrassed moan and covered her face with her hands. Brian stood there with his own hands in his jeans pockets, glancing around nervously, glad that the Cove was deserted that afternoon, but wishing he could get the hell out of there, just disappear or something, before she opened her eyes and looked at him again. He hated it when girls started crying and coming apart on you.

But when she took her hands away from her face, her eyes were dry and dead serious. "I didn't think about this very much at the time—I guess I didn't *want* to think about it, okay?—but when I got home later that night and started getting undressed for bed, I noticed that my right bra strap was twisted around so the little buckle rubbed against the skin, you know? I hate it when it does that! I never wear a twisted bra strap." She stared hard at Brian. *"So why was I wearing one that night?"*

Brian shrugged. "Good question."

"Look." Heather grabbed his *Miami Vice* shirt by the neck. "Did some sleazoid take my clothes off while I was out of it?"

"Not exactly."

Heather released her grip on his shirt and turned toward the open ocean. "I can't believe this! My best friend just stood there and *watched* while some pervert . . . Sherone!" she screamed suddenly at the distant waves, "you *ass*hole!"

Brian cleared his throat. "It wasn't like that."

"Oh?" She turned to him. "How was it, then?"

He told her.

At first she said nothing. Her eyes drifted seaward again. Then she shook her head quickly, several times, as if clearing her vision, or denying an accusation.

"No way," she muttered in a fierce undertone. "There is just no way." She looked up at Brian, a flush rising to her cheeks. "So what happened then? After the free strip show?"

He told her how she had risen several feet off the floor. How she had started turning slowly in midair, naked, swathed in multicolored bands of light. How the great hot wind had roared into the room, blowing glass from the windows, knocking the crystal wind chimes to the floor, filling the eyes and mouths of the coven members with ashes and fear. How the terrible wind had passed, and with it the lights and the levitation. How she had lain crumpled up there on the floor, unclothed, unconscious, Sherone rushing over to her, weeping.

He left out the part about the voice—guttural whispering, the alien sound of a snarling, inhuman tongue, coming from out of nowhere, echoing everywhere inside the darkened, fear-filled room. He left that out because he still wasn't sure it had really happened. He wasn't sure he hadn't dreamed it up, invented it as a nervous reaction to the skin-crawling weirdness of the evening.

When he finished, Heather was looking down at the wet sand underfoot. Breakers crashed against distant rocks. A flock of gulls circled over the dark water. Brian cleared his throat. Heather looked up, a tear trickling down one cheek. She flicked at it angrily with one hand.

"You wouldn't," her voice broke, "b-bullshit me, would you?"

Brian shook his head slowly.

A gull screamed in the distance.

"Oh Jesus." Heather shuddered convulsively. "Jesus, I'm so scared. I'm so fucking scared." She started to cry.

Impulsively, she threw her arms around Brian, burying her face in his shoulder. For several seconds he stood there like a man struck by lightning. He could feel her breasts crushed against him, feel her body shaking with sobs. Gingerly, like a man handling priceless merchandise, he put his arms around her.

"It's okay," he whispered into her long red hair, patting her gently on the back. "Okay?"

She broke away from him suddenly, wiping at her eyes, the sea wind blowing her long hair across her face. She looked at him through the wild red mane.

"Brian," she shouted into the wind, "what can I *do?*"

"Hey, stay cool."

"Help me! I'm afraid!"

"Give me time to think about it, okay?" He took a deep breath. "You can always come up with something if you think about it." *Most of the time*, he admitted to himself, then he said, "We have to talk more about this later, okay?"

Heather nodded, snuffling at her tears.

"Tomorrow. Saturday morning. All right?"

Heather shook her head. "Kurt would be so pissed."

"I'll call you first."

"Brian, we can't talk about something like this over the phone!"

"Then where do you want to meet tomorrow?"

Heather shook her head. "Kurt would find out."

"How?"

"He'd find out."

Brian frowned. "So ask Kurt what to do."

Heather grabbed his shoulder. "Brian! You've got to help me!"

He thought about it. "I'll stop by your place."

Heather let go of his shoulder. "Kurt would—"

"Screw Kurt. I'm not trying to hit on you. Tell him I'm . . . Say I'm comin' by on Saturday morning to wash your car, okay?"

"Wash my car?"

"It could use it."

Heather looked slightly offended. "I can get it washed and detailed any time I want to drive it over to Magic Touch."

"Sure," Brian agreed. "For forty-five bucks you get a bunch of dropouts wipin' on it with grease rags. If I wash it, it'll get done right."

Heather shook her head. "Kurt would be so pissed."

But secretly, she was very pleased.

Not that Heather wasn't used to accepting, and turning down, favors from men. Usually they wanted to buy her things, expensive things, like overpriced trinkets or fancy dinners at hot new restaurants or too many roses in crystal vases. Kurt was into things like that, especially after they had a fight. Sometimes men wanted to go shopping with her and let her pick out whatever she liked and buy it for her. That was more her dad's style. *Just put it on my card,* he'd say to the salesperson, handing over his American Express Gold Card, the one with DAVID ROBERTS, M.D. embossed on it.

What men gave her less often was time, or personal attention. Heather could remember crying alone in her room on birthday evenings because her dad hadn't called. He never forgot to send an expensive present, usually with a singing telegram and a dozen long-stemmed red roses. He always seemed to have a good excuse, like the fact that he was in surgery or consultation or doing hospital rounds. But the point was, he didn't call. Kurt could be the same way. When he didn't want to go out dancing with her or wrestle in the front seat of his red Porsche 928E, he ignored her. If she ever wanted to talk with him about something that was bothering her, he was always busy surfing or riding dirt bikes or getting stoned with Troy Taylor and his other buddies. If she asked Kurt to come over and wash her car, he'd probably give her the forty-five bucks and tell her to take it to Magic Touch. If she asked her dad, through his receptionist, he'd just buy her a new car.

"While I'm scrubbin' down your dirt-mobile," Brian said, "we can talk some more, okay?"

Heather shook her head. "Saturday morning's out. Somebody'll see us." She considered the options. "How about . . . Sunday morning? Everybody in Encino's sacked out or in church then."

"Guess I can tear myself away from High Mass. It's a date. Sunday morning." Brian grinned with delight. "I can't believe it! I've got a date! Me!"

Heather frowned. "Don't get any ideas."

"Heather." Brian did his best bad Bogart imitation. "Somethin' tells me this is the beginning of a beautiful friendship."

Their laughter carried out over the deserted sands of the Cove and up into the rocky cliffs farther down the beach. It carried straight to the top of one cliff where four boys, all Severy Academy seniors, stood partially concealed behind a clump of boulders.

Troy Taylor turned to Kurt Pritchard. "You want to go down now and reset his balls for him?"

Kurt kept staring at the two figures walking along side by side in the distance, a hard, ugly light in his pale blue eyes.

"No," he said in a voice so low you could barely hear it above the breaking waves and crying gulls.

Troy's sneer tightened. "What're you waitin' for, man? Until he fucks her?"

A stocky kid named Garth Wiggins snorted with laughter. "Until he eats her and then fucks her, man."

Kurt turned suddenly and drove his right fist, hard, into Garth's belly below the belt. The air exploded from Garth's lungs in a hoarse groan. He clutched at his gut and doubled over. Kurt grabbed Troy by the collar of his Speedo polo shirt and slammed him up against a flat-sided boulder. Troy cried out in surprise and pain as his head bounced off the rock face.

Kurt's lower lip was quivering. "Don't you *ever* tell me what to do." He pointed a white-knuckled hand at Garth Wiggins, who was on his knees by now making gagging sounds. "Not you or him or *nobody*. Got it, fuck-face?"

Troy stared at him and said nothing, the sneer gone from his face.

Andy Metz, a tall kid with easy moves, stepped forward. "Stay cool, dude," he said to Kurt. "Okay?"

"You keep the fuck outta this, Metz," Kurt snapped at him.

Andy glanced from Kurt to Troy, then back to Kurt, gauging distances, unafraid and ready.

"Stay out of it, man," Troy said to him.

Kurt gave Troy a savage shake, knocking the back of his head against the rock again. "You under*stand* what I said to you, asshole?"

"Sure," Troy said, his eyes on Kurt's. "I understand."

Kurt jerked his hands away from Troy's collar and turned his back on him.

Troy felt the back of his head cautiously with his left hand. "Whatever you want, man. Whenever you want it." He turned to the other two. "Right?"

Garth Wiggins, still doubled over on his knees, managed to nod and make another gagging sound. Andy Metz just stared at Kurt Pritchard.

Kurt was staring at the two figures climbing the wooden stairs at the other end of the Cove.

"We'll fix him," he said softly, nodding to himself. "When the time comes, we'll fix him good."

PART II
wind

chapter 10

warlock

Sherone stood in The Heart of Darkness, alone and frightened.

She had been frightened ever since learning that the tarot cards Heather drew in her bedroom that night spelled out the name of the demon Azgaroth. The fear had stayed with her after Heather left. It went to bed with her, snuggling up close in the dark. She slept with the lights on that night, but light did not banish the fear. It was still there, painful as a throbbing wound, in the bright pale light of morning. It rode to school with her and whispered in her ear during class. It had forced her to call Magda from school, to exorcise the fear.

It had brought her here, to The Heart of Darkness, alone, with the fear like a tumor in her throat.

It was early evening, around 7:15. The Heart was doing brisk business. Occult shop customers, the serious ones, don't start moving until night falls.

The regulars were there. Overweight middle-aged women with short gray hair and shapeless multicolored tent dresses picked over ritual oils and fingered heavy ceremonial bracelets. Older young women with drawn faces and long stringy hair left over from the Woodstock glory days sniffed through jars of magic herbs. Emaciated young men with curly long hair and staring blank eyes wandered up and down the narrow aisles like extras from *Night of the Living Dead*. Ghostly electronic music echoed at low volume throughout the store. There was the occasional yuppie adventurer, daring to find out what this weird occult shit was all about, staring with wide eyes at the shriveled bat wings and desiccated salamanders behind glass counters, and in one separate display case beneath lock and key, with a DO NOT TOUCH sign in red block letters, a sealed jar with a tiny semi-human embryo floating in formaldehyde.

There were also a few kids Sherone's age, curiosity seekers for the most part, lured from the great cruising ground of Van Nuys Boulevard by a glaring pink electric sign:

THE HEART OF DARKNESS

OCCULT BOOKS * SUPPLIES
CEREMONIAL MAGIC * CUSTOM SPELLS
TAROT READINGS * PSYCHIC EVALUATIONS
FREE PARKING IN REAR
VISA * MASTERCARD * AMERICAN EXPRESS

Sherone ignored the other customers and kept her eyes on Magda Prokash, who ignored her, standing behind the *athamé* display counter at the back of the store, talking seriously with two older white-haired women who looked like refugees from a traditional English tea shop with their tweed skirts and jackets, low-heeled shoes and silk ties. *She's deliberately ignoring me*, Sherone thought. Magda could be like that. Get her pissed off at you and she could stay pissed for weeks. She didn't want to hear about Sherone's problems with a bad tarot reading.

Sherone worked her way down the magic herb aisle, pretending to read the jar labels, all the while edging closer to Magda Prokash and her two elderly customers, moving slowly past the labels. Dragon's Blood. Bladder Wrack. Hyssop. Saxifrage. Deer Tongue. Pilewort. Black Cohosh. Dittany of Crete. Lungwort. Jaborandi. Bloodroot. Queen of the Meadow. Black Malva. Heather . . .

Heather, Sherone thought, and her own fear was heightened by an even greater fear for her friend. She had wanted to talk with her about it earlier today at school. They needed to talk about it, about what had happened that night. If Heather hadn't acted like such a bitch on wheels, shutting her down before she even got a chance to open her mouth, maybe they could have talked about . . . everything.

A sharp sense of guilt pricked Sherone as she moved slowly down the magic herb aisle. She was sorry now, very sorry, that she had ever invited Heather to the Wicca that night. She had done so only because Magda asked her to. *And because you wanted to share it with her*, she admitted, *you wanted to let Heather in on the Power.* That was why Sherone admired Magda, because she had the Power. People with it, Sherone knew, didn't take shit from anybody. What they wanted, they got. That was all Sherone wanted from witchcraft, the Power. The rest of it—the spells, the rituals—were nothing. Only the Power mattered.

But she never dreamed the Power could be turned against her, against Heather. *Magda's a white witch*, Sherone told herself, *and she uses the Power to help people, not hurt them.* But it wasn't Magda's Power anymore. The hairs prickled on the back of Sherone's neck as she realized this.

"Sherone! How *are* you?"

Sherone looked up, startled, expecting to see Magda. The girl in front of her, about Sherone's age, had dark olive skin and long dark curling hair. Her low-cut tank top revealed a generous expanse of well-developed bosom.

"Hi, Tamara," Sherone said warily. "How's it goin'?"

Tamara Devon smiled, her hard dark eyes glittering like black diamonds. "Sherone, you look *so* beautiful tonight." She raised a long-fingered hand to touch Sherone's cheek. The nails were painted black. The little fingernail of the left hand was decorated with a sequin-encrusted pentagram.

"*Really* beautiful." Tamara held the skin contact longer than necessary, her fingers tracing lightly down Sherone's cheek to the side of her neck.

Sherone twisted away from the caress. She did not like being touched by Tamara Devon. Tamara was one of the more prominent members of Magda's coven. The daughter of an alcoholic actress and a burned-out director, she also claimed to be the reincarnate form of a demonic sixteenth-century Italian countess burned at the stake for witchcraft. According to coven rumors, she kept several lesbian lovers, one an older woman, the other a thirteen-year-old girl. You never knew if rumors like that were true, and you were supposed to be real chill about alternate sexuality anyway, and Sherone knew this, but Tamara Devon still gave her the creeps.

"It's been so long since we've seen you," Tamara said. "Why didn't you bring her with you?"

Sherone frowned. "Who?"

"Your little friend with the Samantha Fox body."

Sherone's stomach churned as she remembered how Tamara and the other coven members had seen Heather nude, hanging suspended in midair, encircled by lights. "She's not into this kind of shit," Sherone said curtly.

Tamara smiled again. "Too bad. Why're you here?"

"To see Magda."

"Nothing I can help with?"

"Afraid not." Sherone pushed past her, right up to the *athamé* counter where the taller of the two older ladies was describing an object in the air with her thin white hands.

"... *enormous* field of light," she was saying in a clipped British accent. "And even though one knew one was out of the body, of course, still there was this *extraordinary* sense of warmth, as though one were—" She noticed Sherone and stopped, turning to Magda. "Oh dear, I'm afraid there's someone here for you."

Magda smiled a hard smile. "Nobody who can't wait."

"Nonsense!" said the shorter woman, patting Magda firmly on the hand. "We've taken up so *awfully* much of your time as it is. And if we'd known you had patrons waiting, we never should have done."

"Gwendolyn's quite right, you know," the taller woman agreed. "We'll let you get on with it."

"Right." The shorter woman nodded. "I'll send you a copy of that channeling videotape. Come along, Felicity."

As the two women made their way down the magic herb aisle, Magda turned on Sherone. "What do you want?"

"I have to talk with you."

Magda regarded her coolly. "Another night would be better. Perhaps next Thursday. I'll call you."

Sherone's mouth dropped. "It can't wait that long!"

"I think it will have to, Sherone." Magda looked away from her, pretending to straighten one of the *athamés* on display beneath the glass countertop.

"Bull*shit!*" Sherone slammed a fist down on the countertop, rattling *athamés* in their cases. "I am not going to just stand around and watch while my best friend gets possessed by a demon!"

The other customers in The Heart of Darkness froze, then turned with one movement to the back of the store where Sherone stood glaring at Magda Prokash across the glass countertop. The two older British ladies, Felicity and Gwendolyn, looked up from the front cash register where they were purchasing a small bag of saxifrage.

"You stupid girl," Magda hissed at her. "Keep your voice down!" Magda looked up and smiled at the other customers. "I'm going to step into the back for just a moment. If you have any questions, Tamara here will be glad to help you. Remember, amulets are on special, half-price, tonight only. Blesséd be."

In back of The Heart of Darkness was another room, almost another world. Where the main showroom gave forth a kind of spooky good cheer, with its bizarre display items and eerie music and carnival parade of shoppers, the back room was dark and empty, illuminated by nothing more than a pale blue light issuing from a hidden source. The way to the back room was concealed by heavy black curtains and, behind those, an even heavier door.

It slammed shut with the hollow sound of an iron coffin lid. Sherone felt her stomach churn. She had been in the back room only once before and it reminded her of being locked in a closet. But she had to talk to Magda.

She *had* to.

Magda turned from the heavy door, her cold gray eyes almost phosphorescent in the blue light. "This had better be good, Sherone."

Sherone coughed. Something in the room was burning, giving off a sweetish, gagging smell. Sherone cleared her throat, then started to tell Magda about Heather and the tarot cards.

Before she got very far, Magda stopped her. "We've been over this before, Sherone. It's nothing. I told you that. A Sensitive duplicates a set of cards spelling out the name of an entity with which she's had previous contact. This is to be expected."

"But Magda—"

"It merely confirms my original evaluation. The girl is very good, a completely open channel. But then," Magda paused, "virgins often are."

"Magda," Sherone insisted nervously, "she called him up again, without even trying. Right in my goddamn bedroom! You understand what I'm saying?"

"Impossible. She can*not* channel Azgaroth at will. He must be summoned, deliberately."

"Magda, he was *there*. Like he's following her, or maybe waiting for her . . ."

Magda smiled a hard, unforgiving smile. "Why would a powerful demon like Azgaroth be so interested in an ordinary teenage girl?"

"Perhaps," said the voice from the darkness, "we can find out."

Sherone screamed at the sound and backed up against the door, groping for the handle. Something she had mistaken in the blue half-light for a stack of boxes stood up and turned around. Sherone screamed again.

The face was white, dead chalk-white, so blank white that the long white hair straggling across the pale skull seemed almost dark by comparison. The face was narrow and sharp-featured, with a large aquiline nose that seemed to have been chiseled from bleached bone. The eyes were dark and piercing, the teeth so badly discolored that they looked black under the pale blue light.

"Seamus," Magda said hesitantly, as if frightened by the pale man, "don't talk nonsense to her, please. She'll believe it."

Seamus Harrach ignored Magda and spoke directly to Sherone, who was forcing herself to stare at him like someone observing a burn victim without bandages for the first time. "If the demon actually appeared in your presence," he said, "perhaps we can persuade him to . . . reappear."

"Not without the original Sensitive who drew him forth," Magda pointed out.

"But perhaps," Seamus Harrach said, "we can make do with a substitute." He asked Sherone, "Would you let us have some of your blood?"

"No *way!*" She backed up against the door.

Seamus Harrach turned to Magda. "The dark girl, the one outside, she would be more cooperative, no?"

Magda nodded, then left the room.

Holy shit, Sherone thought, panic mounting, *what has she left me in here with?*

As if sensing her question, the pale man said, "I am Seamus Harrach, Warlock of the Ninth Power." He pronounced his first name *Shame-us*. "At your service." He bowed.

But the formality of the bow was belied by the mocking glint of his hard dark eyes.

"Are you a . . . white warlock?" Sherone managed.

Seamus Harrach laughed unpleasantly. "White magic. Black magic. Petty differences for children to squabble over. They mean *nothing*." He spit out the word. "Power is power. Black. White. Or checkered. No?"

Sherone said nothing.

The heavy door squealed open, then slammed shut. Sherone saw Magda's stocky form move into the blue light and smelled Tamara Devon's overpowering Giorgio perfume.

Seamus Harrach turned to Tamara, a slow smile revealing most of his blackened teeth. "For a simple experiment," he said, "we need some of your blood."

"Anytime." Tamara smiled, her teeth brilliant white against her olive skin. "You want it from me skyclad?"

She started to oblige by peeling off her tank top. Her large breasts popped out in 3-D magnitude. The dark nipples were aggressively pointed, surrounded by large dark areolae. She started to unzip her jeans.

"That won't be necessary," Seamus Harrach said. "We need only a small quantity of blood."

Tamara cupped a heavy breast and lifted it toward him. "From here?"

"We'll save that for a hungrier mouth," the warlock smiled wolfishly, "with sharper teeth. Give me the palm of your right hand."

Tamara, still naked to the waist, held out her hand and cast a long sideways glance at Sherone. *She does have great boobs, damn her*, Sherone thought, painfully aware of her own more modest endowments.

Seamus Harrach lighted a black candle. The wick sputtered and flared. He passed the blade of an unusually long and thin *athamé* through the flame several times. Then, holding Tamara's right hand palm upward in his own, he made a series of quick, short cuts. As blood began to well up from the shallow cuts, Sherone could see that they were made in the shape of a pentagram or pentacle, the five-sided star. Mark of the Beast.

Tamara shivered in a kind of ecstasy. Her naked breasts trembled. Seamus Harrach turned her hand palm downward and let the blood drip into what looked like a tarnished bronze chalice. He opened two opaque vials and poured their contents into the chalice. One liquid looked dark and stringy, the other pale gray and jellylike. Sherone swallowed the bile that rose at the back of her throat.

Seamus Harrach turned to her, the chalice in his left hand, right hand held in the Sign of the Beast, middle fingers folded, index and little fingers raised. "Come before me," he commanded.

Her first reaction was to run for it. She did not like this kind of impromptu black magic, not at all. But she stepped forward and stood before the pale warlock, heart hammering inside her chest like an imprisoned, desperate thing.

Seamus Harrach dipped his two upraised fingers into the bowl of the tarnished chalice and dabbed Sherone's cheeks with the mixture of blood and liquids from the vials, two stripes to each cheek. A stomach-turning stench made her nose wrinkle. She could not tell if the horrible smell came from the mess in the chalice or from the open mouth of the warlock, inches from her own, full of black, rotting teeth.

"This is more effective," he murmured, "if the medium's body is anointed skyclad."

"Not on your fucking life," Sherone said between clenched teeth.

"As you wish," Seamus Harrach replied mildly.

He stepped back and raised his hands, holding the chalice, above his head.

"*Satanas!*" he cried out in a deep, ghastly voice.

Heather shuddered at the introit to the Black Mass.

"*Azgaroth!*" he called. "Servant of the Dark Lord! Come before us! *Daemon magnificus!* Grace us with your dark Presence!"

Sherone braced herself for the demon's heat and the hideous voice she had heard—had she really heard it? or just imagined it?—the night Heather hung suspended naked from a nucleus of lights. She braced herself, waiting. Her guts turned to water.

Nothing happened.

Seamus Harrach leaned forward and blew out the black candle. "Well, that's that." He looked up at Magda. "She's definitely not a channel for him."

"Can I go wash this shit off?" Sherone asked, her voice shaking, two bloody stripes dark against each cheek.

"I thought," Magda said, "that you wanted to talk."

"I want out of here."

After Sherone left the back room, Magda turned to Seamus Harrach and said, "You scared her."

"She's lovely," the warlock murmured. "I would like to see her bleed."

chapter 11

the other world

When Karin finally reached Wilton Auditorium on the Hoskins College campus, she found Annie waiting outside the main entrance for her next to a sign announcing that evening's lecture: *The Other World—* Psi *Phenomena and Their Significance.*

Annie waved. "Hey, Karin!"

"Sorry," Karin panted, running up the steps. "I was ready on time, but—"

"Not to worry," Annie reassured her. "Our seats are reserved. They probably haven't even gotten to the good stuff yet anyways."

"It's Heather's fault," Karin explained, as the two sisters walked across the foyer. "I don't know what's wrong with her these days. It's like she's trying to test me or something."

"What happened?" Annie asked, taking two programs from an usher.

"Oh nothing really, I guess. But she knew I had the appointment with you and she got home two hours later than she promised. The second night in a row! She was talking with some boy after school, she said."

"Kurt?" Annie asked.

Karin shook her head. "Some new guy. Some kid I'd never heard of before. Brian Mc— something."

"Sounds like Heather's playing the field."

"I don't think so, Annie." A worried frown crossed Karin's face. "She was upset after talking with him. She wouldn't discuss it with me. But I could tell something was bothering her."

"You don't think it's . . ." Annie hesitated, not wanting to say the forbidden word.

"Do I think she's buying drugs from him? Christ, Annie! I don't know what to think anymore. With Bromley on my case at the museum and Heather acting so damn weird all the time. And Mom waving David in my face like a red flag."

"So you finally called her back, huh?"

"She came over to see me."

Annie gave her an I-told-you-so look. "That's what happens when you don't call her back, K.M. I always call. She's a lot easier to handle over the phone."

"Nothing's easy anymore, Annie." Karin winced at the early warning signs of a major headache.

Annie put a hand on her sister's shoulder. "Lighten up, K.M.! You gotta slow down before you get slowed down." Annie smiled. "It's a good thing you came here tonight. You'll learn lots of useful stuff."

"Sure," Karin said. "Like how to go out of my body and stay there."

As they took their seats near the front of the auditorium, Karin looked around at the other members of the audience. It was a mixed group: students, a few professors, cute suburban mommies like Annie, lots of old folks, the lonely kind who are always seeking messages from departed loved ones. Scattered throughout the audience, like special-effects explosions, were the regular customers of places like The Heart of Darkness, true believers in the occult.

At a podium onstage, a man was speaking. He was tall, about six feet two inches, somewhere in his middle to late thirties, with dark hair and a sharply cut, aggressive-looking beard. With one hand he gripped the microphone like the neck of an antagonist. With the other he gestured as he spoke, pointing at the audience to punctuate his words.

He'd be good-looking, Karin thought abstractly, taking her seat, *if he didn't act so goddamn arrogant*. David Roberts was supremely arrogant, and all men who acted that way were judged by Karin accordingly.

". . . say that *psi* phenomena are nothing more than hallucinations." The speaker repeated the words slowly, with studied contempt. "Nothing more than hallucinations! Have they ever *experienced psi* phenomena? Do they even understand what it *means?*"

Scattered applause greeted these remarks.

Karin whispered to Annie, "So who's this?"

Annie leaned over, reading from her program. "Jeffrey Geller, Research Fellow, IPS."

"Huh?"

"Institute for Parapsychological Studies. You know, the one in Pasadena. I think this guy's been on Carson once, and he got something published in *Psychology Today*. But the really interesting one is over there."

Annie pointed to a small, slump-shouldered man seated at a table beside the podium. With his worn three-piece suit and dark knit tie he looked like a low-grade English civil servant. A thatch of white hair fell across his forehead as he leaned over the table, busily jotting down notes with an outsize black fountain pen.

"Who's he?" Karin asked.

"That's Roland. Dr. Roland Cameron. He's the one who wrote those two books. *In Search of the Other World* and *The Other World in Everyday Life*. He's been on Carson lots of times. He is *so* super, K.M."

"*Psi* phenomena," Jeff Geller continued, "are as real, and as significant, as any other phenomena. We can measure the effects of psychokinesis, or PK. We can test for precognition. We can record the appearances of the

121

disincarnate. We can even photograph the ectoplasm as it leaves a trance medium's body!"

Annie explained, for the benefit of a frowning Karin. "PK, psychokinesis, that's where you move stuff around with just your mind, okay? Precognition is, like, telling the future. And ectoplasm's sort of a spiritual body. The stuff that goes out of your body when—"

"—you go out of your body," Karin finished for her. "Okay, I get that. But what are the disincarnate?"

"The dead."

Jeff Geller pounded on the podium suddenly, making the microphone crackle. "Why won't they accept the reality of *psi* phenomena? They have scientific proof. But they're afraid! Afraid of what people might say. Afraid of what they might find out about themselves!"

Enthusiastic applause from the audience.

"Hiding behind this fear, they refuse to take *psi* phenomena seriously. They attack parapsychology as a pseudo-science. They deny the reality of something they are too ignorant to understand, too cowardly to face!"

Polite applause. But Jeff was starting to lose his audience. They had come to hear about reincarnation and out-of-body experiences, not listen to a defense of parapsychology.

The little man at the desk cleared his throat audibly. Roland Cameron laid down his fountain pen and looked up at Jeff Geller with a slight frown.

Jeff glanced at him, then turned back to the microphone, head lowered slightly. "I don't mean to go on and on. It's just that I get angry when I hear people making fun of parapsychology and *psi* phenomena. I get angry because I know how important our work is and, somehow, I want to make you understand that too."

Annie leaned over to Karin. "Sorry about this guy. He's a real zero. But just hang in there till Roland gets on, okay?"

Karin nodded, but she did not agree. She felt a strong sympathy for Jeff Geller and his outrage at the powers that be—the Milton Bromleys, the David Robertses of this world. It was an outrage Karin had felt for years. She did not know exactly what parapsychology was. What little she had learned from Annie did not make her anxious to find out any more. It all sounded like a grown-up, pretentious version of Heather's ouija boards and tarot cards. But none of that mattered. The tall, angry man at the podium was standing up publicly for what he believed in, no matter how unpopular it might be, and Karin admired him for that.

Trickles of weak applause followed Jeff Geller back to his seat at the table beside Roland Cameron. Jeff sat moodily at the table, drumming the fingers of his right hand on a notepad in front of him, as if he had more to say but had been kept from saying it.

The auditorium broke into thunderous applause when Roland Cameron got to his feet. This was the one they had come to see. Making his way to the podium, a sheaf of papers under one arm, the little white-haired man smiled shyly and nodded at the applauding audience. Once at the podium, he arranged his papers and adjusted the microphone.

"Ladies and gentlemen," he began, in a soft Oxford accent amplified over the P.A. system, "good evening and wel—" *skkrreeeeee*. Roland Cameron winced, fiddling with the microphone as he tried to get rid of the feedback squeal. "Apparently," he continued, speaking carefully into the microphone, "someone has been thoughtful enough to furnish a poltergeist for the evening."

Laughter burst from the audience.

"I shall try hard to keep him, or her, in good spirits. And quiet."

More laughter, followed by applause.

Annie whispered to Karin, "Isn't he *neat?*"

Poltergeists, Karin thought with disgust. *One of those.* But Roland Cameron didn't look like one of those. Unlike Jeff Geller, who had a wild-eyed urgency about him, Roland Cameron looked like some absentminded but completely sane professor of mathematics. He spoke in a quiet, reasonable voice, the voice of a man talking calmly about very ordinary things. *If you had to trust somebody with something important,* Karin found herself thinking, *you'd trust this guy.*

"My colleague and assistant, Dr. Geller," Roland nodded to Jeff, "has spent quite some time tonight attacking the critics of our work. While this has its uses, I should like to open my remarks with a favorable reference to one of our most hostile critics, Sigmund Freud."

Jeff frowned, as if Roland Cameron had suddenly defected to the enemy camp.

"Freud, as some of you know, was quite negative about the whole subject of the supernatural, or what I like to call the Other World. He didn't think much of organized religion. He thought even less of ghosts and clairvoyance, the things we refer to now as *psi* phenomena. Freud regarded the whole lot of it as a kind of overblown neurosis. Rather sad news for people like Dr. Geller and myself who waste our time studying this stuff."

The audience laughed. Jeff Geller, seated morosely at the table, frowned at them, as if they were laughing at him and his defense of parapsychology. Karin, remembering how isolated she had felt at the board meeting with Bromley, wished she could say something to Jeff, who was beginning to look less arrogant to her all the time.

"But Freud," Roland continued, "like most great thinkers, always kept an open mind. Even about things he mistrusted, such as *psi* phenomena. For example, in an essay on the possible occult significance of dreams, Freud pooh-poohs the idea that there *is* any such thing. But then, in the same breath, he goes on to say that there just might be something to reports of telepathic dreams. The kind that communicate messages from one person to another. As when people dream of loved ones in peril and then wake to find, alas, that the dream has become reality.

"Now Freud doesn't come right out and say that he thinks telepathy is real. Or even that he thinks it could be. He simply says, in effect, that he finds the matter interesting and thinks it deserves more study. In short, *he admits to being curious.* Even about *psi* phenomena."

Roland Cameron looked up at his audience. "*Curious.* That's the key. I imagine it's why most of you are here tonight. Because you're curious. About the Other World. About your experiences with that world. Or maybe you're just plain curious. That was roughly my situation when I began my studies in parapsychology forty years ago at Oxford. At the time my experience of the Other World was slight, and I must confess that I was rather skeptical. But I kept an open mind. I neither believed nor disbelieved. I was curious. I wanted to know more."

A hush seemed to fall over the audience. Annie started to say something to Karin, then decided not to.

"We are just beginning," Roland continued, "to understand the complexity—the enormity—of the Other World. Parapsychologists have learned that they are explorers in an undiscovered country. And rather timid explorers at that." He paused, looking down at his papers. "*Telepathy:* direct mind-to-mind communication. *Clairvoyance:* extra-sensory perception, ESP, perceiving objects without the use of the senses. *Precognition:* seeing future events now, before they happen. *Psychokinesis:* PK, the ability to move physical objects without any apparent effort, through mental control alone."

Roland looked up from his papers. "These are the four traditional areas of parapsychological investigation—the official turf of parapsychology, if you will—as established by the English researchers Thouless and Wiesner. How far we have come since then! Especially in the first area, telepathy. Researchers in telepathy used to busy themselves with the conventional kind of experiment wherein one subject sits in a room with the door closed and then 'talks,' without speaking, to a subject in another closed room. Information is given to the sending telepath by one group of researchers. Another group interrogates the receiving telepath to determine if he or she 'heard' the message correctly. Simple. Harmless. Predictable."

Roland Cameron's voice dropped. "But then, things became less simple. Less predictable. Quite dangerous. In London, in 1957, during an experiment to which I was witness, a telepathic subject began receiving messages from . . . beyond."

Murmurs rustled through the audience. People shifted in their seats. Annie gave Karin a What-did-I-tell-you? look and leaned forward to hear better.

Brace yourself, Karin thought. *Here comes the bullshit.*

"At first, we assumed that it was random interference. The telepathic subject, an adolescent girl, was allowed to rest. After a brief interval, the experiment continued. The young subject became increasingly agitated, unable to concentrate on the experimental data. At one point she began to shriek uncontrollably and started ripping loose the adhesive monitoring devices attached to her head. The researchers attempted to restrain her. We also noted down what she was saying. Or trying to say. It was not in any language ever spoken in this world."

Roland Cameron gripped the podium. "The young subject had to be sedated. Then hospitalized. Later, she escaped from the hospital with . . . tragic consequences. Some of you may have read about them in *Night Horror: The West End Demon*, a rather sensationalized account that I understand is still in print in this country. The general reaction at the time was that the girl had been shocked into a psychotic state by the telepathic experiments. GIRL TORTURED, DRIVEN MAD BY FIENDISH SCIENTISTS was how one of the more popular tabloids of the day put it, as I recall. Obviously this had a negative effect on the prestige of parapsychology in England at the time. And our problem in defending ourselves was compounded by the fact that we had no ready answer for what had happened.

"The girl, after all, *had* become psychotic. Not because we deliberately terrified her. But *something* had. Something had invaded her mind during the experiment. *Something had communicated with her from beyond.* Something so unlike anything she had ever experienced or imagined, something so horrifying, that it quite literally drove her mad. And forced her to commit acts of such a hideous and repulsive character that I refuse even to mention them in a public lecture."

There was disappointed muttering from some of the occult shop regulars. Karin felt a dark, ominous dread growing within her, a fear without a name. She put a hand to her forehead and realized that she was sweating.

Annie gave her a worried look. "You okay, K.M.?"

Karin nodded. "I'm fine."

Roland Cameron continued in a low voice. "To find out what that something was became my one goal in life. An obsession. At the time I told myself I owed it to the poor young girl whose life had been so ruthlessly destroyed . . . along with the lives of so many others. But I must admit now that I was driven as much by curiosity as by duty. What had communicated with her? Where had it come from? My search took me far into the dark studies of ancient witchcraft, sorcery, magic, looking for clues, sometimes mere fragments or hints, from earlier explorers of the Other World. I might add that my search also took me far from respectability, both social and academic. My colleagues who had participated in the original experiment were quick to wash their hands of the whole business once it turned to tragedy. They lost all interest in *psi* phenomena and assured press reporters and Oxford officials alike that they intended to restrict their future studies to the more traditional areas of psychology. *Para*psychology became a dirty word. And I became a dirty dog."

There was some laughter from the audience.

"Eventually, my university dismissed me. My wife divorced me. Former friends and colleagues shunned me. I was vilified by the press with various colorful epithets. Crackpot Cameron. Raving Roland. The Mad Doctor of Oxfordshire. But I persisted. And for my efforts, I discovered . . . not the answer I had been searching for, but another question, one of terrifying proportions. I discovered the Other World."

The auditorium was still and silent.

"In my earlier parapsychological studies, I had speculated that, somehow, the energy that manifests itself as *psi* phenomena must be connected with the more readily apparent energy described by physics. In the end, I told myself, it must come down to energy. Modern physics posits energy as the heartbeat of all existence. Psychic energy must interact with physical energy to form one continuous, interdependent universe."

Roland Cameron cleared his throat. "There, of course, I was wrong. Dead wrong."

The audience shuffled uneasily this time, the way people do when they anticipate hearing something they would rather not.

"I had assumed," he continued, "that everything would fit together neatly, like the pieces to an enormous jigsaw puzzle. I had assumed that evil, the dark side of spiritual energy, had no place in this grand scheme of things. Or, if it had a place, it was a distant and restrained one, firmly under control of the good side. I was wrong."

Roland Cameron touched the microphone. Feedback squealed through it. This time several members of the audience started at the sound. Karin felt her stomach burn.

"I began to understand, slowly at first, then with growing conviction, that the Other World was no mere shadow of this one. Rather, it was . . . an anti-world, a world far older than our own, one that precedes ours as death precedes life itself."

Roland Cameron looked out into his audience,

studying them. "The Other World is no place to go wandering, in or out of the body. It is a strange and terrible world, filled with dark, dangerous creatures, some of them ancient as the universe itself, most of them content, thank goodness, to sleep out their dreamless sleep in distant isolation from us and our world.

"But some of them," and here Roland's voice trembled slightly, "*some of them are obsessed by the urge to reach out and pass through from their world into ours.* I wish I could say that this desire to contact us is a friendly and cooperative one. It is not. Their urge is not to communicate, but to possess. Not to nurture, but to destroy. They gather at the dark edges of our known world, peering in hungrily, waiting impatiently for the moment to cross the infinite black gulf," Roland Cameron paused, "and consume us."

The murmuring and shifting in the audience grew more pronounced. Some of the older members began to rise from their seats and steal out of the auditorium.

Karin, staring at the circle of light surrounding Roland Cameron, watched as that light, and then the entire auditorium, began to waver and fade. It was replaced by another image: an endless expanse of black water, flat and glassy like the surface of a mirror, black as obsidian. Before that endless black water stretched a narrow rocky beach on which Heather wandered, naked, head turned toward the dark water, arms raised above her head, blood trickling down her pale white body as she cried out in supplication to something beyond the blackness, something—

Unspeakable.

Karin lunged forward in her seat, grasping at the vanished image.

"Karin." Annie gripped her sister's arm. "Do you want me to get a doctor?"

Karin shook her head, eyes unfocused. "I'm okay."

chapter 12

CROSS FIRE

Karin slept fifteen minutes past her alarm the next day. She awoke with a headache. She had slept badly, harried by dreams she could not remember in the gray half-light of morning.

As she made her way stiffly down the hallway and into the kitchen, she was aware of a low, humming sound. It had a resonating waver to it, like a harbor foghorn. Karin frowned, turning the corner into the kitchen.

She caught her breath.

Heather was bent low over the breakfast table, her back to Karin, in a gesture of strange obeisance.

What kind of ritual? Karin thought, a chill crawling up the back of her neck, and she cried, "Heather!"

Heather snapped up straight, a small yelp of alarm escaping her. She spun around, short nightgown flying up from her legs, blue eyes wide with shock. Then she slumped with a visible sigh of relief.

"God*damn* it, Mother!" She sounded more tired than angry. "Would you quit sneaking up on me?"

"That sound," Karin said. "What was it?"

Heather shrugged. "Blowing on a bottle."

"What?"

Heather bent over a half-full orange juice bottle and blew across the mouth. The low note vibrated throughout the kitchen. "See?"

Karin poured a cup of coffee. "Where's Gabriela?"

"Ironing my silk blouse."

"Don't you have another you can wear?"

"They get all wrinkled in the closet." Heather took a bite of toast and leaned over the comics section of the *Los Angeles Times*, her long red hair falling down onto the tabletop.

Karin studied her daughter. She was truly beautiful. The traces of baby fat that had made her look almost pudgy two years ago were gone now, leaving in their place the firm, sleek lines of radiant young womanhood. The face was lovely, the eyes bright and intelligent, the body gracefully proportioned. The breasts were larger than average and would have to be attended to with diet and exercise as she got older or they might get too heavy. *A problem we should all have*, Karin thought.

Heather tapped a bare foot against the linoleum as she read the comics. P.T. Barnum rubbed his fat Persian body against her other leg and purred.

Karin walked over and put an arm around her daughter. "Hey." She hugged her. "You okay?"

Heather looked up from the comics, a small frown on her face. "Sure. Why'd you ask?"

"You've been kind of upset for the last few days." Karin brushed back a strand of red hair. "And then the business with that boy yesterday."

Heather flushed. "That's nothing. I'm just great, okay?" She looked down at the comics.

"If you say so, okay. I just like to check now and then." Karin kissed her lightly on top of her head. "I *do* love you, you know. I don't always act like it. And I'm sorry about that. But I do care."

Heather squirmed uncomfortably. "Okay, Mom. I know you do. You don't have to go into all that crap."

Karin stiffened. "It's not crap, young lady. You're not

131

too old for me to tell you I love you. And you'll never be." The minute she said it, Karin seemed to hear an echo of Maureen Magnusson saying the same thing and she thought, *Christ, am I turning into her?* She pulled back from Heather.

As she did, Heather turned from the comics and threw her arms around Karin's neck. "I love you too, Mom. You know that."

"Yeah." Karin hugged her tight in return. "I guess I do. But it's still nice to hear it once in a while."

Heather broke away and went back to her comics, embarrassed now.

She's afraid of showing love, Karin thought, *because she's afraid what she loves might be taken away again.* Guilt pierced Karin's heart. Whose fault was it? David's? Hers? She knew it was no one's fault. But that easy answer never made things any easier to live with.

Karin was trying to eat her own breakfast, a bowl of high-fiber cereal that tasted like sawdust, while making a to-do list for the Barringer, when she heard the sounds from outside. First the loud whining of a power saw followed by the muffled roar of Heather's four-cylinder Suzuki Samurai engine turning over. Then voices raised in angry argument, rising from there into a shouting match. One of them was Heather's.

Karin got to her feet, pencil in hand, a paper napkin clinging to her skirt. She opened the front door and looked out. And dropped the pencil.

Heather, dressed in black tights, high-top Reeboks and a green silk shirt, was screaming at Hyung-Joon Kim. Her face was flushed with anger, her fists clenched in front of her. The small elderly Korean gardener was holding a lethal-looking chain saw in both hands, his Dodger Blue baseball cap tilted back on his head.

"*Move* it!" Heather screamed at him. "Or I'll move it *for* you!"

She pointed angrily at Hyung-Joon Kim's faded red Toyota pickup parked sideways on the drive where it blocked Heather's Samurai.

Hyung-Joon Kim was trying to say something, but it was impossible to hear him over the loud whine of the chain saw. Only Heather was audible, screaming at the top of her lungs.

"I'm late for *school!* Move your fucking truck!"

"Heather!" Karin called from the front door. "Hyung-Joon!"

They turned to her. Hyung-Joon Kim snapped off the chain saw. The piercing whine died to a muted *whirrrrrr*.

"He's *blocking* me!" Heather shouted to her mother, pointing at the old man.

"Meesa Robbers." Hyung-Joon Kim bowed. "I try explain Meesee Hedder—"

"I'm late for school, you jerkhead!"

Karin stepped out onto the drive. "Heather, let him finish."

"You're takin' his side, huh? Thanks, Mom! Thanks a lot!"

"Heather." Karin shot her a warning glance.

"Assholes!" Heather muttered under her breath. She stomped off to her Samurai, got inside and slammed the door shut. The little jeep rocked under the impact.

"I try explain," Hyung-Joon Kim continued, "how I gotta cut down tree." He pointed to a withered jacaranda. "Tree die. I cut him down."

Karin's heart sank. She loved the jacaranda with its wealth of purple blossoms. David had hated it when the blossoms blew over onto his silver Lamborghini. He said they stained the finish. There were no blossoms now.

"You should have moved the truck for her, Hyung-Joon," Karin reproached him gently. "She does have to get to school, you know."

Hyung-Joon Kim frowned indignantly. "She go round, no probalem." He nodded at the Samurai, his rimless glasses flashing with reflected sunlight. "There plenty room for go round."

It was true. Although Hyung-Joon Kim's truck was

133

parked behind Heather's jeep and technically blocking it, there was room to pull forward and back out around the red Toyota. It was a large driveway.

Karin walked over to the Samurai where Heather sat sulking in the driver's seat, the jeep's FM turned up to blasting on a new music rock station.

"Honey," Karin shouted over the music.

"What?" Heather snapped back without looking up.

"Can't you just back out around the truck?"

"Sure." Heather looked up, eyes red. "I can go out of my way in my own driveway to do whatever makes *him* happy. 'Cause he owns the outside, doesn't he?"

"Heather—"

"And Gabriela owns the inside. And you run her and him, just like you run everybody at work. 'Cause you own it all!"

"*Heather.*"

"But what do I own?" Heather's lower lip trembled. "Nothin'! I just *live* here."

She turned on the engine and gunned it. Then she rammed the gearshift into reverse. With a squeal of rubber she swerved out past the red Toyota. Karin jumped back. Hyung-Joon Kim hopped nimbly to one side to avoid getting sideswiped.

"Heather Michelle!" Karin shouted at her. "You could have hurt him!"

But Heather was not listening. Out in the street she reversed again, then threw it into first and lurched forward, tires squealing.

Damn her! Karin thought bitterly. *What's wrong with her, anyway?* Her own heart was pounding with an adrenaline rush. She turned to Hyung-Joon Kim. "I'm sorry. I hope she didn't scare you."

Hyung-Joon Kim nodded agreeably. "No probalem, Meesa Robbers. I go cut down tree."

He started up the chain saw. The sharp whining sound filled the morning air. Karin watched as the old gardener walked out toward the wasted jacaranda tree, its barren limbs reaching upward like crippled arms.

chapter 13

the Return

Sherone twisted in the grip of a nightmare so horrible it made her earlier fears seem like sweet dreams.

Magda Prokash was drinking blood. She smiled and it ran from the sides of her mouth and down onto her naked withered breasts. Her gray eyes glowed hellishly in the shifting blue light. The two old English ladies, the tall and the short, were squeezing blood like orange juice from severed human limbs, children's arms and legs. *Here, my dear*, the tall one said, lifting a goblet of steaming blood, *this is just right*. She spoke in a crawling voice, like a tape at slow speed. She laughed. Snakes slithered out of her mouth. The short one clapped her hand against a severed hand. Magda Prokash laughed.

Sherone tried to run away. She could not. She was naked, spread-eagled on some kind of table, ropes cutting into her wrists and ankles. Tamara Devon was bending over her. She was naked too. Her large bare breasts rubbed across Sherone's belly. Sherone tried to squirm away, but the ropes held her fast.

Don't struggle, darling, Tamara said in that same draggy, slowed-down voice. *You'll hurt yourself*. She dipped her hands into the blood and started rubbing it over Sherone's naked body. Sherone could feel Tamara's long, black-nailed fingers rubbing the blood onto her breasts. To her horror and disgust, she found herself becoming aroused. Her breath came faster as Tamara massaged the blood into her erect nipples. Sherone tried to scream at her, tried to scare her away. But she had no voice.

Seamus Harrach appeared from out of nowhere, his gaping mouth filled with outsize razor-sharp teeth. *The breasts are anointed, Master*, Tamara said, stepping back from Sherone's blood-smeared body. *They await the Mouth with Sharper Teeth.*

Sherone tried again to scream.

Seamus Harrach fell upon her.

Sherone sat up in bed, clutching at her breasts, damp with sweat beneath her nightgown, relieved to find them still there, but trembling all over, halfway between the dream world and waking reality. *It's only a dream*, she told herself, glancing wildly around her bedroom, disoriented, *it's only*—

Someone was breaking into her room, shouldering open the door, tearing down the strings of bells and amulets hanging across her doorway like strands of a spider's web.

This time she screamed with full voice.

And kept screaming, shrinking into her bed, her back pressed up against the wall, pillow clutched tight to her breasts, screaming until her throat ached and her ears rang with the echoes of her own screams bouncing off the bedroom walls.

The intruder sat down on her bed.

He put a hand on her shoulder. "What's the matter, Skipper?" He shook her gently. "Bad dream?"

Wes Livingston sat there with a concerned look on his lined, sun-browned face. His hair was starting to gray and recede slightly above the forehead. He had on jeans and a khaki work shirt, rolled up at the elbows.

Sherone stared at him for almost a full minute, her

mouth hanging open. Then she threw her arms around him, burying her head in his shoulder.

"Daddy," she whispered. "Oh, Daddy."

Wes Livingston patted her on the back. "We all have bad dreams once in a while."

It wasn't until she pulled away that Sherone realized she was crying. She wiped at the tears, embarrassed. "When'd you get back?"

"Just now. The Red Eye in from Papeete." He stood up. "Where's Glenda? Still at the lab?"

Sherone nodded, wiping at a stray tear. "She came home late last night. Then she left real early this morning, before I got up."

"I don't know if I'd call that real early," Wes said, "seeing as how it's already past ten."

"Ten o'*clock?*" Sherone leaned over and squinted at her bedside alarm clock. "Ah, shit! I'm late for school."

"A bit," her father agreed. "Guess it won't break your heart in two. But you better get going, late or not."

"Okay," Sherone sighed. She felt like a cigarette, but she wasn't up to one of her father's anti-smoking lectures. "So how was Bora Bora?"

"Beautiful as ever. Despite a lot of serious attempts to screw it up." Wes lifted one of the broken strings of bells and amulets trailing down the door frame. "Got yourself barricaded in here pretty good, Skipper. Planning on a midnight vampire attack?"

Sherone remembered Seamus Harrach's teeth and shuddered. "That's just some . . . stuff. You know, Wicca stuff. Good luck charms, sort of."

"I know what it is. I've seen your hocus-pocus doodads before." He jingled a string of bells. "What I want to know is what you're doing with them here."

Sherone shifted uncomfortably in bed. "Guess I just got scared last night. All alone here . . ." *Almost alone*, she thought, remembering the Presence she had felt after Heather drew the tarot cards.

He smiled at her. "You think all this happy crappy's

really going to protect you?"

Sherone looked at him seriously. "It's better than nothing."

Later, after Sherone left for school and Glenda McGuiness returned from the lab, she and Wes Livingston sat over two cups of coffee at the small kitchen table.

Glenda, an angular woman with short brown hair, looked up from her coffee. "I don't like the looks of that occult garbage she has looped across her doorway, Wes. What's she afraid of anyway?"

He shrugged. "Kids are afraid of lots of things that don't seem very scary to adults. Part of being a kid, I guess."

"Wes, she's sixteen years old. And very intelligent for her age."

"She's still a kid."

"Do you like the looks of that shit?"

He put down his coffee cup. "Glenda, I don't like lots of the things Skip does. But if I called her on every one of them, I'd be a cop, not a father. I call her on the important ones."

They drank their coffee in silence, until Glenda said, "I can't help it, damn it. I never liked her messing around with this occult bullshit in the first place. And now she's getting deeper into it."

"We're not sure about that, Glen."

"What are you waiting for? Black Masses in her bedroom?"

Wes frowned, but said nothing.

"It's irrational, Wes. Worse than that. It places a premium on irrationality. It makes crazy superstition some kind of guiding moral force."

He smiled faintly. "I think your scientist side's coming out there, Glenda. Lots of people who attend First Methodist in the Valley are just as crazy superstitious as Skip. Down in what's left of the South Seas, superstition makes about as much sense as unchecked real estate development or above-ground nuclear testing." He took a sip of his coffee. "Maybe more."

Glenda put down her cup so hard the saucer rattled. "We're not talking about happy natives selling tiki idols. We're talking about a nutball pseudoreligion that's one step away from Satanism and that's obsessed with pain, mutilation and murder."

Wes looked up. "Murder's a strong word, Glen."

"You got a better one for ritual sacrifice?"

"We don't know that Skip's Wicca people are into anything nearly that heavy."

"You want to take the risk of finding out?"

He did not answer, but the uneasy look on his face answered for him.

chapter 14

the warning

Heather was sitting at one of the outdoor tables in the Quad, picking at a school-approved nutritionally balanced lunch: bacon, tomato and alfalfa-sprout sandwich, low-cholesterol French fries, Diet Coke and a multiple vitamin tablet. She was not very hungry. She had felt out of sorts all morning, ever since blowing up at the gardener and then yelling at her mom.

Why did I do that? she asked herself one more time. She didn't hate Hyung-Joon Kim. He was a weird old guy, but he was okay. She didn't hate her mom at all. She loved her. *I really do,* she told herself, even as she felt the familiar anger rising within her, the anger at her mom never being there, at her never being available when Heather wanted to talk about something important, something really important.

Like right now.

Whatever had happened at Magda Prokash's that night was still going on. A chill came over Heather and she shivered, despite the brightness of the afternoon sun. Then she flushed as she remembered Brian McNulty's description of her turning around naked up in the air like some dancer at an all-nude sleazo bar. *At least I didn't get raped or anything*, she thought. But something happened. Something had messed up her head, and was still messing it up. Something had made her see blood on the dresser where there was no blood.

She looked out to the blue Pacific lying calm and smogbound in the distance. It looked the way it always did. She could barely make out the white sail of a small craft cutting through the waves.

She was scared and alone. There was no one she could talk to about this, no one to turn to. *Except Brian*, she thought, *and I don't even know him*. She couldn't talk to her mom about it. She wouldn't understand, even if she had the time. And she never had the time. She couldn't talk to her dad, because she really didn't have a dad. Her eyes misted over as she stared at her sandwich. She knew she was feeling sorry for herself. But her dad never called, almost never came by. And when he did, they never talked about personal things, important things. She couldn't tell him what happened at Magda's.

And she couldn't tell Sherone, because Sherone had already lied to her about it. *My best friend*, Heather thought despairingly. If she hadn't been at school, she would have started crying.

A can of Diet Pepsi and a bag of Doritos plopped down on the table across from her. Sherone sat down behind them.

Heather's heart leaped up, but she forced herself to assume an air of chilly indifference. "I was just leaving," she said, gathering up the remains of her lunch.

Sherone put a hand on her wrist. "We have to talk."

"Oh really? What about?"

Sherone looked over her sunglasses. "You know."

"Hmmmm. Let's see. Maybe about what happened at this certain place, on this certain Tuesday night?"

Sherone sighed. "Give me a break."

"Except *nothing happened*." She stared at Sherone across the table. "Nothing except I took off all my clothes and got lifted up in the air like—mmmphf."

Sherone clapped a hand over Heather's mouth. "Not so loud, okay?"

Heather pushed the hand away. "You lied to me!"

"I didn't lie." Sherone popped open her Diet Pepsi. "I just didn't tell you the whole truth."

"Oh wow! Big difference."

"I didn't tell you everything because," Sherone swallowed with difficulty, "because Magda told me not to."

Heather leaned forward. "Why not?"

"Because she said it'd work better if you weren't, like, aware of everything, okay?"

"Aware of *what?*"

Sherone coughed on the Diet Pepsi. "You know . . . what happened."

Heather's eyes narrowed. She started to say something, then got up to leave.

"She thought," Sherone said in a voice so low Heather had to bend over to hear her, "that if you knew a demon was actually called up and had contact with you, you might freak out and tell your mom or call the cops. Or something."

"What do you mean, 'had contact'?" Heather asked, dreading the answer.

"Not that kind of contact," Sherone said quickly. "I mean, like, all the lights and you going up in the air and everything. Something made that happen. It wasn't Magda."

Heather thought about it, then asked. "Why me?"

"Because you ran out of the circle and he could get to you then. But I think," Sherone hesitated, "I think he *willed* you to step outside the circle. Like he knew you were a Sensitive."

The thought of some dark force luring her outside the salt-lined circle made Heather sick to her stomach. "What's a Sensitive?"

"Someone who, you know, channels psychic energy. Someone who serves like a medium for spirit forces."

"Me?" Heather said, trying to make light of it, even though her eyes were frightened. "God, did you guys ever pick the wrong person! I've never had a psychic experience in my *life!*"

Sherone shook her head slowly. Then she told Heather about the tarot cards she had drawn that night in her bedroom, about how they had spelled out the demon's name.

Heather stared at her, disbelief and fear in her face. "You wouldn't bullshit me about something this serious, would you?"

"Cross my heart and hope to die," Sherone pledged solemnly. "Stick a million—"

"Okay. Okay." Heather shuddered. "Jesus, Sherone. Maybe it's time to go see your friend Magda."

"I've already seen her." Sherone's voice was flat. "She doesn't know what to do. She doesn't think something like this could even happen."

"Great." Heather ran a hand nervously through her red hair. "So what am I supposed to do in the meantime? Just wait around till this thing shows up in my bedroom one night?" She tried to laugh, but she was on the verge of tears, her lower lip trembling.

"Hi, guys!" Brian McNulty stopped beside the table, a *Teenage Mutant Ninja Turtles* comic book in one hand, a physics text in the other. "How ya doin', Heather? Sherone?"

Sherone stared at him with the curious contempt of someone viewing a repulsive alien life form. Heather's face went blank. She looked down at her sandwich.

"Well." Brian cleared his throat awkwardly. "Don't want to keep you guys. I see you're sort of busy here right now. So, if it's okay with you, I'll just, like, move on down the road, okay? Bye!" He stopped, and looked back. "See you later, Heather!"

She turned a quick, shy smile on him, then went back to her blank expression. She kept it until he was gone, then heaved a great sigh of relief, eyes closed.

"Have you gone out of your head?" Sherone asked her. "Does Kurt know about this?"

Heather shook her head. "He would be so pissed if he found out."

"Pissed," Sherone took a swallow of Diet Pepsi, "is not the word."

Brian was on the way to his locker, taking a shortcut behind the gym and thinking about how weird girls could be, nice as hell one day and then freezing you out the next and no transition in between, when he turned a corner and found himself face-to-face with Kurt Pritchard and three other guys.

Kurt had an odd, distant expression on his face, as if he was looking straight through Brian and not liking much what he saw there. The other three closed in, encircling Brian. He knew two of them. Troy Taylor was a world-class prick, the son of coked-out T.V. director Buzz Taylor, who sometimes worked for Kurt's dad, Jack "Mr. Miniseries" Pritchard. Andy Metz's dad was a super agent and part-time star fucker, and Andy, a tall, moody kid, was pretty normal, considering. The third guy, the gross fat one, Garth Wiggins, Brian didn't know so much about. But rumor had it that Garth was some congressman's kid and that he'd got himself kicked out of a military academy in Virginia for screwing somebody's dog. Seeing him up close like this, Brian began to believe it.

"How's it goin'?" Brian said, careful to keep his voice and expression perfectly neutral.

"Pretty heavy, dude," Troy Taylor said, "for you."

"Pretty goddamn fuckin' heavy, man." An evil grin spread over Garth Wiggins's blotched, pasty face.

"Shut up," Kurt muttered to him.

The grin vanished.

Kurt said, "Troy thought he already told you somethin', McNulty."

Brian kept eye contact but said nothing.

"He thought," Kurt went on, "he told you to stay the

fuck away from Heather. Maybe he didn't say it loud enough. Or maybe you just didn't hear." Kurt stepped in closer, so close Brian could smell his stale cigarette breath. "Now I'm tellin' you myself, I see you with her just one more time—I even see you *talkin'* to her like back there at the Quad—and you are fuckin' *dead meat*, asshole. Understand?"

Brian knew he was in a critical situation, about to get the living shit pounded out of him. He knew the right thing—the only thing—to say in a moment like this was, *Sure, Kurt, I understand.* Or something like that. Some bullshit act of buckling under so Kurt Pritchard could go off thinking he was still the biggest cock in the Quad and you could walk away with all your teeth and none of your pride. There was no other way out of it, not unless you wanted to risk broken bones and multiple lacerations and maybe even permanent damage of the kind that might seriously affect your ability to have children later on. Brian knew all this.

But what he said was, "Your girlfriend was the one who asked me to talk with her."

A muscle twitched violently below Kurt Pritchard's left eye. "I don't give a shit who started it, asshole! Alls you gotta remember is, if she ever asks you again, you just say no. Understand?"

Brian said nothing.

"Under*stand?*"

"All right, Pritchard. Back off!"

The voice was not loud, but it cut like a lead-tipped whip. All five boys looked in that direction. A man of average height, ruddy complexion and clipped moustache, stood watching them with hard, no-nonsense eyes. Jeb Howard's official title was Assistant Headmaster of Severy Academy. School rumor said he had been a CIA agent who got shot up bad and that was why he walked with a limp in his right leg. Brian didn't believe that part. But CIA or no CIA, Jeb Howard was one tough son of a bitch. Once he had overpowered some crazy big kid strung out on angel dust just by doing something funny to the kid's wrist, the whole thing over so fast you never even saw it happen.

Kurt smiled a shit-eating smile. "No law against a friendly discussion is there, Mr. Howard, sir?"

"Four on one there is. Break it up. All of you. I catch you ganging up on anybody else, Pritchard, and I am personally kicking your butt down to Detention for one solid week. And you," he nodded at Garth Wiggins, "are high on my shit list to begin with. Don't push it."

As Kurt and his buddies sulked away, casting occasional glances back over their shoulders, Jeb Howard nodded to Brian, "Over here, McNulty."

Brian obeyed.

Jeb Howard stared at him. "Any special reason why you decided to start messing with Pritchard's girl all of a sudden?"

"I didn't know he owned her, sir. I thought they abolished slavery a long time ago."

"Cute, McNulty. But it won't keep you from getting your ass busted. It won't happen on my watch. But after school, you're on your own. There's lots of other pretty girls in the world. You sure this one's worth it?"

"She's worth at least two busted asses, sir."

Jeb Howard frowned and shook his head, then walked away, limping slightly.

But there was something in the frown that made Brian think a younger Jeb Howard had once faced the same kind of situation and made the same kind of choice.

chapter 15

the cannibal god

Workmen pulled apart the fifteen-foot upright crate with crowbars. Boards squealed as they came loose. The crate had been constructed solidly to protect its precious cargo during a journey of more than eight thousand miles.

Milton Bromley frowned at his watch and asked Karin, "How much longer is this going to take, my dear?"

"Just a few more minutes, Mr. Bromley. Isn't it exciting?"

"Hmmphf." Bromley adjusted his designer silk tie. "The show will be opening soon. How many more surprise packages do you have in store for us?"

"We almost didn't get this one," Karin explained. "It's on loan from the Museum of Antiquities in Cairo."

"Karin." Dodge Andrews spoke in a loud stage whisper. "What about those fifteen statues from Madrid?"

Bromley's head snapped up. "Fifteen—"

Dodge batted his eyelashes. "Just *teas*ing!"

"Dodge." Karin shot him a death-ray glance, then smiled nervously at Bromley. "He really is just kidding, Mr. Bromley. We're not expecting even one statue from

Madrid. Honest."

Bromley frowned at his watch again. "I have an important meeting in half an hour."

"Jim!" Karin called to the short, dark foreman supervising the uncrating.

Jim Rice looked up. "Yo, boss?"

"Can we speed it up a little?"

"Try and blast 'er loose. Sucker's a real bitch kitty, pardon my French."

Karin shrugged at Bromley. "Sorry."

"Quite all right, my dear," he said in a voice that made it clear nothing was right. "But perhaps the next time you invite me to see a new showpiece you can advise me if it's going to take all day."

Karin looked humbly apologetic, but thought, *If it was up to me, I never would've asked you to see it in the first place.* Robinson Parker, the boardroom diplomat, had suggested that it might be a good idea if Bromley saw any new pieces before Dodge Andrews went to the trouble of setting up their lighting displays. An increasingly finicky Bromley was interfering more and more with Karin's actual staging of the show, slowing down preparations and fraying nerves by making lots of last-minute, unnecessary changes. *He's doing it just to piss me off*, Karin thought. *And if he keeps it up, I'll quit on him, show or no show*, she promised herself, even though she knew she would never walk out on an exhibition in progress.

An explosive *pop* was followed by the sound of loose boards clattering down onto the marble floor of the main exhibition hall. Murmurs of surprise rose from the museum personnel watching the uncrating.

Jim Rice gave a low whistle and pushed his red BEER DRINKERS MAKE BETTER LOVERS baseball cap back on his head. "God*damn!* Take a look at that."

The uppermost boards of the crate had fallen away in one large section to reveal a massive head carved out of rough, dark stone. It stood erect, but it was not human. Two huge ears jutted out from the head like bat wings.

The forehead was low and slanting, the shape of the whole face loathsomely reptilian, with slitted eyes and flattened nostrils. The monstrous saurian mouth gaped wide, bristling with teeth. Protruding from the carnivorous mouth were stone sculptures of half-eaten bodies. Heads and arms dangled limply from one side, lifeless legs from the other. Slitted eyes stared out at the observers. The saurian mouth seemed to grin as it swallowed the half-chewed corpses.

"Karin," Dodge said, in a real whisper this time, "he is just super!"

Sandy Weatherford gave a discreet A-OK sign from a vantage point near the sculpture.

"Revolting." Bromley raised his nose in the air.

"He's Kraadar," Karin explained, "a fertility god of Ancient Sumeria."

"Mrs. Roberts . . ." Bromley turned on her aghast. "He is *eating* human beings!"

"Sacramental cannibalism formed an important part of the Kraadar cult," Karin said. "By eating the sacrificed bodies of the faithful, Kraadar cleansed the world of corruption and weakness. Then by regurgitating what he had eaten, he cast forth the faithful into a new life."

Karin hesitated. She could see that Bromley was working himself up to a fever pitch, getting more outraged with every second that passed.

"It's a priceless work of art," she went on hurriedly. "We're lucky to get it. It's been shown only once before in this country, at a private exhibition in New York in 1961."

"It is *not* art!" Bromley spluttered. "It's—an obscenity! A blasphemy." He shook his head, livid with indignation. "I'm sorry, my dear. But I cannot—I simply *will* not—allow this . . . travesty to be displayed here at the Barringer."

Groans of disappointment rose from the staff.

If you're serious, Karin thought, *I'll kill you, I really will.* "Mr. Bromley," she began, trying to control the catch in her throat. "Aside from its value as a work of art, please think of the cost involved in bringing—"

Bromley cut her off. "Consider it an expensive lesson in how *not* to plan an exhibition."

Controlling herself with great difficulty, Karin said, "We haven't paid yet for shipping it back."

"And we can't send it C.O.D.," Dodge pointed out.

"Pay whatever's necessary," Bromley snapped. "Just get it out of here." He grimaced at the staring eyes, the gaping, corpse-stuffed mouth.

"Mr. Bromley," Karin pleaded, "as long as it's already here, can't we use it for something? Like a study piece for seminars?"

"We could at least make back our mailing costs," Dodge suggested, "by renting it out for parties in West Hollywood."

"You," Bromley turned on him, "shut up!"

Even Dodge could see that Bromley was dead serious this time. He shut up.

"Disgusting." Bromley cast another contemptuous glance at the staring stone head. "Get rid of it."

The stone head started to tremble. Very slowly at first, then with gradually increasing momentum, the huge wooden crate containing Kraadar began to rock back and forth, a trembling monolith ready to tip over.

"Quake!" Jim Rice bellowed, hopping down from his stepladder next to the crate. "Get back!" He motioned to the astonished museum staff, most of them staring up open-mouthed at the rocking crate. "Everybody back from the box! Stand clear!"

"Look out for falling glass!" Karin shouted to her staff as she glanced up at the large skylight overhead.

"My God!" Dodge gasped. "It's the Big One at last! 9.9 on the Richter!"

Karin looked quickly at the other statues in the main exhibition hall—Baal, Kali, St. George and the Dragon—to see if they were being affected by the quake. They stood rock steady. The Kali statue had real ceremonial bells dangling from its wrists. They were not even swaying slightly. Karin frowned, glanced up at the skylight again, which showed no signs of vibration, let alone imminent breakage.

She realized then what was happening.

An L.A. native, Karin had been through earthquakes of all kinds, from tiny temblors to major convulsions. Most start the same way: a low, thrumming vibration that feels like a trash truck rumbling by outside, then, building in intensity, starts rattling floors, walls, loose objects on shelves and tabletops, glass, especially large panes of glass. *Like skylights,* she thought, staring up at the still glass panels overhead.

Only one object was vibrating in the Barringer Museum.

The statue of Kraadar, the cannibal god.

The huge wooden crate containing Kraadar lurched forward suddenly, scraping across the marble floor. Cries of alarm burst from the museum personnel.

Bromley raised his voice above the mounting chaos. "All staff members will follow emergency evacuation procedures! Leave this room at—"

"Ain't no quake, sir," Jim Rice said.

Bromley turned to him. "What the devil do you mean?"

"Only thing jumpin' in here," Jim Rice nodded at Kraadar, "is th' ol' bogeyman himself."

Bromley was starting to respond when the crated statue stopped moving. Everyone in the main exhibition hall grew suddenly silent. The corpse-filled, devouring mouth of Kraadar seemed to grin back at them.

There was a loud, percussive POP! like a .38 at close range. A board sprang loose from the crate and went flying across the large hall, spinning end-over-end. It reached the fall of its trajectory and clattered down onto the marble floor. POP! Another board shot out into empty space, this time passing close over the heads of several museum workers near a ladder. They ducked. POP! Another board snapped loose. POP! And another. POP! POP! POP! People ran screaming for the exits. Others dropped to the marble floor, covering their heads.

"What in the name of God," Milton Bromley muttered, unable to believe his eyes. "Mr. Andrews," he turned to Dodge, "if this is your idea of a practical joke—"

Dodge, pale with fright, shook his head. "I don't know anything about it, sir."

The boards continued to pop loose from the crate, snapping like rubber bands. And before the astonished eyes of those still watching, the crate began to dismantle itself, revealing in full the statue of Kraadar, the cannibal god. A hulking, heavily muscled torso was covered with scales. Hands and feet like huge claws were tipped with horned talons, and below the heavy belly, an enormous phallus stood fully, grossly erect.

"Disgusting!" Milton Bromley cried, his voice hoarse with shock. "Absolutely disgusting!"

A final board snapped loose and hurtled across the room, striking Bromley a glancing blow on the forehead. He cried out and covered his face with both hands, stumbling backward. Karin and Dodge both turned to help him, but it was too late. His legs gave out. He fell heavily and lay sprawled across the marble floor.

"Sandy!" Karin shouted at Sandy Weatherford, who was standing near one of the exits. "Call the paramedics!"

As Jim Rice and several other workers rushed toward Bromley, Karin and Dodge tried to help the wounded museum director to a sitting position. A groaning shudder passed over him. He took his hands from his face. The cut above his left eyebrow, caused by a nail in the flying board, was only superficial, but it bled copiously. Blood ran down Bromley's fat face in marbled streaks.

Dodge Andrews took out a scented handkerchief and

began dabbing fastidiously at the trickles of blood. "Hold still, Mr. B. We'll wipe off all this nasty nasty."

Bromley recoiled in horror. "Get your hands off me, you filthy little faggot!" He pointed a bloody finger at Dodge. "You're fired! Get out of here!" Bromley turned his blood-streaked, quivering face to Karin. "And you, get that... obscenity out of here." He pointed to Kraadar. *"Now!"*

A small cry of pain escaped Bromley. He covered his face with his hands.

Even though she knew he was hurt, and in pain and shock, and therefore not entirely accountable for what he had just said, Karin still had to hold herself back from picking up one of the loose boards and whacking Bromley over the head with it. *That's what all rich, spoiled men need*, she thought furiously, *when they act like cruel little boys.*

She went over to where Dodge Andrews stood apart from the group gathered around Bromley, a hurt look on his small, bearded face. "Don't worry, Dodge." Karin put a hand on his shoulder. "He's upset. He didn't mean it."

"I wish I could believe you, Karin." Dodge sighed. "It's going to look just wonderful on my résumé. *Reason for Leaving Previous Position:* Fired by museum director in front of assembled staff."

"Mom! You okay?"

Karin looked up in surprise. Running across the wide marble floor through an obstacle course of scattered boards was Heather, long red hair streaming out behind her as she ran. *What's she doing here?* Karin wondered, feeling a sharp stab of anxiety. Heather never came to the museum unless it was a major emergency, like the time she and Sherone rear-ended a Maserati on Rodeo Drive. But Heather did not look guilty. She looked scared.

She ran up to her mother, breathing heavily. "What *happened?* Your hands! Your clothes!"

Karin looked down at her hands and saw that they were smeared with Bromley's blood. Several streaks stained the right arm of her white wool jacket.

"Mr. Bromley got hurt," she told Heather. "Dodge and I were trying to help him."

"Holy shit!" Heather gasped, noticing the statue of Kraadar for the first time. "Where'd you get *that?* It looks like somethin' from a horror movie!"

Dodge Andrews smiled wanly. "This whole experience has been something from a horror movie."

"What happened with all the boards?" Heather asked, glancing around the littered floor.

Karin was in no mood to explain, not just then. "What are you doing here, Heather? What's wrong?"

Heather turned from Kraadar, eyes cast down. "Nothing. I just . . ." She looked up. "I guess I just wanted to say I'm sorry, okay? For the way I acted this morning. Yelling at you and Hyung-Joon. I didn't mean to." Heather looked down again, embarrassed by her apology.

Karin hugged her, being careful not to get her bloody hands on Heather's silk shirt. "You're forgiven."

Heather looked up. "You're not mad? Honest?"

Karin smiled at her. "Honest."

Dodge sighed. "It's nice to see *some* happy faces around here."

A tall, burly man in a guard's uniform came up to Karin, touching his visor brim as he approached. "Sorry about keepin' your young 'un outside, Miz Roberts. She wanted to rush right on in. But the minute she got to that door there," Elmer Burtis nodded at the main entrance to the exhibition hall, "was just when all hell started a-breakin' loose inside here. Didn't think it was safe to let her go on in till things had settled down a mite, ma'am."

"You did the right thing, Elmer," Karin said to him. "Thanks."

A chill crept up the back of Karin's neck as she turned and looked at her daughter, who was staring again at the grotesque statue of Kraadar the cannibal god, her mouth open slightly, blue eyes unfocused with the intensity of her gaze.

chapter 16

the locked room

Three half-naked young men with long hair and painted faces made threatening, histrionic gestures to a mostly naked young woman chained to what looked like either a dungeon wall or the back of an underground parking garage in a bad part of town. All this was presented in quick flashes of images—some in extreme close-up, some in rapid motion, some upside-down, all of them disorienting.

Heather sat on a black leather couch in the living room, wearing white shorts and a MADONNA—THE VIRGIN TOUR T-shirt, legs curled up under her, eyes slightly glazed as she looked at the MTV channel without really watching it. On the other side of the room Gabriela Garcia was trying to dust a convoluted piece of abstract metal sculpture resting on top of a side table. Gabriela looked over at Heather's expressionless face, bathed in flickering colored lights from MTV on the seventy-two-inch Mitsubishi rear-projection screen. Heather's eyelids drooped. Her head started to nod.

Gabriela put down her dustrag. "You gettin' tired, maybe you should go to bed, *mija.*" That was her favorite pet name for Heather, "mee-ha," my daughter.

Heather snapped awake, frowning crossly. "Don't tell me what to do."

"I ain't tellin' you what to do. I tellin' you what you oughta do if you smart."

"I'm not tired, Gabriela."

"Then how come you eyes fallin' shut on you, huh?"

"Just drop it, okay? I don't feel like going to bed yet."

Gabriela sighed and went back to dusting the abstract metal sculpture. *I can't talk to her no more*, she thought sadly. *She's mad at everybody, me included.* There was a time when Heather would tell Gabriela everything, even things she wouldn't tell her mother. They had been very close, almost like granddaughter and grandmother. But after Karin divorced David Roberts and he left the house, Heather seemed to draw up inside herself and cut off close relations with everyone, even Gabriela. Heather rarely spoke to her these days, and when she did it was usually to snap at her. *Disrespectful as hell*, Gabriela thought, *just like my own damned kids.*

She sighed again and looked at the wall clock. She knew she should be home now, worrying about her own kids, wondering who Carmen was going out with and what Mario was up to. On an ordinary night, she would have been home hours ago. But Karin had been worried about Heather lately, about the way she was acting, and she asked Gabriela to baby-sit for her while she went out to dinner with . . . *What's his name*, Gabriela tried to remember, *the young lawyer so stuck on himself.* Karin did not ask for baby-sitting services often. So Gabriela agreed.

But she was to do no more housework for the rest of the evening. Karin had been firm on that point. *I don't want you knocking yourself out*, she told her. *Just kick back, watch television, whatever, and keep an eye on her for me, okay?* But Gabriela Maria de Lourdes Ortega Garcia had worked hard all her life, from the time she picked lettuce in the fields as a little girl with her parents through the long years at the tuna cannery as a young wife and mother up to when she started as a housekeeper for David and Karin Roberts after divorcing a man who had drunk up most of what she earned. She did not know how to kick back. If you were alive and breathing, you worked.

Besides, she had been meaning to get to this thing, this metal sculpture, for over a week now and had been putting it off because she hated even looking at it. It was so ugly. Karin called it a free-form metal sculpture. To Gabriela Garcia, it looked like a scrap pile of twisted coat hangers and crushed tin cans. And it was the devil to dust. When she was finally finished to her satisfaction, she stepped back and caught her breath, and glanced over at Heather on the black leather couch.

She was fast asleep, slumped to one side, her head resting on a black leather cushion. Gabriela crossed the deep-pile white carpet toward her, stepping lightly. As she got closer, she could see a strange-looking metal amulet on a black necklace draped over one of Heather's well-rounded thighs. The necklace had slipped from her hand where she had been gripping it tightly before she dropped off to sleep. The amulet was a circle inscribed with a pentacle, a five-pointed star. *Brujería*, Gabriela thought. Witchcraft. She shuddered, and crossed herself. Then she shook her head, out of pity more than fear. This *brujería* was bad business, very bad. *Diabólico*. She crossed herself again.

She had known that the amulet was evil when she saw Heather bring it home earlier that evening. When Gabriela was only a child her mother had told her of the horrors of *brujería:* the spells cast, the curses brought down on individuals, families, whole villages. The priests had reinforced this terrible warning. Those who practice *brujería* are damned eternally, cut off from the love of Almighty God and forced to dwell in fire with their master Satan forever. Gabriela's heart ached at the sight of the amulet. She loved Heather. She hated to see a thing of evil resting on her leg like a poisonous *escorpión*.

She moved closer to the sleeping girl. The distorted images of MTV flashed across the giant television screen. She reached out a hand toward the amulet, glinting evilly there against the soft white flesh of Heather's thigh. Gabriela lifted the amulet with its necklace carefully, recoiling at the actual feel of the thing in her hand.

Heather awoke with a start.

"Give me that!" she demanded, not fully awake yet, eyes unfocused as she grabbed at the necklace.

"Is no good for you, *mija*." Gabriela released the necklace with reluctance. "Is evil. *Diabólico*."

"Quit tryin' to rip off my stuff!"

"I ain't rip off nothin'." Gabriela looked indignant, but also concerned. "I just tryin' to keep you from gettin' hurt bad, *mija*. I tell you, is no good."

Heather slipped the necklace on over her head.

Mother of God, Gabriela thought, then asked, "Why you wear it all the time, huh?"

"None of your business." Heather glared at MTV.

"What you think it do for you?"

Heather sighed. "It's like a good-luck charm, okay? A friend gave it to me. And I'll wear it if I want to. So just get off my case about it, all right?"

Gabriela shook her head. "The only kinda luck that bring you, *mija*, is bad luck. Real bad."

Heather snapped off the television and jumped up from the black leather couch. "I don't need this kind of bullshit. Not tonight. I really don't."

She stomped off angrily down the hall to her room.

"What you gonna do?" Gabriela called after her.

Heather turned around, bristling. "I'm going to take a bath, then go to bed. That okay with you?"

The part about going to bed was okay. That was fine. She was young and needed her sleep. But it was not okay that she was going to bed wearing a piece of *brujería*. It made Gabriela sick to see that evil thing around her neck. But what could she do?

Heather's bedroom door slammed shut.

Gabriela dusted the rest of the living room. Then she turned on the large television screen, tuning it to an L.A. Spanish-language channel. A Mexican soap opera was on. Gabriela watched it for a while. Then she shook her head and turned off the television. Everywhere it was the same. Sex. Drugs. Violence. Dirty language. It didn't matter whether it was in Spanish or English. She started for the kitchen. There was a load of laundry that needed ironing. She had planned to save it for tomorrow because she liked to iron in the morning. But she could do part of it now.

She heard the sound then.

Something was hitting the side of a wall, or being thrown against it. Gabriela frowned, cocking her head to listen. The sound seemed to be coming from Heather's bedroom. It stopped. Gabriela listened for another full minute, then shrugged her shoulders and headed for the laundry room.

WHAM! The sound hit with the force of an explosion, as if someone had driven a compact car into Heather's bedroom wall.

"*Mija?*" Gabriela called out. "You okay?"

WHAM! This time it seemed to rattle the very foundation of the house. Gabriela set her jaw and marched down the hall to Heather's bedroom. She knocked loudly on the door. No answer. She tried to open it. It was locked. She rushed to get a key. She put the key to the lock and turned it. The door would not open. *She's done something to it,* Gabriela thought, getting angry now.

She hammered on the door. "*Mija!* You open this door right now or I come in there and whip your ass good!"

WHAAAAAAM! The sound seemed to knock Gabriela back from the door. She stumbled, then regained her footing. Her heart was pounding wildly. For the first time it crossed her mind that Heather was not alone inside the room. Someone was in there with her. The thought did not frighten Gabriela Garcia. She was no coward. Once, when she was younger and pregnant with her third child,

159

Estela, a man had tried to rape her on a dark winter night outside the tuna cannery as she walked to her bus stop. He was big and fat, but she picked up a broken beer bottle from the sidewalk. She cut him bad. The police found him later in an emergency room.

She shook the doorknob fiercely. *"Mija!* Open up!"

The door seemed to lurch forward in its frame, as if something huge had pushed against it, something immensely powerful. The door moved again. It seemed to bulge outward. Gabriela stepped back, eyes wide, the first shiver of real fear gripping her as she remembered the evil thing glittering like a metallic serpent against Heather's pale thigh.

The door started rattling suddenly like a tin roof in a windstorm. Then, just as suddenly, it stopped. Gabriela stared at it. And as she stared, she felt the warm wetness at her feet. She looked down. Blood rushed out from beneath the locked door—not a trickle, not several tiny rivulets, but a torrent of blood, spilling out from underneath Heather's locked bedroom door, pooling around Gabriela's feet, washing over them, soaking them with blood, spreading out across the deep-pile white carpet.

"Mija—" Her throat was drying up, her voice falling to pieces. "MIJAAAAAAAAAAAAAAAAAAAAAA!"

What came next was a sound Gabriela had never heard before in her life, not even in a nightmare. A low roar began building rapidly to the howling, demonic wail of some utterly inhuman thing, some creature from beyond the mortal night.

Gabriela's nerve shattered.

With a strangled cry she turned and ran, floundering in the blood, sloshing down the hallway. She stumbled and fell onto the deep-pile white carpet, arms thrust forward. As she scrambled to her feet, pulling back her right hand from the carpet, she left a dark red print on the heavy white fabric.

She continued to run, screaming in helpless terror.

And the inhuman wailing came after her.

chapter 17

sushi à deux

The lovely young Japanese waitress at Tokugawa was dressed in formal kimono and full ceremonial accoutrements, long black hair swept up dramatically like something from a classic Kurosawa film. She bowed to Brett Courtney and Karin Roberts, smiling at them graciously. They smiled back. Deftly she replenished their drinks, Kirin beer for Brett, *sake* for Karin.

"*Domo arigato*," Brett said, thanking her.

Before leaving their table, she bowed to them again and smiled. Behind the sushi bar one of the chefs, wielding a large butcher knife as he chopped up pieces of raw fish, nodded and smiled at Brett and Karin.

If just one more person smiles at me, Karin thought, smiling, *I'll kill them, I swear to God.*

Brett pointed with his chopsticks at the bite-size pieces of octopus tentacle wrapped in seaweed on Karin's plate. "You haven't even touched your *tako*."

"I have so." Karin pushed the plate away. "I think it moved."

"*Tako*'s not really raw," Brett explained. "It's boiled before they serve it."

"I'm glad to hear that," Karin said, thinking, *Raw*

octopus, boiled octopus, does he really think it makes a difference?

"Sushi's like anything else," Brett went on. "It just takes some getting used to. Here." He picked up a piece of seaweed-wrapped raw fish with his chopsticks. "Try this. *Hamachi,* yellowtail tuna. Very mild flavor. Lots of people like this who think they hate cooked fish, let alone raw."

I'd like to let it alone, Karin thought, staring uneasily at the limp, bright pink slice of fish dangling from Brett's chopsticks like an eviscerated organ. Brett used chopsticks with an almost native ease. Karin never could get the damn things to work right. It was like trying to eat with two unsharpened No. 2 pencils.

She reached out gingerly and picked up the slice of yellowtail with her fingers. She stared at it for a few more seconds, then popped it into her mouth quickly, like someone eating a bug. She chewed it, suppressing a small shudder of disgust. It actually didn't taste all that bad. But it felt awful, sort of flabby and oily, like semi-soft margarine with a faint fishy undertaste. If she had been alone, she would have spit it out into a napkin. She tried to think of something else as she swallowed it.

Brett said, "You have to admit that's pretty tasty."

Karin smiled gamely. "It's okay."

Brett returned her smile with real warmth. He was a handsome man, especially so when he smiled, with all-American Robert Redford good looks and a pleasant disposition. Several women at nearby tables cast admiring glances. But he only had eyes for Karin. *He really is drop-dead gorgeous,* she thought, *the kind of guy you could take on a leash to parties.* That was why Annie liked him so much. Annie was very married to her husband Sam Newmar, and even in love with him. But Sam was solid reality. Brett was pure swooning fantasy, the dream date of every *Cosmopolitan* reader.

But there was the problem. Guys like that didn't interest Karin. Sure, they were fun to look at and flirt with, great companions at boring parties. But they were accessories, like diamond earrings. Ever since she was a teenager, Karin had been attracted to men who did things, men who were defined by what they accomplished, not by how they looked or how much money their parents had. When she first met David Roberts, she had been overwhelmed by the all-consuming desire of this scholarship student from a broken lower-middle-class home to become not just a surgeon, but a great one. At first she had thought that devoting herself to such a man would be enough, more than enough. Later she realized that her fascination with driven men was in part an unconscious expression of her own desire to do important things. And so began her graduate studies in art history that led eventually to the Barringer Museum. But even after having done the big things on her own, Karin still found herself drawn to ambitious men. It was not a case of simple hero worship. It was more like intense identification, a sense of shared destiny.

Brett Courtney was successful by ordinary standards, a full partner on a fast track to the top of a major Los Angeles law firm. But he was what Karin thought of as a put-up job, the kind of superficially successful man she had known all her life growing up in L.A.'s moneyed echelons. His track to the top had been laid down and well greased by his father, A. J. "Cap" Courtney, who had inherited his money and social position from his father, pioneer oil producer Maxwell James "Buster" Courtney. Brett would get to the top of his law firm one day. But it would not matter whether he went standing up or lying down. All he had to do was continue being what he was: handsome, pleasant, rich and powerful. He did not have a destiny. He was his destiny.

"Heather doesn't like sushi, does she?" Brett asked. "If she does, we can take some home to her."

Karin shook her head, laughing at the idea. "She's a very normal kid when it comes to eating. Her idea of a good meal is a Big Mac and fries. A great meal is a Big Mac and fries and someone to share it with."

Karin glanced down at her seaweed-wrapped octopus tentacle, and for some reason an image popped into her head of her and Jeff Geller, the tall, bearded parapsychologist, sitting together in a car at McDonald's like a couple of kids, eating Big Macs and fries while Jeff explained something about ESP to her, an intense look in his dark brown eyes. *Why am I thinking about that crazy ghostbuster anyway?* she wondered, pushing the image from her mind. But it lingered, like the aftermath of a good dream.

A concerned frown crossed Brett's face. "Does she really eat like that all the time? It's not good for her to eat so much red meat and fried foods, you know."

Karin felt herself starting to bristle the way she always did when health food nuts got up on their soapboxes, but she forced a smile. "She eats pretty well most of the time. We have this wonderful little lady, Gabriela Garcia, who's been with us for years. So we get lots of real home cooking."

Brett shook his head. "Mexican cooking. More red meat and fried food. And lard." He snagged a piece of sushi with his chopsticks. "You know, my dad—everybody calls him The Captain, or Cap—anyway, Cap always says it's strange how even though mothers take care of the cooking, it's fathers who have the biggest influence on what kids eat. I think that's true. Sure was in my case." Brett chewed his sushi, looking closely at Karin. "I think kids need dads to teach them those things, don't you?"

Karin saw where this was leading. "Heather's wasn't much help in that department, even when he was home. He's the original junk food junkie. He'll eat anything, as long as he can swallow it standing up."

Brett shook his head again. "Doctors. The worst offenders. Telling us the rules, then breaking them."

"His work schedule didn't leave him much time for worrying about what he ate," Karin said, noting with astonishment the defensive tone of her voice. *My God,* she thought, *I'm actually defending Dr. David Roberts, Prick of Pricks.* She hated David's arrogance and selfishness, his crass insensitivity, but she still admired his fierce dedication to his work.

"When we work so hard that we don't have time for our families," Brett said, "then maybe we're working just a little too hard."

He meant it innocently enough, but it cut Karin to the bone. She knew she didn't spend enough time with Heather, hadn't ever, really. She knew she should put her daughter first and the Barringer second. But she didn't want anyone else suggesting that.

"A man's got to work to take care of his family," Brett continued. "Security's important. But like Cap always says, sometimes you lose sight of what you're working for in the first place."

Karin poked savagely at her octopus tentacle with a single chopstick. *He's trying to be nice,* she told herself, *so you be nice too.*

Brett took a sip of his Kirin. "Cap took good care of our security. Still wants me to work hard, of course. You're only as good as your work, Cap says. But he also says you work a lot better if you know your rear end's covered. Grandpa Buster left all his money in oil wells. Cap diversified it, spread it around. He figured you can't keep all your eggs in one basket, no matter how big it is."

Brett smiled his Robert Redford smile. "Good thing Cap was so farsighted. Otherwise we might have felt this oil glut a lot more than we did. You see, we're not just into energy anymore . . ."

Karin gave a long sigh. She couldn't help it. She had been through this many times before. When you grow up a rich little girl, especially in Los Angeles, you learn early about what Maureen O'Connor Magnusson called chicken pluckers—penniless, scheming young men out to get their hands on fine family fortunes. You are encouraged, strongly encouraged, to date men from your own moneyed class. As a result, rich young men trying to break the ice with rich young girls of their dreams learn to make it clear early in the game how much they're worth, assetwise. This is especially important in a place like Los Angeles where everyone poses as a millionaire as a matter of course. Karin and her girlfriends used to call this assetflaunting ritual Shooting the Silver Moon.

Karin tried to listen politely as Brett Courtney itemized his holdings and managed somehow to make it sound like casual dinner-table conversation rather than a financial review. He was pretty good at it. She had to give him that. Some guys turned into droning CPA's when they started going through the ritual dance steps. Karin remembered one horrible date where the ardent suitor had read from notes on 3 x 5 index cards. But regardless of Brett's skill, there was only so much she could take.

"Brett," she interrupted him in mid-statistic, "I don't give a damn about this bullshit, okay?"

He sat with his mouth open, staring at her.

She went on quickly, "I think you're a nice guy and I know you have money and I don't think you're trying to take me for any of mine. So let's drop the *Wall Street Journal* jive, okay?"

Brett recovered, trying not to look hurt. "I wanted to be totally upfront with you, Karin. I'm serious about you. I don't want you to think I'm playing games."

Karin had been dreading this, but now that it was out in the open there was no turning back. "I know you're not playing games, Brett. But isn't it a little early for either of us to be getting serious?"

"Considering the circumstances," he said slowly, "I don't think it's one minute too soon."

Karin raised her eyebrows. "If that's a subtle hint that I'm thirty-eight and counting in a tough market for used merchandise, thanks a lot."

"I was referring," Brett said, "to myself. I'll be forty next August. I've known lots of women, but I've never met one I wanted to get serious about. Until now."

Karin poked a chopstick into her *sake* cup. "Seems I've heard that one before somewhere on the late movie."

Brett leaned forward. "When I say it, I mean it."

He probably does, too, damn it, Karin thought, wishing there was some easy way out. "You don't even know me."

"I know you're the only woman for me," Brett said. "That's enough to know."

"Oh, the hell with it." Karin threw down her chopstick, dug a cigarette out of her purse, and lit it.

Brett looked concerned. "You're doing that just because you're nervous."

Karin blew a cloud of smoke away from the table. "If you want me, you have to take me as is, dirty habits and all."

"Deal." Brett smiled. "But it's easy to quit."

"Sure," Karin agreed. "And it's easy to start eating raw fish and health foods and running five miles a day and working out every night, if that's what you want."

"You don't have to do everything I do," Brett said. "I like you just the way you are."

"Brett," Karin sighed, "that sounds beautiful in a song, but it doesn't play in real life. We are very different people. That's okay, if we stay just friends. But if we start getting into something more serious, we'll drive each other crazy."

"If you love someone, the differences don't count." Brett turned very serious. "I love you, Karin."

She looked down at the octopus tentacle. *In a sushi bar, for God's sake,* she thought. When something like this happened in a romantic novel, at least it took place in a romantic setting. *Raw fish,* Karin reflected dismally, *raw emotions.*

"I love you very much," Brett went on, impassioned. "I want to make you part of my life. Forever."

She looked up at him. "That's why it would never work, Brett. Because you want to make me *part* of your life. Something to fit in nicely with what's already there, like a replacement part."

Now he did look hurt. "This isn't fair, Karin. I never said—"

"You don't have to. It's just there. You want me to be part of *your* life. You've got your plans all laid out. But what about *my* life? Do I leave it behind? Or bring it along with me?"

"Bring it along," Brett said, trying to muster up a Robert Redford smile. "You'll be bringing along a sixteen-year-old daughter anyway. You see, I've thought about these things, Karin."

She shook her head. "I don't have time enough for Heather as it is. And she's my own daughter!" Karin looked straight at him. "I'm not giving up my work at the Barringer. What makes you think I'd have any time for you?"

"If you loved me," Brett said quietly, the hurt look still on his face, "you'd make the time."

But I don't love you, Karin thought, not wanting to hurt him any more, *can't you see that?* "Brett—"

"Excuse, please."

Karin looked up. The pretty Japanese waitress was standing by their table, a grave expression on her lovely face. She said something that sounded like *amarjansi*. Karin was going to ask her what it meant when the waitress repeated the word and Karin understood.

"Emergency. Terephone for you. Housekeepah. Ver' important. Emergency."

Karin stubbed out her cigarette on the octopus tentacle and followed the waitress to a telephone.

She took the receiver, holding it tight to her ear. "Gabriela?"

She heard a soft moaning sound, like a puppy with its head bashed in.

Karin gripped the receiver. *"Gabriela!"*

The entire restaurant turned in her direction.

No one was smiling now.

168

chapter 18

nightmare country

Burning with anger at Gabriela Garcia, Heather slammed her bedroom door and locked it, thinking furiously, *How dare she tell me what to do! Who does she think she is?*

But the moment she closed the door, Heather's irrational anger seemed to dwindle and die.

And the fear returned.

Dark. Heavy. Terrifying.

It was the fear that had kept her in front of the television screen long after her eyelids had started to droop. She wanted to go to bed and sleep for a few years, sleep long enough to forget everything that had happened at Magda's. She wanted to sleep long enough to wake and find that everything had been only a dream.

But somehow she knew that it would be unsafe to dream tonight. She sensed that what she might find—*might find her*—in a dream tonight could be worse than any reality.

She fingered the amulet Sherone had given her. *It'll keep you safe*, Sherone said, placing it around Heather's neck. *If he's trying to get at you, this'll keep him away.* Pentacle. Five-sided star. Talisman of the occult.

Heather felt the rough edges of the crudely worked metal, the chill as it rested on her flesh. *It's like a good luck charm*, she repeated to herself. *It'll protect me.* She had believed that when Sherone gave it to her, believed it despite what Gabriela had said.

She wished she could still believe it now.

The hissing came from the other side of the room.

Heather gasped, turning quickly.

P.T. Barnum, the fat Persian cat, stood watching Heather, his tail twitching. He hissed at her again, then flicked a tongue across his whiskers.

"God*damn*, P.T.!" She heaved a shaky sigh of relief. "Warn me the next time, okay?"

She went over and picked up the cat, nuzzling him. The creature hung limp in her arms like a long sack of flour. Heather flopped down onto her king-size bed, the cat in her arms. She stared up at the imitation 1920s ceiling fan. She was so tired. A heavy drowsiness crept over her. Her eyelids fluttered.

She snapped up into a sitting position at the edge of the bed. P.T. Barnum leaped out of her arms with a disgruntled snarl. Heather shook her head, trying to knock the drowsiness out of it. *Can't fall asleep now*, she thought.

That was why she had walked out of the living room, why she had yelled at Gabriela. She knew that if she stayed there in front of the giant television screen she would have fallen asleep, sooner or later, no matter how loud she played MTV. And then, it would find her, sleeping there on the living room couch, as surely as it would find her sleeping in her own bed.

I'm not falling asleep tonight, she told herself with renewed resolution, *not until after Mom gets home.*

She walked into her bathroom and turned on the bathtub taps. As water splattered noisily against porcelain and steam rose into the air, Heather peeled off her T-shirt and shorts. She was not wearing a bra. She looked at herself critically in the long mirror above her makeup counter. *I'm fat as a pig*, she thought despairingly. It was not true. Her body had a direct, almost overpowering sensuality to it. The breasts stood out full and firm, the ends completely covered by the huge pink areolae of her nipples. All the other curves were breathtaking but sleek. The long red hair fell like a cloak over her pale white shoulders.

She turned off the taps and eased herself into the steaming water, wincing at first, then sighing with pleasure as she sank in gradually up to her neck. She leaned back on her elbows against the underwater side rests, her legs sprawled out comfortably in the large circular tub. Her long hair floated lazily on top of the water like red seaweed. *I should've put it up*, she thought, *but the hell with it; I'll wash it*. She stretched luxuriantly in water that no longer felt hot but deliciously warm. Her eyelids drooped.

A jolt hit the bathtub. Water slopped up over the side and down onto the tile floor. *Shit*, Heather thought, her eyes still closed, *earthquake*. She did not like tremors, but she wasn't afraid of them. Usually they just shook for a few seconds, then went away. She shifted position in the warm water.

The second jolt rocked the whole bathroom, slamming Heather back against the porcelain. Hot water splashed up onto her face, stinging it. She felt a chill between her breasts, so icy cold it almost burned her flesh. She opened her eyes and looked down. She still had on the necklace. The amulet with the pentacle hung against her chest. The metal seemed unnaturally bright, almost iridescent. Heather started to take it off.

The third jolt knocked her underwater. Hot water burned her face. She spluttered, trying to raise her head. The bottom of the bathtub dropped out from under her. She thrashed about frantically, panic gripping her as she struggled in the suddenly deep water, legs kicking out, reaching for the porcelain bottom that was no longer there. She tried to scream. Hot water rushed into her mouth. She broke surface, choking and gasping for air.

She opened her eyes.

The panic was replaced by absolute bewilderment, then fear. Deep fear. The slow, paralyzing kind that overtakes you when the real world turns unexpectedly into something . . . unreal.

She was treading water, hot water, in a massive body of dark water inside some kind of cavern. The splashes of her treading movements echoed against distant stone walls. Huge clouds of steam floated low over the dark water. Strange bubble patterns broke the surface. Looking down, heart pounding inside her naked chest, she saw the jerky movements of her own white limbs, pale as a fish's belly in the dark water. Deeper down she saw—or thought she saw—giant dark forms gliding slowly beneath her.

Closing her eyes, she repeated rapidly to herself, as if in prayer, *This isn't real, this isn't real, this is not real . . .* With a quick extension of the treading movement, she pinched herself hard on the upper left arm.

"Ow! *Shit!*" she cried out, her voice echoing into the stony distance.

The pain of the pinch was real. It burned on her arm. But the dark water, the low clouds of floating steam, the strange bubble patterns moving closer and closer to her all the time—none of these had changed or disappeared. Her legs and arms started to tire and grow heavy as she kept treading and treading, and beneath her she felt a flurry of agitated currents as something rushed up out of the dark water toward her. A whimper escaped her.

A jolt like an explosion threw her up out of the bathtub and onto the bathroom floor, banging her knee. She cried out and tried to get to her feet, wincing as she put weight on the injured knee. About an inch of water had splashed out onto the bathroom floor. Her legs slipped out from under her. She grabbed for the sink, stopping her slide just before she fell. She glanced into the mirror over the sink. The face that stared back at her from the misted glass looked insane. The eyes were wild and terrified. The mouth hung open. Dark red hair lay plastered flat to her skull and dripped down onto her naked shoulders like streaks of slime.

A gust of hot dry air burst into the bathroom, fluttering towels on the rack, knocking over bottles on the countertop, unreeling half the toilet paper roll, lifting the long strands of tissue up into the air, spinning them around like streamers before dropping them down into the standing water on the floor. The hot wind blew over Heather's naked wet body, chilling her at first, then drying her rapidly like a gigantic air blower. She turned toward the source of the wind, her long red hair blown back from her face.

Astonished, she stepped from the bathroom into her bedroom, unable to believe her eyes. The room was filled with pieces of paper, small stuffed animals, video cassettes, computer discs, bras, Polaroid snapshots, felt pens, panties, T-shirts, necklaces and bracelets—all whirling around like objects caught in a pint-size bone-dry hurricane. Heather stared open-mouthed.

"Who *are* you?" she screamed into the parching windstorm. "What're you doing to my *room?*"

As if in answer, the wind stopped. The blown objects dropped, or floated slowly down, to the thickly carpeted bedroom floor. Then came a jolt that knocked Heather to her knees. She screamed as she fell on the injured knee. But the scream was lost in the deafening sound of a large, heavy object slamming into a barrier at high speed. At first Heather thought a car had spun out on Camino de Oro and crashed into her side of the house. She covered her breasts with both hands and looked over at the outside wall, fully expecting to see the headlights and grill of a car come smashing through into her bedroom.

The sound came again, loud enough to rock the whole bedroom and pop all the drawers out of her dresser onto the carpet. The mirror above the dresser cracked. Ragged shards of glass tinkled down onto the dresser top. The explosive crashing sound came again. More glass fell out of the mirror. The sound seemed to be coming from Heather's walk-in closet, as if someone was hitting the door from inside with an atomic-powered battering ram.

She rose unsteadily to her feet, not even noticing the pain in her banged knee as she started slowly toward the closet door where the sound was coming from. Her throat seemed to close on her. Before she reached the door, the carpet started to move beneath her bare feet. *This time it really is a quake,* she thought, looking down. But what she saw was not caused by anything known to geology. The carpet was . . . *rippling,* undulating, as though living things were moving slowly, sinuously beneath it, things like snakes or moles or lizards—burrowing, squirming things. *Oh Jesus,* she thought, looking up from the carpet, *oh shit.* She stared at the wall, unable to look down again as she *felt* them, felt the things moving beneath her bare feet.

They were moving on the walls too, wriggling underneath the expensive gilt-patterned wallpaper, causing it to buckle and fold. She glanced up at the ceiling. It was alive with crawling things, bulging underneath the ceiling plaster like giant throbbing tumors. Nauseated with horror, Heather closed her eyes, put a hand to her damp forehead, her naked body trembling all over. She took the hand away and opened her eyes. The walls and ceiling were flat and still. She felt no movement beneath the carpet. The hot wind was not blowing. The room was silent. She stepped closer to the closet door. And opened it.

The inside of the large walk-in closet was running with blood. It dripped down off her hanging dresses and into her shoes, running them over, forming wide, spreading puddles on the closet floor. It ran down the sides of the white closet walls in jagged streaks, like rain on a plate glass window.

"Oh Jesus," Heather whimpered, shaking her head to clear it of the vivid slaughterhouse image.

The thing burst from the back of the closet, knocking

dresses to the floor, kicking shoes to one side. Heather jumped back from the closet, screaming. Except she could not scream. Her throat was shut tight. All that emerged was a desperate, frightened hissing.

The thing was huge and livid pink, membranous, coated with slimy red mucus, like a flayed body or an embryo still wrapped in its placental sac. The thing had a shape and no shape as it walked or rolled or crawled toward her, emitting a high-pitched, ear-piercing squeal. Heather turned and ran. Her injured knee gave out. She fell to the soft carpet. The thing fell on top of her. Bloody slime oozed over her naked breasts and thighs. She twisted out from under it and away, striking at it with her fists, kicking at it with her bare feet.

"*Away* from me!" she screamed at it, her voice returning suddenly. "*Get away from me!*"

The whole room seemed to go gray and flat like a faded black-and-white photograph, then fold up on itself, flipping over as it did so, spinning around in a 360-degree turn, taking Heather with it as it turned. The movement stopped. The colors returned. Heather felt rough pavement beneath her naked skin. She scrambled to her feet, glancing around, disoriented. She was on some kind of dead-end street, a crumbling warehouse on one side, a row of shabby stucco bungalows on the other. The colors had faded from the cracked and flaking stucco walls. Bars covered broken windows. A savage black dog crouched on the sidewalk, sharp canine teeth bared, snarling. Heather cringed and tried to cover herself. She blushed as the realization sank in that she was naked on the street in some scabby part of town. But there were no people to see her.

Then, suddenly, there were. A short, fat Mexican woman, shorter even than Gabriela, came running across a burned-out stretch of lawn in front of one of the stucco houses, arms raised above her head, crying out in a loud, frightened voice to the gray-haired woman leading away a small child by the hand. The child, a boy of three or four, raised a pudgy hand imploringly to the short woman.

"*Mamá,*" he whispered.

"*¡Roberto!*" his mother cried; then she called to the gray-haired woman, "No take away! *Señora,* please!"

Heather saw the hard gray eyes then and knew who it was. *The witch lady!* she thought with horror, recoiling at the sight of Magda Prokash.

"The bargain has been made, Maria," Magda said coldly. She turned to leave, tugging at Roberto.

Maria fell to her knees, opening her arms wide. "*Roberto, venga acquí!*" she cried, calling him to her.

The little boy twisted in Magda's grip, trying to run to his mother's embrace.

Heather watched all this, hating and fearing Magda Prokash more than ever. A stray tear gathered in the corner of one eye.

"Leave him alone," rumbled the dark voice behind her. "The boy is ours."

Heather gasped and turned around, trying to cover herself. She screamed at the sight of the chalk-white face, the mouth full of blackened, rotting teeth. Seamus Harrach looked directly at her, his dark eyes burning into her naked flesh. Then he turned to Maria on her knees.

"*¡El Malo!*" she cried, crossing herself. The Evil One.

Seamus Harrach raised a sharp-nailed hand and pointed it at Maria. She screamed, cupping her eyes with her hands. The scream rose as blood started leaking out from between her fingers, trickling down onto her broad bosom and spotting the sidewalk where she knelt.

Heather turned to the warlock, appalled by what she had witnessed. "What'd you *do* to her?" she demanded. "Who *are* you?"

The light of day faded suddenly, as if the sun had been turned off. Only Seamus Harrach, Magda Prokash, Heather and the little boy were visible, like figures spotlighted against black velvet. Magda Prokash was stuffing Roberto, kicking and screaming, into a dark brown burlap bag. Heather started to move toward them.

Seamus Harrach laid an iron hand on Heather's shoulder, the sharp nails digging into her flesh.

"Bring us another child," Seamus Harrach hissed. "A purer child. *Bring us the Perfect Blood Offering.*"

Heather backed away in terror. White light exploded. The hot wind began to blow again. Heather was in a long, low corridor, like one of the terminals at LAX, the walls blinding white and endless. The corridor was filled with people, naked like herself, shuffling about aimlessly, bumping into one another, saying nothing, eyes open, seeing nothing. The mindless, milling crowd parted to reveal Maria crawling on her hands and knees, blood dripping from her gouged-out eye sockets, blood on the corridor floor. Beside her stood a small blond boy dressed in a spotless white robe. He looked down at the blind woman crawling around in her own blood.

"*Roberto,*" she whispered, pawing at his white robe, leaving bloody handprints on the hem.

The blond child looked up at Heather. "I am the Perfect Blood Offering." His large blue eyes turned red.

He laughed, and his lips pulled back from long, pointed teeth. Filth oozed from his mouth.

Heather screamed, falling back against a wall.

Her own bedroom wall. The room was filled with the white light of the corridor. The terrible pounding had returned, louder than ever. The wall she was leaning against trembled under her naked back. This time the pounding was coming from the bedroom door. Something was hammering against it brutally from the outside, howling like a fiend as it tried to tear the door from its hinges, tried to get inside.

Tried to get at her.

chapter 19

mark of the beast

Brett Courtney's slate-gray BMW 320i turned hard right off Camino de Oro and bounced up onto the driveway. Karin had the passenger door thrown open before the car came to a full stop.

"Karin," he turned to her, "wait!"

She was out and running, high heels clattering across concrete. He got out and followed her, catching up just as she put her key in the lock, muttering something obscene when the key stuck and would not turn. She slammed the heel of her hand against the wood.

The door opened. Gabriela Garcia stood in the frame, mouth quivering, tears trickling down both cheeks. Her brown eyes were bright with terror, glancing nervously to one side as if something lay waiting for her, just outside the range of Karin's vision.

"Where's Heather?" Karin grabbed hold of Gabriela's shoulders. "What *happened?*"

Gabriela tried to speak. "Karin . . ." She shook her head, pointed with a trembling hand to the hallway that led to the bedrooms.

Karin knocked loudly on Heather's bedroom door.

"Heather?" She knocked again. "*Heather!*" She rattled the doorknob. "Gabriela, get the key."

"Is *there*," Gabriela said in a frightened voice. "Is no good."

Karin turned the key, forcing it. The metal twisted off in her hand. "God*damn* it!" She pounded on the door with a clenched fist. "Heather! Open this door!" She kicked it. *"Heather Michelle!"*

The door began vibrating on its own, like a glass pane in a storm. Karin fell back, heart pounding inside her chest, not able to believe what she was seeing.

"Heather!" she called, voice slipping out of control. "What's going *on?*"

Brett stood behind her, his eyes troubled. "Want me to try and force it open?"

Karin turned to him, holding up the twisted-off key. "It broke."

Brett walked up to the vibrating door. When he put his hand on the doorknob, the vibration stopped. He frowned. He turned hard on the doorknob and threw his shoulder into the door. He let out a small *oooff!* and bounced back from the door.

He stood there rubbing his shoulder.

He tried the doorknob again. Nothing. He pulled back, still holding onto the doorknob, and hurled himself against the door, throwing all his weight into it. The doorknob turned smoothly, as if it had never been locked. He stumbled into the bedroom, off-balance, grabbing for something to catch onto, anything to slow down his headlong momentum. He fell forward onto his hands and knees. A dark shape, like a large rat, slithered past his fallen body and out into the hallway. Karin screamed, backing off, until she recognized P.T. Barnum, fur standing on end. She rushed past the terrified cat and into the darkened bedroom. The only light was moonlight spilling in through the window. Karin fumbled for the wall switch.

And gasped at what she saw.

Heather sat against the far wall, legs spread open. The

room was a shambles. Scattered objects lay strewn across the carpet and bed like debris from an explosion. It looked as if the whole place had been turned upside down, dresser drawers trashed, clothes closet gutted, chaos everywhere.

Brett Courtney, still on his hands and knees, stared open-mouthed at Heather's naked body, full bare breasts and large nipples, firm young thighs spread wide like something from a *Penthouse* pictorial. Then he came back to his senses and turned his head sharply, blushing a deep, embarrassed red beneath his year-round tan.

He got to his feet, rubbing at a bruised shin. "Want me to call a doctor for her?"

Karin ignored him. Putting her hands under Heather's arms, she lifted her to her feet. Heather leaned back against the wall, eyes glazed as she stared at something far beyond the ransacked bedroom. Karin shook her by the shoulders. Heather's head knocked loosely against the wall. Some of the glaze went out of her eyes.

Heather blinked, trying to focus on the reality of her brightly lighted bedroom that looked as if a hurricane had swept through it and her mom shaking her and her standing bare-ass naked while Brett stood back there pretending not to look. It was a strange reality, but almost welcome compared to what had happened—what she *dreamed* had happened. But it was no dream! It *happened!*

"What've you been doing in here?" Karin demanded, her voice rough with fear.

"Sleeping." Heather blinked again. "Dreaming. I had these . . . dreams. Bad dreams. Really awful dreams." She broke into tears. "Oh, Mom, I'm so *scared!*"

She threw herself into her mother's arms, sobbing, her face crushed against Karin's chest. Karin could feel the hot tears wetting her silk dress.

She stroked the tangled red hair. "It's okay, honey. Everything's okay now." *Bad dreams?* she wondered, looking around the trashed bedroom, the clothes and shoes thrown every which way. *What kind of dreams make you do something like this?*

A shudder passed through her. *What kind of drugs cause dreams like that?*

Behind them, Brett cleared his throat. "If she doesn't need a doctor, I guess I better go."

He turned to leave, hesitating, as if waiting for Karin to tell him not to go, please not now, because she needed him, needed his strength and his determination.

Karin flashed him a distracted, apologetic smile. "Thanks, Brett. Thanks for everything."

"Sure," he nodded, moving to the door. "You need anything, just call. I'll be right over."

"Thanks."

"I'll call you Monday, okay?"

"Goodnight, Brett. Thanks again."

He hesitated again. *She needs me right now*, he thought, *whether she admits it or not.* Then he left.

Karin picked up a T-shirt with MAUI SPRING BREAK printed on it and wrapped it around Heather's naked shoulders. Heather snuffled, wiping at her eyes, then pulled on the T-shirt. It hung down below her bottom like an oversize nightshirt. Heather stumbled over to the bed and sat down, still snuffling, her head in her hands.

Karin sat down beside her. "Honey, I want to ask you something. I'm only asking, not accusing. Okay?" She took a deep breath. "Have you been doing drugs?"

Heather lifted her head from her hands, eyes red from crying, and stared at her mother.

"Remember," Karin said, "I'm only ask—"

"I was taking a *bath*. I was taking a bath and I must have fallen asleep in the bathtub and—" Heather's voice caught. "I started to dream." She tried to repress a shudder, then looked at her mother again. "Now you think I'm doing drugs." She indicated the trashed bedroom. "You think all this is just drugs, huh?"

That was pretty much what Karin did think, but she kissed Heather on the cheek and said, "Don't be silly."

We can get an appointment for next week if I tell Norm Goldstein it's an emergency, she thought. *He can test for drugs then.*

Karin smoothed out the tangled locks of her daughter's long red hair. "I think you better get some real sleep."

Heather snuggled up close to her. "I don't want to sleep here by myself. Can I sleep with you? Just for tonight?"

"Sure." Karin smiled at her. "But fair warning: I steal blankets."

Heather laughed, wiping at her eyes; then she sniffed and made a face. "Yuuch! Now I *really* need a bath." She looked at her mother hopefully. "If I take a shower in your bathroom, will you sort of, like, you know, wait outside for me? In case I fall asleep again?"

"You won't fall asleep in the shower," Karin said. "But sure, I'll stand watch for you."

If she knew what she was watching for, Heather thought, *she wouldn't be smiling.*

Heather pulled off the MAUI SPRING BREAK T-shirt. "I'll put this on after I shower. I'll just get it all grody if I wear it now."

Karin started to get up from the bed, then stopped and sat back down. "Where'd you get that?"

She touched what looked like a small scratch or cut on Heather's left breast. There were several lines to it, running at different angles to one another. If you stared long enough, it almost looked like a crude representation of a five-pointed star.

"Oh great!" Heather looked down at her breast. "Just *great!* Now I'm scarred for life!"

"It doesn't seem all that deep." Karin looked up at her. "Sherone didn't talk you into getting a tattoo, did she? Because, trust me, you really don't need anything extra to get guys to look at them."

"Mother!" Heather blushed, embarrassed. She covered her breasts with the MAUI SPRING BREAK T-shirt. "Can you come watch for me while I take my shower now, please?"

"Sure." Karin got up from the bed. "Keep an eye on that scratch and let me know if it doesn't get better."

Later, after Heather had showered and fallen fast asleep in Karin's bed, Karin lay awake at 3:00 in the morning. She got out of bed, quietly, so as not to wake Heather, who lay snuggled up against her, breathing softly with the steady rhythm of good dreams.

As she turned on the hall light on her way from the living room into the kitchen, Karin happened to glance down at a side table holding a vase with the rose blossoms she had snipped from a dying rosebush the day her mother stopped by. The blossoms had turned black and loathsome. Slimy tendrils sprouted from them like long, stringy tumors. They spilled out of the vase and onto the dark polished wood of the table.

Karin grimaced in disgust and stepped closer.

She saw it clearly then.

Carved raggedly into the expensive dark wood finish, like an obscene graffiti scrawl, was a large, five-pointed star.

Pentagram.

Mark of the Beast.

chapter 20

GARDEN PARTY

Parking is a nightmare in most of Los Angeles and it can be a problem even in residential Beverly Hills. But the near-palatial estate of Harald and Maureen Magnusson boasted a circular driveway so large it could hold a full party's worth of cars and still leave room for stray delivery trucks.

Karin pulled her white Jaguar XJ6 up behind her sister Annie's pale gray Peugeot station wagon, the French Lunch Bucket, as Annie called it. Karin looked out over the long oak-lined driveway, checking for the other cars she knew would be there: Regina "Curly" McEwen's souped-up black Cherokee Chief, Father Patrick Donovan's heavily oxidized vintage '60s red-and-white Volkswagen van, Jinx Sedlow's lemon-yellow Maserati, Robinson Parker's sedate dark gray Mercedes-Benz 500 SEL sedan, her father Harald Magnusson's modest maroon Saab, Celeste Corby's bright red Acura Legend, Maureen Magnusson's white Rolls Royce Silver Shadow, waxed and polished to a blinding shine.

For some reason Karin did not notice the silver Lamborghini parked near the driveway's end. If she had, she would have left at once.

"Well." Karin glanced over her sunglasses at Heather. "Time to go in and get it over with."

"There's lots of people here already," Heather said, looking at the other cars. "No one'll notice if we don't show."

"Your grandmother will."

"I don't want to go."

"Neither do I. That's beside the point."

"Mom, please." Heather sighed. "I don't want anyone staring at my scar." She tugged at the top of her low-cut Italian sundress.

"Nobody can even see your scar, Heather. Unless you point it out to them."

"I'm still bummed out over my nightmare." Heather clutched at her stomach. "I'll get sick if I have to go in there."

"You and Kurt still planning on going out tonight? Maybe someplace like Diablo?"

Diablo was L.A.'s trendy nightspot for that month.

Heather tried to appear nonchalant. "Guess so. Don't know where, exactly."

"Doesn't matter." Karin pulled her keys out of the ignition. "If you feel well enough to go to McDonald's, you can make an appearance at your grandmother's party."

The front door to the Magnusson house was an imposing affair of carved wood and polished brass. A large knocker ring hung from the mouth of a glaring bronze lion's head. But the door was overpowered by the house itself, a large white-frame Southern mansion with pillars that towered above the wide front porch. Karin grabbed the ring in the lion's mouth and gave it a good whack.

The door was opened by Trevor Capstan, Maureen Magnusson's perfect English butler, correctly attired in tuxedo and black tie. He had a narrow bald head with white fuzz at the sides and hard blue eyes that sized up callers quickly and mercilessly.

The hard eyes softened upon seeing Karin. "Good afternoon, madam. A pleasure to see you again. And you too, miss." He nodded at Heather.

Karin smiled. "Nice to see you, Trevor. Sorry we're a little late."

"Not so late the others have started talking yet." He glanced back over his shoulder. "This way, please."

"Thanks, Trevor," Karin said. "We know the way."

But Trevor Capstan insisted on leading them through the entrance hall with its brilliant red carpet and glittering crystal chandelier, past the overstuffed chairs and massive fireplace of the grandiose living room, on past the banquet-size dining room with its imitation rococo ceiling fresco of the Virgin Ascending to Heaven in the style of the Spanish Master Murillo, and out into the half-acre backyard landscaped with cobblestone walkways, ornamental fruit trees and rosebushes, and an olympic-size swimming pool with an artificial waterfall.

A large blue-and-white-striped canvas tent had been set up for the garden party to keep the constant Southern California sun off the outdoor diners and the members of the small jazz combo hired to play for the occasion. White-jacketed waiters circulated with trays of champagne, liquor, hors d'oeuvres and designer water. The supervising caterer, a jowly man with thick white hair, stood smiling at the guests and glancing about nervously, waiting for the caviar to hit the fan.

"Karin! Heather!" Curly McEwen, a drink in one hand, waved at them from over by the barbecue pit where she was busy flirting with a Filipino chef's assistant half her age.

Regina Constance McEwen was a short, vivacious woman with a retired boxer's build and curly dark hair that had now gone almost completely gunmetal gray. Her husband, Frank, was an aerospace manufacturer who often acted as a consultant to the Pentagon and the White House. Curly's daughter Ashley used to be Heather's best friend until, in Heather's opinion, Ashley turned into a total shit.

"Hey!" Curly embraced Karin, then Heather, without letting go of her drink. The Filipino chef's assistant grinned and smeared more barbecue sauce on a rotating side of beef. "It has been a long time. I mean a *really* long time. You girls forget the way to Belair or what?"

Karin shrugged. "You know, the work at the museum."

Curly shook her head. "Ain't healthy to hang around there too much, babes. Only men you see at a place like that tend to swish when they walk."

The Filipino chef's assistant giggled.

"Got a cigarette on you?" Curly asked.

"Sure." Karin dug one out of her white cotton jacket.

Curly exhaled a lungful of smoke. "Thank God somebody else still smokes in this town besides me."

"Karin! How *are* you?" Jinx Sedlow extended a suntanned manicured hand, a glass of iced Perrier and lime in the other. She was a tall, lithe woman with light brown hair pulled back from her face and a fashionable tennis outfit, lemon-yellow to match her Maserati. "Heather, you're looking lovely." Jinx kissed her on the cheek. "You're a senior now at Severy, aren't you?"

Heather looked glum. "I wish. Still a junior."

"Don't ever wish for old age, babes." Curly McEwen blew smoke out her nose. "It's all over you before you know it."

"Even sooner than that," Jinx agreed.

"You girls don't know what you're talking about," said the tall, stoop-shouldered man with thin white hair and a white moustache. "I'm the only one around here old enough to complain about old age."

"Hi, Granddad!" Heather brightened up a little.

"How's my girl?" He put an arm around her and his other arm around Karin. "How're both my girls?"

"Okay, Daddy." Karin smiled at him. "A little surprised to see you here. I thought you'd still be at the lab."

"Well," Harald Magnusson lowered his chin, "just between you and me, Karin, that's where I'd rather be. But when your mother goes to this much trouble for a party, guess the least I can do is show up."

"Gee, Mr. M.," Curly McEwen said, "I wish I could send Frank to the same school where they trained you."

Jinx Sedlow extended a suntanned hand, bracelets jangling. "Harald, you're looking wonderful."

Harald Magnusson took Jinx's hand graciously. "Thank you, my dear. You're looking awfully well yourself."

Heather snagged a tulip glass of champagne from a roving waiter's tray.

Karin put a hand on her arm. "Since when did you start drinking in public?"

"Mom!" Heather protested. "It's a *party!*"

"One won't do much harm, Karin," Harald Magnusson said.

"Thanks, Granddad." Heather beamed at him.

"Daddy." Karin turned to him. "How can I ever teach her discipline if you keep undercutting me?"

"Sorry. Grandparents just seem to be that way." Harald took out a pipe filled with tobacco. "I think it's in their job description somewhere." He raised a hand in mock defense. "Just kidding! Don't hit me."

Karin stood on tiptoe to give her father a kiss. "You're an old softie and you spoil her rotten. But I love you anyway."

"Why, I love you too, Karin." He hugged her. "I tried to spoil you pretty good, come to think of it, but your mother sort of held me back."

Karin tried to smile. "Yeah."

"*Gram*pa!" Blond five-year-old Adam Newmar came running across the lawn toward his grandfather, arms outstretched, blue eyes sparkling.

"Whoa!" Harald Magnusson stuck the pipe between his teeth and leaned over to pick up his grandson. "How's my boy?"

Adam stuck out his left hand. "I got a new watch."

Harald examined the digital display watch with its miniature video tic-tac-toe game. "Say, that's pretty swell, Adam."

Annie Newmar, dressed in shorts and a T-shirt announcing THE GREAT NEW ZEALAND ESCAPE, came up and slapped her father on the back. "Hiya, Pops! How's it goin'?"

"You don't want to hold that bag of bricks too long, Hal," Sam Newmar said, a margarita in one hand, sunglasses tilted up on his receding hairline. "Kid's gettin' fat on us."

"I am *not!*" Adam said.

"Sure you are." Sam tickled his son in the ribs. "Fat as a little ol' piggy!"

"*Gram*pa!" Adam cried. "Make him *stop!*"

"Just ignore your parents, Adam," Harald Magnusson advised him. "That's what your mom did, and look how nice she turned out."

"Daddy!" Annie protested in mock indignation.

Heather looked away from the fun-and-games with Granddad and Adam and Aunt Annie and Uncle Sam—away and over to where her mother stood talking with Robinson Parker and his wife Estelle. Her mom had on that serious look she got whenever anyone brought up the Barringer.

This party is such boring shit, Heather thought. But the champagne tasted okay and at least she didn't have to think about anything—especially not about the dreams she'd had last night. She sipped at her champagne. It tasted cool and sweet and tingly, even though it was starting to give her a slight headache, right above the eyes.

"Well, look who's here," said a hard little voice.

Heather turned and saw Ashley McEwen, who was not little but looked even tougher than she sounded. Ashley was tall and angular with a girl jock's springy stance. Her hair, curly like her mother's but dirty blond instead of gray, hung down to her shoulders with a loose, go-to-hell look to it.

"Hi, Ash," Heather said. "How's it goin'?"

"So-so. You and Kurt still close?"

Heather shrugged. "Not that close."

"Somethin' better come along?"

Heather thought of Brian but looked at Ashley and said, "Not yet."

"Sherone Livingston still up to her old tricks?" Ashley asked with a slight sneer. "Calling up demons in her spare time?"

The earth seemed to shift under Heather's feet. She staggered and looked for something solid to grab onto, but there was only Ashley watching her with hard, penetrating eyes. Heather turned away. The sun felt hot on her face now, burning hot. But the tulip glass in her hand seemed ice-cold and slimy. She glanced at the Filipino chef's assistant basting the rotating side of beef. She stifled a gasp. He was swabbing it with blood, thick, stringy bright red blood. It was running down the side of beef, which no longer looked like a side of beef but more like a split human torso, the guts hanging out, blood dripping down onto the hot barbecue coals, making them sizzle and smoke.

I'm dreaming it again, Heather told herself, fighting back the panic. *None of it's real.*

The barbecue coals became the burning charcoal briquets inside the salt triangle on the floor of Magda Prokash's dark house. The coals burst into flame. The side of beef—the split human torso—caught fire and began to writhe in agony on the spit, screaming.

"—okay? *Heather!*"

She blinked her eyes, staring at Ashley McEwen.

"You startin' to gonzo out on us or what?"

"I'm—" Heather blinked again. "Okay. I—"

Ashley nodded at the champagne. "Easy on the juice, babes."

"—darling grandchild!" Maureen O'Connor Magnusson's voice carried above the loud party conversation and the soft strains of the combo's fusion jazz. "*She* has time for her grandmama! *Un*like her mother, who is so wrapped up in shop talk with Rob Parker about that damn musty museum she doesn't even know the rest of the world exists!"

Heather looked up at her grandmother approaching in a pink chiffon party dress. With her was Celeste Corby, a woman near Maureen's age with gray-streaked shoulder-length dark hair and thin expressive hands that fluttered about her face like great jungle moths.

"I'm not surprised Karin's chatting it up with Rob Parker," Celeste Corby said, casting an admiring glance his way. "He is such a handsome man."

"The world's full of them." Maureen turned to Heather, arms spread wide. "Is my only granddaughter in all the world too grown up now to give her only grandmama a big kiss?"

Ashley McEwen muttered, "Go hang one on 'er, babes."

Heather dutifully submitted to Maureen's smothering embrace. She did not flinch as heavily made-up lips planted a kiss on her cheek with a resounding smack.

Celeste Corby smiled at Heather and Ashley. "You know, young girls today are so much prettier than we were at their age."

"Only because of what they've learned from us." Maureen smiled at Heather. "Honey girl, it's so *good* to see you! Do you know I actually began to worry that you and your mother might not show up for your grandmama's little party?"

"Maureen," Celeste said, tugging lightly at her sleeve, "maybe we interrupted a private conversation."

Ashley McEwen smiled sweetly. "No big buzz. We were just talkin' witchcraft."

"Oh!" Celeste Corby's hands fluttered.

"Witchcraft!" Maureen rolled her eyes heavenward. "Holy Mother of God preserve us!" She stared hard at

Heather. "No grandchild of mine had better have anything to do with that kind of . . . *rubbish!*"

Heather and Ashley both shook their heads *No way.* But Heather felt the ground shift beneath her feet again.

"Black magic hocus-pocus nonsense!" Maureen fumed on. "Absolute nonsense! And what's worse—"

"It may be nonsense," Celeste interrupted quietly, "but an awful lot of people are taking it seriously these days. Why, just this morning in the *Times*—I'm almost sure it was *this* morning's paper and not yesterday's— there was a story about the kidnapping of a child. Dreadful." Celeste shuddered delicately. "Actually, it was more like an abduction. The kidnappers just came up and took him—some little Mexican boy, almost an infant. Poor child. The kidnappers just took him away in broad daylight, right from under his mother's nose. With the whole block just standing there watching. Somewhere in East L.A. or Watts or one of those places. You know how those people can be. But the mother, poor dear, did at least *try* to protect her child. So the kidnappers cut out her eyes."

Maureen grimaced. "Celeste, that's disgusting!"

"I'm not making it up," Celeste said defensively. "It's right there in this morning's *Times*. You can look it up for yourself."

"Nothing," Maureen assured her, "could interest me less."

"They found the mother crawling around on her hands and knees," Celeste went on, "with her eyes cut out. The LAPD found her, that is."

"There must be more interesting topics of conversation," Maureen said, turning deliberately from Celeste Corby. "Heather dear, do—"

"But the strangest part of all," Celeste continued, sure of her listeners' interest, "is the reports of the people who saw the kidnappers. They described them as an older, heavyset woman with short gray hair and cold eyes. One of those pushy fat women. You know the type.

And the man she was with was tall and pale, *very* pale, and his teeth were bad, the way some men will let their teeth just *go* if they don't have anyone to make them see a dentist—"

"*Celeste,*" Maureen interrupted firmly.

"But the really strange thing is that this odd couple was accompanied by a lovely young girl who was *stark naked.* Can you believe it? I mean, this is L.A. and anything goes. But still, a pair of kidnappers with a naked accomplice? Of course the poor girl might have been drugged or something. One of the witnesses said the girl's eyes looked glazed and she did seem disorient—"

The sound of glass shattering on stone made Celeste look up. Maureen and Ashley looked with her. Heather stood with her right hand outstretched, a dazed look to her eyes. On one of the cobblestone walkways lay the remains of her tulip champagne glass. A passing waiter stooped down and began to pick up shards of broken crystal.

Heather turned to her grandmother, the dazed look giving way to helpless fear. "Grams," she whispered.

Maureen threw her arms around her granddaughter. "Honey girl! Don't give it another thought! May all our bad luck go with it. Damn cheap glass."

The nervous white-haired caterer appeared, nodding anxiously. "Are you okay?" he asked Heather. "Do you want me to call a doctor?"

"She's my grandchild!" Maureen announced. "*I'm* taking care of her."

"Mother, is she all right?" Karin asked, a cigarette burning in her right hand, wine slopping over the glass in her left. "What happened?"

"Nothing her grandmama can't handle," Maureen said confidently, brushing some long red locks from Heather's still panicked face. "It's just too much sun and too much champagne on an empty stomach."

"She shouldn't be drinking that anyway," Karin said. "Daddy was the one who let her have it."

"Harald Magnusson!" Maureen called sharply to him. "I'll talk with you later!"

Harald, who was playing Transformers on the lawn with Adam, looked up. "What'd I do now?"

"You okay, honey?" Karin asked Heather, feeling her forehead. "Want to lie down?"

Heather twisted away from her. "I'm okay."

"Her grandmama will take good care of her." Maureen began to lead Heather toward the house, pausing to snap at the white-haired caterer, "Make sure your people pick up every bit of that damn cheap glass."

As Karin watched her mother and daughter walk away, she took a quick swallow of her Chardonnay. It almost gagged her. She extinguished her cigarette in what was left of the wine, thinking, *Who's going crazy around here, her or me?* One of the omnipresent waiters silently whisked away her glass.

A concerned Robinson Parker asked, "Are you sure we shouldn't call a doctor?"

"Thanks, Rob, but I don't think she needs one," Karin said. *Not that kind of doctor, anyway.*

"Besides," said a deep, rich-toned male voice behind them, "there's already a doctor in the house. And he happens to know a hell of a lot about this patient."

Robinson Parker and Karin turned around to see Dr. David Roberts looking handsomer than ever, green eyes dark under the bright Beverly Hills sun. He was dressed in that carefully casual tennis-resort style favored by successful Southern California doctors: imported white golf shirt, white duck trousers, cordovan topsiders. He held an iced glass of gin and tonic.

"Hello, Dave." Robinson Parker smiled. "You're looking good."

"Rob." David shook his hand. "It's been too long. Still getting out on the golf links?"

"Not as often as I'd like. No time. It's not true what they say, you know. About having more time when you're older. Get in the good stuff while you can. Time runs like a rabbit when you're old."

David laughed his warm, hearty just-between-us-men laugh. "Rob, you're not old!"

"I'm goddamn old," Robinson Parker said defiantly, then glanced down at his empty glass. "And if I don't get a refill, I'll start acting my age. You two will excuse me?"

Karin put a hand on his arm. "Don't go, Rob. I'm not finished bitching about Milt Bromley."

Robinson Parker patted her hand. "Karin, don't worry it to death. Show's looking great. I'm with you. The board's with you. Even Milt."

Sure, Karin thought, watching Parker walk away, *you're all with me, as long as I do exactly what I'm told.* She turned and faced her ex-husband.

"Hello, Karin." He gave her a winning smile. "Don't I even rate a Hello-David-you're-looking-good-how've-you-been?"

"Hello, David."

He laughed. "Okay. So I'm not looking good and you don't give a damn how I've been. I can handle it. *You're* looking good, lady. You're looking very good." His voice dropped into what she used to think of as his radio-announcer mode: deep, resonant and empty as an unfurnished room. "I've never seen you look better."

She pulled a cigarette out of her white cotton jacket and lit it.

David smiled reproachfully. "Not that you deserve to look good, as much as you smoke."

Karin looked away and blew a stream of cigarette smoke in the general direction of the blue-striped canvas pavillion.

David sighed, a hard light beginning to flicker in his dark green eyes. "You know, Karin, there's no law that says people who are legally divorced have to treat each other like shit. You don't need a court order to talk to me."

Karin turned to him. "What do you want?"

"What do I *want?* Christ!" He took a stiff slug of gin

and tonic. "I want to talk to you. I want to find out how you've been."

Karin drew heavily on her cigarette.

"It's been a long time since I've seen you." David shrugged, a modest-little-boy's look on his face. "I missed you, that's all."

Karin exhaled a lungful of smoke. "Look, I don't come around trying to sneak back into your life—"

"I'm not *sneaking* into anything," David interrupted, his voice rising. "Your mother invited—"

"—and I don't appreciate you trying to trick me into cute little meets like this one."

"Hey! Just one minute, okay?" The dark green eyes were angry now. "Nobody's trying to—"

They both fell silent, the space between them heavy with embarrassment as they realized how easy it was, no effort at all, to slip back into their familiar domestic combat roles. The sounds of the party carried on around them: smooth, icy rhythms from the jazz combo, loud chatter of guests, an occasional barking dog or laughing child.

David let out a long sigh. "Can we maybe start this over? The conversation, I mean?"

Karin kept smoking and said nothing.

"You really worried about Heather?" he asked. "Want me to take a look at her?"

"Maybe you could even say something to her while you're at it. She'd like that. She thinks about you from time to time. Not as often as she used to. She's come to accept the fact that you hardly ever think about her."

Anger flared in David's eyes, but he controlled it. "Come on, Karin. I don't deserve this."

She looked at her father playing Transformers with his grandson.

David asked, "Is this a one-shot thing, her dropping the glass? Has she been dropping other things?"

Karin turned back to him. "Thank you, Doctor. I think I know how to look for obvious symptoms."

He stared at her. "Back off, Karin. I'm not trying to pick a fight. She's my daughter too. And I care about her. Even if I don't have time to take her to the zoo."

Karin smiled bleakly. "The zoo days are long gone."

"You win all the points, Karin. Okay? Karin six, David zero. Just tell me if she's been having other problems or if this glass-dropping is an isolated incident. Can you do that for me? Even if you hate my guts?"

Karin hesitated. "No other real problems. She can be moody and hard to get along with, like any teenager. But nothing unusual. Except—"

"Except what?"

Karin shrugged. "Some sort of sleepwalking. I guess that's what it was. I came home last night and found her room messed up and she didn't remember doing it. She said she just had a bad dream."

How could she remember? Karin thought, shuddering at the memory of the devastated room. *She couldn't have done something like that by herself, not if she worked at it all day.*

"Sleepwalking's usually not serious," David said, assuming his best professional manner. "Not unless it gets out of hand. But it can be a symptom of some deeper-seated unrest."

"Thank you, Doctor. If I want a medical opinion, I'll have Norm Goldstein take a look at her."

"Norm's a G.P. If she's sleepwalking she needs to see a good psychiatrist. Someone like Bernie Rausch."

Karin grimaced at the thought of trendy, gold-necklaced Dr. Bernard Rausch, Headshrinker to the Stars. "I can't stand that man."

"Bernie's one of the best. If I talk to him, he'll see Heather next week."

Karin lifted her chin. "If I need help running my life, I'll give you a call. But don't sit home waiting for the phone to ring."

David's eyes narrowed. "You *are* looking for a fight, aren't you? But I'm going to disappoint you. I don't want to fight with you. I'm trying to talk about the physical and emotional well-being of our daughter."

"Now that you never see her, she's *our* daughter. That really is convenient, isn't it?"

David's control snapped. "You goddamn—"

"Well, look who's actually talking with each other," Maureen Magnusson interrupted. "Almost like old times, isn't it?"

Karin turned to her, a brittle smile on her face. "Yes. Almost exactly."

Maureen stared back with her own hard smile. "Both of you should be pleased to hear that your only daughter and my darling grandchild is now one hundred percent recovered. Thanks to some good food and a nice little bit of girl chat with her grandmama."

Karin looked over to where Heather stood watching her cousin Adam Newmar run around in circles on the lawn, a Transformer in the shape of a jet fighter held high in his right hand.

She looks okay, Karin thought gratefully. *Maybe she really is okay.*

But Heather was far from okay.

As she stared at Adam, she saw again the long, low-ceilinged, white-walled corridor of her dream, airless as a sealed tomb, but empty this time, empty of everything except Roberto's mother, Maria, on her hands and knees, blood oozing from her gouged-out eye sockets, bloody hands fumbling at the hem of the white robe worn by the little blond boy, the one who spoke to Heather in the dream, saying, *I am the Perfect Blood Offering.*

Her five-year-old cousin, Adam Newmar.

chapter 21

STORM WARNING

Sherone sat at the small dining-room table with her father Wes Livingston and Glenda McGuiness and picked at her dinner, take-out linguini with clam sauce and garlic bread and salad, as she pretended to watch the National Geographic special on wild chimpanzees flickering from the cheap television set in the living room.

She did not have much of an appetite.

When Heather first called, she was crying so hard Sherone had trouble even understanding what she was trying to say. When Sherone finally understood, she brushed it off as just another bummer of a bad dream, like her own horrifying nightmare of Seamus Harrach and the Mouth with Sharper Teeth. Then Heather told her about the story in that morning's *Times*. Sherone did not believe it. Heather told her to go read it for herself. Sherone went to look for the paper and found that Glenda had already thrown it out. She drove to a nearby 7-11 and bought another paper.

Then she believed.

The terror that came with the belief was still with her now, hours later, as she sat at the dining-room table. Magda Prokash had lied about being into the Dark Side of witchcraft. Black Magic, Satanism, whatever you wanted to call it, Magda was deep into it, and dragging Heather in along with her. *And me too,* Sherone thought, shuddering, *and all of—*

Azgaroth.

Stop it! Sherone ordered herself, trying to push the hateful name from her mind, where it sat and rasped against her brain like the claws of an unclean thing.

AZGAROTH!

Sherone's fork slipped off her plate and skidded halfway across the Formica tabletop. Wes and Glenda looked up from the National Geographic special. Glenda picked up the fork and handed it back to Sherone.

"You okay, Skip?" Wes asked her.

Sherone stood up from the table. "Sorry. I'm just not . . . very hungry." She pushed out her chair and walked away.

Wes started to get up from his chair. "Skip?"

The back door opened, then slammed shut.

"Let her go, Wes." Glenda looked up at him. "She wants to be alone for a while."

"She's been acting funny all afternoon. Ever since that little friend of hers called, Heather."

"It'll pass."

Wes thought about it, then shook his head. "Sorry, Glen. I've only got one daughter." He tossed his paper napkin onto the table and headed for the back door.

Outside it was dark. The lights of Los Angeles on one side and the San Fernando Valley on the other glittered in the distance. The deep arroyo behind the Livingston house yawned dark and forbidding. Sherone stood near the edge, staring down into darkness. Sean O'Casey, the red-haired Irish setter, sat beside her and licked his chops, whimpering anxiously.

Wes picked up his pace, calling out to her. "Hey, Skipper!"

She turned and looked at him, then turned back to the black gulf of the arroyo.

Wes came up beside his daughter and put his arm around her. "How's it goin'?"

Sherone shrugged. "Okay, I guess."

Father and daughter stared into the dark canyon, listening to the night sounds of small animals moving in the underbrush and distant cars grinding up steep roads. Sean O'Casey thumped his tail cheerfully and tried to nuzzle Wes's left hand.

"You and Heather going out somewhere tonight?"

"Heather's got a date with Kurt Pritchard."

Wes frowned to himself. That could be part of the problem. These days, Saturday nights for him were special pockets of privacy to be savored like rare wine, time apart from work and travel when he and Glenda could be together and perfectly happy just doing nothing. *But that's because we're a couple of old married folks*, he thought, even though they weren't married and Glen wasn't that old. Wes hadn't quite forgotten yet what it was like to be young and restless on a Saturday night, especially when your best friend had a date lined up and you didn't. Maybe that was the whole problem right there. Maybe that was what the phone call from Heather was about.

"That what you and Heather talked about this afternoon?" he asked tentatively, hugging her again.

"Jesus, Daddy!" Sherone squirmed loose from his arm. "Kurt Pritchard is a total *asshole*, okay?"

"Guess you know more about that than I do."

Sherone stared into the black depths of the arroyo, which were starting to take on shape and even some color now that her eyes were slowly becoming adjusted. She could see clumps of manzanita, cacti, a tree here and there, overhead the night sky with its stars made pale by smog, and black clouds building out toward the ocean.

Wes waited a few more minutes before adding, "Whatever you two talked about, I think maybe it upset you a little."

Sherone turned to him. "Daddy." She hesitated. "If

you made a mistake, a really *big* mistake, if you got yourself into, you know, something you didn't mean to, but now you're in it whether you want to be or not . . ." She struggled for the right words, then looked at him imploringly. "You know what I *mean?*"

The usual parent's list of possible horrors unrolled in Wes's mind as he prepared to answer his daughter. Was she pregnant? Hooked on heroin or worse? Had she committed a serious crime? Or contracted AIDS? A more nervous parent might have started yelling, demanding an immediate answer. But Wes Livingston's father hadn't raised his son to panic in a crisis, and that son wasn't going to raise his daughter any differently.

"I think," Wes answered slowly, "I know what you mean by making a big mistake and then having to live with the consequences, see it through to the end. We've all done that." He looked carefully at Sherone. "But I don't know exactly what your mistake was, Skip."

Sherone nodded quickly. "Okay. It's like you've worked with something before and it's always turned out cool. But this time it goes too far and gets out of control and you can't . . ." She swallowed. "You can't stop it. Even if you want to, you can't."

Drugs, Wes decided, a cold lump forming in his gut. The question now was what kind and how bad. "Skip," he probed gently, "this thing that's got out of control, it wouldn't be something you bought from Heather, would it? Or some other friend?"

Sherone shook her head, staring in bewilderment at her father. Then she realized what he was driving at. "Daddy, do I look *that* bad? Like I'm strung out on coke or crack or something?"

"Skip, I never said—"

"It's not that, okay?" Sherone insisted. "It's *nothing* like that. What it is, it's more like a power. It's like you knew there was this power and you wanted to work with it, see what it was like. You know, sort of experiment with it. But now—"

Now it was Wes's turn to realize what was going on. "Skip, this wouldn't have anything to do with that Wicca hobby of yours, would it?"

Sherone stared at him and said nothing.

"Because if it does—"

"If it does," Sherone finished for him, "it's just a lot of black magic bullshit."

"That wasn't exactly what I was going to say."

"You were *thinking* it."

Father and daughter fell silent again. Wind from the sea began to blow across the ridge they were standing on.

Sherone looked up at him. "Daddy, if I *did* get myself into something awful—something *really* awful . . ." She took a deep breath. "And if it was coming after me . . . Would you still stand by me?"

Wes Livingston was not a man given to displays of emotion. But he hugged his daughter close to him and kissed the top of her head. "You think being a father's some kind of part-time job? Where I can just step back when the going gets a little rough and say, 'Hey, sorry, I didn't sign up for this part of the tour'?" He hugged her again. "Of course I'll stand by you, Skip. If anything's coming after you, it's coming after me too. You know that."

Sherone did not answer. She was crying softly.

As he held his daughter close, Wes thought that maybe Glenda was right and it was time to do something about this occult hobby of Sherone's. He did not believe in the occult himself. But he was a thoughtful man who had traveled widely and seen much, and he knew that what people believed deeply could create realities for them. If you thought something was real, whether it was or not to begin with, it could become that way.

A cold wind from the sea whipped across the ridge, making an old oak tree nearby creak with a mournful sound.

Storm's coming, Wes thought. *Bad one.*

And suddenly, for no reason he could understand, he

wanted to take his family, take Skip and Glen, and run, get the hell out of there, leave this quiet home he loved so much and never look back. Just run. And keep on running.

The cold wind blew again. This time it made him shudder, with a chill that was deep inside, beyond the cure of ordinary warmth.

A storm was coming all right. But it was not the storm itself that made him shudder, made him go cold with fear inside. It was what drove the storm. It was something taking on the shape of the storm, its darkness and fury, but no more the storm itself than a nuclear explosion is merely the light that makes it visible.

Wes Livingston raised his head defiantly to the oncoming storm and the darkness that rode with it, seeking out his daughter and himself.

PART III
WATER

chapter 22

Diablo

"What if we can't get in?" Heather asked Kurt Pritchard.

His bright red Porsche 928e screeched to a halt inside the parking lot of the disco nightclub Diablo.

"We'll get in." Kurt opened his door. "Watch."

Diablo was the hot new night spot of the moment in L.A. where everybody who was anybody wanted to be seen. Six months later it might be a forgotten name, its doors and rooms empty, a crumbling relic of popular culture lost and mysterious as a Mayan temple. But for now, Diablo was it, the only place to be when night fell.

Getting in was tricky. It wasn't just a matter of paying the high-price cover charge or slipping the doorman a few extra bucks. At Diablo you had to pass visual inspection. Standing at the entrance, along with an over-muscled doorman-bouncer, was the manager or one of his assistants, sometimes with a punk princess of the boulevards. This select committee looked you over as you stepped up to the neon-spangled doorway. If they liked what they saw, you got in. If not, you were turned away. No out-of-town geeks or local nerds allowed. On any given night the sidewalk outside Diablo was filled with bitter, quarrelsome couples, rejects all, arguing sullenly about where to go next.

As Kurt and Heather made their way through the rejects and into the long line of hopefuls, they kept their faces frozen in the Perfect L.A. Look: eyes slightly glazed, mouth closed tight, jaw hard with steely determination and an out-of-my-way-asshole arrogance. Kurt had on a soft leather jacket with designer shirt and slacks. Heather had left the house wearing a long black coat buttoned up to the neck. She had unbuttoned and discarded it long before they reached Diablo. Underneath she wore baggy black trousers tucked into calf-high black riding boots. Her white silk long-sleeve blouse, set off by a wide red sash, was unbuttoned almost to her waist. What wasn't in plain sight could be seen without a bra through sheer silk.

Heather sighed. "I hope this line goes fast. I am *so* dragged out."

Kurt looked at her. "It's not even eight yet."

"I was at a party all afternoon," Heather explained.

Kurt's expression did not change. "Who with?"

"With my mother, Kurt. The party was at my grandmother's. Okay?"

"Sure, Heather. Whatever you say."

He knows, she thought, *about Brian*. Then she dismissed the idea. *That's bullshit, because he can't know.*

The select examining committee eyed them as they moved up to Diablo's baroque front door. The neon sign overhead flashed hot pink and blood red. The assistant manager surveyed them with small dark eyes, pausing to linger over Heather's heart-stopping décolletage. He was somewhere in the no-man's-land between twenty-five and thirty. He wore a silver metallic jacket and short dark hair oiled flat to his skull. The bouncer beside him had a shaved head and opaque shades that reflected Heather's and Kurt's distorted, shrunken images back at them. The punk princess of the boulevards for that night had spiky dyed-black hair sticking out from her head like shrapnel.

She wore a Madonna glitter coat over a black tube-top and black tights with rhinestone spike heels. Her shades, propped up on the end of her nose, were the see-through kind. She smoked a cigarette languidly, heavy red lipstick staining the filter tip.

The assistant manager glanced at the bouncer, then the punk princess. "Go? Or pass?"

"Pass," the bouncer growled softly, barely moving his lips.

"Hey!" Kurt objected. "What the fuck? I mean, I've been here be—"

The bouncer took one quick, calculated half-step toward Kurt. He did not raise an arm or clench a fist. But his whole body tensed into readiness. Kurt stepped back. He worked out on a fairly regular basis and was not in bad shape. But the bouncer was in great shape, the end product of free weights and steroids.

The punk princess leaned forward, her skin pale under flashing neon. "You been here before?" she asked Kurt.

"Lotsa times," he lied.

"Fuckin' shit," the bouncer muttered.

The punk princess exhaled a cloud of smoke, then smiled at Kurt with yellow teeth. "You're kinda cute. Go. Both you and your friend."

The bouncer objected. "I said Pass."

The princess arched her eyebrows. "So fuck you."

The assistant manager shot her a blank glance. "Later." He nodded at Heather and Kurt. "Pay the cashier. No checks. No drugs on the dance floor. Keep it cool. Any problems and you're outta here."

The bouncer whispered to Kurt, "He means *you*, dude."

Inside, Diablo was divided into three main dance floors and as many bars. Concert-size screens flashed huge videos on the walls. Hidden speakers made the floors vibrate. A billowing fog machine and harsh-colored, contrasty lighting gave everything the look of an early Roger Corman American-International Pictures horror movie. The dance floors, the bars, the waiting areas in front of the restrooms—the whole place was packed.

Heather and Kurt scanned the crowd of punkers, yuppies, cruisers and random celebrities, trying hard to keep their faces frozen in the Perfect L.A. Look. Occasionally, the masks slipped.

Heather nudged Kurt's arm. "Don't stare, but I think that's Eddie Murphy over there with that girl."

"Or some wanna-be asshole."

"No, it's really him. I can tell."

"Bullshit. How?"

"He looks, you know, sincere."

"Hey, dude!" called a voice from the crowd, shouting to be heard over the heavy pounding music.

Kurt and Heather looked in that direction.

Troy Taylor, in shades and striped shirt, moved toward them, accompanied by his girl, Paige Benson, her best friend, Belinda Leonard, and Belinda's date, Andy Metz.

Troy punched Kurt playfully on the shoulder. "Lookin' good, dude." He took off his shades to check out Heather's plunging neckline and sheer silk blouse. "Lookin' *real* good. How's it goin', Heather?"

"Okay," Heather said in the kind of voice you answer a cop with.

Paige Benson, in a glittery bare-shoulders disco dress, took in Heather's outfit at a glance. "Heather, what a *darling* little shirt." Paige smiled sweetly. "Did you make it?"

Heather smiled back. "I stole it."

"It's so cute. But you forgot the buttons."

Troy held up his glass. "Guys been to the bar yet?"

"We just got here," Kurt said.

"*Go* for it, dude!" Troy encouraged him. "They got this new shit—The Desert Wind—that'll put you fuckin' *under*. Guaranteed!"

Heather remembered the hot wind that had blown through Magda Prokash's house that night, the hot wind that had whirled through her bedroom, making all the loose objects in the room dance like leaves in a storm. Her skin prickled into gooseflesh. She had to tense her muscles to keep from shuddering.

Paige Benson's friend Belinda Leonard, whose fat face and turned-up nose had led more than one unkind observer to compare her to Miss Piggy, smiled at Heather. "We're *so* glad to see that you and Kurt are still, you know, together. We thought—"

Heather turned on her. "You thought what?"

"We thought maybe you were, like," Belinda looked carefully at Paige, then Troy, "seein' someone else."

Heather did not look away. "Who?"

Belinda smiled. "Oh, no one special. Just, you know, someone."

Heather moved in close on her, making the fat-faced girl step back. "Any names, Belinda?"

Paige stepped in to defend her friend. "You know, Heather. That nerdy little boy genius with the beak nose. The one who sits around reading comic books in Physics."

Troy laughed at the description.

Heather stared at Paige. "How would you know? You couldn't get into Physics unless they charged admission."

"McNulty." Andy Metz said it in a flat, just-the-facts-ma-am voice. "Brian McNulty."

Heather stopped short, bringing her anger under control, aware that Kurt was staring at her, aware that tension was passing like an electric current through the six people in this tight little group. *They know*, she told herself. *Somehow they all know*.

She tried to shrug it off. "I've heard the name. Maybe I've even seen him in the Quad once."

"Maybe," Paige Benson smiled sweetly, putting a hand on Kurt's shoulder, "you met him down at the Cove."

Kurt shook off her hand, but Paige kept smiling. This was too much fun. And Kurt's growing anger was the best part of it.

Heather set her jaw defiantly. "If you'll excuse me, the

shit's getting pretty thick around here."

Heather turned her back on them and walked away, pushing through the noisy, jostling crowd. Kurt called out her name over the throbbing music. But she did not look back.

When she reached the nearest women's restroom, the waiting area outside was filled with guys, singly and in groups, talking, smoking, waiting. Several of them looked Heather over. One of them, a Mexican guy with an Errol Flynn moustache, gave her a look that said, *If you're pissed at him, why not try me?* Irritated, she looked away and pushed open the door to the restroom.

Inside most of the girls were crowded around the washbasins beneath the long mirror, laying out lines and snorting up cocaine. Some of them were fussing with their hair or adjusting their clothes. Some were talking, loud and hyper, flying on coke. A few were doing jerky dance steps and mouthing silent lyrics to songs playing inside their heads.

Heather found a place in front of the mirror. A girl offered her a free line. She shook her head. The girl stared at her, unable to believe that anybody would turn down primo shit when it was offered free. Heather stared into the mirror. A small tear hovered on the eyelash of the face that stared back at her. The tear broke and trickled down her cheek in a lazy, graceful pattern like a skater on an empty pond. *How did they find out?* she wondered, wiping at the tear. *How the hell did they find out so soon?* Not that it mattered anymore. They knew. Kurt knew.

What happens now? she silently asked the face in the mirror. *Does he just dump me? Or go beat the shit out of Brian and then come back and dump me?*

She turned from the mirror, pushing back a loose strand of red hair from her face. This was bullshit. It was worse than bullshit. It was pure piss-your-pants gutlessness. Whatever was going to happen would happen. Kurt knew. She would go back and they could talk about it. If he didn't want to talk—

"Heather! How *are* you?"

She looked up to see Tamara Devon smiling at her two washbasins away. There were no coke lines laid out in front of her. But Tamara's dark eyes glittered with a heightened intensity.

She came over to Heather and embraced her, kissing her lightly on the cheek. The fragrance of Tamara's Giorgio perfume was overpowering. Heather backed away. She tried not to believe all the rumors she heard about Tamara, but she still didn't like being kissed by her.

"You are *so* beautiful tonight." Tamara's dark eyes stared into Heather's, her long black hair shining beneath the fluorescent lights of the restroom. "Almost too pretty to be real."

Heather smiled uneasily. "You look okay yourself, Tamara."

She did. Her large breasts, larger even than Heather's, were displayed enticingly by a skimpy white tank top with a racing back. The white fabric set off her tawny skin to stunning advantage.

"But you've been *crying,* haven't you?" Tamara touched a black-painted nail to Heather's face, tracing the dried track of the tear down her cheek.

Heather squirmed. "It's noth—"

"And you *cut* yourself." Tamara pressed the small scar on Heather's left breast, the one that had appeared after the horrible nightmare in the shape of a pentagram, the five-sided star. The scar lines were a light puckered pink now, barely visible under the fluorescent lights. Tamara's finger rested on Heather's breast, feather-light as it traced the outline of the tiny five-sided star. The sequin-encrusted pentagram on the black nail of her left little finger glimmered with its own strange light.

Heather shivered at Tamara's touch. The shiver turned into a shudder of disgust. She broke away from Tamara, pulling her silk blouse closed.

She blushed fiercely. "It's starting to heal. It looks

better now than it did last night."

Even with the open neck pulled shut, Heather's breasts were still visible beneath the silk blouse. The large pink areolae of her nipples seemed to poke right through the sheer fabric. Tamara stared openly at them, an amused, catlike hunger in her dark eyes. Heather's blush deepened.

"Your breasts are perfect," Tamara whispered. "The little scar makes them even lovelier." Tamara moved in closer until her own large breasts were almost touching Heather's. "We could be sisters, couldn't we?" She smiled lazily at Heather through half-closed eyes. "The dark sister and the fair sister. Who knows? Maybe we *were* sisters once. In some other life . . ."

Heather felt nauseated at the thought of being related in any way to Tamara Devon. She turned away from her.

"Here with Kurt?" Tamara asked, still smiling.

Heather nodded, repressing another shudder as she headed for the restroom door.

"If you get tired of dancing with him," Tamara called after her in a low voice, "just let me know, okay?"

Outside the restroom, Heather was stopped by the Mexican guy who had given her the eye earlier. He was a good-looking kid with light olive skin and dark brown Spanish eyes.

"You look sad," he said, a quiet smile on his handsome face. "You're too pretty to look so sad, you know?"

Heather shook her head. "Not now. Please."

He put an arm up against the wall, blocking her. "I mean, the way I see it, okay, is you're sad, and I'm lonely. All right. So why don't we—"

He was grabbed from behind, spun around and thrown back hard against the wall. His dark eyes flashed with anger. Then he saw Kurt Pritchard standing there in front of him, not entirely sane, his blue eyes deadly pale, fists trembling slightly with anticipation. The Mexican kid reviewed his options. The *huerta* with the big tits was a knockout all right, a real fox. But this coked-up

214

boyfriend of hers was fucking crazy. He thought about it for another second or so, then left.

Heather stiffened as Kurt came over and put his arm around her.

He kissed her, gently, on the tip of her nose. "Just tell me where you're goin' when you leave all of a sudden, okay?" He glanced at her half-exposed breasts, rising and falling rapidly. "You could get into trouble dressed like that, you know?" Kurt's face was smeared with a sickly smile, his eyes glittering with The Desert Wind or coke or something.

As they walked back toward the dance floor, Kurt's arm still around her, Heather asked, "Where's everybody?"

"Gone." He kissed her again, on the mouth this time. "You want to dance? Or find a table?" He kissed her again. "Or maybe go someplace else?"

What she really wanted to do, she realized with sudden clarity, was go home and sleep—*and please not dream, please God*—and wake up tomorrow morning refreshed and happy and looking beautiful and watch Brian McNulty wash her Suzuki Samurai jeep.

But the music was pounding inside her head, making it vibrate. Kurt's glittering blue eyes reminded her of Tamara Devon's shining dark ones, and being kissed by Kurt was almost as disgusting, as slimy to the touch, as being kissed by Tamara. And over the throbbing music and the crowded, claustrophobic closeness of Diablo came the high-pitched voice of the golden-haired child *(Adam)* announcing to her *(Adam Newmar): I am the Perfect Blood Sacrifice* . . .

She turned to Kurt. "Let's go someplace else."

They parked in a turnout on one of the side roads off Mulholland Drive in the Hollywood Hills. Thick brush and low-hanging branches hid the red Porsche 928e from the outside world. Cars buzzed through sharp curves along Mulholland. The lights of Los Angeles lay spread out below them like an electric carpet of winking, multicolored jewels.

Inside the Porsche, Heather's silk blouse was off and down around her waist as Kurt bent over, his mouth fastened on one erect nipple while he rolled the other one between his fingers.

"Ouch!" Heather pushed him away. "Not so rough."

Kurt stared at her breasts, his eyes glittering as he breathed heavily through an open mouth. Pale moonlight filtered in through the Porsche's tinted windows, making Heather's naked white skin look blindingly bright against the black leather seats of the interior. Her large pink areolae swelled out from the ends of her breasts, the nipples themselves standing up red and erect from Kurt's eager manipulation.

"I thought you liked it like that," he said, his voice husky.

"I don't like it so rough, okay?"

He bowed his blond head, as if in submission, but his glittering blue eyes grew hard. "You don't mind it when *he's* rough, do you?"

Heather frowned. "What do you mean?"

"You *like* it when he's rough, don't you?" Kurt grabbed one of her breasts and ran his thumb heavily across the stiff nipple and its velvety spreading areola. "You like it when *he* does it, don't you?"

She hooked her fingers around his wrist and tried to push it away, but his hand stayed heavy on her breast. "What are you talking about?" she demanded, almost shouting.

"McNulty." Kurt gripped her breast harder. "Brian McNulty. Your little boyfriend. The one who gives it to you the way you like it." He pinched her nipple. Hard.

"*Ouch!* Goddamn it, Kurt! You *hurt* me!" She tried to push him off her.

He leaned against her until his face was on top of hers, his heavier weight crushing her naked chest, making it difficult to breathe. His blue eyes glittered crazily.

This is another nightmare, Heather told herself, fighting back the panic. *It's not really happening.*

On the drive from Diablo up to the secluded turnout Kurt had been polite and attentive, sweet as could be. And when they started messing around, even though Heather hadn't planned to go very far tonight, hadn't even planned to take off her shirt, he was so sweet and gentle and loving about everything that she got turned on and before she knew it—

Kurt leaned into her, his breath rancid with strong alcohol and stale tobacco, beads of sweat standing out like crystals on his forehead, blue eyes glittering like neon. "He got to you first, didn't he? You let him. Didn't you? Because you knew he's such a fuckin' limpdick wimp you could run him like a robot. *Didn't you?*"

"Kurt, let go of me."

"DIDN'T YOU?"

Fear clutched Heather's heart. She knew Kurt had a temper. That's the way he was. She also knew he'd never really hurt her. Sure, he hit her once, or sort of hit her. Nothing serious. He apologized for it right away, even cried about it like a little boy, then sent her a dozen red roses the next day. So it wasn't like he knocked her around or anything. But now . . .

The face glaring at her with glittering crazy blue eyes and beads of sweat popping out on his forehead and lips drawn back from his teeth was not the same Kurt she had always known, the one she knew for sure would never hurt her.

"Cunt." He growled the word at her, like someone swearing at a dog. "Sleazy little fat-ass cunt."

"Kurt, would you please listen to—"

"Fuckin' *cunt!*"

Heather was crying now, unable to believe this was really happening.

"Fuckin' little dirty-cunt whore!" Kurt's breath came faster. "Holdin' out on me and playin' Little Miss Cherry and all the time *he's* stickin' it up your fuckin' sleazy hole!"

Kurt yanked her pants down around her knees with one fast, violent move. Heather screamed and tried to hit him. He grabbed both her hands in his left hand and pinned her back against the black leather seat. The heavy smells of sexual rut and rising fear filled the cramped interior. Heather was sobbing, pleading with him. He unzipped his pants with his right hand and fumbled out his penis. It rose erect and throbbing, veins standing out in the pale moonlight.

Roughly he shoved his fingers up her vagina, thrusting deep inside her. Heather cried out in pain.

"You're drippin' wet, you slut. You want it *bad*, don't you? Huh, Miss Cherry?"

"Please, Kurt," she sobbed.

"Fuckin' whore." He spoke through gritted teeth. "That what you said to him, huh?" He mimicked her in an ugly falsetto. "Oh, *please*, Brian! Please, please, *please* don't fuck me! 'Cause I'm still a *viiiiiiiirrrrgin!* Fuckin' *whore!*"

He shoved his penis hard up against her labia and started to thrust inside her like a man digging into packed dirt with a blunt trowel. She turned her head to one side and sobbed with pain and humiliation, and rage.

A shock wave hit the Porsche, knocking it several yards forward. Kurt almost pitched over Heather and into the backseat.

"What the *fuck?!*" He looked up, dazed.

It hit a second time. Kurt's head knocked against Heather's. Her front teeth cut his left cheek. Blood welled up and trickled down his face. His erection went limp. Furious, he raised a hand to strike her.

Then he realized that the Porsche was still shaking, vibrating almost, like a gigantic tuning fork, building steadily to a climax, as if getting ready to explode.

He moved off Heather, stuffing his limp member back into his pants and looking out the windshield.

The windshield cracked then in a huge starburst pattern, lines radiating across the curved glass.

"Fuckin' *shit!*" Kurt roared, zipping up his pants.

"Asshole's fuckin' with my goddamn *car!*" He reached for the door handle, turning pale with rage beneath his year-round tan.

Heather sat hunched over in the far corner of the front seat, arms folded across her naked breasts, tears still glistening in her blue eyes.

She found her voice, with difficulty. "Kurt, just stay inside. Please?"

He threw open the door and stumbled out.

The first thing he noticed was the ground beneath him. Rock solid. Not even the slightest tremor disturbed it.

Then he noticed the darkness, thick and intense, as if a black cloud had rolled in suddenly from the mountains or the desert, wrapping the turnout in dense, smoky fog, obscuring the lights of Los Angeles winking down below, making everything seem dark and hopeless and dead.

He felt something staring at him from behind, felt it burning into the back of his head.

He turned around.

The scream rose in his throat like vomit forcing its way up and out into the open, bursting forth in a series of shattered gasps.

"*U-uh. U-u-uh. U-u-u-u—*"

Kurt scrambled back inside the Porsche, slamming the door so hard a few shards of glass fell from the cracked windshield. He twisted the key in the ignition, floored the gas in neutral until the engine cranked up whining to almost 7000 RPM.

Heather, wrapped in her long black coat, wiped at the tears streaking her cheeks. *It's coming,* she thought numbly. *It's coming for me again.*

Kurt switched on the headlights with such force that he pulled the knob off in his hand, then pointed at the shattered windshield. "Look!" he cried, his voice cracking into sound fragments. "LOOK AT THE MOTHERFUCKER!"

Heather looked.

And saw nothing but darkness.

chapter 23

INTERLOPERS

Karin was on her way to the front door, attaché case in one hand, car keys in the other, when she stopped at Heather's bedroom door and looked in.

Heather was still asleep, arms and legs curled up in the fetal position, long red hair sprawled out across the pillow. Early Sunday morning light filtered softly through drawn curtains. Karin had intended to wake her and let her know she was leaving for the museum, but seeing her sound asleep like that changed her mind.

Let her sleep, she thought. *She needs it.*

Heather and Kurt had come back early last night, both of them on edge about something. Heather had seemed detached, frightened and unfocused. Kurt looked terrified, like someone who had seen the worst thing he could possibly imagine come to life before his eyes.

Later, Karin promised herself, closing the bedroom door softly. *I'll talk with her about it after I've finished up at the Barringer, and I'll get some real answers.*

She was almost out the front door, checking to make sure she hadn't forgotten anything, when the telephone rang.

Shit! she thought. *Let Gabriela get it.*

But Gabriela wasn't there the way she usually was Sunday mornings, stopping by after early Mass to take care of Saturday night dishes and help get things ready for Monday. She had been badly upset by Heather's sleepwalking incident Friday night and asked for the weekend off. Karin had given it to her without a moment's hesitation.

Gabriela said nothing to Karin about the incidents of that night: the pounding at the door, the blood rushing out from under it, the inhuman howling that followed her down the hall. Karin, in her turn, said nothing about the vibrating bedroom door she had seen. Neither woman wanted to discuss the subject of what had happened in Heather's bedroom.

But it hung between them like an unspoken dread.

Karin's answering machine picked up the ringing telephone. "Hi. You've reached (818) 986-4433. We're not in right now. But if you leave your name, number—"

Karin lifted the handset. "Hello?"

"Karin? This is Brett."

She suppressed an irritated sigh. "Hi, how are you? I was just on my way out the door."

"Look, I know it's sort of early to be calling on a Sunday." It was not quite 8:00 A.M.

"No problem, usually. It's just that I have this big show coming up, the one I told you about, and I'm down one person now." She hesitated, remembering painfully how Milton Bromley had fired Dodge Andrews. "I was just on my way to the museum to take care of some last-minute details." *So why don't you take the hint*, she prompted him silently, *and hang up?*

"I know it's a bad time to be calling," Brett repeated. "I'm sorry. But there were things I didn't finish saying to you Friday night."

"Sorry about that," Karin cut in, jiggling her keys impatiently. "Things turned into kind of a mess." *Christ, did they ever*, she thought, remembering Heather's trashed bedroom and Heather cowering naked against the wall.

"Karin," Brett interrupted, forcefully for him. "I've *got* to talk with you."

"After I get there. Call me, okay? At the museum."

"Karin—"

"Thanks, Brett. You're a sweetheart. Bye."

She hung up on him, reached for the front door handle and almost made it before the telephone rang again. Her shoulders slumped. She let out a long sigh. Then she got angry. *The hell with it!* she thought, and opened the door.

". . . back to you as soon as possible. Remember, wait for the beep. Thanks for calling. . . . BRREEEEEEP."

Karin started to pull the front door shut.

"Karin Marie?" Maureen Magnusson's voice boomed out from the answering machine's speaker. "Are you even checking this damn machine of yours anymore? I can't believe you are. Because I left messages all last night and you *still* haven't had the common courtesy to call me back!"

That was true. Karin had been worried sick about Heather and did not answer the phone or return calls. Besides, after wasting half a day at her mother's party, she felt no obligation to spend the rest of the night arguing with her over the phone.

"I wouldn't be calling," Maureen went on, "if I didn't have something important to tell you."

Karin gritted her teeth and picked up the handset. "Mother, I'm on my way to the museum."

"Is that any way to answer a phone?" Maureen demanded. "'I'm on my way to the museum.' Damn it, Karin Marie! You are *not* going to lose all your manners and start talking like some . . . vulgarian. Not if *I* have anything to say about it!"

"I'll call you later." Karin started to hang up.

"*Don't you dare hang up that phone!*" Maureen ordered. "And if you do, don't *ever* try to call me again. No daughter who hangs up on her only mother is a daughter of mine."

Karin's finger hovered over the disconnect button. "Mother, I really do have to leave. I've got lots of things to take care of before the show opens."

"Do you think you're the only one who does, Karin Marie? Do you think *I* don't have things to do myself?"

If you did, Karin thought, *maybe you'd butt out of my life for a few minutes.*

"Certain things take priority," Maureen continued, "such as the health of my only granddaughter. After our Davie told me about these horrible sleepwalking seizures—"

"They're not seizures!" Karin snapped at her. "They're just . . . nightmares!" *I'm arguing with her again,* she thought. *I'm yelling at her.* "Did he say they were seizures?"

"He said—"

"Because if he did, he's a goddamn—"

"He said," Maureen interrupted firmly, regaining control of the conversation, "that Heather had been having sleepwalking incidents and that you ought to have Dr. Rausch take a look at her."

"I'll set up an appointment with Norm Goldstein," Karin said. "I can't stand Bernie Rausch."

Maureen rose to his defense. "Dr. Rausch is a highly respected—"

"Don't tell me what doctor to send her to, Mother! She's my daughter, not yours."

Maureen bristled. "How *dare* you talk that way to the mother who loves you! Ungrateful, ill-mannered—"

"Call me all the names you want!" Karin shouted into the phone. "It won't make one damn bit of—"

"Mom!"

Karin turned to see Heather standing in the hallway, clad only in a long U2 T-shirt. "Who're you yellin' at?" she asked, rubbing sleep from her eyes.

Karin turned back to the phone. "Look, Heather just got up. I'll call you back later, okay?"

"No, Karin Marie, it is *not* o—"

As Karin hung up the phone, she turned to Heather. "I'm sorry, honey. Did I wake you up?"

"Was that Grams?" Heather nodded at the phone.

"Yes. How're you feeling? Sleep okay?"

"Why does Grams want me to see Dr. Rausch?"

Karin tried to smile. "Because she's confused and she doesn't understand what happened and it doesn't matter what the hell she wants. If I don't want you to see Dr. Rausch, then you're not going to."

Tears formed in Heather's blue eyes. "She thinks I'm crazy, doesn't she?"

Karin went over and hugged her, feeling her heart thump through the thin T-shirt. "No one thinks you're crazy, honey." She kissed Heather lightly on the cheek.

Heather was sobbing now. "I'm *not!*"

"You need some more sleep." Karin patted her on the cheek, then smoothed down some of the more unruly locks of long red hair. "Go on back to bed. I'll be home from the Barringer by about 2:00 or 3:00 this afternoon. Gabriela's not here today. But there's food in the fridge ready for the microwave, okay?"

Heather walked off toward her bedroom, rubbing at the tears in her eyes.

"I love you, honey!" Karin called after her, thinking, *I really do, too.* Then she thought, *If you loved her, you'd stay home and talk with her.*

A spasm of guilt swept over Karin.

Then she left.

chapter 24

the drowning pool

After her mother drove away, Heather got out of bed, where she had been crying facedown on a pillow. She went out to the kitchen. None of the prepared microwave food in the refrigerator looked any good. She took out a frosted cinnamon donut and a Diet Pepsi and returned to her bedroom.

She sat on the bed, legs crossed under her, and ate the donut. *They all think I'm crazy*, she thought, her eyes still red from crying. *Mom, Dad, Grams, everybody*. She didn't know if Kurt thought she was crazy, but it didn't matter much anymore, not after last night. She shuddered at the memory. Afterward, when Kurt was driving her home, he kept looking in the rearview mirror and back over his shoulder, looking for whatever it was he had seen in the darkness at the turnout. He almost ran them off the road once. Heather offered to drive. But Kurt didn't even hear her.

The only one who didn't think she was crazy was Brian McNulty. *And Sherone*, Heather reminded herself. *Don't forget good ol' Sherone*. She frowned as she thought about her best friend. If it hadn't been for Sherone, none of this would be happening, because she never would have gone to Magda Prokash's that night and they never would have summoned . . .

The Diet Pepsi can clinked against Heather's front teeth. Her heart started beating hard and fast. She looked around her bedroom, suddenly aware that the house stood silent and empty, waiting. It was not a good idea to say the name, she knew, not even good to think—

(AZGAROTH)

Heather choked on a mouthful of Diet Pepsi, some of it dribbling out her nose. She wiped at her face, trying to push the name from her mind as her anger at Sherone dissipated like smoke in the wind. It was not really Sherone's fault anyway. Heather knew that. Sherone had tried to keep her from stepping outside the circle. Sherone had even gone to Magda to get help. Sherone was her friend. She wanted to help. But she couldn't. Not even Magda, the great and powerful witch, could help. They both believed in it, the reality. But there was nothing they could do to stop—

(AZGA—) *Stop it!*

Brian believed too. But all he could do was wash her Suzuki Samurai, if he did that. He had promised to come over on Sunday morning and here it was Sunday morning already. Heather glanced at her bedside clock. 8:20 A.M. *He's already forgotten about it,* she thought, licking some donut crumbs from the corner of her mouth. *Either that or Kurt's out after his ass and he's hiding somewhere.*

That was probably it. Kurt went after him and Brian ran. It would be the smart thing to do. But Brian didn't act like someone who frightened easily. He had stood up to Magda Prokash that night, had tried to get her to stop—

(AZGAROTH) *STOP IT!*

He had been the first to tell Heather what really happened that night, after her best friend Sherone had lied about it. And he was the one who had insisted on the Sunday morning date, even after she warned him about Kurt.

Heather tossed the Diet Pepsi can into a wastebasket. She lay back on the bed and stretched out across the cool sheets. She wriggled out of her U2 T-shirt. There were small purple bruises on her nipple where Kurt had pinched it. Kurt was such a bastard. Brian wouldn't be like that. He'd be gentle with her. Somehow she knew that. The thought of it gave her a tiny shiver of erotic anticipation. Then she frowned and pulled the sheet up over her nakedness. She couldn't start seeing Brian now, not seriously, not while she was still going with Kurt. *Maybe I can keep him as a friend,* she thought, warming to the possibility. *He'd make a good friend.* But it would never work. Guys were either dates or pains in the butt. You couldn't keep one just as a friend, no matter how much you liked him.

She was back at Diablo, on the main dance floor. It was crowded, as usual. But everyone was naked. Dark smoke whirled across the large room, driven by dry, scorching winds. Distant fires burned through shifting smoke. Music screeched from loudspeakers like stuttering sirens. *Eeeee—eeeee—eeeee—eeeee—* Troy Taylor danced naked with Paige Benson. Magda Prokash stood naked on a tabletop, withered breasts hanging down from her chest, vulva shaved and gaping. Heather watched all this from up close and far off, drifting over the dance floor like a miniaturized Goodyear television blimp, seeing everything, touching no one.

Then she was lying naked, spreadeagled on a long bar top. Paige Benson and Belinda Leonard, grossly fat in her pimply white nakedness, held her wrists down. Her ankles were held down by Andy Metz and Troy Taylor. Troy stuck his tongue out at her, making obscene licking and sucking sounds. Tamara Devon knelt over her, Giorgio perfume rich and cloying as the scent of dead men's flesh. She pulled on Heather's bruised nipple with her long, black-nailed fingers. Equal parts pain and pleasure jolted through Heather's body.

Kurt stood over her. But he was not quite Kurt. His

penis extended huge and throbbing before him, dripping discharge the color of bloody pus. He bent down close to her, and as he did, his face . . . changed.

The lower jaw dropped and pushed out. Long, pointed teeth rose from within. The shape of the whole head became elongated, reptilian. The eyes narrowed into slits. The nose flattened back into two gaping holes. Hands curled into misshapen claws. Hooked talons sprouted from splayed fingers.

Heather screamed.

In the distance, a bell began to ring.

She woke up screaming, arms and legs thrashing out wildly in all directions. She tumbled off the edge of the bed, catching herself just before she hit the carpet with her head. She hung there, half in bed and half out, gasping for breath, her naked body slick with sweat, the sheets soaked through. The bell was still ringing in the distance. Dread gripped her as she lifted her head, damp hair plastered to her face, expecting to see the dream continue into the real world, like the last time, bringing with it the thing that had been Kurt.

The bell continued to ring.

Heather recognized it as the doorbell. *Shit,* she thought, the back of her throat aching from the tension of the dream. Maybe if she didn't answer it whoever was ringing would go away. Then she remembered Brian and his promise to stop by and wash her car. She glanced at the bedside clock. 10:48 A.M. She had been asleep for more than two hours.

"Coming!" She pushed herself up off the floor and into a sitting position on the bed.

She grabbed the U2 T-shirt, sniffing her nightmare sweat. *Jesus!* she thought, wrinkling her nose. *I stink!* The doorbell rang again, several times in succession. *All right, all right,* she thought, and pulled on the U2 T-shirt. Then she climbed into a pair of shorts and ran barefoot to the front door.

She recognized Brian through the distorting fisheye

lens of the security peephole, but she asked over the intercom, "Who is it?"

"Jehovah Witness!" Brian called back, leaning up against the peephole until one eye filled the lens. "Open up in the name of the Lord!"

Heather opened the door and leaned back seductively against the doorjamb. "What if I don't want to buy a Bible?"

Brian's mouth fell open. The sight of Heather Roberts clad only in a thin, clinging T-shirt and tight white shorts would have left any red-blooded American boy at a loss for words, even if he wasn't in love with her.

He cleared his throat. "We wash cars, too."

Heather laughed, blue eyes sparkling. Then she stopped suddenly, looking behind Brian for Kurt's red Porsche 928e or Troy Taylor's black Nissan 300 ZX.

Catching on, Brian said, "Not to worry. No sign of the axman or his buddies."

Heather frowned. "It's not funny."

"Do I act like it is? Listen, it's my life on the line." Brian stepped over the threshold, looking around. "Nice place. We can sell it fast. Two weeks. Guaranteed. Or your broker's fee cheerfully refunded." He turned to her. "You wouldn't have anything to eat, would you? Every time I come to Encino I feel starved. Must be all the fast money."

Heather smiled at him. "I thought you came by to wash my car. Now I have to feed you too."

"Not very much," he admitted. "And not very good."

Heather sat on the tailgate of Hyung-Joon Kim's faded red Toyota pickup and watched Brian wax down her dark blue Suzuki Samurai jeep. She had helped him wash it. Sort of. Actually she squirted him with the hose and started a great water fight, suds and spray flying all over the driveway, both of them shouting and laughing, her chasing Brian with the hose. Then Hyung-Joon Kim came running up and told them to stop it because they were getting water on his garden tools in the back of his pickup. Heather told him to go fuck off and Hyung-Joon Kim started jabbering excitedly in Korean. Brian stepped in as peacemaker. He apologized to Hyung-Joon Kim and calmed Heather down and the whole situation defused itself in a matter of seconds. Heather knew that if it had been Kurt instead of Brian, Hyung-Joon Kim would have got the shit beat out of him. Not that he didn't have it coming, in Heather's opinion. But she liked the way Brian had taken over so smooth and easy and together and made everything real chill. She liked that a lot.

She liked Brian too. He was sort of funny-looking when you thought about it, with his skinny, gangly arms and legs and his sharp nose and lank dark hair and that intense, concentrated look he got whenever he was doing something, whether talking or waxing a car like he was now, applying the wax in a thin, even coat, not missing any spots, taking as much meticulous care with it as he would with a physics experiment. Funny-looking all right, by ordinary standards. But Heather thought he looked great. She felt comfortable around him, totally relaxed, even in awkward situations, like when they were both soaking wet from the hose, laughing about it, and Heather realized suddenly that she didn't have on a bra under her damp, now almost transparent U2 T-shirt and Brian realized it too. If it had been Kurt, there would have been a lot of leering and cheap jokes. As it was, Brian looked, liked what he saw, blushed, and Heather blushed too. And that was it.

He makes me feel . . . happy, Heather realized, with something like shock. It had been so long since anyone or anything made her feel happy, truly happy, that her eyes started to mist over.

"Soon's we get it all covered," Brian explained, continuing to apply the wax, "we wipe it off and buff it down and then we're done. And then it's time to eat again!" He looked up and grinned. "I don't know why, but waxing cars always makes me feel *starved*. Must be the chemicals in the wax or something."

He moved around to the other side of the small Suzuki jeep, closer to where Heather was sitting on the pickup's tailgate. She reached out a bare foot and touched Brian on the back of his leg. "Brian . . ."

"What?"

"Do you think what happened to me that night . . ." Heather stopped and stared down at her bare thighs on the rusty tailgate. "Do you think it could keep *on* happening?"

Brian stopped. "Depends."

She leaned forward. "On what?"

"On what really happened. I saw what happened. The lights and all that shit. I don't *know* what happened."

"Brian!" Heather said impatiently. "They called up a demon." (AZGAROTH) *Stop it!* "It . . . had contact with me, *touched* me. Something."

Brian looked up. "That's been happening again?"

"Sort of." She hesitated. "I guess."

"Want to tell me about it?"

She shook her head. She hadn't told anyone about the horrible dreams, about what happened at the turnout with Kurt. She couldn't.

Brian went back to his waxing. "If you don't want to even tell me what happened, how can I tell you what I think about it?"

She was silent for several minutes, then said, "Sherone gave me an amulet to wear. She said it'd protect me."

"Has it?"

She shook her head. "I haven't been wearing it all the time. I—" *I wore it once and almost got killed in my own bathtub.* She looked up at him, blue eyes filling with tears. "Brian, something's coming after me. I'm scared. I am really scared."

Brian put down his waxing sponge, a dead serious look in his dark brown eyes. "Maybe we better check out this amulet. After I finish the car and after we eat."

Brian was sitting on the black leather couch in the

231

white-carpeted living room playing with the VCR remote control while he waited for Heather to come back from her bedroom and show him the amulet she was so nervous about. He fast-forwarded through the dialogue scenes from *Top Gun* to get to the good stuff, filling the huge seventy-two-inch Mitsubishi big screen with barrel rolls and power dives and other screaming high-altitude acrobatics. He got so wrapped up in it that he didn't even notice Heather until she stepped between him and the screen.

Then he noticed her.

She was wearing one of those Darling Rio string bikinis. Two patches of pale blue rayon barely covered her oversize nipples, while down below a skimpy triangle of the same material turned into a thong strip in back, leaving most of her buttocks exposed. With her lush, full-breasted figure, she was simply breathtaking, a Playmate of the Year come to sudden three-dimensional life.

The VCR remote control dropped from Brian's numb fingers. He tried to speak, could not.

Around her neck she wore the amulet, the pentagram hanging cold and metallic between her firm pale breasts. In her right hand she carried a rolled-up pair of men's swimming trunks.

"So?" she asked him. "What do you think?"

He found his voice. "The suit's a knockout, Heather. And so are you."

She blushed. "Thanks. But I mean—"

"Does your mom actually let you wear that?"

"Not to the beach," Heather admitted. "But she says it's cool if I wear it at home." *Provided there's no one else around*, Karin had added, but Heather left out that part. "But Brian, what about the amulet?"

He forced himself to look at it. His eyes took on that intense look. "You're not gonna be too jazzed about this, okay? But it looks like a piece of el cheapo crap from some discount magic store."

Heather's eyes narrowed. "If Sherone's *lying* about this—"

"Maybe she's not. You told me it hasn't done zip to protect you. Of course," Brian shrugged, "I don't know what it didn't protect you from, because you still won't tell me."

Heather stared at Brian, feeling very comfortable with him, even in this totally outrageous bikini that she'd never wear in front of anyone else. "Maybe," she said, "I will tell you. Let's take a swim first."

"Like this?" Brian gestured at his own shorts and T-shirt.

Heather tossed him the rolled-up trunks. "These were my dad's. They might not fit just right. You can change in that bathroom down the hall, okay?"

Laughter rang off the concrete walkways surrounding the swimming pool, amplified by splashing water. Brian still hadn't heard Heather's story. When he walked out to the pool, tugging at the drawstring of David Roberts's slightly too large trunks, Heather ran up from behind and pushed him into the water, gangly arms and legs sprawling. She was bending over the side, pointing and laughing at him, when he pulled her in. That was followed by dunking and splashing and squirting people with mouths full of water.

They were stopping to catch their breath, still joking and laughing, Brian out in the middle of the deep end treading water, Heather near the side hanging on to an inflated plastic seahorse, brushing wet red hair back from her face, when she said, "Brian, it's gone!"

"What?"

"My amulet!" She felt her neck. "It was there just a few seconds ago. I *know* it was. Now it's probably at the bottom of the deep end. Shit!"

"Not to worry." Brian shook some damp hair out of his eyes. "I'll go down and look for it."

Brian moved more gracefully underwater than he did out of it. He skimmed along the bottom of the pool using a modified frog kick, scanning the aquamarine cement for any sign of the amulet and its black necklace. When his lungs started to hurt he surfaced, took a deep breath, and went down again. He resurfaced about forty seconds later.

"It went down the drain," Heather said gloomily, still hanging on to her inflated plastic seahorse. "I just know it did."

Brian shook his head, spraying water like a wet spaniel. "Swimming pool drains have safety grids. Something that big would've got caught. It's still down there."

The third time under he saw it: lying on the bottom, not far from the drain, the amulet glinting sharply, the necklace itself undulating slowly like a loose strand of kelp. Brian still had enough air left. He kicked downward, feeling the pressure build on his eardrums as he neared the drain. He reached out for the necklace and pulled it and the amulet toward him. Then he started for the surface.

It hit him like a riptide.

The hand holding the necklace with the amulet was snapped back so hard it nearly broke off. Brian was dragged back rapidly through the water to the drain, sucked in toward it like a leaf in a whirlpool. His hand slammed down against the drain grating, bruising his wrist. He lay twisted on his back, water rushing into his nose as he stared up at the surface, impossibly distant now.

He had lost air when he was jerked back down to the drain. His lungs started to burn, aching for oxygen. He tried to pull his hand away from the grating. It stuck fast, as if held by a powerful magnet. He let go of the amulet. The necklace stayed wrapped around his fingers. He pulled hard at his hand, jerking his shoulder until he almost dislocated it.

Brian did not panic easily. But he was starting to now. The pain in his oxygen-starved lungs became excruciating. He looked up through the water at Heather's graceful legs as she kicked languidly now and then, floating on her inflated plastic seahorse.

I'm going to drown down here, he thought, his brain starting to scramble, *and all because—*

Because a demon was trying to kill him.

Brian grew desperate. He knew that in another few seconds his body would take over from his brain and he would open his mouth to breathe in water. He tore at the black necklace twisted around his fingers. He had read of animals gnawing off their own legs to escape from traps. If he had been wearing a sharp knife then, he would have cut off his trapped hand at the wrist.

He felt the blackout coming over him as he glanced up toward the surface one last time. Heather was underwater, trying to swim down to him. Clouds of bubbles floated up from her mouth as she released air from her lungs. But she was kicking wrong and was still only a few feet below the surface. As the blackout washed over him, Brian could see her face far above him, tense with fear.

Suddenly, his hand came free. He clawed his way up to the surface, rushing toward the air. The ascent seemed agonizingly long and slow, the surface hovering up there like the insubstantial ceiling of a dream.

He gasped as he broke surface, drawing in almost as much water as air. He coughed water from his lungs and moved to the side of the pool where he clung like a drowned rat, choking and gasping for air.

Heather came splashing over to him, a panicked look on her face. "Brian! Are you okay?"

He nodded, still choking on the water in his lungs.

"What *happened?*"

He coughed again. "Got your amulet."

"I thought you were drowning! Your face turned all *red!* You looked like your hand was caught. Would you *please* tell me what happened?"

Heather moved in close to him, hanging on to the side of the pool, her inflated plastic seahorse drifting loose out in the deep end. Her barely covered breasts pushed up against Brian's naked shoulder. The slick feel of wet skin against wet skin shot through him like an electric current. He turned toward her. Her breasts crushed into his chest. The things that happen when healthy young bodies come close together started to happen. Neither of them turned away.

"I'll tell you what," he said.

"What?" she asked, voice barely louder than a whisper.

"I'll tell you what happened to me down there if you tell me what this," he lifted the amulet, beads of water dripping from the black cord necklace like blood, "didn't protect you from. Okay?"

She said nothing.

Their faces were so close together now they could feel the heat of each other's breath and the world was silent, except for the sounds of their breathing, their hearts beating, breast to breast, and the echoing slosh of water against the concrete sides of the pool.

chapter 25

floater

Maureen O'Connor Magnusson roared up Camino de Oro early Sunday evening in her white Rolls Royce Silver Shadow, honking impatiently at an Acura Legend that dawdled along in front of her.

When the Acura did not speed up or pull over, Maureen floored her gas pedal and moved out and around the slower car, shaking her fist at the driver, then cutting back dangerously close in front of her. The driver of the Acura, a sedate gray-haired lady with a Shih Tzu dog beside her, took no notice.

"Rude people!" Maureen muttered to herself.

The world was full of them. Even her daughter Karin, her first-born darling child, was becoming one, hanging up on her own mother, cutting her off in mid-sentence like one of those snippy young girls they hire as clerks in the finer stores these days.

I won't allow myself even to think about it, she decided. *It will only raise my blood pressure if I do.*

But ever since Karin had hung up on her this morning, Maureen had thought of nothing else. She poked at it, like a doctor probing a wound. She fussed with it, like a breeder grooming a show dog. She agonized over it, like a broker tracking a stock. It was the best kind of insult, one that demands vengeance in the form of interference. Karin's hanging up like that, Maureen reasoned, was her way of crying out for help.

Lord knows she needs it, Maureen thought. Karin's life had not been running smoothly—had plain not been working out—ever since she and Davie separated. Maureen liked to think of it that way, as a separation rather than a divorce. Davie had been running desperately from one woman to the next, trying to find someone to soothe the hurt of losing Karin. But the only cure for it was to get them back together again. Maureen knew that much, even if her son-in-law the doctor did not. Her Davie was a one-woman man at heart, appearances to the contrary, and his one woman was her darling daughter.

Karin, Maureen knew, wanted to get back together again too, in her heart of hearts, deep down inside. All that kept her from realizing it was the damn musty museum. If she'd just leave those faded paintings and broken statues alone for a few weeks, she'd start feeling and acting like a real woman, instead of some mousy librarian. No real woman could resist Davie Roberts. Besides, who did Karin have to take his place? Certainly not Cap Courtney's poor scrawny pup Brett. Maureen smiled sadly at the idea. Poor Brett, he might make a respectable dinner date for a fund-raiser banquet. But he wasn't the kind of man women dream of, like Davie.

If it's so obvious to me, Maureen thought, swerving around a double-parked Volvo, *why can't she see it?*

Maureen had never been patient with people slow to see things her way. But she knew that Karin was made of weaker stuff than her mother. Davie went chasing after some little tart and it threw Karin into a tailspin. She dumped the man of a lifetime and went slinking off to her damn musty museum like a nun burying herself alive in a convent. *God help her if she ever has to face a real challenge,* Maureen thought, *because she'd fall to pieces.* It was sad to think that she and Harald had produced two such wishy-washy, spineless little girls as shy Karin and flighty Annie. *God knows I love 'em both*, Maureen thought, gunning the Rolls up a steep hill, *but I wish they'd show a little more spunk!*

Like Heather.

Maureen smiled as she thought of her beautiful redheaded granddaughter, the favorite, if the truth be told, of all her children. Heather had spunk. You could sense it, just looking at her. She had more spirit at sixteen than Karin had at over twice that age. Heather was up to the big challenges of life, even if her mother was not. Heather was polite and modest, as became an innocent young girl. But if you pushed her, she'd push back twice as hard. Just thinking about it made Maureen's heart glow with a fierce Irish pride.

The first thing she saw on pulling into Karin's driveway was Heather's Suzuki Samurai, its dark blue body glistening with a newly polished coat of wax, reflecting the headlights of the approaching Rolls like a mirror. Parked beside it was Hyung-Joon Kim's faded red pickup.

Maureen frowned as she came to a stop, setting the emergency brake. She would have to have a talk with that little Chinese gardener of Karin's. They were good workers, but you had to keep them in line. Service vehicles were always parked at the servants' entrance, if the house had one, in the street if not, but never, under any circumstances, in the main driveway, ever. Let something like that get started and the next thing you know they're addressing you by your first name.

Maureen walked briskly up to the front door and rang the bell, noting as she did so the dying plants Hyung-Joon Kim had uprooted near the house. *Let them park in the main drive*, she thought, *and their work starts going to hell.* She rang the doorbell again, holding the button down longer this time. No lights were on inside. *Probably have them on at the back of the house*, Maureen thought. But the absence of visible lights bothered her. She frowned as she rang the doorbell a third time. Both Karin and Heather liked lots of light at night. Dark houses frightened them.

After getting no response from the third ring, Maureen lost her patience. Doubling up her fist, she pounded on the front door, rattling it in its hinges.

"Karin Marie!" she called out in a loud, carrying voice. "Heather Michelle!"

No sounds came from the dark house. A car horn honked several streets away. Across the street a front door opened.

Maureen pounded with renewed fury. "*Karin!*" she shouted. "*Heather!*"

A dog barked. Maureen turned and saw the silhouette of a neighbor standing framed in the lighted rectangle of his front door across the street.

Nosey old fool! Maureen thought irritably, and resumed her pounding.

Still no answer.

The hell with it! she thought, angrier than ever now with Karin, angry because Karin kept screwing things up, even simple things, like being home on Sunday evenings so you could open the door when your only mother stopped by for a nice surprise visit.

Maureen went around to the back of the house, being careful not to step in any of the mud holes made by Hyung-Joon Kim when he dug up dying plants. Karin was probably sitting there by the pool right now with all the lights turned off around her, except for the underwater pool lights, just sitting there by the water's edge, brooding. She had always been like that: moody, introspective, rather be alone than with people who loved her.

Maureen was almost at the back of the house and ready to enter the interior courtyard surrounding the swimming pool when she noticed it.

The smell.

She sucked in her breath as the rush of nausea hit her. She had always hated bad smells, dirty, disgusting things.

But this was worse than bad. It made the small hairs on the back of your neck stand up. There was a sweet, putrid undertaste to it, like pork that had rotted in heavy syrup.

Maureen stopped and put a hand to her stomach. The smell was making her physically ill. Had Karin forgotten to have the pool cleaned? She knew that Karin's pool boy, Esteban, came by once a week. If he ever got sick or took an infrequent vacation, Javier or Ramón or one of Esteban's other brothers or cousins would come by and clean the pool on schedule. But what was causing the smell? Had some animal fallen into the pool and drowned? Bubbling up into a soggy mess after several days beneath the white-hot Southern California sun . . .

Maureen stifled a belch. The rotted pork taste seemed to come right up her throat. She swallowed hard to keep the bile down.

Aware now of a thumping inside her chest, she walked on toward the pool, badly frightened. Something had happened in the swimming pool, something bad. There was no doubt about it. *Please, God, let Heather and Karin be all right*, Maureen prayed fearfully.

She entered the courtyard at the back of the house, high heels echoing off the cement sidewalk. All the lights were off, inside and out, except the underwater pool lights, which gave the still water a ghostly aquamarine look, like a vision shimmering in darkness.

The smell was worse than ever now, heavy and raw. Maureen started breathing through her mouth. She noticed the heat then, humid heat, like when you step out of a shower and the air is so moist you can hardly breathe. But the California night was not hot or humid. *Why in the name of God,* Maureen wondered, *is she keeping the whole pool heated like a damn spa?* Maybe that accounted for the horrible smell. The water was too hot and the moss, or whatever grows on the sides of swimming pools, was in there reproducing like rabbits. Maureen moved quickly toward the pool.

Toward the source of the smell.

She was still a good ten feet from the water's edge when she saw the dark shape floating near the side, drifting with the slow current caused by the pool's circulation system. It was a man's body, arms and legs spread-eagled, facedown, the classic position for a drowning victim.

Maureen's heart kicked into overdrive, beating so furiously she thought she'd faint. The first thing, she knew, was to see if the poor soul, God help him, might still be alive. She stepped to the edge of the pool, sweat beading her forehead as the air seemed to grow hotter and more humid. She knelt down, being careful not to lean too far out over the water, and reached a hand toward the drifting corpse. She caught the sleeve of a faded denim jacket. Breathing through her mouth, she lifted the head and shoulders up out of the water.

The dead face of Hyung-Joon Kim stared up at her. It bore little resemblance to the way it had looked in life. The elderly Korean gardener had been boiled alive, like a lobster in a pot. His skin had turned beet-red and puffed up until the face was a doughy mass, the features almost indistinguishable. His eyes had crusted over like poached eggs until they burst, dribbling aqueous humor down over the boiled face. Blood had oozed out from the ears, mucus from the nostrils, undigested food from the mouth.

As Maureen held the boiled glistening head up out of the water, a large slab of cheek tore loose from the face like a slice of well-done pot roast. It dropped into the swimming pool with a liquid *plop*.

Maureen uttered a hoarse groan and let the boiled head fall back into the water. It fell with a noisy splash. Drops of swimming pool water, scalding hot, flecked Maureen's face and hands, burning like carbolic acid. She screamed, pitifully at first, like a frightened child, then full-throated. Then she vomited. She had never vomited in public before in her life. It was a spontaneous, uncontrollable reaction. She leaned over the pool and vomited into the boiling water.

And began to lose her balance. *Christ save me!* she prayed silently, too terrified to scream, knowing that if she fell into the pool she too would be boiled alive, screaming for mercy as the hot water cooked her flesh.

She fell back hard onto the cement and rolled away from the pool, tearing her designer dress, already splattered with vomit, her dyed red hair flying loose, eyes wide with terror as she stared at Hyung-Joon Kim's boiled corpse drifting slowly once again with the current of the pool's circulation system.

chapter 26

monolith

"But don't you see?" Heather's voice caught. "It's like it's . . . part of me."

Brian looked up at the dark metal structure looming overhead and said nothing.

When Heather finally tried to tell him about the dreams—the whirlwind in her bedroom, the near-drowning in her bathtub, the kidnapping of the child—she had trouble even getting started. Brian suggested they go for a drive somewhere in his Mazda RX-7, anyplace away from the house, away from where the dreams with their horrors had happened.

Brian drove carefully and well, unlike Kurt—no popping clutches, no laying rubber at stoplights or challenging other drivers, *Road Warrior*-style. They drove along Mulholland past Encino until the pavement ran out and the road became a gravel washboard. Brian drove slowly. Heather moved in closer to him and started, hesitantly, to talk about the dreams. During the bad parts, he put an arm around her. She did not move away.

They finally pulled into what looked like a fenced-off, weed-choked vacant lot. Faded signs warned against trespassing on U.S. Government property. In the middle of the lot stood a hulking metal monolith, an imposing array of steel beams and girders rising stark into the night sky. Close by, on a steep hillside, grew a weathered old oak tree, its wide-spreading limbs gnarled and twisted like crippled arthritic fingers. On the ground beneath the tree was a large fire-blackened circle, a reminder of how quickly fires can burn and spread in the dry, scrub-covered hills and canyons of Southern California.

But the precision of this circle made it look as if the fire that burned it had been deliberately set and carefully tended.

The whole area, Brian told Heather, was an abandoned Nike ballistic missile station with an underground silo and launching pad. Built during the Cold War in the late '50s, the station had gradually fallen into disuse with the passing of time and technology. In later years it had become a secret meeting place for the enactment of magic ceremonies, Wiccas and Sabbaths, with its ancient oak tree and the dark monolith raised to dark gods.

Scrawled unevenly across one of the girders of the monolith in blood-red paint were the words HAIL SATAN!

He had brought her here, Brian explained to Heather, because this was a Passageway, one of the magic corridors connecting this world with the Other World. If they were going to get rid of the demon, take him out of Heather's life once and for all, they would have to do it at a Passageway, a place where he could not play tricks with dreams and sound effects.

A place where he would be forced to appear before them in his true form.

"But how can I get rid of something that's *me?*" Heather asked, her voice trembling.

Brian turned from his silent scrutiny of the black monolith. "It's not you. It's just using you."

Heather shuddered. She had changed into a sweat shirt and jeans before they went driving, but she was still cold.

Everything in this witches' trysting ground was cold, dark, unsettling.

"You can't run away, Heather." Brian paused, seeing the real fear in her eyes. "You've got to stand up to it."

"How?" She started crying. "It's a *demon!* A *monster!*"

Brian nodded sympathetically. "Whatever. It's still subject to certain laws and restrictions, okay? I mean, maybe not natural laws, like in physics, because it's not really part of, you know, nature. But—"

"What can we *do* about it, Brian?"

"Send it back to wherever it came from."

Heather was so surprised by this answer that her mouth fell open and she just stood there, open-mouthed, staring at him.

"I'm serious," Brian assured her. "It didn't get here by accident, you know. Somebody called it up, summoned it. Deliberately." *Magda did*, Brian thought, *after I warned her not to.* "Now that it's here, it's having a great old time smashing up stuff and scaring the shit out of you, like some asshole poltergeist. But if it can be called up, it can be sent back."

Heather wiped at a tear. "You think so?"

Brian nodded. He did not know for certain, but it seemed probable, and he had learned that probabilities have a way of turning into realities, if you give them enough room.

Heather was silent for a few moments before she asked, "You going to help me with this?"

"Sure."

"You won't leave if it gets bad?"

"Not unless you tell me to."

"What if I don't tell you to?" She put a hand on his shoulder. "Ever?"

"Then I guess I won't leave. Ever."

They stood there facing each other beneath the dark monolith, Heather's hand resting lightly on Brian's shoulder. He put his arms around her, very slowly, and drew her closer to him. Their lips touched, softly, then once again. The embrace tightened. Heather locked her arms around Brian. Their mouths met hungrily, tasting deep of each other.

Heather broke away. "We better stop."

Brian kissed her again. "Why?"

"Because we just better."

He kissed her again. "If you say so."

Heather blushed in the darkness. "I think we better."

He kissed her again. "Whatever you say."

"Why don't you just fuck her and get it over with?"

Heather let out a startled scream. Brian turned toward the mocking voice.

Kurt Pritchard stood close by, watching them, his face tight with fury, eyes glittering like blue diamonds. Behind him stood Troy Taylor, Andy Metz, Garth Wiggins. *Followed us here with their lights off,* Brian thought, trying to make some sense of it even as his heart started rattling out of control.

"Kurt—" Heather began.

She never got to finish. Moving with the precision of a SWAT team, Kurt grabbed Brian while Troy Taylor and Andy Metz held on to Heather. Brian tried to defend himself. He landed a hard kick to Kurt's upper shin, missing the kneecap he was aiming for. Kurt cried out in pain and threw his fist flat into Brian's face. Brian turned to deflect the blow. It smashed into the side of his head, making his ears ring. Blood trickled from his nose.

Kurt hit him again. Brian thought he felt a tooth break loose. Blood filled his mouth. Kurt hit him again, full in the chest this time. Brian staggered. He could hear Heather screaming for Kurt to stop, but she sounded a long way off. Kurt hit him again, below the belt. Brian doubled over. Kurt hit him on the back of the neck. Brian's knees buckled. He sprawled out across the hard, dry earth. A booted foot caught him on the right side below the ribs. Kurt was wearing heavy-duty hiking boots with steel-reinforced toes. A second kick connected with the rib cage. Brian cried out, twisting on the ground.

Another boot hit the back of his head, shoving his face into the dirt.

Then he was yanked to his feet and dragged backward, legs trailing limply across the hard ground in front of him. They threw him up against one of the steel girders of the monolith, pinning his arms back behind him and over the girder in a do-it-yourself crucifixion. Andy Metz and Garth Wiggins held Brian's arms. Troy Taylor hung on to Heather.

Kurt limped up to Brian, favoring his kicked shin. "I told you to stay the fuck away from her." Kurt was breathing heavily. "You were *warned,* McNulty. Twice." He spit into Brian's face. "Motherfucker!"

The spittle dribbled down Brian's face. He returned Kurt Pritchard's stare without blinking.

"This time," Kurt pulled out a knife from a sheath at the back of his belt, "this time we're gonna *help* you remember, cocksucker." The blade was eight inches long and almost three inches wide, with an ugly serrate edge. "This time we're gonna make sure you don't forget."

"*Real* sure, asshole," Garth Wiggins hissed in Brian's ear, soft enough so Kurt could not hear.

Kurt waved the serrate blade slowly in front of Brian's face. "We're gonna carve the warning on your fuckin' dick!" Kurt glanced down contemptuously at Brian's crotch. "And if there ain't enough room on that little pussy sticker of yours ..." Kurt looked up, his lips pulled back in what was meant to be a smile. "Why, we'll just *make it fit!*"

"Kurt!" Heather screamed at him, breaking partially free from Troy Taylor's grip. "*Stop* it!"

Troy swore at her under his breath and pulled back hard on her arms. Heather yelped with pain, then lowered her head, long red hair falling down over her face.

Brian said to Kurt, "Let her go."

Kurt Pritchard brought the point of the serrate knife up against Brian's left cheek. "You don't tell me *nothin'!*

Under*stand?*"

Brian held Kurt's stare. "She hasn't done anything. It's not her fault. Let her go."

"Don't tell me what to do, you *fuckin' shit!*" Tiny flecks of froth appeared at the corners of Kurt's mouth. The knife trembled in his grip.

A tight smile crossed Brian's face. "Why so hot, Kurt? You've got your big knife. Afraid to use it?"

The blade nicked Brian's cheek. He tried not to wince. Blood trickled down his cheek, collected in his collarbone hollow and began soaking slowly into his T-shirt.

Kurt pulled back the blade, several of the serrate teeth smeared lightly with blood. "I'm gonna cut your fuckin' prick up into hamburger!" Kurt's chest was rising and falling, the muscles in his neck standing out like cords. "When I get done, you'll have to piss through a fuckin' straw! Under*stand?*"

"We'll save a piece for your girlfriend here," Troy Taylor called out. "We'll make her eat it!"

Harsh laughter broke from the onlookers. Troy let out a rebel yell. Brian ignored the laughter and the jeers, ignored the blood still trickling sluggishly down his cheek and the pain only now starting to burn along the shallow cut. He tried to ignore everything and force himself to think.

He was running out of options. They had them where they wanted them. The missile station was isolated. No L.A.P.D. cruisers patrolled this area regularly. The nearest house was beyond screaming distance. He could try to talk with Kurt and the others, try to reason with them. But they didn't want to talk. They weren't interested in doing a deal. Brian knew what they wanted.

He made himself look over to where Troy Taylor was holding Heather, pinning her arms back, hurting her unnecessarily. He could see where Troy's fingers were digging into her shoulders as he pulled her in close to him, whispering something in her ear, rubbing his crotch up against her backside as he did so. He could see

Heather's face, empty of expression, lips tight with suppressed rage.

He could see everything.

Brian felt a rough jerking at his waist as his belt was unbuckled and his pants pulled down. Kurt brought the serrate knife edge in close. The onlookers whooped with animal delight. Kurt's ugly grin slid backward into his skull. The knife edge moved in closer.

Brian could see everything. And do nothing.

Heather saw nothing, except for the monolith, rising dark and hideous above the four boys clustered at its base. Everything else was washed out by a red haze of rage and hatred—everything except the dark monolith, terrifying in its immensity as it began to take on shape and movement like a living . . .

Something.

The cold steel of the serrate blade touched Brian's naked genitals. He twitched. Kurt grinned at him, his smile sliding sideways off his face.

"Hey there," Kurt crooned. "I ain't even *started* cuttin' yet! But maybe I'll start with your balls. Yeah! Yo' *balls*, boy!" Kurt's glittering blue eyes turned up like a light on a rheostat. "Yeah! I'll start by makin' you sing fuckin' soprano!"

Troy Taylor let out a high, loonlike laugh. *"O solo mio!"* he screeched, breaking off with crazy laughter. "Singa, Brian! Pleasea singa the songa for us! Singa *O solo mi—eeeeeeeeeeeeeeeeeeeeeeeeeeeeeeeeeeeeeeeeeeeeeeeee—*"

At first, no one noticed anything. Troy's shrill, out-of-tune high note kept rising like a siren. Then it stuck there, wailing long and forlorn over the empty landscape the way the missile station's emergency warning system had been originally designed to do. It was only when Troy kept on screaming, without stopping even to draw a breath, that Kurt turned—Andy Metz and Garth Wiggins and Brian turning with him—

And saw.

Troy was no longer holding Heather. He stood apart

from her, trembling violently like some kind of holy man filled with the divine ecstasy, his arms outstretched as if in adoration.

But it was not adoration that made him scream.

His hands and arms were being systematically flayed. The skin rolled back from his fingers and wrists like peeling paint on a burning wall. The receding skin revealed blood-soaked muscles and nerves and bones. Blood fell like rain from the flayed hands, spotting the dry earth below. Fingernails popped loose. Bones began to break and detach themselves. Nerves and muscles shriveled up into twisted, useless things.

And still the flesh receded, rolling up Troy's forearms. Bones cracked open. Living marrow twitched and dropped out. Troy kept on screaming. The excruciating pain crushed his face into a monkeylike visage, red and wrinkled, eyes bulging from their sockets. His voice squealed like a rusted hinge.

Heather stood back from the horror, flecks of blood on her sweatshirt, her face a pale mask, only the eyes revealing any reaction to what was happening before her.

Kurt turned back, his own eyes wild with fear and hatred. With one hand he grabbed Brian's testicles, hard, making him cry out. With the other he pushed the serrate knife edge up against Brian's throat, the sharp teeth pressing into sensitive flesh.

"What the fuck you doin' to him?"

Brian spoke with difficulty. "Noth—"

"Stop it now!" Kurt's voice broke like a frightened girl's. *"Stop it now, McNulty!"*

The monolith began to tremble. The huge dark structure started to vibrate with a low, resonating hum.

Andy Metz looked up. "What the fuck—"

Garth Wiggins dropped his hold on Brian's arm and backed off, his mouth open, eyes watery with fear. Kurt's own crazy blue eyes had gone almost transparent with a deep, primitive terror. He remembered how his Porsche had trembled at the turnout, vibrating until the windshield cracked. He remembered what he had seen, there in the black fog. He had put it from his mind after the terror passed, letting it all wash out like bad drugs. But now it was coming back, the vibrating, the goddamn fucking vibrating again. And Troy getting his arms chewed up like he stuck them in a rotary lawnmower blade. Only this was happening right in front of his eyes and there was nothing he could do about it.

Nothing at all.

Kurt's mind was skidding out of control, onto the treacherous soft shoulder of insanity. He wanted to stick his fingers in his ears, stuff them up with dirt and rocks, anything to block out Troy's hideous, tortured screams. But instead he was standing there holding on to McNulty's nuts like some kind of fucking homo. He decided then to go ahead and really do it. *Just do it!* he told himself. Cut McNulty's throat open and save Troy. McNulty was the one causing it, the one behind everything, taking away Heather, doing a *Texas Chainsaw Massacre* number on his best buddy. Kurt didn't know how the fuck McNulty was doing it, but that didn't matter now. He was doing it. Cut his throat open! Saw off the motherfucker's head! Bury it like a fucking vampire's heart! Stop it!

"Stop it!" he shrieked at Brian, pulling back the serrate knife arm's length to strike. *"Stop it! You fucking son of a bitch!"*

Kurt Pritchard's whole body twitched violently, jackknifing backward. The huge knife flew out of his hand. A guttural groan issued from his throat, the kind of gut-wrenching sound you make just before you vomit up everything you ever ate. The groan became a roar, a mindless blind bellowing. Kurt began tearing at his shirt, ripping it open, baring his chest, which was pumping in and out like a terrified bird's.

The ripping sound came then, like the tearing apart of heavy canvas or bound books. Kurt's entire torso, from neck to crotch, split open along a jagged line down the middle of his chest. Blood sprayed out into the night, spattering Brian and Andy Metz and Garth Wiggins and the dark metal of the monolith. Lungs and heart and other vital organs tore loose from inside Kurt's body and flopped down onto the dry dust of the empty field. Intestines jerked out of the gaping cavity in long, bloody strings. Blood gushed from his open mouth. Then Kurt's whole body began to collapse in upon itself, crumpling up like a deflated plastic doll. The bloody husk floated rather than fell down to the ground.

Heather, who could smell the heavy stench of Troy Taylor's disintegration still like the rank odor of rotten meat held under her nose, lost the battle with her heaving stomach when she saw what was happening to Kurt. Hot, burning vomit forced its way up her throat. She spit it out into the weeds. More followed.

Garth Wiggins cowered near the monolith, whimpering with fear. Andy Metz stepped forward to help what was left of Kurt, then stopped, then stepped forward again, moving like a run-down automaton, unable to get any kind of fix on what had just happened.

And was still happening.

A shattering scream broke from Garth Wiggins. Brian could smell the smoke and something worse burning beneath it before he turned to look. Andy Metz stopped and turned around, a look of pure dread on his tear-streaked face.

Garth Wiggins was on fire, burning from the top down like a human torch. His greasy long hair blazed like a gasoline-soaked rag. His eyeballs burst into flame. His shirt caught fire, then his jeans. He staggered forward in agonized slow motion, wrapped in flames like a stuntman in a disaster movie. Andy Metz stumbled after him, shouting something hoarse and unintelligible.

"Heather!" Brian shouted to her. *"Get back!* Don't let him touch you!"

Heather, still nauseated from her vomiting fit, fell back as Garth Wiggins streaked past, the heat of his flames rushing over her like the hot wind at Magda Prokash's. *Like the whirlwind in my bedroom,* she thought numbly, and then all at once she knew that Kurt was dead, horribly dead, killed for her by—

Don't say it! (AZGA—)

Don't even think it! (AZGAROTH)

A sound like thunder boomed inside her head.

Terrified, she looked up.

And saw the huge red eyes against the night sky. Saw some kind of dark and gigantic face, hovering insubstantially above the monolith, almost part of it now, like a nebulous, smoky extension of the dark metal itself. They were not human eyes. It was not a human face. But it had come for her.

Through the Passageway, she thought mechanically to herself. *Down the Passageway from the Eternal Darkness beyond space, beyond time.*

It had come for her and done her bidding.

It had served her.

Heather knew then a fear so deep and ancient that it seemed to obliterate her. She became a window for the Fear, a dark glass through which it looked out of the Passageway and down into the world of the living.

She started to scream. She put her hands to her face and fell to her knees on the hard, dry earth, screaming. Beside her, Troy Taylor writhed helplessly, groaning softly, two stubby, bloody fins sticking out from his shoulders like the malformed limbs of some monstrously deformed child.

Brian stumbled over to her, pulling up his pants, his head swimming with the horrors. He dropped to his knees beside her and put his arms around her.

"It's okay." He kissed her repeatedly, desperately. "Everything's okay."

A scream rose from the far end of the abandoned missile site where a patch of weeds burned around Garth Wiggins's motionless body. Andy Metz pulled off his own burning shirt, which had caught fire while he was trying to help the other doomed boy. His hands and chest were burned, but he was not on fire. He wept brokenly over the smoldering body of Garth Wiggins.

Closer to Heather and Brian, what was left of Kurt Pritchard's body hissed and smoked as if someone had poured carbolic acid over it.

"Brian." Heather looked up at him, her eyes dulled with shock. "This time . . ." Her voice trailed off. "Did you *see?*"

Brian nodded, blood still oozing from his cheek.

He had seen everything.

chapter 27

homecoming

Karin's white Jaguar XJ6 whined through its gear changes as she took the sharp curves of Camino de Oro, the Golden Road that Leads to Home. She had told Heather she'd be back sometime by the middle of the afternoon. *And now it's*, she glanced at her gold Rolex, *almost nine P.M., for Christ's sake*. She was getting as bad as Heather about coming home late. *No way to set an example*, she thought.

But there were extenuating circumstances. Her show, the Barringer's show, The Forgotten Gods, was opening in a matter of days. Now that she was down one person, Dodge Andrews, thanks to Milton Bromley's interference, there were things that simply weren't getting done, things that had to be done by someone if the show was going to open on time. *And it will open on time, by God*, she promised herself, gripping the Jaguar's steering wheel, *Bromley or no Bro*—

She almost hit the roadblock before she saw it.

It stood there blinking monotonously in the middle of Camino de Oro—on-off, on-off—like a railroad crossing sign. Karin hit her brakes. The Jaguar swerved slightly as it squealed to a violent stop, throwing Karin back hard against the leather seat. She leaned forward over the steering wheel, heart thumping, trying to see past the roadblock.

A small crowd stood scattered across her front lawn: two paramedics, at least six police officers. Neighbors from the entire block had come over to see what was going on. One officer stood guard at the front door. Two others kept onlookers from working their way into the backyard.

Heather! Karin thought, shaking herself out of an open-mouthed trance. *She fell into the pool and drowned!*

Karin jumped out of the Jaguar and started running across the street and over the curb and up onto the grass and straight into the arms of Brett Courtney.

"Whoa!" He grabbed hold of her, turning halfway around with her as she stumbled to a stop. His smile was tense. "Where've you been? We called the museum—"

She twisted loose from his grasp and ran for the pool. She heard David Roberts calling to her. Her sister Annie yelled something. Karin kept running, thinking, *Christ, what happened? She can swim!*

This time a cop stopped her.

She almost ran him down. But he stepped nimbly to one side and brought her to a halt with a quick, almost casual move.

"No one's allowed back here right now," he said.

"I *own* this place!" Karin gasped, breathless from running.

"There's no use getting—"

"If you don't let go of me right now," Karin warned, "I'm calling the police!"

To his credit, the officer did not laugh. But the absurdity of it hit Karin all at once. Her right hand, clenched in a fist, dropped to her side. Tears filled her eyes.

"What happened to my daughter?" she asked quietly, feeling suddenly weak and sick.

"It's okay, Mike." A Hollywood-handsome man

somewhere in his middle forties with a dark blue pinstripe suit and a head of styled black hair nodded at the officer restraining Karin. "Mrs. Roberts?" He extended his hand to Karin. "I'm Captain Becker."

She ignored the hand, craning her neck to look around him toward the pool. "My daughter, Heather . . ."

Becker's blue-gray eyes turned cautious. "That's something we'd like to talk with you about, if you wouldn't mind, Mrs. Roberts. Do you know where Heather is?"

A look of mingled terror and bewilderment crossed Karin's face. "She's not here? In the pool?"

Becker paused. "No one's in there right now. Water temperature's come down a bit. Still pretty near boiling, though."

Stunned, Karin looked at the pool again.

She noticed the body then.

It lay stretched out beneath a dark gray tarp beside the pool. Several officers stood around it. A forensics expert took Polaroids. Karin started to walk slowly toward the gray tarp, her hand stretched out in front of her.

"I wouldn't lift that up, Mrs. Roberts," Becker called to her. "He was cooked for quite a while."

Karin shuddered, asking in a low voice, "Who is it?"

"Gardener who used to work here." Becker walked over to her. "Elderly Korean party by the name of . . ." Becker consulted a note card. "Hyung-Joon Kim."

Karin raised a hand to her mouth.

"Know anybody who might have hated him enough to do something like this?" Becker asked.

Karin shook her head. "He—" Tears filled her eyes. "I can't—" Her voice caught and stuck.

"Quit picking at her, damn you!" boomed a loud female voice from the far end of the pool.

Heads turned in that direction.

Still disheveled from her own recent ordeal, designer dress torn and stained, dyed red hair tangled, Maureen Magnusson nevertheless stared straight at Captain

Becker with fierce disdain. At her side stood Harald Magnusson, his own blue eyes somber, one hand laid gently on his wife's shoulder. He whispered something to her.

She tossed her head, glaring at Becker. "You've already asked me those questions, Captain Becker. Over and over and over again! Not that *I* mind. I'm tough!" She raised her chin defiantly. "But now you're starting in on my darling daughter, the child of my own heart."

"Mrs. Magnusson," Becker began.

"What can she tell you? She wasn't even here when it happened! *I* found the body!"

"We understand all that, Mrs. Magnusson," Becker said evenly. "But your daughter owns the property and was the employer of the deceased. We'd just like to ask her a few questions."

Harald Magnusson tried once again to whisper something to his wife.

She brushed him aside. "What do you want from her? A confession? A public admission of guilt? 'I did it! Take me away!'" Maureen raised her hands as if handcuffed. "Is that what you want, Captain Becker? Would that make you happy?"

Becker sighed. "Mrs. Magnusson—"

A piercing scream tore through the nerves of everyone near the pool. Karin backed away from the boiled corpse of Hyung-Joon Kim, half-exposed by the turned-down dark gray tarp. An officer hastily covered up the disfigured corpse again.

"Forensics about finished with that?" Becker asked one of his officers.

"Yes, sir."

"Then get it out of here."

Maureen went to where Karin stood with her hands over her face, weeping. She embraced her daughter.

"There, there," she crooned. "It's not a very pretty sight, is it? Don't even think about it, honey girl. They're taking it away now. You should have seen it when *I* found it." Maureen shuddered delicately. "But your poor gray-headed mother's a pretty tough old bird."

Karin broke free from Maureen's embrace. "Where's Heather?" she asked Becker.

He looked up at her. "That's what we'd like to know. Her car's still in the driveway. She planning on having anyone over this afternoon?"

Karin shook her head, still taking in the fact that Heather's jeep was there and she was not. "She's been kidnapped, hasn't she?"

Becker paused. "I wouldn't go quite that far. Not yet, anyway."

A muscle twitched in Karin's cheek. "Then where is she?"

Before Becker could answer, his attention was distracted by two officers trying to restrain Brett Courtney and David Roberts from entering the pool area. Behind them, Annie and Sam Newmar peered out anxiously.

Becker turned to Karin. "Friends? Or family?"

Karin swallowed. "Both."

"Mike," Becker called to one of his officers, "let those people through. But keep the rest of the rubberneckers out of here."

David Roberts pushed forward with a self-important stride. Brett Courtney charged past him, rushing up to Karin, then stopping short, waiting for her to recognize him. She was still staring at Captain Becker.

"Has anyone administered a sedative to either of these women?" David demanded, indicating Karin and Maureen.

Becker looked at him. "We've got paramedics."

"I'm not a paramedic," David informed him. "I'm a doctor of medicine."

"He's also my daughter's husband," Maureen added.

"Ex-husband," Brett said, politely, but loud enough to be heard.

David turned to him. "And just who are you?"

"A friend of Karin's."

David forced a smile. "Well, friend, you've just stepped into the middle of a very private family matter, okay? So maybe you better step on back a few paces."

"Maybe you'd better consult your divorce papers, Doctor. Your community property rights may have lapsed."

David's lip curled. "Listen, you—"

"Cut it out!" Annie Newmar ordered, frowning beneath her blond curls. "Both of you!"

All the fear, frustration and rage that had been building up inside Karin, growing worse with every run-in with Bromley, every argument with her mother, every deadlock with Heather, every fencing match with Brett or David—all of it came bursting out at the impassive, rock-steady Captain Becker.

"Where *is* she?" Karin screamed at him. "Where's my *daughter?*"

"Mrs. Roberts, if we knew that—"

"Why don't you know?" Maureen demanded, jumping onto the dogpile with relish. "Isn't that what we pay you for? To know things like this? She's only sixteen years old! She was here this morning! How far could she have gone?"

Annie put a hand on her sister's shoulder. "Cheer up, K.M. They'll find her. Okay?"

Karin shook her head, tears trickling down her cheeks. "Annie . . ."

"Captain!" One of the officers came walking quickly across the pool-side cement, holstered .38 service revolver jiggling at his side. "Just got this in. They found her."

"*Where?*" Maureen cried.

"Is she hurt?" Karin asked.

Annie leaned forward. "Can we pick her up?"

David asked, "Is she in shock?"

"QUIET!" Becker bellowed, startling everyone into absolute silence by the unexpected loudness and anger of his voice. "You'll get your turns. One at a time." He turned to the officer. "How is she?"

"Okay, far as they know. Guy with her seems okay too."

"Where'd they find 'em?"

The officer told him.

"What the hell were they doing out there?"

"Don't know. Few miles back down the road, at the old missile station, they found three bodies. Pretty bad shape. Flayed, chopped up, set on fire."

Karin felt the earth shift beneath her feet. She put a hand to her forehead. Her knees buckled. Annie screamed. Maureen cried out. David shouted something.

Brett caught Karin as she toppled forward.

chapter 28

PROGNOSIS

Dr. Norman Goldstein, thin-faced, somber-looking, somewhere in his late thirties, stepped into the private waiting room at Cedars Sinai. He carried a medical clipboard and several stacks of computer printout paper.

The private waiting room had been reserved by Maureen Magnusson at no small expense. Karin looked up from where she sat in a straight-backed chair, face pale, cigarette burning in one hand. Most of her immediate family was there with her: Maureen and Harald Magnusson, Annie and Sam Newmar, all trying to mask their concern. Five-year-old Adam Newmar wandered around the room, looking at windows too high for him to reach. David Roberts and Brett Courtney sat stiffly on opposite sides of the room, avoiding even looking at each other. On occasion, when their glances met accidentally, they locked stares with open malice.

As Dr. Goldstein stepped into the room, Maureen rose to her feet, clutching a handkerchief. "Well?" she asked in an unsteady voice. "What is it?"

Dr. Goldstein cleared his throat.

"Tell us!" Maureen demanded, anxiety giving way quickly to indignation. "We can take it! Whatever it is.

Just *tell* us! *Don't try to protect us from the truth!*"

Harald Magnusson got to his feet, put an arm around his wife's shoulders and, with uncharacteristic firmness, pulled her right back down into the seat beside him. He glanced at her sternly, but did not say a word.

Dr. Goldstein smiled at Karin with a professional doctor's smile, tight-lipped and more than a little grim, the one that says this hurts him more than it hurts you. "Karin?"

"Yes?" Her voice sounded raw. She was trying hard to keep herself under control. But her eyes started filling with tears because, damn it, you could tell from the look on his face that the news was no good.

"Karin," Dr. Goldstein said quietly, "we have almost all the test results back now."

She nodded. A sob escaped her.

"There are some others we could still run. But I don't think they'd tell us anything new."

So what's wrong with her? Maureen wanted to scream at the damned waffling fool of a doctor. You could almost see the question written in block letters across her face. She would have asked it, had Harald Magnusson not given her another stern glance. She dropped her eyes and began dabbing at them dramatically with her handkerchief.

"We've done the important tests," Dr. Goldstein continued quietly. "We know what's wrong now."

Karin swallowed another sob. "Wh-what?"

"Nothing. She's fine."

Maureen's mouth fell open.

David Roberts half rose from his chair.

Annie and Sam Newmar smiled at each other.

Karin looked up at Norm Goldstein, her eyes swimming with tears. "What do you mean?"

"I mean she's okay. Still a bit upset from . . ." Norm Goldstein hesitated diplomatically. ". . . whatever happened out there. But in all other respects, she's a perfectly normal, healthy sixteen-year-old girl."

"What about . . . drugs?" Karin managed the forbidden word.

"Nothing. Not a trace. Not even amphetamines."

"What about EEG's?" David asked, suspicion clouding his green eyes. "CAT scans?"

"All negative, Dave."

"You checked them?"

"The specialists did. Twice. I checked again."

"What about the possibility of cerebral bleeding?"

"Dave." Norm Goldstein smiled again, a tired one this time. He knew how difficult it was to be a doctor when your own child was the one at risk. "We looked for everything. Tumors. Aneurysms. Blood clots."

"Chronic intracranial pressure?"

Norm Goldstein nodded. "Everything."

There was a sudden deflation in the room, something you could feel like an unexpected drop in temperature. They had all been waiting for hours, preparing themselves for the worst. Extensive hospitalization for Heather. Painful, even dangerous therapy. Risky surgery. Possible institutionalization. Even death, slow and terrible, stretched out over endless hospital vigils while her young life leaked out, drop by drop, through plastic tubing . . .

And now this. Nothing.

Nothing to account for what had happened.

For what she said had happened. She had tried to explain in words that did not match up or make sense, disconnected images, whimperings of fear. Through it all, there was a look of terror in her pale blue eyes like darkness in the eyes of someone who has looked into an abyss—

Deep into the abyss.

David slammed his fist against a padded armrest. "There's something wrong with her, Norm. Just because you can't find it now doesn't mean it won't show up later."

Norm Goldstein's tired smile vanished. He knew that it

was Dave's daughter and that any man is a father first, a doctor second. But he also knew that David Roberts was pulling one of the real asshole tricks of medical one-upmanship: world-famous heart surgeon, saver of lives and talk-show celebrity, versus the aw-shucks, plain-folks family doctor out of a Norman Rockwell painting, standing there scratching his head, trying to figure out just what might be wrong with the little girl.

It took all Norm Goldstein's professional experience to keep his voice level. "I'm only a doctor, Dave. Not a fortune teller. You and I both know there can always be something wrong—even something seriously wrong—that just won't show up, no matter how many tests are run, until it's farther along. But for right now, *there's nothing physically wrong with your daughter.*"

Karin's heart felt like it was going to burst. It hurt to draw even a shallow breath, and her face felt tight as a clenched fist. She wasn't going to start crying now. She couldn't. If nothing was wrong with Heather physically, then something was wrong with her mentally. Very wrong. Karin knew she would have to be strong enough to help her daughter face whatever that was.

She bit her lower lip to stifle a sob.

David's chin had a belligerent tilt as he stared at Norm Goldstein. "So now it's time for a little psychotherapy, eh? A little counseling. The long road to nowhere."

David Roberts loathed psychiatry and its practitioners. As a surgeon, he could actually fix something that was wrong. He could make a patient better, sometimes against a patient's will. He was the one in control, the doctor, not the patient. With psychiatry, it was fifty-fifty at best whether the patient would ever be cured or not. And even when it did work, the cure was a joint effort by patient and psychiatrist, a patchwork compromise. Except for the newer chemical therapies, it was all a lot of highclass voodoo.

"Some kind of counseling or psychotherapy might be appropriate," Norm Goldstein suggested cautiously.

"But I think Karin should make that decision." He nodded to acknowledge her.

Thanks, Norm, she thought, grateful that there was still one doctor left in Los Angeles who respected her opinion.

"I know Karin wants the same thing I do," David said, "and that's what's best for Heather. If that means psychotherapy or counseling, fine. If it means some kind of brief institutionalization . . ." David shrugged. "If necessary, that's fine too."

Karin paled at the thought of locking Heather up in an institution, even the Beverly Hills kind with color television and scenic views. She started to object.

Maureen beat her to the punch. "Davie." She rose to her feet. "I love you like a son. But damned if I'm going to let you or anyone else drag my beautiful red-headed granddaughter off to some funny farm when all she needs is a little rest." Maureen cast a sharp glance in Karin's direction. "And some love and attention."

Karin's eyes widened with hurt, then turned hard.

David, aware that he had marched into a minefield, began his retreat. "Maureen, darling, I don't know if it's even necessary to consider institutionalization at this stage. That's for Bernie Rausch to—"

"Who brought Bernie Rausch into this?" Karin demanded, turning all her anger at her mother toward David.

Annie looked worried. "Easy, K.M."

David stared at his ex-wife. "Bernie Rausch, for your information, is one of the finest psychiatrists—"

"In whose opinion?" Karin snapped. "Yours?"

"Look—"

"She's *my* daughter!" Karin shouted at him.

"And just when did she become *your* daughter? Did I get written out of her life in the divorce order?"

"You think your monthly installment payments make you some kind of real father?"

Harald Magnusson, a pained look on his face, took his pipe out of his mouth and tried to say something. But it was already out of control.

"I know I'm her father!" David was shouting now, green eyes blazing. "But sometimes I wonder if you're her real mother!"

A steady male voice said, "Why don't you quit trying to bully her, Doctor, and just let her make her own decision?"

David turned in open-mouthed astonishment to where Brett Courtney had risen from his chair, earnest indignation clouding his patrician good looks.

"Who the hell asked you?" David advanced on him. "This is a family argument, asshole!"

"Dave," Norm Goldstein warned him, "we're in a hospital, remember?"

"You used to be family," Brett said reasonably, looking David straight in the eye as they squared off. David was taller and heavier than Brett. But Brett was in better condition and unafraid. "I think I have just as much right to be called family now as you do," Brett continued. "Maybe even more."

David swung on him. It was a clumsy right hook that clipped Brett across the left jaw and bounced off his nose. Brett hit back with a quick punch to the solar plexus that left David doubled over and gasping for breath. David charged, slamming his head into Brett's stomach. Both men went down, sprawling across the thick-pile light beige carpet of the private waiting room, knocking over the Danish modern end table and designer lamp, spilling copies of *Architectural Digest* and *Vogue* and *Forbes* and *People.*

Sam Newmar, Norm Goldstein and Harald Magnusson rushed to separate the two men. Maureen screamed louder than her daughters, louder than anyone else in that madhouse of a waiting room. No one paid her any attention. Adam Newmar stood wide-eyed as he watched the adults wrestle on the floor, just like Hulk Hogan versus André the Giant.

Norm Goldstein and Sam Newmar pulled Brett and

David apart. A trace of blood trickled down from Brett's nose. He breathed fast but easily, ready for more. David's mouth was bloody and one eyelid was starting to puff up. He breathed with difficulty, letting air whistle out through his clenched teeth.

"You motherfucker," he wheezed at Brett.

"Davie!" Maureen gasped. "There are *children!*"

"I'm gonna sue the shit outta you!"

"Go ahead." Brett smiled a bloody smile. "You haven't got a leg to stand on. You swung first."

"Fuck you, asshole!"

"Davie!" Maureen glared at David, then Brett. "And *you*, Brett Courtney—"

"*Stop it!*"

They all turned to Karin, who stood white-faced, trembling with fury as she stared at David and Brett.

"If you want to fight," she said, her voice breaking, "because it's more fun than wondering what to do about Heather, then please go do your goddamn fighting somewhere else."

There was a stunned silence.

Then the faces moved in on her. Concerned faces. Sympathetic faces. Caring faces. Harald. Norm. Sam. Annie. Brett. David. Maureen. They all wanted to show Karin that they really cared, that they understood.

A whole roomful of compassionate faces.

Karin had never felt more alone in her entire life.

Chapter 29

GUINEA PIG

About a year ago, when she was a sophomore at Severy Academy, Heather had been required to take part in a biology experiment involving a rat. At first she was disgusted by the idea. But after a while she realized that he looked more like a mouse than a rat, with his soft white fur and sad pink eyes. She started to feel sorry for him as he hopped around his cage while student experimenters zapped him with random jolts of electricity. Her teacher told her she was acting silly about it because the rat, being a rat, didn't feel things the same way they did. But Heather couldn't help wondering what it would be like, locked up in a cage, frightened and miserable, tormented by powerful creatures beyond her comprehension or control.

Now she knew.

The police found them when she and Brian were still in shock from what had happened at the monolith. They shone a powerful light inside Brian's Mazda RX7, blinding them. They made Brian lie spread-eagled across the hood while they frisked him for weapons.

They kept asking questions, hammering away as though they thought maybe it would all start to make sense if only they were rude enough. Brian tried to explain things in that careful, exact way of his. But he was just some punk kid out cruising unauthorized with a rich doctor's daughter and they didn't want any more noise out of him. They kept asking Heather for her version of what had happened. But how could she tell them about . . .

Inhuman red eyes gleaming high above the monolith.

Fear looking down at her through the long Passageway from the very edge of the universe.

Power exploding out of the darkness, killing Kurt, killing Troy, annihilating them . . .

Power that did her bidding.

Heather opened her eyes. Her face was damp with sweat. The nurse on duty in her private hospital room was reading a paperback novel. Heather swallowed. It seemed to stick in her throat.

After the police finished with her, after that good-looking older guy had talked with her, Captain Becker, who was really pretty nice for a cop, they turned her over to the doctors. She told them she was fine, just a little tired. All she needed was some sleep. But her dad told her, in that faky doctor voice of his, that they had to make sure first that nothing was wrong.

Something was wrong all right. But the doctors would never find it. They poked her full of needles, x-rayed and CAT-scanned her, made her drink barium, rigged her up with electrodes, just like the poor rat in her biology class. And like the student experimenters, the doctors, specialists all, studied their computer printouts and compared notes and discovered nothing they did not already know. They tried to smile and be nice. Dr. Goldstein, her family doctor, was very nice. It was just that they did all these things to her, some of them embarrassing, all of them painful, and they still didn't know what was wrong or how to fix it.

And it needed fixing. Heather tried not to think about it, because whenever she did she got so scared she wanted to start screaming and never stop.

Kurt. Troy. Some kid she didn't even know. Poor old Hyung-Joon Kim. All dead . . . and all her fault, every one of them. Heather choked back a sob. The nurse on duty looked up from her paperback novel.

Heather wanted to talk with Sherone about it. Not that Sherone knew what to do. And her great witch pal Magda Prokash couldn't care less. But Sherone was the one who had started all this. Maybe, Heather stubbornly clung to the hope, maybe she could help end it. Besides, Sherone was her friend. And right now she needed a friend.

But she was allowed no visitors. There was a phone in the room that could not make outgoing calls. All incoming calls were blocked at the main switchboard.

We want you to rest, honey, her dad had explained, smiling down at her as he held her hand, *and we don't want you wearing yourself out talking on the phone all the time.*

They allowed her to go for a walk twice a day. But the only place she could walk to was one of the private waiting rooms where her mom and dad and grams and granddad and Aunt Annie and everybody looked at her like she might die any minute on them and spoke in low voices and sort of crept around with sick smiles on their faces until she wanted to shout at them that she was fine, totally okay, just great.

Except she was possessed by a demon who killed people for her when she got angry enough with them.

And whenever that thought sliced into her mind like a burning razor's edge, she became so terrified that she started crying and the nurse took her back to her room, leaving everyone just standing there looking at her like she was going to die.

Heather shuddered beneath the hospital blanket. She needed someone at least to hold her and tell her everything was going to be all right. But there was no one. A tear rolled down her cheek.

The knock at the door came then.

The nurse got up to answer it, smoothing down the seat of her uniform with one hand, holding her place in the paperback novel with the other. She opened the door only partway, confronting whoever was out in the corridor.

Heather leaned forward to hear.

". . . sorry, sir. Only family members are allowed in right now."

The visitor in the corridor mumbled something Heather could not catch.

The nurse turned to her. "Got a cousin named Adam Newmar?"

"Yeah." Heather nodded. "Sure."

"He's here to see you." The nurse opened the door all the way. "Remember the time limit. Fifteen minutes and not one second more."

Heather wiped the tear from her cheek, wondering why Adam would want to visit her and why Uncle Sam would bother to bring him by. Adam was a cute little kid and all, but he was only five and . . . *the Perfect Blood Offering.* Heather heard the awful voice again, rasping inside her head, saw the chalk-white face with the rotting teeth, the death's-head from her nightmare. She shut her eyes.

When she opened them again, she almost cried out in surprise.

Brian sat down on the edge of her bed, Kurt's knife scar stitched tight across his left cheek, a twelve-rose bouquet in one hand. "Dear cousin Heather! We've been so worried about you."

Heather shook her head in astonishment, a slow smile spreading over her face as she realized that this was the one she needed to see—Brian, not Sherone—but she hadn't even hoped for it because guys were never there when you really needed them. "Brian . . ."

"Adam! Adam! Your dear cousin Adam. It hasn't been that long, has it, cousin Heather?" Brian turned to the nurse, handing her the rose bouquet. "Put these in some water for us, would you? Thanks so much."

As the nurse walked off with the flowers toward the bathroom, Heather leaned forward, blue eyes bright with excitement. "How'd you even find me here?" she whispered.

He whispered back, "It wasn't easy. But vee haff our vays. Listen, we better talk fast." Brian glanced at the bathroom where the nurse was running water noisily into a pitcher. "I don't think the Bride of Frankenstein's kidding about her fifteen-minute limit."

"It's so good to see you!" Heather squeezed his hand. "What've you been doing?"

"Talking to cops and dodging lawyers."

"Lawyers?"

"I am getting the ever-lovin' shit sued out of me. By Kurt Pritchard's pop and Troy Taylor's old man. But the worst is that pervert, Garth Wiggins, the reformed dog fucker. His dad's some congressman and he's trying to make a federal case out of it."

Heather looked bewildered. "I can't believe their parents are actually suing you."

"Believe it. Probably suing you, too. You just haven't heard about it yet."

Her eyes widened. "Suing me?"

"Heather, three guys died out there. And not from old age. The cops had to scoop 'em up with shovels."

Heather dropped his hand and shuddered. "Brian, don't."

"The cops have this funny idea someone may have killed them. And they're right. Only they think we're the ones who did it."

"*I* didn't kill them!" Heather shouted.

Brian put a finger to her lips. "Not so loud, okay? Neither did I. But trying to convince the cops that a demon did is going to be a very tough sell, believe me."

Heather reached up and touched his hand to her lips, kissing it softly. "Hold me, Brian," she whispered.

He put his arms around her.

"You two kissin' cousins watch yourselves," the nurse said. "Lots of AIDS goin' around these days."

Heather blushed. Brian turned and nodded gravely to the nurse. "I'm just consoling her. We're a very close family."

"Yeah, right." The nurse gave them a hard stare before returning to her paperback novel.

Heather rested her head on his shoulder. "Brian, I am so scared. What are we going to do?"

"Whatever it is, we better do it fast." He stroked the hollow of her back. "Before it turns on you."

Heather pulled away from him. "It doesn't hurt me. It . . ." The words caught in her throat. "It hurts other people."

"So far. But it's not like having an attack dog on a leash. The thing's dangerous, okay?"

She stiffened. "I know what it can do, Brian."

"You think you do. So far it's only sent you on an out-of-body nightmare trip, rattled Kurt's Porsche, boiled your gardener, split Kurt in half, chewed up Troy's arms and set that dog-fucker on fire. No big deal."

She swallowed, fighting back the sudden nausea in her stomach. "You don't have to get ugly about it."

He raised her chin until they were staring each other in the eye. "This thing is not your friend, Heather. You think you control it, just a little, but that's part of its game. To make you think that."

Heather frowned. "I never *made* it hurt anyone!"

"I never said you did."

"Besides, you're wrong. It doesn't hurt anyone unless . . ."

"Unless you really hate them?"

"You're putting words in my mouth!" She turned away from him, angered by his remark, but terrified by the idea that maybe she did want those people to be killed, to die horribly. "I'm not talking to you anymore, Brian."

"Fine. I'll do the talking. But you've got it all wrong,

you know. Your pet demon doesn't just go after people you hate."

Heather glared at him. "Quit calling it that!"

"Remember when it tried to drown me, at the pool drain? When I was down there diving for your demon-buster amulet?"

Heather stopped, her mouth open, as the images came rushing back of Brian trapped and struggling underwater, his hand stuck to the drain grating, her trying to swim down to him . . .

She looked up. "God, you're right. I completely forgot about that. It tried to kill you."

Brian shrugged. "Just a little practical joke, really. As we both know by now, it can do a lot more than that once it gets excited." He paused. "And it can do it to you, too."

Heather's face turned pale. Tears welled up in her blue eyes.

"Hey, it's not that bad." Brian brushed away some of the tears. "There's always a way out of something. Somehow. We'll find it." He drew her close to him.

"What the hell are *you* doing here!"

Heather shrank back into her hospital bed. Brian jerked around toward the thundering male voice, his nerves more shot than he liked to admit after what had happened at the monolith. David Roberts stood glaring at him from the open doorway of the hospital room, one eyelid still puffed up from Brett Courtney's fist, an enormous bouquet spilling out over the crook of his right arm like something that had fallen off the back end of a float in the Rose Parade.

"Who the fuck let him in?" David turned to the nurse. "You?"

The paperback novel dropped from her hands. "Doctor, he said he was her cousin."

"He said *what?*"

Brian stood up. "Sir, I can explain."

David turned on him. "The only thing I want you to do, sonny boy, is get out of here. Okay?"

"I had an obligation to come here, sir."

"I don't give a shit what you had or didn't have! Get the fuck out of here! Now!"

Heather sat up in bed. "Daddy, please . . ."

"You stay out of this!" He turned back to Brian. "You going to do what I say?" David took a threatening step toward him. "Or do I have to throw your sorry ass out of here?"

"Daddy!"

Brian stood his ground. "I think—"

The windows in the hospital room started rattling. The floor underfoot began to vibrate with a low, resonating hum.

The nurse got to her feet. "Earthquake, Doctor."

A glass of water on Heather's bedside table was rattling like a castanet, liquid sloshing up over the brim. It started to move, skidding across the table, slowly at first, then faster, like a car pulling out from a light. It shot off the end of the table, flying through the air toward David Roberts. He raised his right hand. The glass struck his forearm and shattered, splashing water into his face and down his shirtfront.

Heather screamed.

The fluorescent light overhead hissed and sizzled. A long tube broke loose and fell to the floor, narrowly missing David and Brian. The floor continued to vibrate and now seemed to be tilting slightly to one side. The door behind David slammed shut, making him jump.

Then it all stopped as suddenly as it had begun.

"Oh God." Heather covered her face with her hands. "Oh my God."

David, water dripping from his face, stared at Heather, then Brian, then down at the shattered glass on the floor.

The room was silent now, except for the sound of Heather's weeping.

chapter 30

night callers

Sherone sat watching the rain come down.

Sean O'Casey, the red-haired Irish setter, sat beside her thumping his tail on the living-room carpet, whimpering mournfully. Sherone reached out a hand and patted him. The rain had been coming down all afternoon. It was almost evening now. The rain drizzled across the living-room window in twisted patterns as Sherone stared out into the gathering darkness. Her reflection stared back at her from the window glass, the sharpness of the image increasing as the light slowly disappeared and the rain continued to fall.

Sean O'Casey trotted over to the front door and scratched at it, whimpering.

Sherone turned from the window. "Come on away from the door, Seanie baby. Dad and Glenda won't be back for hours."

They had gone to a show at some gallery on La Cienega. The photographer mounting the exhibition was a friend of Wes Livingston's. Sherone had stayed home alone because gallery shows bored her and because the aging trendies who attended them made her sick.

And because she was still trying to get in touch with Heather.

She had called the damn hospital all afternoon. The bitch at the reception desk wouldn't let her through to Heather's room and wouldn't take a message. She had called the house and left messages on Heather's mom's answering machine, but no one called back. She called Heather's grandmother's house, even though Sherone thought Maureen Magnusson was a real Geek from Geeksville. The phone was answered by some frosty English-butler type with a rod up his ass who said Madame was away for an indefinite period of time.

Sherone called Brian McNulty, the original world-class Geek from Geeksville, but his mom was not accepting any calls on the advice of her attorney.

The only person she had not tried to call was Magda Prokash.

But Magda had been calling her.

The first time Glenda answered the phone and took a message: *Magda wants to see you, at The Heart, now.* The second time there was a message on the answering machine. It was brief and ugly. Magda had even mentioned . . . the name, right there on the tape. Sherone erased the tape and turned off the machine. The third time Sherone picked up the phone herself, hoping it might be Heather. When she heard Magda's voice, she hung up the phone and disconnected it.

Sherone shivered and walked over to check out the thermostat. Seventy-eight degrees. It didn't feel like it. She was cold clear through, chilled to the very center of her heart. She shivered again and sat back down on the couch, pulling an afghan up around her. Sean O'Casey came over and lay down at her feet, looking up at her with mournful dog eyes.

It had gone too far this time, whatever it was. White magic. Black magic. Sherone no longer cared about the fine distinctions. It was out of control, way out of Magda's or anybody's control. Sherone remembered the eleven o'clock news story with the three body bags in the middle of a burned-out field, all that was left of Kurt,

Troy, that other kid.

She shivered again.

This time it was so pronounced that a muscle cramped in her back. She winced with pain, swearing sharply. Sean O'Casey licked his chops and whimpered. Then, unaccountably, his ears pricked up. His whole body took on that tense, hostile look dogs get when they hear a strange sound. He lowered his head and growled.

Sherone stopped rubbing her cramped muscle. "Whatsa matter, baby? Hear somethin'?"

The dog growled again, a warning growl this time, deep in his throat.

A knot formed in the pit of Sherone's stomach.

Damn stupid dog, she thought, *probably smells a cat or something*.

Her own reflection continued to stare back at her from the living-room window, and beyond that the darkness of the night. She wished she had drawn the curtains when it started to get dark, the way Glenda was always reminding her to do. She started to get up and close them.

Sean O'Casey leaped to his feet suddenly and began barking with full, deep-throated barks. He trotted over to the front door, still barking.

"Shut up!" Sherone yelled at him, her nerves on edge. "Quit actin' like a jerkhead, okay?"

The dog ignored her and kept on barking loudly, scratching at the front door with his right paw, tail twitching aggressively.

She stepped over to the front door. "Would you just *shut up* for one second?"

The dog kept barking, but there was a new, frightened urgency to it now.

Sherone knew then she was not alone.

It was not a question of hearing things. She could hear nothing above Sean O'Casey's noisy barking and the steady patter of falling rain. But she could smell it—the rough smell of wet leather, the fibrous odor of damp denim. She could also feel the moisture from whatever it was, not far away, water dripping softly off it and down onto the carpet.

Her heart seemed to slow down, then stop. She forced herself to turn around.

He was tall and thin, about her age, maybe a few years older, dressed in faded denims and worn leather, his head shaved bald except for a hank of hair hanging limply down one side of his naked skull. He stared at her with empty eyes. A pentagram, the five-sided star, was tattoed across his left cheek, right below a pale gray eye.

Sherone fought back a scream when she saw him, but it came out anyway.

The front door burst open, banging against the living-room wall. Wind and rain swept in from the dark night outside, knocking over a lamp on a side table, ruffling the pages of a magazine. Sean O'Casey's barking reached a frantic pitch, then faded suddenly to a frightened whimper as the dog backed off, tail between his legs, cowering before the figure at the threshold.

Sherone did not even try to hold back her scream this time.

The chalk-white face glistened with cascading drops of water. Seamus Harrach smiled, exposing his mouthful of blackened, rotting teeth. Water from his shapeless dark robe dripped down onto the cheap hardwood entryway. Behind him, Tamara Devon stepped in from out of the rain.

She wore a thin white sheath that had been soaked through and now clung to her voluptuous body like a second skin. Her large dark nipples stood tauntingly erect through the sheer fabric, the outline of a dark triangle lush and provocative below her waist. Tamara stared at Sherone with dark cat eyes, a sly cat smile forming on her face.

Sean O'Casey crouched against the far wall, caught between a growl and a whimper.

Sherone backed off from the sinister trinity: Seamus Harrach, Tamara Devon, the boy with the shaved skull and the Sign of the Beast tattoed below his left eye. "What are you doing here?" she demanded, her voice breaking. "What do you *want?*"

"We want," said the rough voice behind her, "to talk with you."

Sherone gasped, turning toward the voice.

Magda Prokash stood clothed in her damp brown monk's robe, heavy cowl thrown forward over her head. Rainwater dripped from the robe. Her gray eyes burned with a feverish light. Trickles of water dribbled down the gnarled wooden staff in her right hand.

Like blood on a stick, Sherone thought, and she grew afraid.

"Things have happened," Magda said, throwing back her monk's cowl. "Contact has been made."

Sherone forced herself to stare at Magda—anywhere except at Seamus Harrach with his crumbling black teeth and his dead white skin. "You can't just walk in here," Sherone said, some of her confidence returning as she stared Magda down.

"What would you have us do?" Seamus Harrach's voice had an unpleasant edge. "Wait for an invitation? Stand on . . . ceremony?" He smiled another black-toothed smile.

"You never returned our calls," Magda said reproachfully. "You never shared the joyous news with us. We had to find out about it on television."

"You made us think you didn't *care* anymore," Tamara whined. "We thought you forgot about your friends."

"Look." Sherone glanced from Tamara to Magda, avoiding Seamus Harrach. "If you're talking about whatever happened out there at the Meeting Place, I found out about it the same way you did. On the eleven o'clock news."

"But you had warnings." Magda's gray eyes hardened. "You knew contact had been made."

"I tried to tell you, Magda!" Sherone exploded. "I

called you up that day and asked you what to do about it and you said it's nothing, just forget it!"

"You called," Magda said, "about some childish trick with a tarot deck. If you had specified . . ."

Sherone did not listen to the rest of it. Magda was just covering her ass, probably to impress her Dracula wannabe buddy, that warlock what's-his-name. Sherone glanced at Seamus Harrach, then looked away immediately, shuddering. *Christ*, she thought, *he gives me the creeps!*

Magda was still talking when Sherone impatiently interrupted her. "So what do you want from me? I haven't had any contact with . . ." She hesitated.

"Azgaroth," Magda Prokash murmured.

Sherone winced. "Don't say it!"

"Azgaroth," Magda murmured again, her voice caressing it like a hand fondling a knife blade. "Are you afraid, Sherone, to hear us speak his name?"

"I don't ever want to hear that fucking name again for the rest of my life!" Sherone was good and scared now, truly frightened by the presence of the four intruders, here in her own house, and by the unseen presence, growing stronger all the time, of . . . (AZGAROTH). "I didn't have anything to do with it!" she protested to Magda.

"Ah, but you did." Seamus Harrach flashed his rotting teeth at her. "You participated in the original ceremony. You helped raise the great and powerful demon. All of your own free will." The white-faced warlock took a step toward her.

Sherone saw again the Mouth with Sharper Teeth from her horrible nightmare, Seamus Harrach's gaping mouth, and real terror took hold of her. "Stay away from me!" she cried, backing off.

"Your little friend," Magda said, "the Sensitive. She told you about the contact. About the dream journeys. But you didn't tell us, did you?"

Seamus Harrach took another step toward her, his face a bone-white death's-head.

"Get away from me!"

The boy with the shaved skull stepped toward her.

"We're your friends." Tamara Devon moved forward, licking beads of rainwater from her upper lip. "But you don't trust us."

Sherone was backed up against the living-room wall now by the three advancing intruders: Seamus Harrach, Tamara Devon, the boy with the shaved skull and the Sign of the Beast. Magda Prokash stood back, leaning on her wooden staff, observing.

"Leave me alone!" Sherone screamed at all three of them.

Sean O'Casey, startled, leaped into action in defense of his owner, barking fiercely at the intruders, baring his teeth at Seamus Harrach and growling. The warlock raised his right long-nailed hand and pointed it at the barking dog.

Sean O'Casey shifted in mid-bark to a frenzied whining. He curled up on the floor and started batting clumsily with his paws at his face, whining constantly.

Sherone looked in horror from the warlock to her suffering dog, then back to that cold, dead-white face. *"Stop it!"* she ordered him. Then, frantic, she turned to Magda. "Make him stop it, Magda! Please!"

Magda smiled a razor-thin smile. "Please is better. Seamus, enough."

The warlock lowered his right hand.

Sean O'Casey stopped clawing at his face. He lay curled up on the living-room floor, whimpering. Sherone fell to her knees and put her arms around the dog, burying her face in his neck.

When she looked up again, her face was wet with tears. "What do you want from me?" she whispered brokenly.

A gust of rain-laden wind blew in through the open front door.

"We want you to come with us," Magda said.

Seamus Harrach smiled. "Of your own free will."

chapteR 31

confessional

Karin's eyes started to fill with tears as she stared at the priest sitting on the other side of the desk. "Then there's nothing the Church can do."

Father Patrick Michael Donovan folded his hands. "The Church can do many things."

"But you won't do anything to help me."

"Karin." He paused, the office lights reflecting off his wire-rimmed glasses. "There's not much I can do. Not with what you've told me."

Karin leaned forward, a tear coursing down her right cheek. "What do I have to tell you? That some— something supernatural— I don't know what it is! I still have trouble believing it myself. But *some*thing is trying to take my daughter away from me. Trying to hurt her . . . make her hurt other people." This last was said so quietly as to be almost inaudible. Karin wiped the tear from her cheek, and as she did, another trickled down to take its place. "What more can I tell you?"

Father Donovan gave a quiet, patient sigh. This was difficult, truly. He liked Karin Roberts, always had, ever since she was a bright-eyed, dark-haired, inquisitive little girl, the kind of child you look at and say to yourself, *Now that one's going to go far someday.* Karin had gone far, and it had not been easy. Sure she had the money, but she had Maureen Magnusson to go with it, and David Roberts, and then the divorce.

At the time of the divorce, Father Donovan had counseled Karin to go back to David Roberts. As a priest, he had no choice. But he had quietly admired her when she rejected his advice and went on with her life, working at the museum and raising Heather by herself. It takes a special kind of courage to face a difficulty alone. Father Donovan admired Karin for her courage as much as if she had been his own child.

Now he faced his own difficulty: turning her away when she came to him for help.

Of course he was not literally turning her away. He was still offering her the solace of confession and the sacraments, the abiding consolation of the great and ancient Church. But he was refusing to do what she had asked of him. He was not going to take up his shield of faith and sword of the Spirit and do battle with a demon for the immortal soul of Heather Roberts.

Because the demon did not exist.

Except in Heather's imagination.

And now, to a limited degree, in Karin's as well.

"Karin . . ." He began slowly, because it worked better that way when they were upset. "The things you've told me, the things Heather's seen and felt . . ." Father Donovan paused, choosing his words with care.

He doesn't believe any of this really happened, Karin thought, still wiping at her tears, but starting to get angry now. *He thinks Heather made it all up and I bought it like a fool.*

"These are grave matters," Father Donovan continued, "highly disturbing, potentially dangerous. They must be looked into. I'm thankful you came to see me now instead of putting it off."

"I didn't have much choice," Karin said bluntly. "The doctors were no help. I came to you because you're my last hope."

Father Donovan nodded as if he understood. "Our Lord directs our actions to the right end, if we put our full trust in Him. The time was right for you to bring this burden to Him, Karin, and you did the right thing."

Now I have to do the right thing, he thought, hesitating, though he knew hesitation did no good.

He cleared his throat softly. "These upsetting incidents she's been experiencing lately—especially the tragedy at the abandoned missile site—these things must be addressed immediately, Karin. By a competent medical professional, a psychiatrist or licensed psychotherapist."

"We've been to one," Karin said, bristling at the memory of Heather's and her brief visit to the Beverly Hills office of Dr. Bernard Rausch, M.D., Analyst to the Stars.

Bernie Rausch had a short, chunky build that made him look like a dwarf wrestler. Bald on top with fringe on the fenders, he wore a graying beard, gold neckchains, flower-print shirt, white painter's pants, topsiders without socks and the laid-back, goofy grin of someone slightly but permanently stoned. He listened rather absently to Heather's account of what had happened, then grew excited as he outlined ways she could break free from her "crippling inhibitions." By the time he reached nude group therapy, Karin had had enough. She thanked him and they left, with almost forty minutes still to go on their initial hour.

"I can talk with Heather about her problems," Father Donovan said. "I can counsel her. But I can't help her the way a medical professional could."

Karin sat back stiffly in her chair. "You mean you can't give her prescription drugs and shock treatments."

"No, Karin, I don't mean that."

"Father, something supernatural—okay, a demon—a demon is trying to destroy my daughter. That's her only problem. These things are really happening to her. I've seen some of..." Karin stopped, remembering the withered rosebushes and dying grass and Hyung-Joon Kim boiled alive. "What am I supposed to do about it? Nobody else believes in demons except—"

"—except the great gullible Church," Father Donovan finished it for her. "Ghostbusters R US. Call 1-800-XOR-CISE."

Karin blushed. "I didn't mean it like that."

The priest smiled gently. "I know you didn't. I was making some bad jokes at your expense." He sighed. "The Bible does tell about Our Lord casting out demons. At one point He learns a demon's name: Legion. Obviously, the Church recognizes their existence. In that respect, we haven't changed much in almost two thousand years." Father Donovan frowned. "But in another very important respect, we've changed a lot. Unlike our medieval ancestors, we are no longer quite so ready to attribute most of the afflictions of this world solely to evil supernatural powers. That's why we don't waste our time trying to exorcise demons from people disabled by brain tumors or psychiatric disorders, for example. Sick people need doctors, not exorcists."

"Heather's not sick!" Karin insisted.

"How do you know?"

Because if she's sick enough to be making up something like this, I'm not sure I can handle it right now, Karin thought to herself, but she said, "Because something killed those kids and it wasn't Heather. Something killed my gardener, a sweet old man who's been with the family ever since..." At the thought of Hyung-Joon Kim, tears came to Karin's eyes again. She fished around in her purse for a handkerchief.

"I agree with you, Karin," Father Donovan said quietly. "I don't believe Heather would ever hurt anyone intentionally. But, as you point out, someone did. Someone butchered two boys, set a third on fire and boiled your elderly gardener like a lobster in a pot.

Appalling acts of unmitigated evil. Who committed them?"

"A demon," Karin said, her voice muffled by the handkerchief pressed up against her face.

"Possibly. Anything's possible." Father Donovan folded his hands on the desktop. "But not very likely."

"Why not?" Karin's head snapped up, tears glistening in her eyes. "Heather got mixed up with this damn flaky witch cult and they tried to call up a demon and, somehow, they did, because— *I've already told you this!* About what happened to my plants, about what happened to Heather's room that night . . ."

Karin gulped back a sob. "I didn't expect the police or the doctors to take me seriously. But I thought at least you would. I thought you'd understand. But you don't! You don't understand at all!" Karin bowed her head and began to weep.

Father Donovan sighed deeply and passed her a box of Kleenex.

When she finished, he said, "I think I do understand, Karin. But maybe you don't fully understand my position. I have duties to God, to my Church and to you, my parishioners. These duties overlap. I can't take care of you without serving God and vice versa. Do you see what that means?"

Father Donovan took off his rimless glasses and stared myopically but intently at some undefined point in the distance. "It means I can't humor you. I can't say to myself, 'Oh go ahead and tell her what she wants to hear, as long as it makes her happy.' Either I do it right or I don't do it at all."

He tapped the rimless glasses on the palm of his left hand. "You tell me you've got a daughter who's possessed by a demon and you want me to say, 'No problem, my child, we'll just schedule her for an exorcism—how's next Thursday morning sound?"

Karin snuffled. "It's not that simple."

"Nothing ever is. That's the problem. How do we know we're dealing with a demon? And before you interrupt, Karin, let me emphasize that word *know*. How do we *know for a fact?*"

Karin wiped at her eyes. "What happened in Heather's bedroom that night . . ."

"Anything that couldn't have been done by an ordinary human being?"

"You didn't see her bedroom."

"No, I didn't. You did. That's why I'm asking you."

Karin thought about it, remembering Heather crouched naked against the bedroom wall, her eyes blank with some kind of uncomprehending terror, the room and its furnishings in total chaos.

She shook her head fiercely. "She *couldn't* have—"

"Maybe she didn't. Maybe someone else did. You've expressed concern about the company she's been keeping of late, especially Sherone Livingston. But that's not my point." Father Donovan leaned forward. "I'm not interested in assigning blame. The point is that there are solid, plausible explanations for everything that's happened so far—even the terrible murders—and not one of those explanations has anything to do with demons."

The priest settled back into his chair. "If the Church is going to treat a case of demonic possession, it had better be the real thing. Otherwise . . ." He paused. "Otherwise, if it turns out to be a psychological problem, or anything other than genuine possession, we're leaving ourselves open to attack from every anti-religious bigot in the country. And believe me, Karin, there are lots of them out there, just waiting for things like this."

Karin's tears were dried now. "You care more about the Church than you do about Heather."

"I care for both of them, equally. But it's not going to help anyone if we diagnose this situation incorrectly. It won't help Heather. It certainly won't help the Church."

Karin closed her eyes. It all made sense, damn it. That was the worst part. It just plain made good sense, the kind of good sense that had held her back at first when Heather came out with all this hocus-pocus, black magic bullshit, babbling, half out of her mind with fear after what . . . after whatever had happened out there at the goddamn deserted guided missile station—which the government should have had brains enough to get rid of now that they were not using it anymore so things like this couldn't happen . . .

Whatever it was that really did happen . . .

Whatever cut Kurt Pritchard to pieces and shriveled Troy Taylor's arms . . .

Karin shook her head sharply to get rid of the mocking voice, the one that was asking her now, with a razor's edge to its whisper, *What if she's right?*

What if she's right and it all really happened?

Karin looked up at the priest. "If she's making this up—just inventing it—I don't think I can handle it right now. I just can't!" The tears started again.

He reached out across the desk and put a comforting hand on her arm. "She's not making it up deliberately, Karin. She may be troubled. But there's help for that kind of trouble."

Karin looked up at him through her tears. "It's like I'm the one who's being tested, or tempted, or whatever."

Father Donovan closed his eyes, quoting from memory. "Paul's First Letter to the Corinthians, Chapter 10, Verse 13. 'For God keeps his promise, and he will not allow you to be tempted beyond your power to resist; but at the time you are tempted he will give you the strength to endure it, and so provide you with a way out.'" He opened his eyes to find Karin staring at him.

"Do you think that's really true?" she asked.

"It's God's promise, not mine."

Karin swallowed hard. "Then maybe I'll make it after all."

Father Donovan smiled. "I'm sure you will."

But as he gave her a consoling embrace, and the rest of

the box of Kleenex to take with her, and helped her with her coat because it was still raining hard outside, Father Patrick Michael Donovan was not entirely at peace with himself.

He knew there was a slight possibility, however remote, that actual demonic possession might be at work in such a case as this.

And that possibility terrified him.

He remembered the case several years back in Michoacán, Mexico, the one with the old woman who breathed fire, according to witnesses, and fornicated with demons, according to her own report. Two priests died in that investigation. A third went mad. The woman disappeared. The presiding bishop ordered the case closed. But it was never truly closed. Such things never are. Rumors persisted from Michoacán, rumors of demons appearing in the forms of an old woman and two priests, breathing fire, rumors of a mad priest blinding himself, then continuing to scream in horror at the things he still saw with his sightless eyes.

Father Donovan shivered as he closed his office door after Karin left.

He looked up at the crucifix on the wall, seeing not the glory of Christ Triumphant but the horror of Christ crucified: blood, wounds, suffering, death. He thought of Karin and Heather coming under the dark shadow of a demon from Hell and he grew afraid, mortally afraid.

He would pray for them.

chapter 32

dark road

The same rain that had fallen on Wes Livingston's house in Topanga Canyon with Sherone sitting alone inside was still falling harder than ever as Karin and Heather got into Karin's white Jaguar XJ6 in the almost deserted parking lot of Our Lady of Mercy.

Karin shivered as she closed the car door. Heather stared blankly at the rain running in streaks down the windshield. Karin flicked on the wipers and started out of the parking lot.

"Guess I better turn on the heater before we catch pneumonia." She looked over at Heather. "You okay?"

Heather shrugged. "I guess."

"You'll be just fine, honey. I promise." She reached out to stroke her daughter's long red hair.

Heather twisted away.

Karin sighed. *If she's acting difficult*, she told herself, *just try to be a little more understanding, okay?*

They drove in silence for several miles before Heather said, "Father Donovan didn't buy it, did he?"

Karin hesitated. "I wouldn't exactly say that."

"But he doesn't believe it, does he?"

Karin took a deep breath. "He thinks maybe we should

check out some other things first."

Heather looked at her mother. "You didn't stand up for me, did you?"

"What are you talking about?" Karin's voice rose. "What do you mean I didn't stand up for you?"

"I knew you wouldn't." Heather turned back to the rainy windshield. "You never do."

For God's sake, don't yell at her! Karin told herself, hands tensing as she gripped the Jaguar's steering wheel. *If she's sick she needs love and understanding, not yelling.*

Several more rainy miles went by in silence. Karin turned onto Mulholland Drive, the twisting ribbon of a road that winds through the Santa Monica mountains. They were driving to Annie and Sam Newmar's house in the Hollywood Hills not far from Laurel Canyon. Annie had insisted at the hospital that both of them come over as soon as Heather was released. *Go see Bernie Rausch and Father Donovan first if that's what you think you have to do*, Annie told her, *but then come see me, okay?* Karin did not want to talk with her little sister about what had happened. She was in no mood to handle a truckload of New Age bullshit. Annie meant well and Karin knew that, but she didn't need any more advice just now, no matter how well-intentioned. What she needed was a way out.

If there was a way out.

She braked on a steep curve on Mulholland, one that swung out toward the edge of the mountainside then cut back in sharply. The brake pedal pressure felt normal to her foot and there was no funny sound to signal anything wrong. But nothing happened. The Jaguar XJ6 kept up its straight-ahead acceleration into the curve.

Heather's head snapped up. "Mom! Slow down!"

Karin's heart seemed to lurch inside her chest. She jumped on the anti-lock disc brakes. Again, nothing. The Jaguar kept hurtling into the curve full speed, radial tires hissing on the rain-wet pavement. Heather started screaming. Karin, fear closing off her throat, turned the steering wheel just enough to make the Jaguar track the curve instead of shooting off the shoulder and down into the canyon.

Don't jerk it! she commanded herself, her frightened brain keeping pace with the out-of-control car, pulsing with great adrenaline charges of fear. *Jerk on the wheel and you'll never stop flipping down the mountainside.*

The Jaguar shot out of the curve like a hockey puck on ice.

"*Mother!*" Heather's blue eyes went wide with terror.

The Jaguar raced forward on the rain-slick road. Trees and houses lining Mulholland streaked past in a dizzying stroboscopic blur.

"Slow *down!*" Heather screamed.

Karin found her voice. "I'm not . . . speeding. I— My foot's not even on the gas."

Heather glanced down at the pedals and her stomach seemed to drop away. Karin had both feet pushed down on the brake pedal, holding it to the floor. The gas pedal was also crushed to the floor—by some other, unseen weight.

"No," Heather whispered, recoiling from the sight, shaking her head slowly in denial and fear.

The next curve almost got them. The Jaguar skidded into it, tires squealing on wet pavement, and started to spin. Karin had only a few seconds in which to steer out of the spin. She made it, barely, the back end of the Jaguar fishtailing madly back and forth across the center line. A car coming fast around the curve on the other side swerved just in time to avoid colliding with them head-on, horn blaring loudly, the other driver's face white with terror.

Karin felt paralyzed by fear. The Jaguar's engine seemed to be accelerating with every curve, going faster and faster like some insane windup toy spinning out of control. She glanced at the speedometer: seventy-five, the needle bouncing up toward eighty.

Christ, Karin thought helplessly. *Dear Jesus Christ!*

The next curve came at them without any warning.

Karin oversteered slightly. The Jaguar cornered on two wheels, knocking Heather into her mother despite the seatbelt. *We're going to flip,* Karin thought grimly. But the car held the road and came flying out of the curve like a bullet from a gun barrel.

"Heather," Karin managed, her voice a hoarse whisper, "if you're doing this . . . stop it, please."

Heather, in tears, gripping the dashboard with white-knuckled hands, turned to her. "I'm not doing *any*thing! Why do you *always* blame—"

It was two cars coming at them this time, one trying to pass the other on the wrong side of a curving mountain road, in the rain and at night—just your typical L.A. driver in a hurry. Everything happened at once. The two cars started to scramble, but there was no place to go. Heather screamed and covered her face with her hands. The four sets of blinding headlights came rushing up on them. Heavy rain hammered on the windshield. One of the oncoming cars started honking desperately. Karin gripped the wheel, eyes wide and staring straight ahead, like someone in terminal shock.

In fact she was thinking clearly, very clearly. Something her father, Harald Magnusson, had told her long ago, when she was six or seven, came back to her now with the formal precision of words appearing on a digital display: *When things get dangerous, s-l-o-w d-o-w-n.* She remembered him sitting there telling her this, a pipe in his mouth as usual. *You want to move fast in an emergency,* he told her *but most people move too fast, and that can kill you.* She knew what he meant now. She saw the two cars coming toward them and she knew that if they met in a head-on collision they would all die, but she was not panicking. She was strangely calm as she watched the blinding headlights fill the windshield, heard the rain drumming on the Jaguar's roof, considered whether she should take the shoulder and go over the side, and if she did—

She saw the driveway then.

Dark, narrow, obscured by bushes and low-hanging tree boughs, it stood there by the side of the road, visible only for an instant under the headlights in the rain at the speed the Jaguar was moving. Karin did not hesitate. With that same strange calm, she turned hard left and cut across the path of the two oncoming cars.

It did not look as if there would be enough time. From where Heather sat on the shotgun side, the bumpers of the oncoming cars seemed less than a foot from the Jaguar's side door. She closed her eyes and braced herself for the bone-jarring, glass-shattering impact of collision.

What happened instead felt like the middle part of a very rough roller coaster ride. The Jaguar rattled and shook, jerking Heather from side to side in her seatbelt. She opened her eyes. They were skidding down a long gravel driveway, still going fast, incredibly fast. Karin pulled hard left on the wheel and threw the car into a deliberate spin. The dark rainy world outside revolved like a carousel on fast-forward. Gravel sprayed up across the windshield, along with mud, flowers, chunks of lawn. Heather started to feel sick to her stomach as she hung on to the dashboard and the car kept spinning around and around and—

It finally stopped with a jolt that shuddered throughout its metal frame. Both Karin and Heather pitched forward violently into the windshield, stopped short only by their seatbelts. The Jaguar's engine was still running, but the car had spun itself into a clump of trees on the front lawn of a spacious estate. Karin, her heart pounding and nose running, looked out through the rain-streaked side window and saw a white-haired man in a satin robe and silk pajamas running across the wet grass toward them. Her hand trembling, she pressed the button that lowered the window.

"—the fuck you think you're doin' anyway, bustin' in here ripped on coke and tearin' up other people's property like a bunch of fuckin'—"

He stopped when he saw Karin staring out at him,

raindrops beading her pale face, eyes still wide with terror, Heather sitting beside her red-eyed and weeping. He paled beneath his own deep tanning-parlor tan.

"You girls okay?" he asked cautiously, wary of lawsuits now that he was beginning to see how serious this thing might be.

"We're fine." Karin tried to smile at him through the heavy rain. "We're just fine now." She hesitated. "Could we please use the phone?"

PART IV
FIRE

chapter 33

memento mori

"I don't give a shit about your goddamn procedures!" Her knuckles went white as she clutched the telephone receiver. "I want to report a kidnapping!"

Glenda McGuiness was not in the habit of yelling at people, not even at the half-wits they seemed to be sending her as lab assistants these days. She had a temper and she knew it, and she tried to control it. Usually she succeeded. But tonight was different.

Tonight they had come home to a nightmare.

They were walking to the house from the driveway in the rain, deep in discussion of a photograph they had both admired at the gallery show, when Glenda looked up and knew immediately that something was wrong. The front door was standing wide open. Most of the lights were on. Sherone never left the door unlocked, not even when she went sneaking out late at night without permission. Wes was fairly tolerant about things like cutting curfew. But Glenda was an absolute fanatic about locking up. *I ever find you gone and this place burned down,* she told Sherone once, *and the door's locked, you're okay, but if it's unlocked, God help you, kid.*

Rain blowing in through the open door had soaked the

entryway. Lamps were overturned on side tables. Drenched curtains hung beside an open window. Sean O'Casey, Sherone's dog, crouched in a corner licking at a puddle of his own vomit. When Glenda tried to see what was wrong with the animal, he bared his teeth and snapped at her, refusing to let her come near.

"No, I am not the next of kin!" Glenda shot back at the officer on the other end of the line. "Look, what does this have to do with anything? A young girl's been kidnapped! Her life's in danger and all you care about is getting your goddamn forms filled—"

Glenda stopped when she saw Wes Livingston step back into the room. He was holding what looked like a shiny piece of paper in his right hand. He was pale beneath his Tahitian tan, pale with a kind of terrible anger she had never seen in him before. When they had walked into the unlocked house and learned that Sherone had been kidnapped, it had hit Wes hard. He turned his face from Glenda so she would not see how hard. But she saw. It was as if someone had cut him open and ripped out his insides and left him standing there, a husk of the man he had been.

But all that was nothing to the anger that burned within him now.

Glenda turned her attention back to the officer on the phone. "Look, I know details are important, okay? But we've got a time factor here that—"

Wes yanked the receiver from her hand. Glenda stepped back, stunned. Wes had never made a violent gesture toward her in the years they had been together. She felt violated and insulted, as if he had slapped her across the face. But then she saw his troubled eyes, consumed by anger, and her own eyes filled with tears.

"Yes, I'm the father. No, she's never done anything like this before. She—" The muscles in his neck tensed. "I answered that already. I won't answer it again."

There was a hardness to his voice Glenda had never heard before, and she was glad she was not on the other end of that line.

"No, I'm not mad at you." He was speaking slowly now. "I'm not even mad at the sick son of a bitch who broke in here and took her away. But I am in a hurry. Because I'm going to find her. If you people want to help, I'll be grateful. But we can talk about it later."

He hung up the phone. As he did so, a tremor coursed through his body. He lowered his eyes to the floor and stood there, trembling. Glenda came over to him, her eyes still wet with tears, and put her arms around him.

"Come on, Wes." She kissed him on the forehead. "We'll find her. We'll—maybe she just left. It's not like her, I know. But maybe just this once she went off and left the door open . . ."

There they were again, the little lies, the ones you tell yourself when you know damn well what the truth is but you don't want to face it, don't even want to think about it, because the truth is nothing but a naked, grinning horror. It was no good telling lies, not to someone like Wes. But she did it anyway because she loved him, and she loved the girl too, and she shared his pain and his rage and his deep fear, and she had to say something, because something, even a lie, was better than the mocking nothingness of the truth.

He looked up at her, several tears trickling down the side of his lined, sun-weathered cheek. "Look at this."

He showed her what he held in his hand.

It was a color photograph of Sherone and Heather, taken last winter when they went skiing at Aspen. They must have been cutting up before the picture was taken because they both wore silly grins and stood with the loose-limbed sloppiness of two girls not out trying to look beautiful or impress any guys but just together and having one hell of a good time, their cheeks rosy from the cold mountain air, a glistening snowfield behind them framed by stately evergreens, their eyes sparkling with all the passionate energy and openness of youth.

Someone had carved a pentagram, the five-sided star,

across Heather's face. It cut deep into the glossy finish of the photograph. Smudged across Sherone's body and onto Heather's was a smear of blood, already dried a dark coppery brown, as if someone had picked up the photograph with bloody hands.

"What is this?" Wes held it out to Glenda in an accusatory manner. "What the hell kind of thing is this?"

Glenda shook her head. "Wes—"

"Excuse me, Sherone around?"

They both turned to the high-pitched adolescent voice. It belonged to a gangly boy with a sharp nose and straight dark hair plastered down flat against his skull by the rain. He stood in the entryway, the front door still open to the wet night outside.

Wes came toward him. "You part of that group came by earlier?"

"No, sir." He shook his head. "I've never been here before."

Wes held out the disfigured photograph. "Know anything about this?"

His eyes widened. "Hey, that's Heather! Heather Roberts. She's my— I mean, I sort of know her, okay?"

"Heather's her name, all right. And the girl with her's my daughter, Sherone." Wes's eyes grew hard. "Now who the hell are you?"

Brian McNulty was fast coming to the conclusion that all adults were assholes. Rationally, he knew better. There were good ones and bad ones, like any other age. But experience seemed to be proving otherwise. Heather's dad, the doctor, had acted like a world-class asshole. Of course Heather had warned him in advance, so Brian was ready for that one. But he had expected more of Wes Livingston. Heather had told him all about how totally in control Wes was, an upfront kind of guy without the concentration camp commander's attitude that made most adults act like such . . . well, assholes.

And now Wes was turning out to be just like all the others.

Brian took a deep breath, and told how Heather had been hospitalized after what happened at the missile station, how he had gone to see her in the hospital but they were able to talk for only a few minutes before her dad came in and threw him out.

"So that's why I came here," Brian concluded lamely. "I was hoping maybe Sherone could get me in to see Heather again . . . or something."

Wes studied him. "Know anything about this hocus-pocus group Skip—I mean, Sherone—belongs to?"

"Magda Prokash's Wicca?"

Wes nodded.

"I don't exactly belong to it or anything, okay?" Brian explained. "But I was there with Heather and Sherone the night they raised a demon—"

Wes interrupted. "They *what?*"

"Wes." Glenda glanced up. "Let him finish."

Brian told them what happened that night.

The rain had stopped for now. Excess drops fell slowly from wet lemon trees outside. The only sounds inside the house came from water flowing along roof gutters and down drainpipes. Brian shifted uncomfortably under the intense scrutiny of Wes's stare.

Finally Wes said, "Glen can set another plate for supper. You hungry?"

"Starved," Brian answered truthfully, relieved to be out of the hot seat. "I don't know what it is, but walking in the rain always makes me really hungry."

"Good. We've got lots to talk about." Wes looked at him. "And you're going to do the talking."

chapter 34

fire demon

The Institute for Parapsychological Studies in Pasadena was flanked by several smaller buildings in a campuslike setting of neatly kept lawns and interconnecting sidewalks. Heavy rain was falling again as Annie Newmar led Karin and Heather past the double glass doors of the main entrance and across a low-lighted lobby to the central reception desk.

Annie had finally convinced her big sister to go see Roland Cameron at IPS, now, tonight, before anything else happened. Karin was reluctant about turning to a parapsychologist for help. She had been impressed by the depth of Roland Cameron's commitment that night she and Annie heard him lecture at Hoskins College, and she had been surprised by the older man's calmness and rationality, qualities she had learned to value from her research scientist father but did not expect to find among followers of the occult. Still, as she explained to Annie, she was not entirely convinced that—

It came back to her suddenly, right there in the middle of Annie's living room: the horrifying, rain-slick ride over Mulholland Drive. Karin felt again the Jaguar pitching and rolling, heard the squeal of skidding tires, saw the speedometer needle edging inexorably upward, her feet pressed down on the brake instead of the gas as the speed of the car increased, hurtling out of control like all the events of her life these past terrible days.

She agreed then to go with Annie and see Roland Cameron. Maybe he could help, maybe not. But she and Heather needed help from someone, somewhere.

And there was nowhere else to go.

A nondescript, middle-aged woman at the central reception desk took their names and directed them to a row of chairs against a black marble wall. They did not wait long before the tall, dark-bearded assistant to Roland Cameron whom Karin remembered from the lecture showed up and introduced himself to them. Up close, Jeff Geller did not appear as aggressive or angry as he had standing there on the stage of Hoskins College auditorium, defending parapsychology from its detractors. The intensity was still apparent in his dark eyes and the serious set of his face. But it was softened by a warm smile that came forth unexpectedly.

"I really appreciate this on such short notice," Annie said to Jeff, adding a bit wistfully, "wish I could tell Roland thanks in person."

Karin looked over at her sister and thought, *She's a damn good kid*. Annie would have been on cloud nine if she had been granted a private interview with Roland Cameron. Instead she had gone to a lot of trouble to get an emergency session for her sister and niece and now Annie wouldn't even be allowed to see the famous man.

"We're glad to do whatever we can to help in a case like this, Mrs. Newmar," Jeff told her. "I wish we could include you in the interview. But Dr. Cameron feels that it will be more effective limited to Heather and her mother."

"That's cool," Annie nodded, a little glum; then she perked up into her usual cheerful self. "Thanks again, Jeff." She turned to Karin. "I just *know* Roland's going to help!" A sudden somberness entered her bright blue eyes. "You guys be real careful driving home, okay?"

"Promise." Karin squeezed her sister's hand. "I'll tell you everything he says."

Annie smiled goodbye and left.

Jeff Geller led them down a long gray-walled corridor, their footsteps falling softly on thick-pile blue carpet. Most of the doors they passed were closed. Karin looked into one that was open and saw a bank of electronic machinery with blinking lights. A man sat in silhouette before a screen covered with multicolored geometrical patterns.

A door opened up in front of them and a woman stepped out into the corridor. Somewhere in her late twenties, she had on a long, thick white robe and heavy white mittens. She wore the dark wraparound sunglasses used by persons with vision impairments and her ears were covered with heavy-duty protectors designed to block out all outside sound. She moved along the corridor slowly but surely, without groping for the wall or turning her face to one side to sense pressure waves caused by advancing objects. Karin and Heather, unsure of what to do, stopped walking. Jeff, when he realized this, turned around and rejoined them.

Heather whispered, "Was she in an accident?"

Jeff shook his head. "She's a Sensitive with advanced ESP abilities. She's been testing with us for over six months now and the results, so far, have been spectacular. We have her dressed up like that so we can test her ambulatory navigational skills with minimum sensory input."

Seeing Heather frown, Jeff added, "In plain English, she's trying to find her way around without relying on any of the senses we normally use for that purpose, such as sight, hearing, touch and so forth."

"How's she doing it, then?" Karin asked, transfixed by the sight of the white-robed woman, artificially blind and deaf, moving confidently down the corridor toward them.

"By using the sixth sense," Jeff explained. "She's relying on *psi* power to perceive the world around her."

"You mean she's seeing things with her eyes closed?" Karin's own eyes widened slightly.

"Not exactly. It would be more accurate to say that she's *sensing* them, as if she knows what they look like or where they are without even having to visualize them."

"That's impossible," Karin said flatly.

"Unusual maybe," Jeff corrected her, "but not impossible. When you've been in this business long enough, you get very cautious about calling anything impossible."

The white-robed woman stopped abruptly in front of them and smiled. "Good evening, Dr. Geller."

Jeff returned the smile. "Hello, Catherine."

"I don't mean to detain you and your guests, so I'll be on my way." The woman nodded at Heather and Karin as she passed, murmuring politely, "Your daughter has such lovely red hair."

Karin turned around and watched Catherine's smooth progress down the corridor. Then she turned back and hurried to catch up with Heather and Jeff, who had gone on ahead. *If that's possible,* she glanced back once more at the white-robed figure, *then maybe whatever's happening to us is possible and,* she thought with the slightest rising hope, *maybe something can be done about it.*

Several closed doors bore cryptic signs. PK LAB. PRECOGNITION TEST CENTER. DISINCARNATE COMMUNICATION RESEARCH. O.O.B. CONTROL ROOM.

"What's O.O.B.?" Karin asked Jeff.

"Out-of-body."

The disincarnate, she remembered Annie telling her at the lecture, *are the dead.*

The sign on the closed door across from Jeff Geller's office read PHENOMENOLOGICAL MUSEUM.

Karin frowned. "What's that?"

Jeff looked up from where he was unlocking his office door. "A collection of artifacts. Might even call them souvenirs. Some are from projects we've worked on here at IPS. Others are from famous historical cases. Sort of specialized stuff." Seeing her continue to stare curiously at the locked door, he added, "Not of much interest to the average person."

Karin looked over at him. "I'm not the average person, thank you. I also happen to be a museum curator, so I have a professional interest."

Jeff recovered quickly. "My apologies, Mrs. Roberts. I didn't mean it that way."

"Apology accepted, but I wish you wouldn't call me that," she said, thinking of the sanctimonious Milton Bromley.

"No problem, Karin." He smiled at her. "But it's Jeff, all right?"

She returned the smile. They both held it a little longer than necessary.

Heather looked down at the blue carpet, embarrassed the way teenagers can be when reminded that adults have the same emotions they do.

Inside his office, Jeff interviewed Karin and Heather quickly and professionally. He let them do most of the talking, prompting them with questions and, once in a while, interrupting to clarify a point or ask for repetition of an important comment. He recorded the interview on video but also took notes in what looked like a modified shorthand.

When he was finished, he looked up. "I'm going to show this to Roland. It won't take long. But he'll want to preview everything before he talks with you."

While they waited for Jeff to return, Karin tried to talk to Heather. Heather said nothing. Karin got up and walked out into the gray-walled corridor, where she noticed again the heavy double-lock door to the Phenomenological Museum. It was unlocked and standing open.

She stepped inside. As she did so, a small gasp escaped her. It was unlike any museum she had ever seen. The closest thing to it would have been a combination modern art exhibition and natural history museum. There were strange stones oddly shaped and sized, some with highly polished surfaces like mirrors and others with intricate crystalline structures. Bizarre metal configurations serving no functional or decorative purpose hung above complex electronic devices Karin had never seen before. Throughout the room were strange things under glass: grotesque lizardlike creatures floating in formaldehyde, snakes curled up inside glass balls, and, strangest of all, a naked human embryo preserved inside a square glass box bordered on three sides with wooden walls.

On closer examination Karin realized that it was not an embryo at all but a naked adult human body lying lengthwise, in perfect proportion, reduced to the size of an eight-inch doll. A chill moved up Karin's spine. The skin of the shrunken mummy was gray and shriveled, the small eyes sharp points of black. It was grotesque, but fascinating. Mesmerized, Karin stretched out a hand toward the glass.

Another hand grabbed hers. She cried out in alarm.

Jeff shook his head. "I wouldn't do that."

"Christ!" Karin shuddered. "What is it?"

"One of our more unusual specimens. Perfectly harmless now. Still, I wouldn't touch the glass if I were you." Jeff pulled up a fourth wooden wall, blocking the shriveled mummy from view, then placed another piece of wood on top of the glass box and locked all the pieces together.

Then he said to Karin, "Dr. Cameron's waiting for us in his office."

Despite her earlier misgivings, Karin felt immediately at ease in Roland Cameron's presence. The white-haired parapsychologist had that effect on people. His office, except for overflowing floor-to-ceiling bookcases, was sparsely furnished: inexpensive personal computer, basic telephone, several modest paperweights. He greeted Heather and Karin politely, had them take comfortable chairs, then looked at them quietly, as if waiting for them to start.

Karin came to the point. "Can you help us?"

"We'll have to try, won't we?" Roland indicated Jeff's notes. "Whole thing's got rather out of hand."

"You believe us," Karin said, relief washing over her. "You don't think we're crazy."

"Not in the least. Both seem to be of perfectly sound mind. Why not believe you? Of course," Roland paused, "it's not really a matter of *belief* anyway, is it?"

"I mean the part about the demon," Karin said.

"Demon," Roland mused, as if considering an option. "Well, yes. One could call it that, after all."

Karin looked confused. "That's what *she* called it, that horrible woman who summoned it. Magda . . ." Karin looked at Heather for help, but Heather said nothing.

"Magda Prokash," Roland finished it for her. "Yes, Magda would call it a demon. Part of her Wicca business, a little black magic and a bit of Satanism tossed in for added spice."

"If it's not a demon," Karin asked, "what is it?"

"People still use that term," Roland agreed with her. "In the Middle Ages, they would have called it a devil, one of the minor devils serving the great devil, Lucifer, or Satan. In the pre-Christian era, they might well have called it a god."

Images of the Forgotten Gods at the Barringer came suddenly to Karin's mind, especially Kraadar, mocking and hideous, his gaping jaws filled with the half-devoured corpses of his sacrificial victims. She suppressed a shudder.

"Not a god in our sense of the term," Roland continued, "but a dark and terrible god, one without order or compassion, a savage god for whom destruction, not creation, is the reason for being."

"Where does it come from?" Karin asked hesitantly, not certain that she wanted to know.

"From a world diametrically opposed to ours, a kind of

anti-universe that I call the Other World, a place, or dimension, far beyond the farthest imaginable reaches of our own vast universe."

Karin felt a chill creep over her at the thought of an intelligent evil dwelling deep in the black reaches of outer space.

"So you see," Roland explained, "it's actually more like an elemental force than a god or a demon, more like an energy source similar to heat or light, or nuclear fission. Of course, one can't go around calling it an elemental force all the time. Have to call it something. And demon does seem more appropriate than god. Although fire demon might be more appropriate still, considering what we've seen of its powers thus far."

Karin thought of the hot wind that had blown through Heather's bedroom, the fire that had burned the one boy alive out at the monolith, the boiling water that had turned Hyung-Joon Kim into a viscid mass of floating garbage . . .

She swallowed hard and looked up at Roland. "How could something that powerful and terrible be summoned by one old woman pretending to practice witchcraft?"

The white-haired parapsychologist frowned. "Well, yes. Much of what Magda does *is* merely fraudulent, of course, but not all of it, unfortunately. She's wanted on suspicion of Satanic ritual murder in several countries in Europe. And she's quite capable of summoning a demon like . . . Azgaroth."

Heather reacted visibly to the dreaded name. She shifted in her chair. A sheen of sweat began to glisten on her upper lip. She glanced about the office anxiously. Roland noticed all these things, but said nothing.

"Summoning a demon's not all that difficult," he continued, "if one follows the proper procedure. After all, the basic ritual is quite ancient, goes back to the dawn of humanity, perhaps even farther. There's evidence that powers like Azgaroth may have been worshipped on other worlds preceding this one."

Roland Cameron's office seemed overshadowed suddenly by the Other World, by its ancient gods and their ancient evil, by its dark terrors lying forever in wait at the edges of our own bright and fragile world. Karin looked over to where Heather sat frightened and helpless, and she grew afraid for both of them.

"Okay," Karin said, controlling the tremor in her voice with difficulty. "We know what it is and where it came from. But what does it want with Heather? And how do we get rid of it?"

"Challenging questions," Roland admitted. "Taking them in order . . . The demon, Azgaroth, as noted, is more like an energy source than a creature. However, for reasons not entirely clear to us, when it passes into this dimension it tries to effect something like an energy transfer with a human being. In other words, it tries to find a human body as a means of, well, expression."

Karin leaned forward. "Why *my* daughter?"

"One doesn't want to sound indelicate," Roland glanced at Heather, as if asking permission, "but the fact of her virginity surely has something to do with it. Ever since prehistoric times sexual energy has been closely linked to religion and magic. Hence all the stress on virgin gods and goddesses, even in highly sophisticated religions."

"My daughter," Karin said pointedly, "is not the only virgin in Los Angeles."

Roland nodded. "Right. Another factor, of course, is her having been in simply the wrong place at the wrong time. When she stepped outside the salt circle during the ceremony, she presented herself as an offering to Azgaroth and was, unfortunately, accepted."

Heather shuddered and shut her eyes, feeling once again the loathsome embrace of the darkness that night at Magda's, feeling the way it had passed *through* her naked, suspended body.

Karin's face was pale with fear. "Can you get rid of it?" she asked Roland. "Send it back to wherever it came from?"

He cleared his throat. "They're a great deal easier to call forth than send back, unfortunately."

Karin's voice slipped out of control. *"Can you do anything to protect my daughter?"*

Roland nodded. "We must take precautions. Immediately. With every attack, Azgaroth grows bolder. He's been laying siege to your home for some time now, of course. The dying plants, the burned candles—all unmistakable signs. The house is no longer safe for Heather. It would be unthinkable to let her return there now."

Karin frowned. "Where do you want her to go?"

"We have accommodations here at IPS. It would be most helpful," he added quickly, seeing Karin's negative reaction, "if you would consent to her remaining with us for a short while."

Karin was starting to tell Roland what he could do with his idea and his institute when she realized that he was right. The danger was increasing with every day that passed, the danger to her as well as Heather. *The danger to everyone,* she thought helplessly, remembering again the slaughtered boys, poor Hyung-Joon Kim . . .

"How long?" she asked quietly.

"A few days at least. Enough time to let us observe her while providing a kind of safeguard against . . . any further unpleasantness."

Karin nodded feebly, feeling very tired.

"Mom!" Heather turned to her. "I don't want to stay here!"

Karin put a hand on her daughter's shoulder. "Honey, I don't think we have much choice."

"It won't be all that bad, Heather," Roland added encouragingly. "Rather like a holiday. Food's not so bad. Lots of videos. Some of the experiments are even a bit of fun." He hesitated. "Besides, the whole thing might be cleared up this way. Azgaroth might turn out to be very area-specific, unable to move easily from one location to the next." But he said that without much conviction.

Karin had her arms around Heather, who was crying

now. "Come on, darling. We're doing this for you."

Jeff Geller stepped into the office and handed Karin a note. "Someone from the Barringer Museum called your sister. She phoned here to relay the message."

"Thanks," Karin said with a sigh, as she realized that the outside world was charging ahead with its own deadliness and expectations, completely unaware of her problems. "I'll call them back."

Roland turned to Jeff. "As long as you're here, would you mind awfully escorting Heather to the residential wing? She's going to be staying with us for a few days."

Heather lifted a tear-streaked face. "I have to go home and get my things!"

Karin smoothed her daughter's ruffled hair. "I'll have them sent over, honey."

"You don't know which ones I want!" Heather protested, bursting into fresh tears. "I want my grandmama! She wouldn't let this happen to me!"

That, Karin thought, *is God's truth.* She hoped Annie would not tell their mother about this IPS interview. Not even Roland Cameron, Karin knew, could remain calm and rational when confronted by a loud, bullying Maureen Magnusson.

Jeff smiled at Heather. "When you're ready, we'll walk over there together. Along the way I can give you a guided tour of—"

A glass paperweight leaped up from the desktop and struck Roland Cameron a sharp blow to his shoulder. Books crashed to the floor with a thunderous explosion, startling a scream from Karin. A framed certificate fell with a shattering of glass.

Roland sat calmly at his desk, rubbing his shoulder, eyes alert. Jeff stood poised, arms raised, glancing quickly about the room. Beads of sweat began to appear on Roland's forehead as the temperature in the room shot upward, growing unbearably, suffocatingly hot.

Jeff said quietly, barely moving his lips, "We've got one hell of a force field building up in here."

As more books fell from a high shelf and another paperweight started skittering across the desktop, Roland leaned toward Heather. "He's not your friend, Heather. He's trying to hurt the people who want to help you. Heather? Do you understand me?"

Heather, terrified, shouted at the white-haired parapsychologist. "It's not *me!* I'm not doing it! Quit *blaming* me!"

Roland continued quietly, "Tell him to go away, Heather. Just think it in your mind. Think: go away, be gone, I do *not* want you here."

As Roland spoke, he raised his right hand in a gesture so subtle only someone specially trained would have noticed it. Jeff moved in quickly behind the desk and pushed a button on a wall console.

A stunning flash of white light filled the room. Colors reversed, like images in a photographic negative. Faces became black masks, eyes and mouths white holes. Energy seemed to be sucked out of the room. Everything felt reversed, turned inside out. Then, as suddenly as it had come, it passed. The temperature gradient began to fall rapidly. The air in the room became temperate and breathable once again.

Heather sobbed uncontrollably in her mother's arms. Roland raised a hand to his sweating forehead. Jeff took a deep breath and let it out very slowly.

The office was a mess of dumped books, scattered papers, broken glass. There was a smell of burning, as if wires had melted in the walls.

But no object moved of its own volition.

No Presence remained within the room.

For now.

chapter 35

acolytes

The neon sign advertising the Heart of Darkness glowed like witches' fire through the rain that fell on Van Nuys Boulevard that night.

Wes Livingston parked his camper van in one of the many empty spaces near the front of the occult shop. The rain was keeping customers away. He pulled his bush jacket close around him as he got out of the van, squinting into the rain. It fell on his lined face and into his eyes and made him feel old and tired. Then he remembered the blood-smeared photograph of Heather and his daughter Sherone. A hardness entered his eyes.

He pushed open the grimy glass front door of the Heart of Darkness. A warning bell jingled sharply overhead. Inside, three or four customers milled about the aisles. Ethereal music crackled from hidden speakers. Incense smoke hung heavy and acrid in the air. Wes walked slowly toward the counter at the back of the room, looking around for someone to match Brian McNulty's description of Magda Prokash. The small dark-skinned girl sitting behind the counter glanced up at his approach, then looked back down at the amulets she was arranging on the glass countertop.

"Magda in?" Wes asked casually.

She looked up at him. "'Scuse me?"

"Magda Prokash. She here?"

The girl shrugged. "Gone somewheres. Maybe she'll be back later. Maybe not." Considering the conversation closed, the girl went back to fiddling with the amulets in front of her.

Wes let her fiddle for almost a full minute before he said, "I've got something important for her."

"Oh? Like what?"

"Sorry. For her ears only."

The girl shrugged indifferently. But it was clear that she was interested.

Wes pretended to look at *athamés* and amulets beneath the glass countertop until the girl asked, "How come you know Magda? I never seen you around here before."

"I've known Magda for a long time."

"Oh." Now she was really interested. She started to ask him something, then stopped and went back to arranging and rearranging the same amulets.

Wes let some more time pass before he asked, "She getting ready for the Sabbath?"

The girl did not answer at first. But her fingers tightened around the amulets.

When she finally looked up, fear glimmered in her dark eyes. "How do you know about that?"

"Like I told you, Magda and I go way back."

Suspicion flickered across her face. "I never heard her say nothing about you. What's your name?"

Wes gave her a small plastic smile. "Let's just say I'm the man from back east."

Aracely stared at him suspiciously, then went back to the amulets. But her hands trembled as she pretended to arrange them.

Wes leaned forward slightly. "Hate to think what Magda might say when she learns I came all the way out here to tell her something important and now you won't even let me know where she is." He hesitated. "You know how she gets once she's mad enough."

When Aracely looked up at him this time, there was real fear in her eyes. "How do I know you ain't lyin'?"

"You don't. You take a chance. You tell me where she is. Or you don't tell me, and let her find out the hard way what it is I'm supposed to tell her."

Aracely swallowed hard and looked down at the glass countertop. "She's with Seamus," she mumbled, wincing at the sound of the warlock's name. "They took that girl, the one they got last night, and went to . . ." Her mumbling became indistinct, as if what she was saying was too fearful to be spoken aloud.

It took all Wes's self-control to say casually, "Can't quite hear you there, darling. Mind speaking up just a bit?"

Aracely swallowed again. "I said, Magda's at—"

"Most probably at home," said the voice behind them. "Or at that scruffy little place she calls home."

Aracely's head snapped up. She gasped and shrank back behind the counter. Wes turned around slowly. The voice, distinctively British, belonged to a tall, thin older woman with white hair and a conservatively cut tweed suit. Her companion, though shorter and stockier, was also white-haired and similarly dressed. If Sherone had been there, she could have identified for her father the two older English ladies who had been at the Heart the last time she went there to see Magda.

"Forgive our impertinence," said the taller woman, addressing Wes. "But we have been eavesdropping. The three of us seem to share a common goal: finding Magda Prokash. My name, by the way, is Felicity Perkins. This," she indicated her shorter companion, "is Gwendolyn Dandridge."

Wes nodded, his expression neutral. "The young lady here was just about to tell me where Magda is."

"I doubt if she knows," Gwendolyn said bluntly. "Aracely's part of the Wicca. A very small part. One

320

can't quite imagine Magda entrusting her with important information."

If Aracely took offense at this, she did not show it. She remained behind the counter, glancing warily at Wes and the two older English ladies.

"Magda," Felicity, the taller one, continued, "will most likely be found at the small tract house that she rents here in Los Angeles. In any event, that is where we propose to go. We had been planning to call on her this evening when we overheard your little talk with Aracely and decided to ask if you should like to accompany us."

Wes was taken off guard. The two older ladies looked harmless enough, more like retired librarians than members of a witch cult. But appearances, he knew now, could be dangerously deceiving. The harmless appearance of Magda's Wicca had blinded him to the peril threatening his daughter.

If I'd been half as concerned as Glenda, he thought accusingly, *Skip would be safe at home right now.*

He considered the possibility that the two women were part of a security setup at the Heart of Darkness, instructed to detain anyone who showed too much curiosity about the owner. But if they were working for Magda, then they were part of the pack of jackals that had broken into his home and kidnapped his daughter.

He made his decision.

"I'd be honored to accompany you ladies." He smiled cordially at them. "They say two heads are better than one. Three must be even better."

Both women nodded sharply, as if a deal had been struck.

Gwendolyn, the shorter one, turned to the frightened girl behind the counter. "Straighten up those amulets, Aracely. They look a mess."

chapter 36

BLOOD OFFERING

When the doorbell rang, five-year-old Adam Newmar was on his knees in the living room playing with the plastic figures from his DINOSAUR COMMANDOS® set and chanting to himself a rhyme he had learned in kindergarten.

"Rain, rain, go away!

"Come again some other day!"

"Like next year," said his mother, Annie, from over on the designer sofa where she was watching a videotape of *Fatal Attraction* with her husband, Sam. "It's too early to be raining this much."

"It's the Flood," said Sam. "Better build an ark."

The doorbell sounded again.

Adam lifted his blond head. *"I'll* get it!"

Annie got to her feet and put a hand on top of Adam's head, pushing him back down to the floor. "You don't *ever* open the door at night, mister. And you know that, right?"

"I just want to help," Adam said.

"You can help fold your jeans when they come out of the dryer."

Annie turned on the porch light and looked out

through the security lens. A young girl stood by herself, blond hair matted to her head with rainwater, teeth chattering as she shivered inside a dark blue polyester windbreaker several sizes too large for her. She looked familiar somehow, but Annie couldn't quite place her.

"Who is it?" she called above the falling rain.

"I'm Heather's friend!" the girl answered, shivering.

Then Annie recognized her. She and Heather had stopped by before. She drove that cute little red VW bug. Her parents were divorced and she lived with her father, a wildlife conservationist or something like that. Annie tried to remember the girl's name. Cherise? Yvonne?

Annie opened the door. "Come on in before you catch pneumonia! Don't tell me. It's . . . Shereen, right?"

"Sherone." The girl tried to smile, but the look of helpless fear on her face made that impossible.

Annie stared at the rain-soaked girl with the terrified look in her brown eyes and the too-large jacket. A small alarm started to go off inside her head.

The dark figure rushed at her from out of the rain.

Annie tried to slam the door. But he hit it with his shoulder before it closed, knocking the door wide open, and Annie back away from it. She screamed in fear at what stood in her doorway. He was a young man with his head shaved bald except for one strip of hair hanging wet and limp down the side of his skull. A pentagram, the five-sided star, Sign of the Beast, was tattooed beneath a cold gray eye.

"What the hell—" Sam Newmar turned around on the sofa.

Realizing they were in trouble, deep trouble, Annie moved quickly toward her son, who was kneeling on the floor watching everything with an open mouth and wide eyes, a DINOSAUR COMMANDO® clutched in one hand.

The young skinhead pulled a large-bladed combat knife from beneath his damp blue denim jacket. He reached Annie with one step and grabbed her roughly by the

323

upper arm. She cried out in pain.

Sam flushed an angry red. "Take your hands off her, you punk-ass son of a bitch!" He moved out from behind the sofa, fists clenched.

The skinhead held the wicked-looking knife blade against Annie's throat. Her eyes went wide. Adam started to cry.

Sam came to a sudden stop, raising a hand to his own throat. "Don't hurt her," he pleaded hoarsely. "We'll do what you say."

"No one has to be hurt," said a voice from outside the front door.

Magda Prokash stepped into the room, rainwater dripping from the hood of her dark brown monk's robe. "If everyone cooperates, no one will be hurt."

"What do you want?" Annie cried, her voice shrill with terror.

A cold smile crept over Magda's face. "We want," she said, "the child."

"NO!" Annie screamed, and started to twist loose from the skinhead's grip until he pressed the knife into her throat.

"Don't hurt her, Damon," Magda commanded. "Just restrain her." She turned to Sherone, who stood shivering to one side, tears in her eyes. "Sherone, get the child. *Now!*"

Sherone, still shivering, wiped at her eyes and walked slowly toward Adam. The little boy got to his feet and watched her cautiously as she approached. He gripped the DINOSAUR COMMANDO® in one hand.

"Come on, Adam." Sherone tried to smile at him. "You can come with me, okay? We'll go for a ride."

Adam stood still and watched as she crouched down beside him and put a hand gently on his arm. "Okay?"

"Is she gonna go with us?" Adam asked, pointing at Magda Prokash.

Sherone bit her lip and nodded, and started to cry.

"I'm not goin' *no*where with her!" Adam shouted.

He broke loose from Sherone's grip and started to run for the long hall leading to his bedroom.

"Sherone!" Magda ordered. "Stop him!"

Sherone, still crying, made a half-hearted attempt.

"Wretched girl," Magda muttered, moving quickly to cut off Adam's escape route.

He pulled back, glaring fiercely at her. "I *hate* you!" he said, and threw the DINOSAUR COMMANDO® in her face.

The plastic figure scored a direct hit on the end of Magda's nose. She yelped with pain and grabbed at Adam.

He slipped around her, running headlong for the front door. He was almost out and into the rain when someone stepped in from outside, blocking his way.

Adam looked up and saw Seamus Harrach's bone-white face and black-toothed smile and began to howl in terror. Here was the monster of his worst possible nightmare, come horrifyingly, irrationally to life.

Magda grabbed the little boy from behind and slapped him hard on the side of his head. "Miserable little whelp!" she wheezed, gasping for breath. "Stop that whining or I'll break your worthless neck!"

Seamus Harrach gave her a stare that reduced her to sudden silence. "You'll do nothing of the kind," he said in a voice pitched too low for anyone other than Magda to hear. "You will treat him with the reverence that is his due as the Perfect Blood Offering."

Seamus turned to the skinhead Damon, who was threatening Annie with the knife to keep her from breaking loose to defend her child. "Damon!" Seamus called to him. "Tie them both securely with this." The warlock took out a coil of nylon rope and tossed it to the skinhead. "Remember, no games. Just tie them up, without hurting them."

Magda, balked in her rage to hurt Adam, grabbed Sherone by the hair and pulled on it until the girl screamed. "Ungrateful little slut!" Magda hissed at her. "If you don't start following orders, I'll hand you over to

Tamara as her playmate. Just see if I don't! Wretched girl."

"Mommy!" Adam screamed, his voice breaking with fear. "Daddy!"

"Adam!" Annie turned from where Damon was binding her and Sam together, back to back, sitting on the floor. "Adam, I love you! I—"

She started crying and could not go on.

Through blurred eyes she saw her small blond son being dragged by Magda Prokash out into the rain and the darkness and the unknown.

chapter 37

house sitter

The rain hammered down on the windshield of Wes Livingston's camper van parked on a dark side street off Van Nuys Boulevard. He sat in the driver's seat and finished telling his story to the two older English ladies, Felicity Perkins and Gwendolyn Dandridge, who sat in the front of the van with him. Felicity, the taller one, listened attentively, her long, thin hands folded in her lap. Gwendolyn, the short and stocky one, watched Wes more carefully than she listened, keeping him covered with a 9mm Beretta automatic held rock-steady in her right hand.

After Wes finished, Felicity sighed and said, "I, for one, am thoroughly convinced that Mr. Livingston is telling the truth." She turned to her companion. "Gwendolyn?"

The short woman frowned. "If you're convinced, Felicity, then so am I. But I always say, caution's the watchword." The Beretta did not waver an inch from where she had it pointed at Wes's midsection.

Felicity nodded. "Right. But one can overdo it. Put the gun away, Gwendolyn. We have nothing to fear from Mr. Livingston." She looked at him. "Please accept our apologies. One can never be sure nowadays. For all Gwendolyn and I knew, you might actually have been a friend of Magda's."

"No hard feelings," Wes said. "Do I get to hear your stories now?"

"Ours are not so personally painful as yours, but we have seen much suffering caused by that woman." Felicity leaned forward and lowered her voice, although the van windows were all rolled up. "It's almost four years now that we've been on Magda's trail, so to speak. Gwendolyn and I are what you might call, for lack of a better term, occult investigators. Sounds silly, but the work is quite important and, Lord knows, challenging. Both of us have studied occult phenomena for many years. I can even lay claim to a small bit of individual talent in that area."

Gwendolyn snorted. "Felicity's being falsely modest. She's an extraordinarily gifted Sensitive. Studied with Roland Cameron, formerly of Oxford, now Director of IPS at Pasadena. You've heard of him, of course?"

Before Wes could answer, Felicity said, "Roland's part of the reason we're here in Los Angeles. He offered us a one-year residency at IPS, very flattering and all. But the main reason we accepted, you see, was to enable us to keep an eye on Magda."

"We suspected she would show up here," Gwendolyn explained, "once she started making contact with Seamus Harrach again."

"I keep hearing that name," Wes said. "Who is he?"

"A so-called warlock, and a sadistic villain of the worst order." Gwendolyn frowned fiercely. "One hoped so to nab him, along with Magda."

"We came close to doing just that," Felicity said. "You see, Magda, until quite recently, did not know exactly what we looked like. Thus we were able to approach her directly, posing as two slightly daft spiritualists on holiday. We were set to close the trap on her and end her career of Satanic crime, when all at once she disappeared. Went underground, so to speak. All we could find out from her little minions at the Heart of Darkness was that Magda and Seamus had announced it was time for the Blood Sabbath, the great Witches' Sabbath at which Satan himself is said to appear. Magda's disappearance and the news of the Blood Sabbath all took place right before—" Felicity hesitated.

"Before they kidnapped your daughter," Gwendolyn finished it for her.

The muscles in Wes's face tightened, but he said nothing.

Felicity cleared her throat. "Magda has somehow managed to summon a very ancient and powerful demon, Azgaroth. The same one that has made contact with your daughter's friend, Heather Roberts. We believe that Magda intends to invoke Azgaroth once again at the Blood Sabbath as part of an attempt to call forth Satan himself, the dark center of all Evil."

"I don't believe in God or the Devil," Wes said, his voice somewhat unsteady.

Felicity looked at him somberly. "It doesn't really matter, Mr. Livingston. A central source of Evil exists, whether you choose to believe in it or not. And Magda intends to call it forth into the world, with what dreadful consequences one dare not imagine." Felicity hesitated again. "In order to invoke Azgaroth again she may need the assistance, willing or unwilling, of Heather Roberts. And that might just be why she kidnapped your daughter: to use as a lure for her best friend, as bait for the Blood Sabbath."

Streaks of water drizzled down the van's windshield, distorting the dark world outside.

Wes Livington seemed to have aged several years in as many minutes, but his voice was steady when he asked, "You sure you know where Magda is?"

"As the Evil gathers around her, she begins to radiate stronger and stronger emanations," Felicity said. "I can sense these more easily the stronger they grow. Almost works like an electronic homing device, so to speak. The emanations from her rented house have become very powerful during the last several hours. It is not far from here. I feel certain we shall find her there."

Wes turned on the van's engine. "Which way?"

Magda's house was a shabby-looking one-story bungalow with mildew-stained stucco walls and drawn curtains. A pile of unopened newspapers rotted in the driveway under heavy rain. Wes's headlights flashed off the rain-slick wood of a closed garage door.

Felicity turned to him. "Mr. Livingston, you do understand that there is the distinct possibility of great danger in this, don't you?"

Gwendolyn added, "Mortal danger, she means."

Wes looked at the two women. "Someone just kidnapped my daughter. That makes me a little dangerous too."

Wes pried open the front door with a crowbar from the back of the van. A suffocating stink of mildew wafted out through the jimmied door. But underneath it curled another stench, dark and evil, the kind that makes the small hairs prickle at the back of your neck.

Felicity put her hands on the shoulders of her two companions, her pale blue eyes staring into the darkness of the unlighted house but sensing something else, something waiting within the darkness. "Magda's emanations are still here," she said in a hoarse whisper. "But they don't feel right. Not at all. Something is dreadfully amiss. Everyone, please! Be careful. Be very careful."

Wes felt along the inside wall by the door frame for a light switch. He found none. He switched on a flashlight from the van's glove compartment. The narrow beam revealed a stripped living room. Black mildew speckled the walls. The pilot light was out in the wall heater and a clammy cold enshrouded the entire house. As Wes moved across the scarred hardwood floor, a board creaked underfoot. It seemed to be answered by another sound from deeper within the house: a slight, barely audible shifting of position by someone waiting somewhere in the darkness.

Wes stopped and called out, "Anybody home?"

No sound at all now, except for the *whoosh* of tires on a rain-wet street in the distance.

Wes found a light switch on the kitchen wall and turned it on. A naked bulb glared from the ceiling. The walls and floors were covered with rust-brown streaks and splotches. On the wall near the refrigerator someone had scrawled in rust-brown slashes the words HAIL SATAN! Beneath it was crudely drawn a pentagram, Sign of the Beast.

Wes rubbed his hand lightly across one of the smears on the wall. When he pulled it away, the tips of his fingers were stained with a sticky rust brown.

"Blood's starting to dry," he muttered to himself. "Only a few hours old."

Felicity gapsed behind him and his heart skipped several beats. "Can't you *smell* it?" she asked, poking her head into the kitchen. "It's positively overpow— Oh my God." She put a hand to her mouth. "Ritual murder has been committed here. Quite recently. That's the smell. They've hidden the body somewhere here on the premises. And the only reason Magda would do that— Dear God."

Felicity stepped back into the living room, calling in a loud voice, "Gwendolyn! We must leave here at once. She's set a trap for us!"

Gwendolyn's voice carried back from the short hallway leading to the bedrooms. "What on earth are you talking about? I've found the light switch in the hall and I've already checked the one bedroom and the bath." She headed for the closed door at the end of the hall. "The only trap Magda's set is her usual one of disappearing just when we think we've got our hands on her."

"Gwendolyn!" Panic entered Felicity's voice. *"Don't open that door!"* She turned to Wes. "Please stop her. This is a life-or-death matter, I assure you!"

Wes rushed toward the short older woman as she reached out for the knob of the closed door at the end of the hall. He got to her just as she turned the knob.

The door tore loose from its hinges, accompanied by an ear-splitting, inhuman roaring. A dark blur slammed into Gwendolyn, driving her and Wes down the hall and back out into the living room. Wes staggered back against the unlit wall heater. From what he could see in the weak light cast by the hall and kitchen bulbs, Gwendolyn was being attacked by a short, apelike creature. Wes moved forward and grabbed hold of the thing's rough hairy shoulders.

It turned on him, howling with murderous rage. Wes saw it clearly then and his blood ran cold. It stood hunched and wiry like a baboon, but its head looked more like a jackal's, red eyes and a large canine jaw bristling with fangs. Its long prehensile fingers were tipped with heavy hooked talons. Red eyes flashing, the creature laid its claws on Wes, picked him up bodily and hurled him across the room. He smashed into a bare wall and fell heavily to the floor.

The creature turned back to Gwendolyn, who sat dazed and bleeding on the floor. With one snap of its ferocious jaws, the jackal-headed monster bit off the older woman's head and began to chew it noisily, slobbering gobbets of flesh down the sides of its muzzle and onto its hairy chest. Felicity cried out in anguish, cowering near the kitchen doorway. Wes, stunned and badly bruised, struggled to his feet with the crowbar in one hand. He took an uncertain step toward the feasting monster.

"No!" Felicity called in a low but penetrating voice. "This is a demon familiar that Magda has summoned using the blood of a ritual murder victim. You can't possibly match its demoniacal strength. It would snap that crowbar like a breadstick. Only fire kills it." Despair entered her voice. "And there's no fire here."

Having chewed up the last of Gwendolyn's head, the creature poked its long snout down into the corpse's neck cavity and began to suck out the insides of the body, blood and muscles and tissue and internal organs, slurping up everything noisily and greedily like a child with a straw in a milkshake.

Wes moved slowly and cautiously behind the slobbering creature, inching his way toward the unlit wall heater. Once there, he swung the crowbar and struck the gas jet a crushing blow. The metal head popped off. At first Wes thought the gas had been turned off and his heart sank. Then he smelled the familiar odor. The creature looked up at the sound of the blow, its muzzle dripping blood and viscera, and hissed menacingly at Wes before returning to its hideous meal.

Wes grabbed Felicity from where she stood numbly watching Gwendolyn's desecration, and hurried her out the front door. On the threshold he stopped and lit a rolled-up piece of paper, a letter from a travel magazine editor, and placed the burning fuse on the hardwood floor. He started the van as they climbed in and backed out into the street while Felicity was still closing the passenger door.

They were almost at the end of the street when the escaping gas caught and the house blew. The blast pressure rattled the van's windows. Debris fell out into the street. Wes pulled over to one side and stopped, leaving the engine running. He and Felicity looked out the passenger window.

What remained of the house was burning fiercely.

Through the flames they could see a semi-human form writhing in agony as it blazed like a torch. The creature staggered back and forth among the burning walls and lashed out at nothing with fiery claws. Then, in a prodigious feat of strength, it leaped free of the roaring inferno and stumbled out onto the front lawn, heading for the van.

Felicity drew back in horror from the passenger window.

The burning monster came to a stop, lifted back its

jackal head and let forth a howl that penetrated the closed windows of the van. Then it shot upward in a blur of smoke like a giant roman candle, sputtering in long swooping arcs this way and that across the rainy night sky until it exploded in a burst of flame.

The burning walls of the house began to hiss and smolder under the falling rain. Wes pulled back out into the street.

"Where are you going?" Felicity asked.

"Emergency room, I guess."

"Please drive to IPS in Pasadena." Her pale blue eyes turned hard. "This is war now. We must see Roland."

chapter 38

the ANGER Of the GOD

Kraadar the cannibal god loomed forth from the shadows, more horribly reptilian-looking than ever, fanged jaws overflowing with half-devoured sacrificial victims, huge phallus projecting blunt and heavy as a club.

Jeff Geller let out a long breath and stepped back, his footsteps echoing off the polished marble floor of the empty Barringer Museum. "Pretty impressive, Karin." He looked at her. "Where'd you get him?"

Karin was not as impressed by Kraadar as she had been—tonight, in fact, he gave her the creeping willies— but she was glad of Jeff's interest in the statue. "The Museum of Antiquities in Cairo loaned him to us," she said. "It wasn't easy to arrange."

"I'll bet."

She frowned. "Not that it matters now. This statue won't be part of the show."

Jeff looked surprised. "Why not?"

"The chairman of the board thinks it's tasteless."

"And who's he?"

"Bromley," Karin sighed. "Milton Bromley."

Bromley was the one who had called Annie's with the

urgent message for Karin that Jeff had relayed to her at IPS: return to the Barringer and start taking charge of the Forgotten Gods exhibition again, tonight, or hand the whole thing over to someone else. Karin had been gone all of two days. Bromley's ultimatum was just his way of causing a crisis for his own amusement. Karin could usually handle that. But this time she did not have the strength to battle Heather's demon and Milton Bromley at the same time.

Then there were the Forgotten Gods themselves, Kraadar and the rest. Karin was not up to spending several hours alone with them in an empty museum at night. Not tonight. Not after what she heard from Roland Cameron. Not after what happened on Mulholland...

That was when Jeff Geller volunteered to accompany her to the Barringer and stay with her while she went over some last-minute pre-opening details. Karin refused the offer at first, claiming that she couldn't leave Heather and her job wasn't that important. But Jeff persisted and at last she agreed, mainly because she liked him.

He was easy to like.

But don't start liking him too much, she warned herself, thinking of David and Brett and the way her relationships usually worked out.

Karin leaned over to check the light on the Baal display. She wrote a note asking Jim Rice to have it replaced. Sighing, she reflected that Dodge Andrews should be the one to take care of lighting details like this. But Bromley had fired Dodge.

"Why does Bromley's opinion matter so much?" Jeff asked. "I thought you were head curator."

"I am. But Bromley runs me." She smiled wryly. "At least he likes to think so."

"Ever thought of telling him—nicely, of course—to take his asshole attitude and back off a few miles?"

Karin laughed. "Lots of times! But—"

"But Mrs. Roberts has the good breeding not to use manners as vulgar as yours."

Karin cried out in surprise. Jeff looked up.

Milton Bromley stood there with his Saville Row suit freshly pressed and his designer tie firmly knotted. One eyebrow rose above his black-framed glasses as he stared at Jeff, not much liking what he saw.

"Mr. Bromley." Karin tried to smile. "I didn't expect to find you here so late."

"Nor did I, my dear." He gave her a critical look. "But I can't depend on you anymore. I wasn't sure you'd show up tonight."

"Mr. Bromley!" Karin objected. "I've only been gone two days. You know me. I never take time off."

"Right before the opening of a major exhibition is a poor time to start." He glanced at Jeff. "Who's this?"

Jeff introduced himself and offered a hand.

Bromley did not take it. "Parapsychologists. Hmmmmmm. Aren't they the ones who go around chasing poltergeists and interviewing fortune tellers?"

Karin saw Jeff's eyes narrow. If it had been David, the next step would have been a shouting match or fight.

Jeff answered politely, "Parapsychologists spend their time studying physical phenomena that no one else takes very seriously."

Bromley turned to Karin. "I hope you're not planning on hiring him as a consultant."

Karin shook her head. "He's just helping me tonight."

"I'm somewhat relieved. Now that we're finally rid of that neurotic fag Dodge Andrews, I'm not anxious to bring any more madmen onto the payroll."

"You've got a very nice museum here, Mr. Bromley," Jeff said, looking around at the Forgotten Gods. "Of course, some of the statues are just a bit, ah, tasteless. But that's not your fault, is it, sir?"

Bromley's mouth opened, then closed. He was still trying to think of an appropriate comeback when a distant telephone started ringing.

Karin looked up. "That's my phone!"

Jeff put a hand on her shoulder. "Stay here. I'll get it

for you." He ran across the marble floor toward the ringing phone with long, easy strides.

"Energetic lad." Bromley turned to Karin. "Does young Brett Courtney know about him?"

Karin stepped back as if she had been slapped. "Since when is that any of your business?"

"Only when it threatens to interfere with your professional duties here at the Barringer."

Karin, furious, turned her back on Bromley.

"Brett comes from a good family," Bromley said. "You don't want to string along a boy like—"

Echoing footsteps interrupted Bromley's discourse. He and Karin looked up to see Jeff walking rapidly toward them, grim determination in his eyes.

"Karin," he addressed her quietly, "we've got to get back to IPS."

She looked shaken. "Is Heather all right?"

Jeff started to say something, then stopped. "I'll explain on the way over."

She put a hand to her mouth. "Oh Christ! You said she'd be okay there. You promised!" Tears filled her eyes. "I trusted you!"

Jeff took her hands in his. "Trust me now. We have to leave."

Karin shook her head, tears wetting her cheeks, and hurried with Jeff toward the exit at the far end of the main exhibition hall.

"I was afraid of something like this!" Bromley called after them. "When you let personal problems—"

Jeff looked back over his shoulder. "Shut up, okay? Just this once."

Bromley frowned until the exit door slammed shut. Then he allowed himself a smug, self-satisfied smile. She wasn't a bad little girl, really. But she needed discipline. All women did. Spare the discipline and spoil the girl. True in his father's time and truer now than ever, what with all the rampant feminist nonsense around and the attacks from every quarter on the sanctity of home and family. That's what Karin needed more of. Home and family. Brett Courtney was just the lad to steer her in the right direction there, if she had enough sense to accept him.

Bromley looked around at the Forgotten Gods. The show was shaping up nicely. Karin had done a good job, as always. Some of the objects *were* a bit tasteless, that ill-mannered young spookhunter's snide comments notwithstanding. But except for—

A dark frown settled over Bromley's face as his gaze came to rest on the towering statue of Kraadar the cannibal god, fertility symbol of ancient Sumeria.

It was such a disgusting thing, a lewd priapic demon, shamelessly violating every law of God and common decency. Whatever had possessed Karin to make her think she could include it in the show?

Bromley walked over until he was standing before the huge statue. Here, in an unlighted side recess of the main exhibition hall, shadows and half-lights fell across Kraadar's grotesque stone features. His slanted reptilian eyes seemed to glisten. The bat-wing ears looked as if they might start to wiggle at any moment. Clawed hands appeared ready to reach out and seize more victims for his ever-grasping jaws. And the obscene, aggressively erect phallus seemed to throb with inhuman lust.

Bromley shuddered at the hulking monstrosity, making a mental note to have Jim Rice haul the damned thing away and put it in storage for the duration of the exhibition. After that it would be Karin's problem to ship it back to wherever it belonged.

Still frowning, Bromley had started back to his own office when the statue of Kraadar suddenly moved. Bromley blinked his eyes and looked again, certain that what he thought he saw had actually been nothing more than a trick of the half-lights and the shadows.

It moved again.

Bromley gasped and backed up a few quick steps, his heart fluttering. He recalled fearfully what happened the last time a minor earthquake had rocked the monumental statue. Of course it *had* been an earthquake, no matter what Karin and Jim Rice and those other young idiots claimed. It was a localized quake, affecting only Kraadar and not the other statues.

What else, Bromley asked himself uneasily, *Dear God, what else could it have been?*

The massive statue lurched forward, grinding loudly across the polished marble floor.

Bromley leaped back this time, almost stumbling over his own feet. "Abomination!" he cried out, voice quivering like a feeble old man's. "Abomination before God!"

The marble walls of the main exhibition hall rang with his cries. The gigantic statue lumbered forward again, moving slowly but deliberately toward him. Bromley raised his arms in the sign of the cross, holding them out to ward off the gargantuan block of carved stone that loomed threateningly above him.

"Unclean thing!" he shrieked, losing all control. "Stop in the name of God! I command you!"

Bromley's eyes darted about the deserted museum, his heart hammering wildly as he tried to tell himself that he was overreacting, that there had to be—there *must* be—a perfectly natural explanation for this...

He noticed then that the other statues in the room all seemed to have shifted position slightly, to have turned just enough to let the other Forgotten Gods observe what was taking place here in the main exhibition hall, in the dead of night, with no one around but Milton Bromley and the discarded, silent deities of another age.

The stone colossus of Kraadar the cannibal god began to rock back and forth on its massive base, making the marble floor beneath Bromley's feet tremble.

Terrified, he screamed and fled for his life.

His right ankle gave out. He stumbled and fell facedown onto the polished marble. Blood leaked from his smashed nose. He lifted his head in pain and looked up at the gigantic statue towering above him. Tears came to his eyes, mixed with blood from his broken nose. He raised a pudgy, well-manicured hand in feeble protest against the inevitable.

With one last convulsive movement, the enormous statue of Kraadar the cannibal god toppled forward and came crashing down on Milton Bromley like an avalanche of grinning, solid stone.

chapter 39

the call of azgaroth

It came to Heather while she slept.

Falling asleep had not been easy. The room they gave her at IPS, while nothing like her bedroom at home, was okay—except for all the monitoring equipment, the wall microphones, the ceiling video cameras, the separate aura-sensing machines along the wall opposite the bed. Straight up she told Roland that she would not stay in a bugged room with cameras peeping at her all the time. He was agreeable about it, for an adult. Since she was not under formal observation, he decided there would be no problem with shutting off the monitoring devices, for now.

Heather did not like the "for now" part of it. But Roland was true to his word. He even let her see how they disconnected the cameras and other machines. She did not entirely trust him. He was a doctor, after all. But he was very different from that other doctor in her life, her father, David Roberts. Roland listened to what she said and did not think she was crazy or sick because of what had happened at Magda's. *It's just something we have to deal with,* he told her. And he said it in a nice voice, not a doctor voice. He was a nice guy. So was the other one who went off to the Barringer with her mom. If you had to spend time with doctors, Heather decided, it was better if they were nice guys.

The guy she would rather be spending time with was Brian. But she knew there was little chance of that. Brian did not know where she was now and would not be able to get inside IPS even if he did. Besides, what did they really have between them anyway? Just the fact that he said he loved her and she was stupid enough to say she loved him back. Nobody took shit like that seriously these days.

Except it felt serious.

So she thought about Brian for a while and was miserable, then happy, then miserable again, and somewhere between these alternations, she drifted off to sleep.

She and Sherone were shopping in the Beverly Center, loaded down with shoes, clothes and perfume. But no one would accept their credit cards. Sherone was yelling at some snotty salesbitch with too much makeup and a fish-eye stare. Then Heather was lying nude on her back on the sand beside the ocean. For a moment she thought it was the Cove and Brian was with her, kissing her on the lips, then on her neck, then moving down slowly to the hollow between her breasts, then kissing her breasts, her nipples, the waves rushing and breaking in the distance, sea gulls crying overhead.

Then it was dark. Someone was still kissing her nipples, sucking on them, moving from one to the other, then back again, taking time with them. Heather stretched like a cat, arching her back up off the mattress, shoving her erect nipple deeper into the warm, wet, eager mouth. Then she was awake. A dim blue light burned somewhere in the room. A smooth, white body bent over hers, alabaster skin even paler and softer than her own. She looked at the head on her breast, shiny black hair falling in ringlets about his face, dark eyelashes on closed eyes, lips full and ruby red as they sucked at her nipple, making it large and hard, swollen with passion.

343

She grabbed him by his shoulders and pulled him from her breast. "Who are you?" she asked breathlessly.

The dark-lashed eyelids opened to reveal eyes black as midnight, eyes so black that Heather, staring deep into them, felt herself falling into a vast and bottomless pit, dropping down and down into the darkness, rushing millions of miles beyond the sun and the moon and the stars and all forms of light into an endless universe where there was only darkness and nothing else.

She gasped and shook her head, and looked down at the dark curly head between her thighs, his smooth back and shoulders shining white even against her own pale skin, everything touched faintly by the soft blue light, the only sound the beating of Heather's own heart—at least she thought it was her heart—enormously amplified, pounding slowly, repetitively, like a gigantic drum. One white, veinless hand rested on her breast, caressing her swollen nipple, pulling on it slowly until the sensitive flesh stretched and Heather moaned as a wave of pleasure shuddered through her body, moving up from her loins and her stomach and through her chest and throat and she moaned again.

He sat astride her, his alabaster skin glowing, one hand still on her breast, the other guiding an oversize penis, thick and semi-erect like a pale white worm, as it probed the lips of her vagina. It felt cold as ice, coarse and scaly despite its smooth white appearance. Heather cried out in fear. But no sound came, other than the slow, steady beating of the enormous heart—not her heart, she finally realized with a chill, but *his* heart.

She screamed soundlessly.

His black eyes turned red, burning with a fierce and ancient rage. The soft, veinless white hand on her breast began to stretch and transform itself. Fingernails curved into claws. Scales and lumps crusted over the smooth white flesh, turning it dark and misshapen. Heather opened her mouth and screamed in silent, helpless terror.

She woke up screaming, her ears ringing with the sound. She was naked, her body covered with sweat. Her nightgown lay crumpled at the foot of the bed. Her nipples stood out erect and swollen from her full white breasts. The sheet beneath her was sticky with vaginal secretions. She sat up in bed, breathing hard, long red hair clinging damply to her back. The room was hot and dry and airless as a sauna. A small night-light burned near a baseboard, neon white instead of pale blue.

Over the sounds of her own frightened breathing and rain falling hard against the windowpane, she heard someone shouting outside, the same word over and over, as if calling out a name. Heather got out of bed, the carpet soft beneath her bare feet, and moved over to the window. She drew back the thick curtain.

The voice came again, calling out the name.

Her name.

Naked flesh tingling, she looked out through the rain-streaked glass and two stories down onto the open expanse of lawn where two figures stood, alone, looking up at her.

Downstairs, Roland Cameron stepped out of the elevator into the main lobby of the IPS building, a worn leather briefcase in one hand, a sheaf of papers in the other. He glanced at his watch. 2:45 A.M. It was good after all, he reflected, that his wife had left him these many years ago. Not a day went by that he did not still miss Penelope. But what kind of life could he have given her, leaving work this late? And still leaving too soon, he knew. The business with the Roberts girl was proving very difficult. He had to find a way to anticipate Azgaroth's next move. If not—

The sound of voices from the central reception desk caught his attention. At this time of night the lobby was usually empty, except for Gerald Redmond, a black six-foot-four-inch former L.A.P.D. officer who was head of security for the graveyard shift. Gerald was sitting behind his monitors at the reception desk, listening to a skinny young boy with damp straight black hair and rainwater dripping off the end of his nose.

"Look," Gerald raised a hand, "I understand where you're coming from. But you've got to believe me—what's your name again?"

Brian McNulty told him.

"Brian, you've got to believe me. I don't know which room your girlfriend's in and I have no way of finding out."

"There's always a way." Brian took out his wallet. "If it's a question of showing my gratitude—"

"Son, let's not even get into that. I am not for sale. Not unless the buyer happens to be J. Paul Getty. And because I am such a shrewd judge of character, something tells me you are not J. Paul Getty."

Roland came over to the reception desk. "What seems to be the difficulty, Mr. Redmond?"

Gerald turned in his swivel chair. "Dr. Cameron, good morning. This young man—"

"I'm looking for a friend. Heather Roberts."

"And why must you see her," Roland glanced at his watch, "right now?"

Brian took a quick breath and tried to size up Roland Cameron. He was an adult, therefore an obstacle. But he also seemed to have it all together, like Sherone's dad, Wes. He was older, but he didn't seem to think that made him God.

"I—" Brian hesitated. "You know about what happened at Magda's?"

"Enough for now." Roland looked at him carefully. "You must be the young man who was with her at the missile station, after you barely escaped drowning in her swimming pool. Brian—something."

Brian's eyes widened with respect. "McNulty," he said softly, then in a rush, "Her best friend Sherone's been kidnapped. Magda has to be the one who did it. I don't know why, but if she grabbed Sherone, she might—"

"—come here looking for your friend Heather next. Yes." Roland nodded, considering the problem. "Yes, one is forced to agree. That's quite possible, Brian. Tell me, when she—"

Gerald Redmond's deep voice boomed out across the lobby. "Can I help you, sir?"

Brett Courtney wiped rainwater off his forehead and shook excess drops from the rose bouquet in his right hand. "I'm—" He blinked. "I'm an attorney."

"Municipal building's on the other side of town," Gerald said.

Brett started over. "Sorry. I mean, I'm here to see Karin Roberts."

Gerald looked at Roland. "Thought her name was Heather."

Roland said to Brett, "I'm afraid Mrs. Roberts is elsewhere at the moment. And it's rather past visiting hours in any event. Perhaps—"

Gerald Redmond rose to his feet and lifted a hand radio to his mouth in one swift movement. "S-2. Base. Got a little party here. Need some backup. On the double."

"You got it," crackled the voice on the other end.

Gerald snapped off the radio. "Help you folks?"

Brian turned around and drew a sharp breath.

"Ah," Roland said softly, laying down the sheaf of papers and switching the briefcase to his right hand.

Magda Prokash stood leaning on her gnarled wooden staff, laboring for breath. Beside her, Damon, the tattooed skinhead, bounced on his heels, eyes burning bright from too many drugs.

"Him," Magda whispered, nodding at Roland, "and him too." She nodded at Brian.

Damon drew out a combat knife with a broad six-inch blade and lunged at Roland. The white-haired parapsychologist raised his briefcase like a shield, just in time to catch the blade point as it cut into the worn leather.

Gerald Redmond stepped out from behind the reception desk, unsnapping his holstered Smith and Wesson .38 as he moved.

The force of Damon's knife thrust tore Roland's briefcase from his hand. Damon pulled back the knife for a lateral slash.

"Hey!" Brett Courtney dropped the rose bouquet and grabbed Damon's knife arm with a grip made powerful by regular workouts, every other day, on the Nautilus machines at the L.A. Athletic Club. "What do you think—"

Damon shifted the knife to his other hand and slashed it across Brett's throat, severing his jugular vein. Brett's mouth dropped open. He grabbed his neck with both hands and fell to his knees, blood spurting between his fingers like water from a slit hose. Damon, spattered with blood, moved around Brett and came after Brian.

"Freeze, asshole!" Gerald ordered, .38 raised.

Brian dropped to one side. Damon kept coming. Gerald fired. The bullet caught Damon between his shoulder blades. He jerked to a stop, throwing his arms out wide. The knife flew from his grasp, spinning across the lobby.

Gerald was preparing to fire again when Roland called out a warning. Gerald paused. His mouth snapped open with a guttural groan. A long, thin knife blade burst from his chest like the beak of a mechanical bird. Behind him, Magda savagely twisted her lethal wooden staff into his back with one hand, the false wooden cap held in the other. Gerald's .38 clattered onto the tiles of the lobby. As his body slumped down to the floor, Magda gritted her teeth and wrenched the impaling staff out of his back. Then she turned on Roland.

Brian stooped forward and scooped up Gerald's .38.

Magda raised her staff like a javelin, aiming it at Roland, who stood looking at her, calm and unafraid.

"This sort of thing will do no good," he said.

She drew back the staff.

"Drop it, Magda!" Brian's voice was high-pitched and nervous. But he had the .38 pointed straight at her.

Magda's lip curled into a contemptuous sneer. "Cowardly little boy. You haven't the nerve for it."

Brian pulled the trigger, his eyes squeezing shut involuntarily as the gun bucked in his hand. The bullet went wide of its target, blowing out a fluorescent light fixture in the ceiling. Glass and plaster showered down onto the tile floor. Magda stared at him, a wary look in her hard gray eyes. Then she turned and fled out the front door, her brown monk's robe billowing like a sail behind her.

Roland leaned against the reception counter, one hand on his heart. Brian stood there, staring at the .38 revolver. He looked up, startled, when the front door banged open and two security officers came running into the lobby, guns drawn. They stopped when they saw the bodies and the blood.

"Jesus Christ!" said the shorter of the two officers. "Go help Redmond!" he ordered his partner. "Holy shit. Dr. Cameron! You okay?"

Roland nodded. "See to the victims, though I fear they're past all help." He shook his head. "Madness. Absolute madness. Why would she— Good God!"

He leaned over one of the monitors behind the central reception desk. "Emergency light for 205. Heather Roberts's room. All this butchery was nothing but a pretext—"

He called to the short security officer. "Mr. Jarvis! Room 205. At once. Keep your gun ready."

Jarvis rose from where he had been examining Brett Courtney's motionless body, but Brian was already through the door marked STAIRS—EMERGENCY USE ONLY.

Heather drew in her breath as she stared through the rain-streaked window. Two stories down, in the middle of an open lawn, stood Sherone Livingston and blond five-year-old Adam Newmar, looking up at the window to

Heather's room with Heather standing naked behind it. Sherone called up to her, cold and frightened in the rainy darkness down below.

"Sherone," Heather whispered, her breath fogging the window. "Adam."

A sudden rush of dizziness came over her. She stepped back, grabbing the windowsill for support. The hot, dry atmosphere of the room seemed to be sucking air from her lungs. Images from her erotic dream came flashing back to her—except it had not been a dream. *It felt too real,* she thought, shuddering in the dry heat. She had fallen asleep and had dreamed and then had awakened and—

It was no dream.

He had made contact with her.

AZGAROTH

Panic rose in her throat, threatening to choke her. She stared out the window again. Sherone stood shivering in the cold rain, her arms protectively around Adam, whose teeth chattered visibly even at this distance, while behind them, like a malignant guardian, loomed the vampiric form of Seamus Harrach—the pale-faced terror who had first appeared to Heather in the nightmare in her bedroom, who had kidnapped a little Mexican boy and blinded his mother and then turned to her, black teeth rotting in his open mouth, and said, *"Bring us the Perfect Blood Offering."*

Her five-year-old cousin, Adam Newmar.

He's taken him and Sherone, she thought, *and now he wants me to go with them.*

A savage anger came over Heather then, mixed with a sense of power, a certain knowledge of her own strength. She had not asked for this. She had not called . . . AZGAROTH . . . forth from the darkness. She had not willed the fear and the horror and the deaths. She had *not,* no matter what anyone said! But it was hers now, all of it, whether she asked for it or not.

In her mind's eye she looked out across a vast series of

extended geometrical planes unfolding infinitely into blackness. And across the vastness she saw the horrible events of the past few days, vivid and three-dimensional. She saw Sherone and Magda and the Wicca. She saw the nightmares and the burned doll and the deaths of Kurt and Troy and the others and the attack on her and her mother in the rain on Mulholland. She saw the white-limbed, black-eyed boy seducing her and then becoming a red-eyed thing of darkness. And she knew now that she was Azgaroth's, that he possessed her, and that she possessed him.

And his power.

The glass in the windowpane exploded, blowing back inside the room in thousands of glittering fragments that passed by Heather but did not cut her naked flesh. She climbed up onto the windowsill, crouching inside the frame of the open window. The heavy rain, cold and wind-whipped, beat upon her naked flesh. But she did not feel cold or wet.

Down below, Tamara Devon, soaked and miserable as a drowned rat, lifted a lightweight aluminum ladder against the side of the IPS building, trying to position it beneath the window of Heather's room. Heather looked down at the ladder waving awkwardly in the windswept rain, at Sherone and Adam shivering in the middle of the lawn, at Seamus Harrach standing behind them, staring up at her.

Heather leaped from the windowsill.

Sherone screamed and started to rush forward. Tamara fell back, looking up open-mouthed into the rain, the ladder toppling back from the side of the building and crashing down onto the lawn.

For several seconds Heather stood suspended in midair like a naked goddess in demonic ascension, arms outstretched, pale skin shining in the darkness, long red hair blowing in the wind and the rain. Then, slowly, she began to descend, floating down gracefully until her bare feet touched the damp grass of the lawn. A blinding flash of lightning split the rain-dark sky, accompanied by an earth-shaking clap of thunder. Sherone and Adam shut their eyes against the lightning's glare. Even Seamus Harrach squinted, his black-toothed mouth agape in something like awe.

The lightning came again, snaking down toward the middle of the lawn. Brilliant white light encircled Heather, wrapping around her body without burning her naked flesh. Her white skin shimmered as if lighted from within. Her blue eyes glowed in the rainy darkness. The others on the lawn turned their faces from the brightness of the electical firestorm, shielding their eyes with their hands.

Then, as suddenly as if a switch had been turned off, the lightning and thunder stopped, along with the rain. The wind continued to blow and actually increased in velocity. But it became hot and dry, like a Santa Ana wind blowing down on the city from over the mountains and out of the desert. Heather stood naked before the others, hands at her sides, chin raised, breasts thrust forward, nipples still erect and enlarged, a sense of power radiating from her as forcefully as heat from the blowing wind.

Seamus Harrach regarded her with a look of reverence on his chalk-white death mask of a face. "The sacred virgin," he murmured, bowing slightly to her, then, glancing at Adam, "and the Perfect Blood Offering."

He moved forward, taking off his own heavy dark cloak to wrap around Heather's nakedness.

But the fierce light burning in her blue eyes and the wildness of her long red hair whipping in the dry, hot wind made even Seamus Harrach step back, afraid.

chapter 40

WAR COUNCIL

The conference room in the IPS building was soundproof and windowless, with a long blond-wood table surrounded by comfortable leather chairs. But there was nothing comfortable about the room or its atmosphere, or its occupants, in those early morning hours following Heather's disappearance.

Roland, at the head of the table, appeared to have aged visibly. Jeff Geller sat next to him, tense and concerned. Karin's eyes were red from crying, her shoulders bowed with grief. Maureen Magnusson sat beside her daughter, ashen-faced and grim. Wes Livingston seemed calm, but a dark determination clouded his eyes. Felicity Perkins, sitting beside him, appeared quiet and withdrawn, pale blue eyes lost in thought, as if she could see things not readily apparent to the others. Brian McNulty sat a few chairs off by himself, isolated, but alert to what was going on.

David Roberts, arms folded belligerently on top of the table as if he owned it, leaned forward and demanded of Roland, "Why haven't the police learned anything yet?"

Roland cleared his throat. "The police, as a general rule, take little interest in this sort of thing. They tend to regard occult crimes and Satanic rituals as publicity stunts. They're interested in murder, or course, and they found the murderer responsible for the carnage downstairs in the lobby: Magda's boy, the dead youth with the shaven head, conveniently dead himself. The police now seem to feel that solves—"

"What about the kidnapping?" David interrupted impatiently. "Two teenage girls and a little boy have been abducted by a gang of psychopaths!"

"The police have entered the names of all three children into their missing persons file," Roland said. "One supposes it will be followed up, eventually."

"The kids aren't missing!" David objected.

"Right," Roland agreed. "But the police perceive it that way."

David snorted in disgust.

Karin looked at Roland, tears in her eyes. "They have to do *something*."

"They might," Roland said gently, "but not right away. Whatever the police decide to do will take time. And time, in our case, is rapidly running out."

Roland glanced at Karin before going on. "In all likelihood, the three children will be forced by Magda to participate in a special witches' sabbath. The Blood Sabbath. A dreadful ceremony that may well cost them their lives."

Karin stifled a sob. Maureen began toying with a large emerald ring on her right hand, taking it off and putting it back on again, obsessively, mechanically.

"The small boy," Roland continued quietly, "Adam Newmar, will most likely be offered as a blood sacrifice."

A sharp gasp escaped Maureen. The oversize emerald ring clattered noisily onto the tabletop.

Roland turned and looked at Wes Livingston. "Sherone may be sacrificed as well."

Wes said nothing, but the muscles in his face contracted.

"What about Heather?" Karin asked hoarsely.

Roland took a deep breath. "Heather's fate is more . . . problematical. They almost certainly won't sacrifice her right away. They know, as we do, that she is a channel for Azgaroth, a means of calling him forth to the Blood Sabbath. She is essential to their plans."

Something like hope stole briefly across Karin's strained features.

"However," Roland warned, "she is still in great danger. She is frightened now, upset, in a highly emotional state. This will make her channeling of the demon unpredictable and hazardous in the extreme. Azgaroth's terrible power may be unleashed as it has never been before, at least not on this planet—with disastrous consequences for Heather and the others, for everyone within a given radius of the Blood Sabbath."

Karin covered her face with her hands. Maureen laid a hand gently on her daughter's arm, tears glistening in her own eyes.

David Roberts threw down a pen with weary contempt. "Sorry. There's only so much of this bullshit I can handle." He looked hard at Roland. "We have got a life-threatening emergency on our hands, for which I hold you and your incompetent staff entirely responsible, by the way. Time is running out, like you say, and what are you doing about it? Bullshitting about witches and demons and magic rituals! Jesus H. Christ!"

Karin took her hands from her face. "David, shut up."

He turned on her. "You'd like that, wouldn't you? Let me shut up and let you keep dragging Heather and yourself deeper and deeper into this insanity. Sorry, Karin. You had your chance. You took our daughter away from competent medical care and put her in the hands of these frauds. Now it's time for her to get help from some qualified professionals!"

"Exactly what do you and your qualified associates plan to do about it?" Jeff Geller asked.

David's green eyes narrowed as he stared at Jeff. No one had to tell him about this prick. He had seen him enter the conference room with Karin, one hand on her shoulder as he helped her with a chair.

"If the police are getting nowhere," David answered curtly, "then it's time to hire some security professionals, private investigators."

"Where would they start looking?" Jeff asked.

"Excuse me?" Hostility edged David's voice.

"Knowing where to look," Roland intervened, "is not as easy as it sounds. Magda has taken care to cover her tracks, as we have learned from the heroic investigations of Miss Perkins and Mr. Livingston." Roland nodded to them. "We think we know what Magda is going to do next. But we do not know where she plans to hold the Blood Sabbath. However, from what is known of witches' sabbaths in general, we can deduce three things."

Sensing that the whole room was with Roland and against him, David sat back down in his chair, resentfully.

"First," Roland continued, "we know that a witches' sabbath involving blood sacrifice cannot be held in any place open to casual observation. This rules out backyards, public parks, beaches and the lot. Secondly, we know that trees, especially oak trees, play a crucial role in ritual witchcraft. Thirdly, we know that mountains hold a special place in magical lore. Witches' sabbaths of the past were often held on mountaintops, as in the *Walpurgisnacht* of Central European tradition."

Roland paused. "All three facts would seem to indicate that Magda Prokash and Seamus Harrach will choose a mountainous, heavily forested site for the celebration of their Blood Sabbath. Unfortunately, there are many such places, some of them true wilderness areas, within easy driving distance of Los Angeles."

The telephone at the head of the conference table rang. Jeff excused himself and answered it. As he was replacing the handset, the door opened. A young woman with short dark hair and a conservatively cut suit entered and handed Jeff a stack of papers.

Roland took one from him and glanced at it briefly before going on. "We have tried to map out some of the more likely sites here, using input variables such as forest density, elevation from sea level, difficulty of access and known use by other groups practicing ritual magic. It narrows down our choices somewhat, but the possibilities are still overwhelming. That is when we must turn to Miss Perkins for help."

Roland nodded to Felicity. "Mis Perkins is an extremely gifted Sensitive. She has recently had a rather harrowing encounter with Magda's magic and thus retains a powerful sense of that woman's aura. It should enable her to trace the movements of Magda and her three captives as accurately as a bloodhound follows a freshly laid trail. Even here in this room, she should be able to perceive some sense of our quarry."

Felicity Perkins spoke in a voice so soft that the others had to lean forward and strain to hear her. "They are moving into the mountains," she said. "I can feel the steepness of the ascent and smell the fragrance of pines and other conifers. We are in a motorized vehicle of some kind. I cannot see the faces of all those with us. But the children are there. Two young girls. One with pale skin and long red hair, wrapped in a heavy cloak. The other with sunburnt skin and dark blond hair, wearing a blue jacket several sizes too large for her. The little blond boy is fast asleep, his head resting in the lap of the red-haired girl."

Karin put a hand to her mouth.

David shook his head reproachfully. "Come on, Dr. Cameron. Give us a break. What do we do now? Join hands around the table and pray for their safe return?"

A frown creased Roland's forehead. "We will depart as soon as possible and, with Miss Perkins's help, follow Magda's trail to the site of the Blood Sabbath. Then, when the time is right, we shall rescue the children."

Silence fell on the room. Even David was silent.

Then he said, "Am I hearing you right? All of us here

are going out to track down the kids and bring 'em back alive?"

"Not all of us," Roland corrected him. "That would be both unnecessary and ill-advised."

David smiled cynically. "Plan on taking any weapons with you? Those guys made one hell of a mess downstairs in your lobby. Ever occur to you they might get just a little excited if you try to crash their party?"

"All necessary precautions will be taken," Roland said. "But the most powerful weapons in the world will not protect us from the greatest danger at the Sabbath."

David smiled again. "Oh yeah, almost forgot. The ol' bogeyman. Azmerov. Kalashnikov. Whatever."

Roland did not return David's smile. "Like most people, Dr. Roberts, you seem to have a set of strangely misplaced values. The unfortunate people killed in the lobby were dispatched rather conventionally with knives. The four persons killed to date by Azgaroth have all been destroyed in especially painful and hideous ways."

He studied David thoughtfully. "Perhaps you make light of it because the truth is too horrible for you to face. If that is the case, you have my sympathy. But let me warn you: do not underestimate the reality of the danger." Roland leaned forward. "We go forth to challenge an immense and malignant power. If we fail, things will not go pleasantly with us. Azgaroth will reach inside your mind, Dr. Roberts. He will discover your darkest fears, your secret weaknesses. And he will use them. Be sure of that. He will use them mercilessly to torment and destroy you."

The smile was still fixed on David's face, but it was beginning to resemble the frozen rictus of a lockjaw victim.

He got to his feet suddenly, looking around at the others. "Look, I came here because I love my daughter and I want to help her. I never agreed to take part in any half-assed Halloween pranks. Witches' sabbaths, bullshit like that. If it turns you on, folks, it's all yours. But count me out." He headed for the door.

Karin looked up at him. "I never thought I'd see you act like a coward in public."

He came to an abrupt halt.

"But it just goes to show, you never really know someone."

David's face turned livid. "Look, you little—"

Maureen's stentorian voice drowned him out. "Well, Davie? Is that it? Are you afraid?"

"Goddamn it!" he exploded at Maureen. "You think I'm afraid of some figment of *his* imagination?" He pointed at Roland. "I haven't got time for this shit! I'm one of the top heart surgeons in the world! I had to cancel an emergency quadruple-bypass operation this morning just so I could come here and listen to him shoot his mouth off!" David paused, panting for breath.

Maureen stared him down. "If you're not afraid, Davie Roberts, then why in the name of God are you deserting us at a time like this?"

He opened his mouth, started to say something, stopped, licked his lips, looked at Roland, Jeff, several of the others, carefully avoiding Karin, then turned back to Maureen. "Okay. If it means that much to you, I'll stay. All right?"

"It might be nice," Maureen said, "if it meant a little something to you too."

"Goddamn it, Maureen! You know it does!" He sat down heavily in the leather chair, his face a mask of sullen resentment.

Roland leaned forward. "We have no time to waste, gentlemen. The four of us and Miss Perkins must leave at once. Mr. Livingston has graciously volunteered the use of his four-wheel-drive van—"

"Wait a minute." Karin shook her head, as if she did not understand. "'Gentlemen'? 'The four of us'? What's going on here? Jeff?" She turned to him.

Jeff started to say something, then handed it off to Roland.

"One had assumed," Roland said, "that this was all understood beforehand. The task we are about to attempt is frightfully dangerous. I cannot in good conscience—"

"You're planning on making it a men's club, then, is that it?" Karin asked. "You, Jeff, David and . . ." She blanked out on Wes Livingston's name.

"Wes," he helped her.

"Thanks. So it's just the four of you?"

"It's better this way, Karin," Jeff said gently.

"Better for you, maybe. What about me? She's *my* daughter. Why can't I go along?"

Roland looked taken aback. "Mrs. Roberts, it's not open to discussion. Anyone who accompanies us will be placing himself in a life-threatening situation. Women and children have no—"

"I'm no child!" Brian McNulty called out from the far end of the table.

"You're a brave and intelligent young man," Roland told him, "but you're not going with us."

Brian got to his feet. "The hell I'm not!"

Roland glanced at his watch. "We must get started."

"Hold on." Karin rose from her chair and pointed at Felicity Perkins. "You're taking her with you."

"That's unavoidable," Roland replied. "Miss Perkins is the only person who can lead us to Magda and the captives."

"You're still exposing her to danger," Karin said. "So why can't I go? Why can't we all go?"

A pained look crossed Roland's face. "Mrs. Roberts, please let's don't make this difficult. I share your concern. We are all concerned, even those not with us at present, such as your sister and her husband, who are still in hospital being treated for shock."

Karin winced with guilt at the thought of what had happened to Annie and Sam, and Adam.

"But don't you see," Roland continued, "that it's a matter of logistics as well as safety? A small group can travel faster and, when the time comes, act more quickly.

We must succeed in this attempt. I know you understand that, Mrs. Roberts."

She looked at him glumly. "So the bottom line is, you're still saying I can't go?"

Roland nodded. "I'm afraid so."

"But you're forgetting one thing, Dr. Cameron!" Maureen interjected in a piercing voice. "My daughter and I are not frightened secretaries or browbeaten housewives! We have a bit of money on my side of the family, you know. We're used to getting what we want." The light of battle gleamed in Maureen's green eyes. "Just try and stop us! Go ahead. Leave without us and see what happens! We'll follow you every step of the way! If you go into the mountains, we'll rent jeeps. Every one of us! Karin. Myself. That boy back there, what's-his-name."

"She's right," Karin said. "We'll follow you!"

"Me too!" Brian put in.

Roland let out along sigh. "Mrs. Magnusson—"

"Maybe you ought to give in and let them come along," Wes said to him. "The van can hold eight easy. And if you're right about what kind of trouble we're headed for, we'll need all the help we can get. Besides," Wes added, "if they're going to follow us anyway, one van will be a lot less conspicuous than a whole convoy."

Roland seemed to waver. "But the risk . . ."

Wes shrugged. "Life's a risk. Only thing you can do is weigh it against the value of what you want. In this case, I think we all agree that the goal is worth the risk."

Karin smiled at him. "Thank you." She turned to Roland. "It's very important that I go with you. I have to be there. No matter what happens . . ."

Karin swallowed. "For a long time now, I've felt that Heather's been slipping away from me, that I've been losing her, little by little, the way mothers and daughters can lose each other and grow apart."

She looked over to where her own mother sat watching her, moisture glinting in her sharp green eyes.

"Now, I really *have* lost her. I won't accept that. I can't. I want her back. It's very important to me. It's . . . everything." Karin swallowed again, blinking back tears. "I want a last chance to bring her back again. But it has to be *my* chance! Not somebody else taking the chance for me." She looked at Roland. "Do you understand what I mean? Do you know what I'm trying to say?"

"Yes." He nodded, arriving finally at his own decision. "Yes, I think I do."

chapter 41

the mountains of erebus

The metal floor of the covered truck bed was cold beneath Heather's bare feet and hard on her bottom as the truck bounced over rough road, jolting her back and forth. She was naked under the heavy, smelly cloak Seamus Harrach had wrapped around her and she felt cold, damn cold, and she had to go to the bathroom bad. The godlike omnipotence she had experienced at IPS was fading fast.

She remembered jumping from the second-story window, floating down gracefully to the ground like a dove or an angel, her naked flesh impervious to rain or cold or lightning. But it all seemed now as if it had happened to someone else.

What the fuck was I thinking of? she wondered, massaging her frozen toes. *Why didn't I at least throw on some clothes and grab some shoes before going outside?*

Before jumping outside . . .

She looked down at Adam Newmar sleeping peacefully in her lap. *Poor baby,* she thought, her eyes starting to water, *you shouldn't even be here.* He never would have been, except for her and Sherone and everything that happened at Magda's and everything after that. Heather shook her head. It was all hopelessly screwed up. Everything was tangled up with everything else. Whatever happened to her happened to everyone else she knew.

Because everything, now, belong to Azgaroth.

The thought chilled her, numbing her with despair, until she realized that whatever belonged to Azgaroth also belonged to her.

You can control him, said the voice in her head, *if you can stand against him, if you're brave enough to try.*

She shook off the voice with a shudder and looked over to where Sherone rested against the other side of the truck bed, nestled deep in the old windbreaker Magda had loaned her, head lolling to one side, fast asleep. Next to her sat a gaunt, sunken-cheeked boy with spiky platinum-streaked hair and dead brown eyes. The eyes seemed to be staring at Heather, but they floated over her like those of a zombie, unable to focus on her or any of the other members of Magda's Wicca crammed together there in the covered truck bed, along with assorted weird kids who looked like leftovers from the regular Heart of Darkness crowd.

Tamara Devon sat across from Heather, watching her closely but saying nothing. Tamara had tried to say something as Heather stood naked on the IPS grounds, Seamus Harrach wrapping his cloak around her, but she had been unable to speak, awed by what had happened, wonderstruck by Heather's sudden power.

Let her stay that way, Heather thought.

"We're in the mountains now," Tamara said tentatively, dark eyes on Heather.

Heather frowned. She was not much of a mountain person, not unless it involved skiing. She wanted to ask why they had to do this in the mountains anyway, but she did not feel like asking Tamara.

"See?" Tamara sniffed the air. "You can smell the trees."

Mixed with the truck's heavy gasoline fumes was the

sharp, resinous smell of evergreens. The angle of the truck bed shifted suddenly, throwing Heather into a fat girl sitting next to her. The truck's gears whined as the road grew steeper.

"Aren't you excited?" Tamara asked, dark eyes shining. "We're getting closer to the Great Sabbath site!"

"I have to piss," Heather said.

Concern crossed Tamara's face. "Bad?"

Heather nodded.

Tamara got up in a kind of half-crouch, stepping over the packed bodies, steadying herself with one hand on the truck bed wall. She hammered on the back of the cab. The truck slowed down, then stopped, engine thumping loudly in heavy idle. A bolt scraped across metal and the back door creaked open. The young man standing outside had long dark hair falling to his shoulders and teeth that had been filed carefully to points. He wore a blue workshirt and trucker's gloves. Magda stood beside him, looking red-eyed and irritable.

"What's wrong?" Magda asked Tamara.

"She really needs to pee." Tamara pointed to Heather.

"Harlan," Magda said to the young man with the pointed teeth, "get back in the cab." She turned to the passengers inside the covered truck bed. "We'll take a quick break. Don't wander off. If you need to use the bathroom, there's lots of trees on either side of the road."

Heather shook Adam and Sherone awake. Adam stretched and whimpered, calling out for his mother. Heather kissed him lightly on top of his blond head.

Sherone rubbed at her eyes. "What?"

"Get out. I've got to piss."

Sherone frowned. "Huh?"

"We've *all* got to piss. Get out, okay?"

Karin gritted her teeth as Wes Livingston's van took a sharp curve too fast, almost on two wheels, tires squealing. The force of the turn knocked her into Jeff Geller, who put a hand on her shoulder. She smiled at him, her teeth still gritted. She knew that Magda had several hours' lead time on them and they had to go as fast as possible to catch her. But the harrowing drive over Mulholland in the rain was still too fresh in her memory.

Maureen stared critically at Wes as he negotiated another tight curve. "My son—my *former* son-in-law enjoys driving like this. You must be giving him a run for his money."

"He's still sticking with us," Jeff said, looking out the back window at David's silver-gray Lamborghini as it tracked the van's progress, moving expertly in and out of the difficult curves.

Maureen frowned. "Why in the name of God Davie insisted on driving that overpriced toy of his instead of riding with the rest of us is something I'll never understand."

Because he always has to be the one in charge, Karin thought, but she said, "It's just as well, Mother. We're pretty crowded in here."

The van's interior was packed with blankets, ropes, coats, several odd-looking machines, food and other supplies—all gathered with incredible speed by Jeff and Roland at IPS—in addition to some of Wes's considerable photographic gear and the seven passengers themselves.

Maureen sighed. "I guess Davie knows what he's doing."

"If we hit rough terrain," Jeff said, "he might have to turn back."

Karin shook her head. "He'll never turn back now, no matter what. I know him that well."

Felicity Perkins, seated near the front of the van with Wes and Roland, leaned forward. "They've stopped."

Roland turned to her. "Are they changing their route? Leaving the mountains?"

"No," she said, her eyes seeming to stare vacantly at

the road ahead. "They've driven high into the mountains and are heading higher still. But they have stopped for now. Decidedly."

"Why," Roland asked, "would they stop at a time like this?"

"Maybe they're already there," Brian suggested from the backseat.

Felicity shook her head. "No. Not yet."

"Maybe they had a flat," Wes said, "or engine trouble."

"Or an accident, God forbid!" Maureen shuddered theatrically.

Felicity shook her head again, eyes still staring vacantly. "No. But something's wrong. I can feel it. Something's *not* going according to plan."

Sherone crouched in the dense undergrowth about thirty yards back from a narrow road high in the San Gabriel Mountains. Heather squatted several yards farther off, urinating behind a large pine tree. The other Sabbath members stood in small groups near the idling truck with the words BARSINI BROS. "YOUR QUALITY MOVING SPECIALISTS" painted in block green letters on the van side. Seamus Harrach, Magda Prokash and Tamara Devon stood apart from the others. Magda cast frequent glances in Sherone's and Heather's direction.

"You really screwed this up good," Sherone muttered to Adam Newmar, trying to unstick his jeans zipper.

"I didn't do it," Adam said.

"Jesus!" Heather called out. "There's no toilet paper!"

"What'd you expect?" Sherone said, grimacing at the zipper. "Just drip dry or use some leaves."

"Gross!"

"Haven't you ever been camping before? There!" The zipper came unstuck.

Adam went off behind another tree, calling over his

shoulder, "Don't look."

"Cross my heart," Sherone promised.

She stood up and looked out across the heavily forested valley below them and the barren peaks hazy in the distance. She had been in the San Gabriels many times on camping trips and day excursions with her dad and mom back before the divorce. Serena Livingston hated wilderness vacations and never lost an opportunity to say so. But Sherone liked the San Gabriels; at least she had before the divorce. She liked the way the mountains were right next to L.A., practically a metropolitan backyard, but once you went a few miles into them it was as if the city suddenly disappeared and you found yourself in a world apart, unchanged since long before the first city had ever been built. She did not visit the mountains now as often as she used to. But they still had that effect on her, where the skin prickled at the back of her neck and she realized that she was looking at one of the sacred places of the world.

Even Seamus Harrach was moved by the mountains, but he talked about them in a way that Sherone had found more terrifying than his bone-white face or his rotting, black-toothed grin.

"The Mountains of Erebus!" he exclaimed in awe, after they all got out of the truck and stood there looking around, the hot Santa Ana winds that had begun blowing after Heather's descent from the IPS building blowing still, rustling Seamus Harrach's stringy white hair and making the pine trees creak and groan. "The original home of the Dark Gods, these mountains were not always as we see them now," he told the Sabbath members. "They exist today still dark and mysterious, and potent with magic, but they are mere shadows of their former selves. Once, in the days before the weathering of ages wore them down, these mountains towered higher than the Himalayas, proud and savage, looking fiercely out toward the distant sea. They were as gods themselves and the Dark Gods dwelt upon them and within them. And now," he paused, holding up a sharp-nailed hand, "even now they still possess the strong magic of that time before time, the dark power that moves the world and rules our lives."

His voice rose in exaltation. "They are the altars on which we raise the offerings to our Gods!"

The Sabbath members had stood entranced, eyes wide, lips parted, as if waiting for the spirit of that darkness to enter them and take possession of their souls. Sherone remembered thinking that it was mostly bullshit, just something to get the nerds all hot and excited. But even so she had felt a chill pass over her, despite the blowing of the hot wind.

It was getting hotter. Sherone took off Magda's shabby windbreaker and wiped at the sweat on her forehead. *What totally fucked weather*, she thought, *raining like shit for days and now this.* A pine tree creaked loudly overhead as the hot wind blew through its boughs.

Heather came back from behind the tree, grimacing as she wrung her hands. "I feel so gross!"

"You'll suffocate in that." Sherone nodded at Seamus Harrach's cloak. "It's getting hotter than hell."

"Ain't got nothin' on underneath, remember? Besides, I'm still cold. I was warm when it was raining and now I'm cold." She shivered.

"I'm done!" Adam came out from behind his tree. "But it's stuck again."

"You three!" Magda called out to them. "Come back up here and get in the truck. We're leaving."

"Okay," Heather called back.

Magda turned and started for the truck's cab, where Seamus Harrach was already climbing back in beside Harlan, the pointed-toothed driver.

Heather bit her lip, watching them closely. "Let's run for it," she whispered. "Now."

Sherone's mouth fell open. "Are you crazy or what? You don't even have *shoes!*"

Adam tugged at Sherone's arm. "Unstick it for me."

- 369

"Let's go, you three!" Magda called from where she was starting to climb into the truck's cab. "Hurry up!"

Heather brought her face in close to Sherone's. "What do you think's going to happen once we get there?"

Sherone hesitated. "I— Have the Sabbath, I guess."

"They'll summon him again. Azgaroth."

Sherone winced at the name, but Heather's blue eyes were clear and steady. "He kills people, Sherone. This time he might kill you or Adam. Or me. And he'll come for sure." Heather's voice caught. "He comes to me all the time now. Without being summoned."

Fear pinched Sherone's face. "You knew this back there. Why'd you go with them? Why didn't you stay up there in that room and holler for help?"

Heather looked down at the forest floor beneath her bare feet. "You're my friend and they had you and Adam. I thought maybe I could help you get free." She looked up. "I thought maybe I had some kind of power."

Sherone's eyes were moist. "Am I still your friend? After all this shit I got you into?"

Heather looked embarrassed. "Sure. You know that."

Sherone grabbed Heather's hand and pressed it against her cheek, wetting it with tears.

"What're you doing?" Magda called out harshly from the truck's cab. "Get up here!"

Heather glanced nervously at the truck. "Sherone—"

She nodded. "Okay." She turned to Adam. "Honey, we're going to run into the trees now and we're going to run *fast*, okay? So you just hang onto cousin Heather's hand real tight, okay?"

"My zipper's stuck," he said.

"We'll catch that later." Sherone turned to Heather. "Follow me. Try not to step on any sharp rocks. If anything fucks up, you and him stop running and hide somewhere. All right?"

Heather nodded.

Sherone picked up a round, hand-sized rock. "Let's go for it."

"Hey!" yelled one of the Sabbath members from the truck.

They ran.

The van came to a grinding halt. They had rounded a blind curve and there it was: a rushing torrent of water spilling out across the narrow mountain road. It cascaded off the outside shoulder's edge down into a ravine below. The only way forward was through the torrent, which was over a car's length wide and at least wheel-well deep.

Wes sighed, hands resting on the steering wheel. "That'll teach me to take shortcuts."

"What shortcut?" Maureen demanded.

"Miss Perkins," Roland explained, "has finally fixed Magda's destination: an isolated valley farther up the way with a geological formation known, according to our map, as Altar Rock. Magda's taking the more traveled route, one that climbs slowly with an excess of switchbacks. If we followed her that way we'd most likely lose several hours. Hence Mr. Livingston's shortcut."

"Can we make it across the water?" Karin asked.

"Should be able to," Wes said. "But I'm not so sure about our friend back there in the Lamborghini. This may just be the end of the road for him."

Jeff looked back to where the silver-gray Lamborghini was stopped behind the van and David was climbing out. "I'd better go tell him." He reached for the door.

Karin put a hand on his arm. "I don't think that's such a good idea."

"But—"

"Trust me."

"*I'll* tell him." Maureen handed Roland her large white leather purse. "Hold this."

Outside, David scowled at the rushing torrent. He looked up at the sound of footsteps on pavement and saw his former mother-in-law walking toward him with Karin following.

371

"I thought," he said, "your experts knew the way."

"The road's washed out," Karin said.

"No!" He laughed cynically. "Guess this is where the party ends."

"Wes thinks he can get the van across," Maureen announced. "But you'll have to park your little toy and ride with us. That," she glanced derisively at the Lamborghini, "would float away like a leaf in a flood."

David gave her a boyish smile. "Maureen, you know I love you. But I think I'll just stand here and watch. Someone's got to go for the Search and Rescue Team when you guys wash over the edge."

Maureen stiffened. "Wes Livingston isn't the kind of man who makes rash judgments."

David shrugged. "If you want a professional medical opinion, I'd say you're all risking your lives."

Maureen stepped closer. "The life of your daughter and my granddaughter is at risk, Davie Roberts. We have to do whatever's necessary. Now act your age and get into that van with us!"

David folded his arms and met Maureen's hard stare with his own green-eyed stubbornness. "I'll watch. *If* you get across, I'll be right behind you."

"You're acting pig-headed and foolish and I'm very disappointed in you. But it's not going to do one damn bit of good to stand here and argue about it. Time's a-wastin'." Maureen turned and marched back to the van.

Karin looked at him. "David, when we get across, please turn around and drive back. Please?"

A faint sneer stole over his handsome features. "Your concern touches me deeply."

Her face tightened. "Goddamn it! Can we *ever* talk without fighting? You have a daughter who loves you—"

"But you don't love me." He stared at her reproachfully. "Not anymore."

She took a deep breath. "I used to. Once. I loved you very much. And I think you know that. But Heather still does love you. And if anything—"

"Karin Marie!" Maureen called from the van. "Are you going to come with us or stand there all day and argue with that pigheaded nincompoop?"

She turned back to him. "Please? Come with us or go back."

"Let's see how well you do. Maybe your little friend, the parapsychologist, can levitate you across."

Karin stared at him, and as she did she seemed to see beneath the hurt and resentment the old David Roberts she used to know, the one who had cared so passionately about everything, about work and her and Heather, about being the best and giving them the best. For one brief moment she wanted to reach out and take him back and try to find it again, the love that had been there once before he threw it all away.

But it was gone, buried beneath years of mutual contempt and hateful accusations, calcified into stony indifference.

She turned and walked away.

Inside the van, Wes started the engine and eased toward the rushing water. "It may wiggle us around a bit," he said to his passengers. "But we should have enough weight to plow on through."

And if we don't, Karin thought, but did not finish it. She looked down as she realized that she had Jeff's hand locked in a death grip, the knuckles of her own hand turning white. He smiled at her in a reassuring way, but she could see the tension in his eyes.

The van bucked as the front wheels rolled into the rushing water. Spray hammered against the side panels with a loud *whhiisssssshhh*. The van forged ahead through buffeting water, rocking from side to side.

Maureen gripped the back of the seat in front of her, green eyes wide with alarm. Roland and Felicity sat calm and unmoved, like Zen masters in meditation. Wes steered intently, gauging the gas feed carefully, enough but not too much, his whole attention locked on the task of getting them through. Brian leaned forward in his seat.

Halfway through, the van started to turn sideways, drifting slowly in the rushing water like a boat without a rudder.

"Holy Mother of God!" Maureen gasped.

The van began drifting toward the narrow outside shoulder and the waterfall that cascaded down from it into a deep, rock-filled ravine.

"We're going over the edge!" Karin cried.

Wes turned the wheel. It spun loosely. He gave the engine more gas. The van drifted closer to the shoulder and the drop-off below. He stepped on the gas again. A tire hit something and obtained purchase. The van lurched forward, rolling and bucking through the rough, buffeting water. It broke free from the torrent with a spray of huge water wings on either side.

"Ah!" Maureen pressed a hand to her heart. "Thank you, Dear God Almighty!"

Wes, sweat glistening on his forehead and upper lip, threw open the door and called out to David across the rushing water, "Man, you just bought a ticket home. We barely made it. Don't even think about it in that lightweight."

David stood staring back at him across the water. He turned and walked to his Lamborghini, opened the door and got in. He started the engine, backing up as if to turn around. And kept on backing. When he had backed up all the way to the blind curve, he stopped and revved his engine, making the powerful motor roar.

"God no!" Karin put a clenched fist to her mouth.

"Whoa!" Brian said. "He's goin' for it!"

Jeff turned to Wes. "Can he make it?"

Wes shook his head. "Not unless he can broad-jump it. Once he hits the water that thing'll start hydroplaning like a jet ski."

Karin looked around the van's interior, appealing for help. "We've got to do something!"

Maureen regarded her daughter with hard-eyed compassion. "Honey girl, we tried. He wouldn't listen."

"He'll kill himself!"

David released the brake. With a screech of rubber the Lamborghini leaped forward, shooting straight for the rushing torrent. The silver-gray nose of the car cut through the water like a knife. For several seconds it looked as if he might actually make it. Then the force of the torrent caught him. The Lamborghini began to spin, describing several slow, elegant 360-degree turns. When the back end hit the shoulder, the car began to tip precariously over the edge.

"No!" Karin screamed, grabbing at the van's door.

As the Lamborghini tipped farther out over the edge, David Roberts sat straight and tall in the driver's seat, his precise surgeon's mind fixed on the job at hand, working with the gearshift and the steering wheel, trying one thing after another, his face grim with concentration as he wrestled with this problem the way he would with any other, one-on-one, head-on, no concessions to himself or the opposition.

The car went all the way over and bounced down the side of the rock-filled ravine, the light body crumpling and folding as it rolled. The gas tank blew in a sudden blossoming of flame.

Karin bent over in her seat, sobbing brokenly.

Jeff put a protective arm around her shoulders.

Maureen looked up, makeup streaked with tears. "Such a *fine*-looking boy! And he always tried so hard..."

Heather's lungs were burning, her feet bruised and bleeding. Branches scratched at her bare legs and caught in the folds of Seamus Harrach's heavy cloak. But she kept running, cutting her way through the dense forest.

"Heather!" Adam called from where he was being dragged along beside her. "Heather, slow *down!* I can't run no more!"

Sherone ran ahead of them, following a trail where none seemed to exist. Behind them, Heather could hear the cries and heavy breathing of Magda and her people as they gave chase. *All we have to do,* she told herself, *is just keep—*

She screamed and fell to the forest floor, grabbing at her left ankle. Adam started crying. Sherone stopped and turned around, breathing deeply but evenly.

Magda, Seamus Harrach, Tamara Devon, Harlan the pointed-toothed driver and several other Sabbath members ran toward them through the heavy forest at different speeds. Magda puffed and swore, slashing at branches and undergrowth with the exposed blade of her staff. Leading the pack was a tall, lanky kid with stand-up hair and deepset, hate-filled eyes. He ran well, loping toward Heather sitting on the ground, Adam crying beside her and Sherone standing watching, a heavy club of some kind held easily in his right hand.

Sherone threw the round stone she was holding, taking careful aim and giving her arm a snap as she released the missile. It struck the lanky runner full force on the left side of his forehead. He staggered, stumbled, dropped to his knees, bringing up both hands to his forehead, blood leaking out between his fingers.

The other members of the pursuit party slowed down, as if hesitating. Pointed-toothed Harlan went to the aid of the downed runner.

Sherone turned to Heather. "Can you walk on it?"

Heather nodded, biting her lip. "Think so."

She started to get awkwardly to her feet, Sherone helping. She put weight gingerly on the ankle.

Sherone looked back to Magda and her people. They were rushing at them again, except for Seamus Harrach, who seemed to have disappeared. Sherone searched the ground for another stone. She found one, picked it up, threw it. Harlan ducked, crying out as the rock bounced off his right shoulder. Magda and the others came to a stop. Sherone saw another hand-size rock on the ground, perfect for throwing. She bent over and reached out to

376

pick it up.

A clawlike hand clamped down on her arm and pulled her around in a violent half-turn. She screamed as she saw Seamus Harrach's bone-white face glowering like a death's-head above hers.

"Hold still!" the rotting mouth hissed at her. "Or I'll tear out your eyes and offer you as a blind sacrifice to Azgaroth."

Sherone stared terrified at the sharp-nailed fingers raised menacingly in front of her face.

The others were catching up to them now. Little Adam Newmar stopped his sobbing as he saw Magda and Tamara and Harlan approach. He got up and took off running. Tamara started after him. Heather stuck out a leg in front of her. Tamara stumbled heavily into some sharp undergrowth.

Magda rushed over and grabbed Heather by her long red hair, yanking her to her feet and bringing the unsheathed blade of the staff up under her throat. "Submit!" she growled. "Or I'll cut your pretty face until even your own mother wouldn't recognize it!"

Heather blanched with fear, cringing before the long, sharp blade. But then a light began to burn in her blue eyes, fierce and sudden. Magda saw it and the hand holding the sharp-bladed staff wavered slightly. She let go of Heather's hair. The hot wind whistling through the pine forest started blowing with greater force now. Tree branches swayed back and forth, creaking loudly. Dust flew into the faces of Magda and her people. They coughed and shut their eyes, and still the wind continued to blow with ever-increasing fury.

Seamus Harrach's bulky cloak billowed out from Heather's naked body. She stood there, full breasts bare to the hot and savage wind, long red hair blowing wild behind her, blue eyes burning with a cold, unearthly light.

Magda stepped back, afraid.

A sharp *crack*, like the report from a heavy-gauge rifle, sounded above the howling desert wind. It was followed by a rumbling sound that grew louder and louder, like the rush of an oncoming train.

"Magda!" Seamus Harrach called out a warning.

She looked up to see the tall pine tree falling down toward her, toppling in slow motion through the hot wind. She moved back, sharp-bladed staff raised before her. The huge tree crashed to the forest floor only a few feet from where she stood. One of the branches almost took out an eye. The tremor of impact shuddered through the ground and was felt by everyone there. Magda stood transfixed, staff clutched in one hand, her face a mixture of terror and awe as she stared at Heather.

The girl stood with her naked breasts held high and proud, her blue eyes burning bright as she returned Magda's stare.

Then she gasped and seemed to wilt, drawing her arms up over her nakedness. The hot wind died down at once.

"Daddy!" she cried out plaintively. "Something's happened to my daddy!"

As the girl bent over, sobbing, Magda nodded to Harlan. "Take her back to the truck."

Harlan stood and rubbed his rock-bruised shoulder, hesitating uncertainly.

Tamara came up to Magda, dragging a wailing Adam Newmar by the scruff of his neck. "Fucking little brat!" Tamara shook him angrily.

Magda capped her long-bladed staff with its false wooden head, slowly and deliberately. Then she brought it down hard across Tamara's back. The dark-haired girl yelped and let go of Adam, raising her hands to protect herself. Magda rained down blows on her back and arms.

"Stupid girl!" she hissed, finally stopping. "Bathroom break, indeed!" She turned to Harlan, who still stood rubbing his shoulder, watching Heather warily.

"Take her to the truck!" Magda commanded.

Harlan touched Heather cautiously on the shoulder of the heavy cloak. She lifted a tear-streaked face to him. Harlan jumped back, ready to run for cover.

But she followed him, limping, back to the truck.

chapter 42

sabbath

Altar Rock stood waiting.

A massive stone plateau, nearly level on top, it rose like a giant's sarcophagus from the floor of an enclosed valley high in the San Gabriels. The steep mountainsides that formed the valley walls were densely forested, but the trees thinned out near Altar Rock, leaving it bare and open, hidden from outside eyes by encircling mountains yet starkly visible in the center of its own secluded world.

A commanding ancient oak tree grew up through cracked stone at the north end of Altar Rock. Sharp-toothed Harlan tied Heather to the tree, binding her hands above her head, securing the rope tightly around one of the larger branches. Seamus Harrach's heavy cloak had been removed. She stood naked on Altar Rock, hands lashed high overhead, full breasts thrust forward, long red hair blowing loose about her pale shoulders in the hot Santa Ana winds.

Harlan was naked too, as were Magda and Seamus Harrach and the other members of the Sabbath. "We shall worship skyclad," Magda had announced solemnly upon their arrival at Altar Rock. "The Great Sabbath demands no less."

Shucked clothes lay scattered in piles near trees and boulders on the steep stone path that led up to Altar Rock. Sabbath members adorned their nakedness with amulets, bracelets, ceremonial belts. Polished stones gleamed on skins of different colors.

Sherone and Adam sat naked at the far end of Altar Rock, tied back to back with several lengths of thick rope. Tears glistened on Adam's round cheeks.

"I want my mommy," he sniffled.

"Don't worry, honey," Sherone told him. "We'll be okay."

But she knew better. Naked Sabbath members piled up dry branches near the center of Altar Rock. Fast-fading daylight turned the surrounding mountains purple, the sky above them luminescent pinkish-orange. Sabbath members poured coarse rock-salt crystals from burlap bags, laying out a large salt circle near the pile of branches. A thin boy with long blond hair and suntanned skin piped monotonous atonal music on a wooden recorder.

What will they do with us? Sherone wondered. *Burn us alive? Or leave us outside the circle for . . .*

She winced at the mere thought of Azgaroth's name, and turned to where Magda Prokash and Seamus Harrach stood supervising the Sabbath preparations. Sherone winced again. Magda's flabby nakedness was mottled with rashes and open sores. The skin itself looked coarse, sickly white, diseased. But she was radiance itself compared to the naked Seamus Harrach.

At first Sherone thought he was deformed, horribly scarred from some accident, and she looked away because to stare would have been impolite. Then, with a sense of growing horror, she realized that he was not so much deformed as . . . different. Slits like gills gaped red and raw down his bare sides. What looked like a hump rising from his upper back turned out, on closer inspection, to be two withered stumps that might have been stillborn or mutilated wings.

A chill crawled up her spine, despite the hot winds.

She was frightened now and she wanted her dad. *Where is he?* she wondered, the fear making her despair. *Is he even worried about me?* She knew her dad loved her a lot, and with no strings attached, not just when she was good or respectful, which was almost never. Over the years, Sherone had grown to take that kind of unconditional love for granted, to depend on it, without thinking much about it, whenever she needed it. Exactly how much Wes Livingston loved her, and how much she relied upon his love, were things she had never thought about seriously.

Until now.

Heather twisted naked in the ropes that held her bound to the ancient oak tree. Several Sabbath members crept forward cautiously, trying to get a better look at her. But they kept their distance. Magda's near-miss with the falling pine tree had not been lost on them. They were afraid of Heather, afraid of what she had done and, even more, of what she might yet do. Fear was all that held back Tamara Devon. She stood at a safe distance, staring hungrily at Heather's voluptuous nude body, her own olive-skinned nakedness rich and erotic, marred only by the dark bruises beginning to show on her arms and back where Magda had beat her. Tamara was given the task of anointing Heather's body with witch's oil for the Great Sabbath. The desire to do so burned fiercely in her dark eyes, but she kept back from Heather, fearful of her unknown power.

Heather herself was feeling uniquely powerless at that moment. After Harlan had tied her to the tree, she tried to will the rope untied. When nothing happened, it merely confirmed what she had begun to suspect ever since the euphoria of her magical descent from the IPS building started to fade. The power was not hers. It never had been. It could respond sometimes to her desire or hatred, especially to her hatred, but she could not consciously control it. The power belonged to

AZGAROTH

As the dread name sounded inside her mind, she looked up across the forested valley to the purple mountain peaks turning black with the approach of dusk. Far beyond them, she seemed to see another blackness, separate from the oncoming night. She felt it moving inside her mind, building like a distant storm, advancing slowly toward the wall of mountains and the enclosed valley with Altar Rock standing high and exposed in its center. This advancing blackness was without form or feature, except for two savage burning eyes, dark red and malignant, that seemed to pierce the center of Heather's soul.

She cringed in fear, twisting back against the grip of the ropes. She recognized it now. It was the horror that had come down through the Passageway for her, there at the monolith. It was the power that had taken her that night at Magda's, lifting her into the air, embracing her with loathsome darkness made visible as shining, multicolored lights.

AZGAROTH

Coming for her now across the night sky, coming this time not merely to amaze and horrify, and kill, but coming this time to claim her, to take her back with him.

Heather let out a cry of helpless terror. Tamara and the others moved back, real fear in their eyes.

As if in answer to Heather's cry, a loud, low note sounded across the valley, echoing back from the distant encircling mountainsides. A fat boy stood near Sherone and Adam at the other end of Altar Rock and blew into a large curved horn. Other naked Sabbath members stood next to him holding small harps and strange one-stringed fiddles, primitive cymbals and tambourines, light recorders and heavy leather-covered drums.

Magda stepped forward, raising her wooden staff. "Earth! Air! Fire! Water! Demons of the Four Elements! Come forth and join us in our Great Sabbath, blessed with the blood of innocence!" The hot desert wind blew through Magda's short gray hair. "Let the music and dances of darkness begin! All hail the Prince of Darkness and the Lord of Evil!" Magda's withered breasts trembled as she struck her staff upon the stone. "Hail Satan!"

Sabbath members took up the cry. "Hail Satan!"

A shrill cacophony burst from the assemblage of bizarre instruments. One-stringed fiddles squealed and groaned. Drums pounded into the night. Tambourines shook and cymbals crashed and over it all sounded the deep, vibrating tone of the curved Devil's Horn.

Heather shuddered as the cries in praise of Satan rose from the throats of Sabbath members. The pile of dry branches caught fire, burning hot and bright in the parching wind. Torches were lighted. Naked oiled bodies danced and leaped and whirled on Altar Rock. Firelight glimmered off shining skin. Squeals and laughter intercut the chanted praises of the Lord of Darkness. The music played. The dancers danced. The night grew darker and hotter. And the fires burned.

Magda appeared suddenly before Heather, gray eyes made hard by hatred. "Why isn't she anointed?" Magda called to Tamara Devon.

Tamara stepped forward anxiously, the stone jar of witch's oil in one hand. "I tried, Magda, but she didn't—"

"Wretched girl! What *she* wants is of no importance!" Magda gestured imperiously. "Anoint her!"

Tamara hesitated, then a catlike smile spread slowly across her face. She moved up close to where Heather hung suspended from the oak tree, so close that Tamara's large dark nipples kissed Heather's pale pink nipples, the two girls' bare breasts pressing softly together.

Heather kicked out hard with her right foot. Tamara yelped and backed off, grabbing at her left shin.

Magda regarded Heather through half-closed, hooded eyes. "If you want to play games, child, we can play too. We can break both legs. The pressure on your arms would become intolerable, to say nothing of the pain in your legs. But it matters not at all whether you ever walk again, as long as you're properly prepared for the Great Sabbath."

Heather lowered her head.

Magda turned to Tamara. "Anoint her."

The van made another in what seemed a never-ending series of jolting switchback curves. And then, all at once, there it was: Altar Rock, outlined now in full darkness by the bonfire blazing in its center and the lighted torches that moved irregularly, bobbing and jerking across the stone plateau.

Wes Livington pulled over to one side of the curving road, engine idling. Through an open window the faint cries of the Sabbath members could be heard, along with the harsh notes of ceremonial music and the deep rumble of the Devil's Horn.

Jeff Geller leaned forward. "They've started."

"Yes," Roland agreed. "One had hoped Magda might take her time with something like this, perhaps even wait for the witching hour. Apparently not."

"How far away are we?" Karin asked, fear muting her voice.

"Farther than it appears," Roland said. "Distances are deceiving at this height."

Wes pulled back onto the road and steered with the curve of a new switchback. "How long," he asked Roland, "before they— How long before the sacrifices begin?" He tried to keep his tone neutral, but the deep anguish was plainly there.

"All depends," Roland answered carefully. "These preliminary revels should continue for some time . . . unless something unexpected comes up."

The van wound through switchback after switchback, dropping deeper into forested darkness, coming closer with every curve to the base of Altar Rock itself.

Karin turned to Jeff, bodies jostling as the van pursued its winding course. "If we're already too late—"

He squeezed her hand. "We're not."

"How do you know?"

"We have to believe that."

Felicity Perkins raised a hand. "Stop!"

Wes eased on the brakes. "What is it?"

"Someone is calling to us." Felicity leaned forward, pale blue eyes staring out into the darkness. "A small child in the forest. Can't you hear him?"

Wes turned off the engine. The other passengers strained to listen, hearing nothing except the weird music and frenzied cries of the Sabbath, the pounding of drums echoing through the trees.

Then, softly at first, barely audible, like something from a dream, a child's voice came to them.

"Mommy . . . Daddy . . ."

The voice of a small boy, lost and frightened.

Maureen sat bolt upright. "That's my grandson!" She reached for the door handle.

Roland stopped her. "Mrs. Magnusson, please." He asked Felicity, "Is there danger?"

Felicity shook her head, still staring into the darkness. "Doesn't feel like it. But something's wrong."

They all saw it at the same moment: a small blond boy, naked, his body bathed in blue phosphorescent light as he walked out of the dark forest and onto the road where the van waited.

"Adam!" Karin and Maureen cried together.

Felicity said to Roland, "Let me talk to him first." When Roland started to object, she insisted, "I'm no safer in here than I would be out there."

Outside the van, Felicity approached the child as he stood in the rough dirt road. "Who are you?"

"Mommy," whined the little boy, tears shimmering in the blue phosphorescence.

"You are not what you seem. Who *are* you?"

With a hideous roar, the child stretched its arms and transformed, growing suddenly huge, hands becoming claws, wings sprouting from a humped back, blond head turning flat and saurian, heavy jaw bristling with razor-sharp teeth. Felicity staggered back, hands raised in front of her.

Karin screamed inside the van.

"Dear God in Heaven!" Maureen gasped.

"Felicity!" Roland called, then to Jeff, "The activator! *Now!*"

Jeff grabbed at a machine beside him.

With another nerve-shattering roar, the creature pounced on Felicity, digging its claws into her head. The huge wings flapped furiously, kicking up pine needles and dust, as the loathsome thing lifted Felicity's limp body into the air. Small flames sparked from the beating wings. The uppermost branches of a nearby pine caught fire. The winged monster rose with its burden, howling into the night sky.

"Holy shit," Brian murmured, eyes wide with terror.

Jeff sat there with the activator in his lap, a look of dazed fury on his bearded face. "An elemental demon! Jesus Christ! What does Magda think she's doing? Calling up something as unpredictable as that!"

Roland's face hardened. "She is playing the last round of a very desperate game." He turned to Wes. "Now is the time, Mr. Livingston, to drive as fast—"

Wes turned on the engine and floored the gas before Roland finished speaking. The van took off with a squeal of rubber, throwing the passengers back hard against their seats.

Tamara hesitated, the stone jar of witch's oil in one hand, dark eyes moving from Heather to Magda, then back to Heather again.

"Anoint her," Magda commanded.

Tamara stepped forward.

Heather stiffened, backing up against the ropes. "Don't touch me! Splash it on me if you want. But keep your hands off me, Tamara. I mean it."

Tamara smiled, pouring some oil into the palm of her right hand. "It's not so bad, Heather. Relax. Who knows? You might even learn to like it."

Tamara applied the oil generously to Heather's firm, full breasts, massaging it into her large nipples, working on them skillfully and patiently until they stood up hard and erect from the wide surrounding areolae, gleaming in the firelight.

Heather's face tightened with embarrassment and disgust.

Tamara smiled her cat-smile and let her oil-slick hand trail down languidly across Heather's smooth stomach. Down below, she inserted the hand smoothly between Heather's round white thighs.

Magda watched with amusement and the faint stirrings of her own jaded arousal.

Tamara gasped suddenly, pulling back her hand.

Then she began to scream.

Small flames burned like candlewicks from the oil-slick fingers and thumb of her right hand. The rancid stench of burning human flesh mingled with the heavy ozone smell of the hot Santa Ana winds.

Magda stepped back, hooded eyes wide with astonishment. "The Hand of Glory," she murmured. "THE HAND OF GLORY!"

Seamus Harrach looked up in reverent awe.

Tamara's screams rose in pitch and intensity. She began to wave her hand frantically in the air. But the thumb and fingers continued to burn. Her long dark hair caught fire. She ran in aimless, erratic circles around the surface of Altar Rock, screeching like a maddened animal, her burning hair trailing out behind her like a comet's tail. The terrible fire spread to her neck and shoulders, down her torso and legs. She continued to run, shrieking helplessly, staggering now, then stumbling finally into a writhing heap that flamed and twisted on the hard stone until it gave one last convulsive shudder and lay still, a charred, smoldering ruin.

The Sabbath members stood silent. The musicians were mute. Heather's body was fully anointed at last, dripping with cold sweat, her eyes dark with horror and revulsion as she trembled in her ropes beneath the oak tree.

Magda Prokash stepped forward, clutching her staff, gray eyes feverish with something like ecstasy. "Azgaroth!" she cried out, shattering the grim silence atop Altar Rock. "Satanas!"

She raised the staff above her head, shouting out the names of the great demon and his Dark Lord.

"Azgaroth! Satanas!"

The other Sabbath members took up the cry, feebly at first, still shaken by the horror of Tamara Devon's immolation. Then, as the courage of the crowd grew within them, they raised hands above their heads and cried out to the darkness above.

"Azgaroth! Satanas!"

"AZGAROTH! SATANAS!"

The shouting rose to a wordless, pounding roar, echoing back from the surrounding mountainsides.

Aracely, the dark-skinned girl, was the first to see them. "Magda!" she shouted, breaking off the chant, pointing to the black night sky. "Magda! *Look!*"

Heather looked up, tears rolling down her cheeks.

She saw them then, swooping down on Altar Rock.

The naked Sabbath members began to scream.

The van tracked the outside of a long blind curve, leaning hard into it. Pine trees whirled by under the headlights in a stroboscopic blur. Then, from out of the dark night sky, a brilliant stream of shining multicolored light dropped down and shot across the road in front of the van, striking a nearby pine tree and causing it to burst into full flame.

"Fire Demon!" Roland shouted above the noise of the van's engine.

Jeff leaned forward. "Another elemental?"

"No!" Roland shouted back. "Azgaroth himself!"

Another stream of light blazed across the road ahead, so close this time that it lit up the van's interior like a lightning bolt, momentarily blinding the driver and his passengers. Jeff blinked and turned to watch the light vanish inside the dark forest, clipping pine boughs as it went, instantly starting new fires.

He stared at the burning trees. "Christ . . ."

Then the black sky above and the twisting road ahead seemed suddenly filled with sweeping streams of brilliant light. Trees right and left burst into flame. One fiery stream knocked branches from a tall pine beside the road. They fell down burning in front of the van. Wes rolled on over them. Sparks and flaming bits of wood flew up onto the windshield. Brian watched open-mouthed, dazzled by the pyrotechnics but terrified at the sight of the very same streams of light that had wrapped themselves around Heather's nude body that night at Magda's.

"The whole forest is catching fire!" Karin called out. "We'll never make it!"

"We'll make it." Wes increased his speed.

Maureen took a deep breath, her knuckles white as she gripped the seat in front of her. "We *all* want to make it, Mr. Livingston. In one piece, thank you."

A sharp twist of the road brought them almost head-on into the side of the Barsini Brothers moving truck before Wes had time to see it, parked sideways in the road like a huge white roadblock. He jumped on the brakes and steered to avoid colliding with the truck. The van fishtailed out of control, throwing passengers into one another and down onto the floor as it slid to a grinding stop in thick clouds of dust and gravel, the right front fender barely nicking the sidewall of the truck.

"Hope everyone's okay!" Wes called out.

He opened the door, letting in a blast of dry heat and resinous smoke. Roland straightened his tie, a dark smear down one cheek. Jeff was underneath the seat, hunting for one of Karin's shoes. Brian helped Maureen up from the floor. A thin line of blood trickled from her left nostril.

"Damn nosebleeds," she muttered, dusting herself off. "Had 'em since I was three. Ignore it!"

"Yes, ma'am," Brian said.

Jeff found Karin's shoe and helped her on with it. She sat looking at him, tears dribbling down her cheeks.

He grabbed her shoulders. "What's wrong?"

She shook her head. "We're too late," she sobbed. "We can't save them. We can't even save ourselves."

Jeff put a hand under her chin and gently lifted her face until she was staring into his serious brown eyes. "Hey, we haven't come all this way to give up. On us or Heather. Okay?"

She looked at him for several seconds, her eyes still full of tears, then nodded slowly.

Outside the van, Wes and Roland stood looking through the half-mile of forest that separated them from the stone path winding precariously up the side of Altar Rock. Maureen got out of the van supported by Brian, a bit shaky on her feet but straight-shouldered with determination. Karin and Jeff joined the others. They stood huddled in a small group beneath a dark sky filled with deadly streams of multicolored light. The forest burned fiercely at their backs and before them rose the starkness of Altar Rock.

Wes said to Roland, "Looks like we'll need the gun after all." He turned to the van and the heavy-gauge shotgun he carried there.

Roland shook his head. "No. Not with the powers already set in motion against us tonight."

Wes frowned. "With all due respect to your powers, the people holding my daughter are flesh and blood. And they have weapons."

"Please," Roland insisted, "believe me. Physical weapons are not an option. Not at this stage."

Jeff added, "We can't even use our own specialized gear now, the electronic activators, the energy-field reversers."

Roland coughed on the dry, smoke-filled air. "Mr. Livingston, our main adversaries are no longer Magda Krokash or Seamus Harrach, or that motley crew of deluded adolescents gathered about them. Our enemies now are what used to be called the Powers of Darkness."

A fiery streamer shot close overhead. The whole group ducked. A nearby pine tree burst into flames.

Roland cleared his throat. "These powers work through something like electrical impulses, but at unbelievable levels of intensity. The closest equivalent is the operation of the human mind itself, especially the function we call *psi* power. *That* is our only weapon against them, Mr. Livingston, the only way we can hope to win."

"How?" Wes looked incredulous. "By thinking positive thoughts?"

Roland met his gaze. "By confronting their energy with our own."

"Only problem I see with that," Wes said evenly, "is their energy outweighs ours about a thousand to one." He felt his patience running out. "You go fight the powers as you see fit. I'll handle the kidnappers my own way."

He started for the van.

"Mr. Livingston!" Roland stepped forward. "Their energy is indeed more powerful. But it is less easily directed, less concentrated. It also lacks entirely that bonding of two energy fields that we humans, for want of a better word, call love."

Wes stopped.

"We speak of the power of love," Roland continued. "But do we fully realize, any of us, how great a power it actually is? How much it can accomplish? Tonight, we must believe in that power. It is our only hope. The three children's only hope."

An elemental demon came down on them then without any warning, wings flapping, fanged mouth gaping, its howl piercing the night sky. Wes and Brian ducked under the attack. Maureen cried out in horror. Karin backed off, stumbled. Jeff caught her, wincing as the demon descended upon them all.

Only Roland stood staring straight up at the monstrosity, his thick white hair blowing in the hot wind and the smoke. He looked frail and helpless, shoulders slumped, baggy suit whipping in the winds of the demon's descent. But his eyes burned fiercely, unblinking even as the creature's claws came down within inches of his skull. The elderly parapsychologist locked stares with the monster. It began to howl anew, its furiously beating wings stirring up a minor dust storm. Squinting through dust and smoke, Jeff and the others watched in horror as the demon bared its fangs and lunged at Roland Cameron, standing small but unafraid beneath its awful, howling malignity.

Then, as if in a dream of deliverance, the demon withdrew shrieking and rose rapidly into the night sky. Within seconds, it was nothing more than a shrill fading scream and a vanishing point of light.

Roland staggered, clutching at his heart. Wes and Jeff rushed forward. The older man fell to his knees. He knelt on the dirt of the forest floor, laboring painfully for breath, mouth open, face flushed.

"Christ, Roland!" Jeff muttered, helping him to his feet. "You don't have to show off like that."

"Is he okay?" Karin whispered.

Maureen stood with a hand to her mouth.

Brian moved forward cautiously.

"It was necessary," Roland gasped. "Direct attack. Had to be repelled." He put a hand to his heart again. "But I must conserve my strength. The Great Battle lies ahead."

Wes looked thoughtfully at the exhausted older man. "So that's how you fight them," he said softly.

Roland lifted his face proudly. "That's how you fight them to win."

Another fiery streamer shot by close overhead. They all jumped in startled reaction. Above the crackle of pine boughs bursting into flame, they heard a chorus of terrified screams ringing from Altar Rock.

"Let's go!" Wes led the way, breaking into a run.

Jeff, Karin and Roland followed, walking rapidly, Brian running on ahead of them, when Maureen called out from back beside the van, "Excuse me. I don't think I'm up to this—all this rock climbing. I'll wait here."

They all stopped, except for Brian, who kept running.

"Brian!" Wes called after him. "Come back here and stay with Maureen!"

Brian stopped. "No! I want to help Heather!" He looked defiant but miserable, like a small boy about to cry.

"Sometimes, Brian," Roland said quietly to him, "being a real hero's not all that glamorous. Stay with her, please."

Hating Roland and Wes and Maureen, and all adults in principle, Brian turned around slowly and trudged his way back to the van.

The naked Sabbath members scattered across the stony vastness of Altar Rock, shrieking in terror as the streams of multicolored light fell upon them. The dazzling streamers cut above and around the fleeing naked revelers and began to take their toll. One seemed to pass right through a running girl. She burst into flames. Another hit a tall blond boy in his midsection, blowing him into bloody fragments of flesh and bone. Sabbath members dropped to the rough stone floor of Altar Rock, cowering in mindless fear beneath the streams of deadly light.

Magda, gray eyes bright with delirium as she beheld the carnage on all sides, raised her staff aloft and cried, "Hail Azgaroth! Hail Satanas! Hail the Great Demon and the Dark Lord of the Blood Sabbath!"

A stream of light shot right past her face, so close the heat singed her flesh. The wooden staff wavered slightly in her grasp and something almost like fear entered the glittering gray eyes.

"Fool, enact the blood sacrifices!" Seamus Harrach hissed in her ear. "The minor elemental demons will feast on us all if a greater does not appear to control them. And so far, for all your bellowing, there's no sign of Azgaroth, or of the Great Dark Lord."

Magda pointed her staff at sharp-toothed Harlan, cowering beside Sherone and Adam, still bound back-to-back at the far end of Altar Rock. "Cut them loose!" she screamed. "Bring them forth and begin the Blood Offering!"

Terror burned in Harlan's dark eyes as he crouched naked beside Sherone and Adam, sawing away at their ropes with a trembling hand, cringing each time a stream of deadly light shot past to fall on another screaming Sabbath member.

The moment the ropes dropped, Sherone started to make her escape. A heavy hand locked down on her arm, pressing right into the bone and making her cry out in pain. She looked up to see the sinister runner with the deep-set, hate-filled eyes, the one she had hit with the stone down in the forest. The left side of his face was dark with dried blood from her dead-on marksmanship. He held her easily with one hand, a long-bladed *athamé* gripped in the other, the hatred in his eyes almost as bright as the streams of deadly light passing by them on all sides.

"Sacrifice her now!" Magda cried above the screams of the dying Sabbath members. "Then take the child over there!" She pointed to the oak tree from which Heather hung bound.

"And treat him with the reverence," Seamus Harrach warned, "that is his due as the Perfect Blood Offering!"

A wicked smile came over the blood-encrusted face of the runner. He turned Sherone around toward him, pressing even harder on her arm, making her cry out again. With his other hand he raised the *athamé*. Sherone looked at Adam, whining in the grip of sharp-toothed Harlan. She looked at Magda Prokash and Seamus Harrach, at Heather bound to the ancient oak tree, at the screaming Sabbath members, cowering and dying beneath the streams of savage multicolored light.

It's all over now, she thought with a strange kind of calm, turning to watch the *athamé* as it came down on her.

A stream of light burst overhead with the terrifying brilliance of a technicolor thunderbolt. The head of the hate-filled runner caught fire. He let go of Sherone and hurled away the *athamé*. He raised his hands to his burning head and quickly withdrew them. He stumbled across the rough stone surface of Altar Rock, head blazing, bodily fluids hissing.

A violent tremor shuddered through Altar Rock, like the shaking of a major earthquake. Sherone fell to her hands and knees. Looking up, she saw that the ancient oak tree was on fire. Flames leaped up from its withered branches. Heather stood before the burning tree, the ropes that had bound her lying limp and singed at her feet.

Blinding multicolored lights—harsh reds, bright oranges, cool purples, deep magentas—encircled her naked body as they had done that distant night at Magda's. The streams of light wrapped themselves sinuously about her, seeming at points to pass through her shining white flesh. She raised her arms, naked breasts thrust forward. The oak tree exploded into fragments of flaming wood and all the streams of light suddenly vanished, except for those that still revolved harmlessly around Heather.

In the uneasy silence that followed, broken by cries and groans from the surviving Sabbath members, a distant rumbling could be heard, growing rapidly louder and louder until it became a deafening roar, like the approach of a mighty avalanche. The stone floor of Altar Rock trembled violently again. New screams rose from the terrified members of the Blood Sabbath.

An enormous arc of fire appeared in the night sky, like a burning rainbow bridge. One end disappeared over the wall of the surrounding mountains. The other reached down to rest in front of Heather, who stood with her arms raised, red hair blowing free about her naked white body as she stared up at the fire in the sky.

Behind the fire a darkness began to form, dark even against the midnight blackness of the sky, dark and evil beyond comparison or human comprehension. The darkness seemed to take a familiar shape, as if such evil might try to wear a human face. But all that could be seen clearly in the great dark face were two points of intense, malignant red, burning brighter even than the fire of the arc, burning darker than all the hatred in the world.

Seamus Harrach and Magda Prokash fell prostrate in reverence.

Sherone's soul seemed to shrivel up within her at the sight of so much dark and terrible evil. She wanted to cower blindly on the stone floor of Altar Rock and let the evil take her—let the evil take them all—or let it pass. But then a small hand touched hers and she saw the frightened, tear-streaked face of Adam Newmar. Sherone pulled him close to her, looking back to where Heather stood before the burning arc, her naked body still wrapped in multicolored light as she began slowly, majestically, to rise from the surface of Altar Rock and ascend the path of the fiery arc toward the dark evil taking shape above.

"Heather," Sherone whispered, anguish piercing her heart, although she knew that her friend was now beyond her help, beyond anyone's help.

But she could still save Adam.

Sherone jumped up, grabbing Adam by the arm.

"Stop her!" Magda screamed, rising from her prostrate position before the burning arc. "Kill her and bring back the Perfect Blood Offering!"

Sherone ran naked across the rough stone surface of

Altar Rock, Adam at her side, crying for his mother. Sharp-toothed Harlan got to his feet and went after them, joined by several other Sabbath members, bolder now that the lethal streams of light had ceased. Sherone started down the steep stone path at the opposite end from where Heather slowly ascended the burning arc. Her heart pounded inside her chest and she could hear the shouts and labored breathing, the muttered curses of her pursuers as her own breath came in ragged gasps.

She was more than halfway down the side of Altar Rock when her right foot struck a large stone and she pitched forward, struggling to maintain her balance. She took most of the fall on her knees and right shoulder. Adam started squealing with fear. Sherone tried to get to her feet. The pain slowed her down. Both knees were torn open and bleeding. Her right shoulder was scraped raw.

"Shit," she muttered, then turned to Adam. *"Run!"*

Adam, tears in his eyes, looked at her, then at the naked Sabbath members charging down the steep stone path toward them.

He turned and ran.

Sherone knew they would be on her within seconds and then she would be killed, no fancy ritual this time. But she could run no farther. She could barely stand. She looked out over the edge of the stone path, down to where the forest burned beneath her.

Harlan came running toward her, dark hair flying back from his face, sharp-toothed mouth open wide as he sucked in air.

Sherone hesitated for a second or two, gauging the distance, trying to determine her chances of surviving the fall, then, deciding that all she had at this point was a choice between certain death and possible death, she leaped from the edge of the stone path and down into the fires below.

chapter 43

INFERNO

Heather ascended the burning arc, first in terror, then astonishment.

When the darkness appeared before her at last and became the demon Azgaroth and called to her on wings of darkness that enfolded her and dealt death to the members of Magda's Sabbath, she knew terror. But when she began to rise from the stone surface of Altar Rock—and she realized, this time, that she was actually ascending—then she knew an astonishment even greater than that which had accompanied her descent from the second story of the IPS building. The power, once again, was under her control. It freed her from bondage and scattered her enemies and gave her the freedom of flight.

She looked down upon the dead and dying of Magda's Sabbath, upon the broken and the terrified. She saw Sherone fleeing with Adam across the stony vastness of Altar Rock. But she felt nothing about what she saw. Those she looked at, the living and the dead, seemed transparent as ghosts, vague and insubstantial things that flickered across her screen of consciousness. They were not part of her and she was no longer part of them. The world below was becoming colorless and unreal, disconnected from everything that mattered.

Reality lay beyond the burning arc.

As she ascended farther up the curve of the arc, Heather began to see into the darkness and beyond it. The darkness became a frame and within that frame was fire. The fire that burned in the forest below Altar Rock and blazed on the mountainsides surrounding it became now an endless sea of fire, rolling onward forever in great billows and crests of flame, fire everywhere, fire above and fire below. *Fire as the phlogiston,* Heather thought dimly, wondering what it even meant until she remembered, coming back to her now like a dream from another life, Brian telling her about the history of science and the ancient philosopher who believed that fire was the primary element of the universe: fire as energy and matter, fire as essence and appearance, fire as the beginning and the end.

All the world was fire now and she was in the heart of the flame, like a moth in ecstasy, still ascending the burning arc to the source of the fire, the power that controlled both the darkness and the flame.

She heard someone call to her, calling out her name from far away, just as Sherone had called to her from the lawn beneath the IPS building. But she would ignore the call this time. There was no one she cared about any longer, no one she wanted to see again or be with. The fire would consume them all anyway, in its own time. And she was ascending the arc to become one with the fire.

Adam's bare feet hurt and he felt like throwing up. Instead, he stopped running and started to cry. Within seconds Harlan caught up with him, gasping for breath, air whistling over his sharp teeth. Adam began squalling as Harlan picked him up and headed wearily back up the stone path, the child draped over his shoulder like a sack of grain. He had not taken more than ten steps when he was set upon by what he thought at first was an elemental demon. He turned, terrified, and saw a sight almost as unnerving.

Wes Livingston's face was twisted with rage, his eyes dark with vengeance. He snatched Adam from Harlan's shoulder and set him down out of harm's way. Then he seized Harlan by the throat and began to shake him until his long dark hair flew out in all directions. The other Sabbath members who had joined the pursuit of Sherone and Adam came to a sudden stop at the sight of Harlan in the hands of a madman. Then they turned and ran up the stone path even faster than they had come down it.

When Harlan tried to offer feeble resistance, Wes slammed him back up against the sheer cliff side of the stone path. "Where's my daughter?" Wes demanded roughly. "Her name's Sherone. She's blond. What've you done with her?"

Harlan shook his head. "Man, I don't know who—"

Wes slammed Harlan's head into the cliff side again, tightening the grip on his throat. "She was with the little boy." Wes nodded at Adam, who stood watching everything wide-eyed, no longer crying.

"Her?" Harlan croaked. "Man, she went over the edge!"

"She *what?*"

In a frightened voice Harlan explained what had happened. Wes threw him to the ground. The naked young man cried out as his hands and knees collided with rough stone. Wes turned and walked to the edge of the path and stared down into the burning forest below.

He was still staring when Jeff and Karin caught up with him, Roland bringing up the rear.

"Adam!" Karin cried.

The blond little boy rushed over to her embrace.

Wes turned to them. "I'll take him back down to Maureen. The rest of you go on ahead."

"But Sherone—" Karin began.

"Sherone's down there somewhere." Wes pointed to the burning forest, smoke rising in thick clouds into the night.

"How—"

"She jumped." Wes took Adam from Karin and started back down the stone path, carrying the child in the crook of his arm.

Karin watched him, wanting to say something, but Jeff touched her arm. "Heather's still up there."

She nodded and turned back to the upward path.

Brian ran through the burning forest, heat sweeping over him in waves. His jacket was unzipped and his face glistened with sweat. When the sound of the great roaring came from above Altar Rock and the earth shook beneath his feet, Brian knew something was happening—something that had to do with Heather. He had begged Maureen, pleaded with her, to let him go and help. Maureen Magnusson did not know Brian McNulty very well, and she was not sure that he was the right person for Heather. But she knew what true love looked like, and what to do about it.

"I don't need a baby-sitter," she told him brusquely. "Get on up there. And God be with you."

God be with us all, she thought, as another pine tree burst into flames nearby and she wondered how much longer it would be before the raging fire consumed everything in sight.

As Brian rushed up the stone path to Altar Rock, he could see part of the burning arc far above him, stretching red and fierce across the dark night sky. A chill came over him then, despite the fire's dry, searing heat. Azgaroth. Fire Demon. He thought of Heather and the lights at Magda's, the fire at the monolith. A cold hand seemed to clutch at his heart.

He ran harder and faster.

He almost ran right over Wes Livingston with Adam Newmar riding in the crook of his left arm. Brian came to a skidding, near-colliding halt. He stood with his mouth open, panting for air, sweat dripping from his face, body poised to continue his headlong charge up the side of Altar Rock.

"Where's Maureen?" Wes asked him.

"She let me go! She said she was okay by herself and she *told* me to go. Honest!"

Wes said nothing. The look in his eyes spoke for him. He handed Adam to Brian.

Brian backed off, shaking his head. "I got to help Heather!"

"Three people are doing all they can for her."

"Fuck it!" Brian turned angrily and started up the stone path. "You're not my goddamn father. You don't tell me what to do!"

"Brian." The edge to Wes's voice stopped him. "You had one responsibility and you blew it. You've got another responsibility now." He handed over Adam.

Brian numbly accepted the squirming little boy.

"You blow this one, Brian, you'll answer to me."

Wes turned and started down the stone path, veering off into the burning forest where the path met level ground.

Brian stood watching, the child in his arms.

Sherone lay on her side in the middle of the small clearing, waiting for the end to come. She coughed on thick smoke and watched as the flames crept closer, drawing the circle of death tighter around her. The right leg was killing her now, the one she had broken in the leap from the stone path, shattering it in several places, broken bone poking jaggedly through the skin at one point. She tried not to look at it. But it kept reminding her of its presence, throbbing and burning with a steady, maddening rhythm. She was lucky, she knew, to have survived the fall at all and escaped being impaled on a tree or pulped against some boulder. But the leg hurt so bad. She shut her eyes. A small tear squeezed out from beneath one lid.

She coughed again and opened her eyes, blinking against the stinging smoke. Sweat glazed her back and arms and trickled down between her naked breasts. The fire would close in and that would be it. She started to cry, eyes watering, silent sobs shaking her body. It was not the dying she minded so much, but the thought of dying all alone like this, with nobody even knowing what happened. The fire would burn up everything, leaving only charred bones that no one would ever find. The people who loved her would miss her for a while and then forget about her, and her bones would stay buried in the ashes of a burned-out forest. The tears came faster.

"Skip!"

Sherone looked up through the tears, thinking she had imagined her dad calling to her. That was the way it was supposed to happen, right before you died. Your whole life started flashing before your eyes and you remembered everything. But it was all in your head.

"Skip! Answer if you can hear me!"

The reality hit her like a slap in the face. It really *was* her dad! She started to get up, but the pain stopped her cold, sending a jolt up her right leg that almost passed her out.

She shouted in a hoarse voice, "Daddy! Over here!"

Wes Livingston was cut off from his daughter by the flames. But he came through regardless, running full speed, jacket pulled up to protect his face, holding his breath against the lung-scorching heat. Burning branches fell down on him. Fire seared his hands and legs. One sleeve of the jacket was burning fiercely as he stumbled out into the clearing. He beat out the flames, coughing deep in his chest.

He stared down at his daughter lying naked on the forest floor, right leg shattered by a compound fracture, cuts and scrapes across her back and arms, blood soaking into the earth. She would have to be moved carefully, very carefully, if she could be moved at all. He did not know how he would get her through the flames that were closing in on them, burning hotter and brighter every second, sucking up what little air remained within the clearing. He took off his burned jacket and knelt down to wrap it around her.

"Skip," he said, his voice breaking.

"Oh, Daddy!" She tried to sit up and hug him, but the pain bit into her leg.

"Don't move, honey. Just lie still till we find out how bad you're hurt."

Branches broke loose from the top of a burning tree and fell down into the clearing, igniting scrub grass and twigs.

Sherone looked up at her father, firelight shining off her sweating, tear-streaked face. "Daddy, *leave!* You can't help me now! The fire . . ." She started crying again, helplessly.

"Hush." He stroked her tangled blond hair. "We'll make it out of here. Somehow." Then he added, "But I'm not leaving. You're all I've got, Skip."

"It's my fault!" She coughed. "Everything! I've killed Heather. And you. Oh, God!" The tears overwhelmed her.

Wes squeezed her hand. "It's not your fault, Skip. Things just happen. Sometimes they don't happen right."

A new and violent trembling shook the earth beneath them. A greater fire seemed to appear in the sky. Fire roared through the trees around them and swept above them like the winds of a hurricane in Hell.

Sherone cried out, "My leg, my *leg!* Daddy! Hold me!"

Wes Livingston embraced his daughter gently, pressing his lips to her damp forehead.

"Daddy," she whispered in a broken voice. "I love you so much. But I never told you."

Wes smiled at her, his own eyes wet with tears. "Honey, you never had to."

 ire exploded from the forest and swept through

the clearing. For a moment Wes Livingston and his daughter could be seen through the flames. Then another wave of fire rushed over them and only the inferno remained.

Karin was the first to reach the top of Altar Rock. She ran the last dozen yards, smoke and dry heat and exertion making her throat ache and her lungs burn, her heart pounding inside her chest, blood hammering at her temples hard enough to burst a vein and stroke her out into black nothingness. She gasped for breath as she rounded the last turn in the path and stepped onto the top of Altar Rock.

The hot air stuck in her throat.

Dead bodies lay scattered across the stone plateau. Charred, most of them, burned black beyond recognition, while a few lay flayed and bloody or hacked into pieces like refuse from a slaughterhouse.

Karin's hands rose in front of her, as if to ward off an unspeakable evil. "Dear God . . ."

"Karin!" Jeff called out from behind her.

The red fire burning in the sky above lighted the charnel-house horror down below. Karin felt sick with revulsion and terror. Her stomach lurched and the stone floor seemed to shift beneath her feet.

"Heather," she whispered, not wanting to think—*unable* to think—that her daughter might be one of the burned and mutilated bodies spread out before her.

She looked up then.

And beheld Seamus Harrach, a blood-streaked fragment of a nightmare, and Magda Prokash, hatred and madness triumphant in her gray eyes as she grinned like a death's-head at the end of a dark corridor—

And the great arc burning in the night sky, reaching up from the stone floor of Altar Rock and extending out into the infinite blackness above—

And her daughter ascending the burning arc, multicolored lights encircling her pale naked body, long red hair flying out behind her as she tracked slowly up the curve of the arc like a virgin sacrifice rising into the jaws of Hell.

"HEATHER!" Karin screamed, and all her fear and fury and hopelessness went into that scream, doubling her over with the agony of it.

"She cannot hear you." Magda Prokash grinned at her, standing unsteadily near the base of the burning arc, madness glittering in her gray eyes. "She goes to become one with the Great Demon and his Great Master, the Dark Lord of the Sabbath."

Seamus Harrach moved toward Karin, blood running from his mouth and down onto his naked chest, dark eyes burning with an unholy light. "On your life!" he rasped, sounding more animal than human. "Stand back! Do not interfere!"

Altar Rock shook suddenly with a violent tremor. A great roaring seemed to swell up from deep within the plateau itself. Huge cracks split the surface of the stone floor. In the night sky above, the arc blazed brighter. Heather seemed to stop for a moment, hanging suspended between the known and unknown worlds, surrounded by fire and darkness at the threshold of evil.

Magda raised her wooden staff in a twisted hand. *"Hail Azgaroth!"* she shouted into the hot wind, above the great roaring. *"Hail Satana—"*

"AZGAROTH!" The powerful voice cut above Magda's cries and the great roaring that rose from the bowels of Altar Rock. *"Apage! Daemon exsecratus! Apage!"*

Roland Cameron stood upon Altar Rock like a Biblical prophet, white hair blowing wild in the hot wind, eyes blazing with the wrath of righteous indignation. He raised an arm in front of him, index finger pointing up at the blackness beyond the burning arc. In a voice like a trumpet blast he repeated the ancient Latin words again, words that were old in other languages before the first pyramid was raised, words that were spoken by inhuman ongues in a time before the world was, words that banished an accursed demon and commanded him to depart this world.

"*Azgaroth!*" Roland Cameron called out to the blackness above. "*Apage, daemon! Apage!*"

As he repeated the ancient adjuration, the blackness beyond the burning arc, where Heather hung suspended, began to shift and take on a different shape, inconceivably huge, towering above the mountains that burned around Altar Rock, blotting out the stars that hung pale and distant beyond the fire and the terror. Darkness became a human shape, hideous and lowering, impenetrably dark, dark as the blackness beyond the grave, dark except for two gigantic burning eyes, red and malignant and filled with all the hate that had ever existed, or would ever exist, in this world or any other.

Karin shrank back from the darkness, shaking with a fear she had never known before, a fear of evil so great and terrible that it seemed to blast all good, and all hope of good, into absolute, irredeemable nothingness.

"*Apage!*" Roland cried, pointing his finger at the red-eyed shape of darkness towering overhead. "*Exsecratus, apage! Apage!*"

The hate-filled red eyes seemed to burn darker. The earth shook. Altar Rock trembled anew. The roaring became a deafening howl, the blood cry of a maddened beast. The hot winds blew with the force of a hurricane. Fires exploded in the forest below Altar Rock and on the mountainsides surrounding it. The cracks in the stone floor widened. As Karin looked down in unbelieving terror, she saw monstrous, malformed things crawling up from out of the cracks, scrabbling their way up to the surface of the living world. The flapping of great leathery wings filled the night sky along with the shrieks of elemental demons hunting human prey. The burning arc blazed more fiercely red than ever and all the world above and below was filled with fire and demons.

"*Apage, exsecratus!*" Roland Cameron called to the

red-eyed darkness glaring down upon the burning world.
"*Apa—aaaaaaaaaaaaaaaaaaaaaaaahhhhhhhhhhhh!*"

Roland's head snapped back. His outstretched arm and pointing finger wavered but did not drop. Blood burst from his open mouth. A thin shaft of sharp metal protruded from his chest. Behind him Magda Prokash stood twisting the pointed staff she had thrust into his back, forcing it in up to the blade hilt, turning it viciously like a drill bit in a hole, her mouth open to catch the blood that sprayed from the punctured aorta, her gray eyes mad with evil and darkness and the delight of death.

Through a film of tears Karin saw Jeff rushing forward to help. But it was too late. Roland was dying, or dead. His outstretched arm drooped before him. His body slumped loose in Magda's murderous grasp.

It's not fair! Karin thought miserably, weeping like a lost child. *He was winning and she crept up behind him and killed him and it's not fair, not fair at all!*

Bitter tears burned her eyes. Despair pierced her heart.

Then she understood.

He had been winning. It could be done. You could stand against evil so terrible that it seemed greater than any other power in the world. And if you were brave and stood your ground, you could win.

You *would* win.

It hit her with a shock more violent than the tremor that still rumbled beneath her feet. She looked up at her daughter hanging suspended against the burning arc and then at the monstrous red-eyed darkness towering above them, dwarfing even the mighty arc in its black and evil immensity. She moved closer to the base of the arc.

"Heather!" she cried, looking up. "*Heather!*"

Seamus Harrach stepped in front of her. "Stand back!" he hissed, raising a sharp-nailed hand. "On your life, stand back!"

Jeff Geller slammed into the menacing warlock like a defensive end on the forty-yard line. They went down in a tangle of limbs and blood, rolling around on the rough stone surface of Altar Rock, Jeff struggling to get his hands around the warlock's throat while ducking his head to protect his own eyes from Seamus Harrach's talonlike nails.

Karin came as close to the burning arc as she dared, the heat striking out at her like something from a blast furnace. She looked up into the night sky filled with fire and shrieking elemental demons. Heather was moving again, ascending the burning arc, drawing steadily toward the darkness that controlled the fire.

"God, no!" Karin whispered, her heart sinking.

Then she remembered Roland's defiant stance and she called out to her daughter, shouting above the roaring of Altar Rock and the shrieking of the demons and the howling of the hot winds from Hell.

"Heather!" she cried. "Heather, I love you! Come back to me! Please. I love you so much . . ."

Heather, moving up the fire and into the darkness, moving toward the dark heart of Azgaroth who had sought her out and come for her through the infinite black wastes of intergalactic space—Heather heard her mother calling to her down below, but it sounded strange and distant, like a lost voice from a fading dream. She raised her arms in front of her and continued to ascend toward the fire and the darkness that controlled the fire.

"I love you!"

Heather stopped abruptly, like a ferris wheel carriage rocking to a sudden halt. She looked down. Her mother stood there on Altar Rock at the base of the burning arc, stretching her arms up toward her, looking absurdly small and insignificant, a miserable little insect crying out with a human voice.

If you really loved me, Heather thought, *you wouldn't have ignored me all the time, the way you and Dad always did because your lives were more important than mine and they always came first, always.*

She turned back to the fire and the darkness beyond. "I love you so much! Please!"

Heather stopped. She could feel her heart beating within her naked breast. It seemed the loudest sound in the world just then, louder than the shrieking of the demons and the roaring of Altar Rock and the burning of the fire in the sky. She felt her own heart beating and she looked down upon her mother calling out to her, clearer now, like someone she once had loved, like someone she wanted to love again, calling for her at the end of a long, dark tunnel that kept growing longer and darker.

Her mom loved her. She was trying to save her from Azgaroth now, even though there was no way she could and she would die, but she was trying anyway because—

Because she really did love her.

The tears that came to Heather's eyes changed the colors of the night sky and transformed the patterns of darkness. She could see her mom clear and sharp now and she wanted to be down there with her.

A savage roar broke from the darkness above, deafening her. She turned and looked back, and her heart almost stopped.

The hatred in those burning red eyes.

The intensity of all that evil.

She turned and started to reach out her hand toward her mother calling to her down below, as if she could somehow bridge the gulf of fire and darkness and touch her.

"Mom," she whispered, her voice lost in the vengeful, ear-shattering roar of the Fire Demon.

Jeff Geller drove his fist like a hammer into Seamus Harrach's throat, again and again, until the loathsome deformed body lay still. He got to his feet, breathing hard, and stepped back from the motionless form, turning to where Karin stood below the burning arc.

The warlock rose suddenly to a standing position, rigid as a fallen tree, one clawlike hand extended before him. A force field hit Jeff full in the chest, knocking him backward and off his feet. He fell heavily onto Altar Rock, striking his head against the rough stone. Through blurring eyes he saw Seamus Harrach standing over him, a sharp-pointed *athamé* clutched in one hand.

"Yes," he hissed through his black-toothed, bloody mouth. "You with your little knowledge and less power. You *dare* to attack me! Wretched fool. Die!"

He raised the *athamé* to strike.

Brian McNulty, breathless from his run up Altar Rock, did not have a good strong throwing arm. He had served his Little League apprenticeship in Beverly Hills missing pop flies in left field. But Heather's life was in danger and Roland was already dead. They needed Jeff. Brian drew upon his inner resources and applied what he knew about aerodynamics and threw the baseball-size rock in his right hand as fast and hard as he could, aiming straight at the center of Seamus Harrach's naked, deformed back, just below the two stunted wing nodes.

The rock hit its target dead-on. The warlock stumbled forward, dropping the *athamé*, almost falling to his knees.

He turned around in a kind of limping crouch. When he saw Brian, his mouth opened wide, exposing all his black and rotting teeth. He hissed like a jungle cat and reached out a menacing hand toward Brian. Blue sparks crackled from the ends of his long, sharp-nailed fingers.

In the burning sky above, Heather looked down with dread and whispered, "Brian . . ."

Seamus Harrach jerked backward like a puppet on a string. His neck snapped up toward the burning arc and his mouth dropped open, so wide it seemed as if his jaw had become unhinged. Blood gushed from the gaping mouth, followed by skin and bone and pieces of lung and heart and cartilage and ropes of intestines and everything inside his naked bone-white body. His insides shot upward, defying gravity and sanity, while his empty body crumpled in upon itself like a discarded husk. Then it burst into flame and rose into the night sky in a whirlwind of fire until it disappeared within the greater fire of the burning arc.

"Heather! Reach out your hand to me!" Karin's voice was hoarse from shouting above the chaos of the Sabbath. "Come back to me! I love you!"

Karin stretched out her own right hand until her arm ached. She would have given everything she owned in the world to be able to rise along the path of that fiery arc and touch her daughter. But she remained solidly earthbound, standing on tiptoe, reaching up toward Heather hovering like a demonic Madonna in the burning evening sky.

Heather reached out her own hand toward her mother's, then withdrew it, shaking her head sorrowfully, tears streaking her face in the brilliant light of the fiery arc. There was no way. Azgaroth was too powerful. They were too weak.

"Keep trying!" Karin called hoarsely from below. "I love you! Don't give up! I love you so much!"

Heather reached out her own hand timidly. There was a sudden jolt, like the start-up of an aerial tramway. She started moving again, down this time, down toward her mother, down to a love that called her back.

Karin saw Heather beginning to descend slowly toward her and she stretched out her own hand until the arm began to strain at the socket. All the madness and terror and evil of that Sabbath night seemed to contract and diminish, leaving only the great burning gulf that separated their two hands, hers and Heather's, a gulf that was closing steadily, inch by inch, as they reached out one to the other, mother and daughter, across a universe of darkness and fire.

Brian was bending over, helping Jeff to his feet, when Jeff grabbed his arm and shouted in a thick voice, "Brian! Stop her!"

Magda Prokash rushed toward Karin, sharp-pointed

staff raised above her head like a javelin. Brian ran after her, shouting. When Magda was within striking distance, she stopped and hurled the staff as hard as she could at Karin's back.

The lethal weapon flew from Magda's hand, then stopped in midair and turned around in a complete half-circle. It shot back to where Magda stood watching it with an open mouth. The pointed blade entered her mouth and burst out the back of her neck, spraying blood across her naked back. A flock of elemental demons descended upon her, tearing at her flesh, stuffing it into their mouths, sucking greedily at the blood sticking to their clawlike fingers. Magda screamed over the spear stuck down her throat. Within minutes she was a raw, bleeding carcass being dismembered and stripped to the bone by ravenous winged demons.

Heather drew closer and closer, descending slowly from the burning arc. Karin's heart leaped within her.

"Hang on, baby!" she cried. "I love you!"

I'm winning, Karin thought, ecstatic to the point of delirium. *We're winning!*

The sky exploded then.

A huge wheel of fire appeared, encircling the red-eyed tower of darkness, passing above and beneath the burning arc, blazing in the night sky with the blinding brilliance of a second sun. Jeff and Brian staggered back, shutting their eyes and shielding their faces against the raging fire storm in the sky.

The fire blinded Karin and the heat burned her face, singeing her eyelashes. She could smell her own hair baking in the sulfurous heat. But she kept her eyes on Heather, descending ever nearer through the darkness and the fire, her hand outstretched toward her mother's, the two hands reaching out like elemental forces of good through the deadlock of evil that held Altar Rock in its grip that fateful Sabbath night.

The fury of the fire storm knocked down Jeff and Brian. It tore up boulders and dead bodies and burning trees and howling elemental demons and tossed them all like chaff in the wind, whirling them around before it hurled them down to fiery destruction.

Heather was close enough now for Karin to see her clearly, almost close enough to be touched, surrounded by fire yet unscathed, her red hair blowing free against the fiercer red of the flames, her naked skin pale white, shining bright with sweat and purity in the burning heart of evil. Karin stretched out her own hand toward her daughter's, aching with a love for her that defied the terrors of darkness, a love that cut through the power that was Azgaroth like lightning flashing through a storm-dark night.

And as Heather drew nearer, Karin felt the power extending from her own hand and meeting the power that came from Heather's halfway, the union of the two powers forming a bond so strong that not even the greatest evil in all the dark and unknown universe could break it.

And as this bonding of their powers grew, Karin thought she could actually see it, shining like a band of wide and brilliant light, drawing Heather down from the darkness and the fire, drawing her closer and closer, until at last the fingers of their two hands touched, bridging in that moment the immense gulf of hatred and despair that had separated them, delivering Karin's lost daughter back again from evil.

And in that same moment the Sabbath ceased.

The fires burning in the forests and on the distant mountainsides went out suddenly and completely, like the snuffing of a candle flame. The hot Santa Ana winds stopped blowing. The shrieking elemental demons vanished. The malformed things that had crawled up from out of the cracks in Altar Rock were no more to be seen. The gaping cracks themselves drew close together and melded into wholeness once again.

The burning arc and the giant wheel of fire began to fuse with the darkness that towered above Altar Rock.

The malignant red eyes blazed up momentarily out of the darkness, terrible in their hatred, then disappeared forever. The fused fire and darkness withdrew rapidly into the infinite blackness of the night sky, accompanied by a distant, vengeful howling.

Karin threw her arms around her daughter, pressing her close. Tears spilled down her cheeks and wetted Heather's long red hair.

Heather looked up, tears in her own eyes. "I love you, Mom," she whispered.

Karin hugged her even closer.

Brian stepped forward awkwardly, holding out his jacket to Heather. She broke free from her mother's embrace and took the jacket and pulled it on, turning her back to Brian and blushing as she did so. After zipping it up, she turned back around and hugged him so hard he almost fell over.

Karin wiped the tears from her own eyes. Jeff came up beside her and put his arm around her waist. She squeezed his hand and raised it to her lips, not taking her eyes from Heather and Brian.

Above the smoking forest and the charred mountainsides rose a bright full moon, shining down with soft white light on Altar Rock and a world washed clean by refining fire.

Karin stiffened. "My God." She turned to Jeff. "My mother! She and Adam..."

Brian broke off from a prolonged kiss. "When I brought Adam back down, we found this hollowed-out place between two huge boulders. It wasn't perfect or anything."

"But the fire—" Karin began.

Jeff touched her arm and nodded at something in the distance. Maureen Magnusson walked slowly toward them across the graveyard of Altar Rock, Adam Newmar squirming in her arms. She limped as she walked and her face was smudged with smoke, but her green eyes burned fierce and bright.

"Mother!" Karin rushed over to her.

She hugged her mother and kissed Adam and then hugged them both. "I was so scared! I thought you were..."

"We're alive and well, thank you." Maureen smiled at her daughter and granddaughter and the two men who loved them. "We're all alive. That's all that matters, isn't it?"